GODBLIND

GODBLIND

ANNA STEPHENS

HARPER
Voyager

1

Typeset in Sabon LT Std by Palimpsest Book Production Limited,
Falkirk, Stirlingshire

Printed and bound in Great Britain by
Clays Ltd, St Ives plc

MIX
Paper from
responsible sources

FSC C007454

FSC™ is a non-profit international organisation established to promote
the responsible management of the world's forests. Products carrying the
FSC label are independently certified to assure consumers that they come
from forests that are managed to meet the social, economic and
ecological needs of present and future generations,
and other controlled sources.

Find out more about HarperCollins and the environment at
www.harpercollins.co.uk/green

For my Uncles, David and Graham.
I wish you could have seen this.

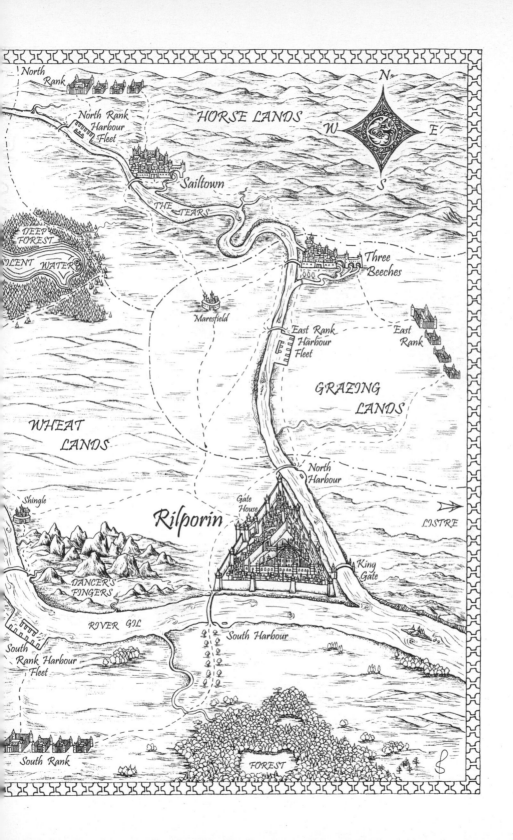

RILLIRIN

Eleventh moon, year 994 since the Exile of the Red Gods
Cave-temple, Eagle Height, Gilgoras Mountains

Rillirin stood at the back with the other slaves, all huddled in a tight knot like a withered fist. Word had been sent days before, summoning all the Mireces' war chiefs from the villages along the Sky Path, drawing them to the capital to hear the Red Gods' Blessed One. Whatever They had told her, it was important enough to bring the war chiefs to Eagle Height as winter set in.

Rillirin glanced towards the Blessed One with an involuntary curl of the lip, and then lowered her head fast. The high priestess of the Dark Lady and Gosfath, God of Blood, spiritual leader of the Mireces, was a remote figure, lit and then hidden by the guttering torches, her blue robe dark as smoke in the gloom, face as closed and beautiful as Mount Gil, rearing harsh and impassable above Eagle Height.

The altar was stained black and the temple reeked of old blood. Most of the Blessed One's sermons ended with sacrifice, with a slave writhing on the altar stone. Rillirin shrank in on herself, staring at the floor between her boots. She had no desire to be that slave.

'Come first moon we will enter the nine hundred and ninety-fifth year of our exile,' the Blessed One said, her voice hard as she paced like a mountain cat before the congregation. King Liris stood at the front among his war chiefs, but she pitched her voice to the back of the temple so it bounced among the stalagtites hanging like stone spears above their heads. All would hear her this night.

'Almost a millennium since we and our mighty gods were cast from the land of Gilgoras with its warm and bountiful countries to scratch a living up here in the ice and rock. Driven from Rilpor, harried from Listre, exiled from Krike.' Cold eyes swept the warriors and war chiefs thronging at her feet as she listed the countries where the Red Gods had once held sway. 'And what have you accomplished in all those years?' Her voice cracked like a whip and the men flinched, hunching lower beneath wrath as sudden as a late spring storm.

'Nothing,' the Blessed One spat. 'Petty raids, stolen livestock, stolen wheat. A few Wolves dead. Pathetic.' Her teeth clicked together as she bit off the word. She raised her left hand and extended her index finger. It commanded a rustle of fear from Mireces and slave alike as she let it point first here, then there. She didn't look where she gestured, as though it wasn't attached to her, or as though it was driven by a will other than hers, a will divine.

The choosing finger. The death finger. How many times had Rillirin felt the brush of its sentience across her nerve endings, wondering if this, now, was the time of her death? It suddenly stilled, its tip pointing straight at her, and Rillirin's vision contracted to its point and her breath caught in her throat. Stomach cramping, eyes watering, she forced herself to look past the finger into the Blessed One's eyes, and saw the calculation there.

She wouldn't dare. Liris would never allow it. Would he?

The finger moved on.

'You disagree?' the Blessed One demanded when Liris dared to look up. Challenge heated her eyes, tilted her chin up, and the Mireces king met her gaze for less than a second. 'No, you would not. You cannot. Each year you swear your oaths to the Red Gods, sanctified in your own blood, promising Them glory and a return to the warm plains, swearing you will restore Them to Their rightful dominion over all the souls within Gilgoras. And each year you fail.'

Her voice dropped to a silky whisper. 'And so the gods have chosen the instrument of Their return.'

Liris was sweating. 'You have seen this?' he managed.

'The Dark Lady Herself has told me,' the Blessed One confirmed, her smile small and cruel. 'There are those in Rilpor who are of more use to Her than any man here.' She swept her finger across the crowd and they leant away from it. 'There are those in Rilpor who hate and fear us, and yet who will do more for our cause than you.'

She accompanied the words with the finger, and for a second it pointed at Liris's heart. The threat was clear and men slid away from him as though he were plagued. The sacred blue of their shirts was dull under the temple's torches, blackening with fear-sweat at their proximity to death.

Rillirin felt a bubble of shock and then sickening fear. What would happen to her when Liris's tenuous protection was gone? *I'll be unclaimed.* She hated Liris, despised him with everything in her, yet he kept her safe from the depradations of the other men. Kept her for himself.

Liris threw back his shoulders and drew himself up to

meet his fate, but then the finger jerked on amid a growing babble of noise. Rillirin breathed out, relieved and disgusted with that relief in equal measure.

The Blessed One hissed and drew all eyes back to her. 'Our gods are trapped on the borders of Gilgoras like us, but They weave Their holy work inside its bounds nonetheless. With the help of my high priest, Gull, who lies hidden in the very heart of Rilpor, They draw one to Them who can finally see Their desires fulfilled.' She bared her teeth. 'Know this now, and rejoice in the knowing. The gods' plans are revealed to me, and soon enough to you. Begin your preparations and make them good. Come the spring, we do not raid. Come spring, we conquer. And by midsummer, we will have victory not only over Rilpor but over their so-called Gods of Light as well.'

She raised both arms to the temple roof. 'The veil can only be broken by blood: lakes and rivers of blood. We will shed it all if it will return our gods to Gilgoras. Our blood and heathen blood, spilt together, mixed together, to sanctify the ground and make it worthy for Their holy presence. We shall have victory, you and I,' she shouted, 'and the Red Gods, the true gods, will be well pleased.'

Rillirin pushed forward, trying to see Liris's face, to see whether he knew as much as the Blessed One appeared to. *They're going to war against Rilpor? They'll be slaughtered. The shadows in the trees will do for them, and the West Rank.* Her mouth moved in something that might have been a smile if she could remember what one felt like.

Amid the cheers and cries of exaltation to the gods, the Blessed One dropped her arms to her sides, before the left rose once more, dragged by that weaving, ever-moving finger.

'You.' It was a single word whispered amid the tumult, but the silence fell faster than a stone. All eyes looked where she pointed, not to the slaves, but to the warriors and women of the Mireces, born and raised within the gods' bloody embrace. 'The Dark Lady demands Mireces blood in return for Mireces failure. She demands a promise that we will stand with our new ally to the gods' glory, that we will bleed and die for Their return. A promise that we – that you – will not fail Them again. The gods choose you. Come and meet them.'

Liris's queen rose to her feet, her lips pulled back. She threaded her way through the crowd with small, stumbling steps, breath echoing harsh in the orange light. Rillirin watched her, her guts swamping with relief. *You poor bitch,* she thought, and then tried to burn out the pity with hate. Rillirin rubbed her stinging eyes, swallowing nausea. Bana was a Mireces and she deserved to die. They all did. Every one of them, starting with Liris and with the Blessed One next. She was pleased Bana was being sacrificed. Pleased.

'Your will, Blessed One,' Liris said as the mother of his children reached the altar and looked back at him, for a kind word or a demand for her release, perhaps. Her face rippled when she received neither. The Blessed One smiled and, tearing the woman's dress down the front, bent her back over the altar stone; the queen's soft, wrinkled belly undulated as she panted.

'My feet are on the Path,' Bana shrieked, and the Blessed One's knife flashed gold as it drove into her stomach.

Gods take your soul to Their care, Rillirin thought despite herself, her fists clenched at the screams. Yet she didn't know to which gods she prayed any more, those of Blood or of Light. None of Them did anything to help her. She looked away as the Blessed One dragged the knife sideways and opened Bana's belly, her other hand pressing on her chest to keep her still. Bana's screams echoed and re-echoed and the Mireces fell to their knees in adulation.

The slaves knelt too, and one pulled Rillirin down to the stone. 'Are you stupid?' he hissed. 'Kneel or die.' Rillirin knelt.

Liris's face was stony and closed as Bana shrieked out the last moments of her life. He stood as soon as it was done and the Blessed One had completed the prayer of thanks. The blood was still running and his war chiefs still knelt in prayer when he shouldered his way through his warriors. Before Rillirin could get away, he reached out a sweaty paw and grabbed her by the hair.

No no no no no no.

'Come on, fox-bitch,' he snarled in her ear, hauling her towards the exit. The slaves melted from their path like snow in spring, eyes blank or calculating – her perceived power was something many of them coveted – and the temple rang with Liris's rasping, angry breath, the pat-pat-pat of blood, Rillirin's muffled whimpers.

Rillirin stumbled up the slick stone steps from the temple, bouncing from the walls in Liris's wake, and when they reached the top Liris shook her until she squealed. He cuffed her face and dragged her through the longhouse and into the king's room, threw her at the bed and dropped the bar across the door.

'Lord, you must not,' Rillirin pleaded, on her knees, one hand pressed to her stinging scalp. 'The Blessed One said that you should not touch me, not for three more days. I'm still sick.'

Liris flung his bearskin on to the floor and brayed a laugh. 'You've had a pennyroyal tea to flush my seed from your belly because you don't deserve a child of mine. You're a slave, not a consort, and you'll do as you're told.'

'Honoured, please,' Rillirin tried as he advanced. She scrabbled away on hands and knees, the weakness a blanket slowing her reactions. *He can't. Bana's still warm, he couldn't want* – Liris pulled her to her feet by one arm and dragged up her skirts, blunt fingers hard against her thigh. The stench of his breath caught at the back of her throat. It was clear that he did want.

Rillirin squirmed and thrashed, but he was too big, too strong. Always had been. 'No,' she screamed in his face. 'No.'

Liris jolted back in surprise, piggy eyes narrow. His breath sucked in on a whoop of outrage, and Rillirin clenched her jaw and screwed up her eyes. *Stupid. Stupid!*

She was convinced the punch had broken her jaw, and the impact with the stone floor sent shards of white pain through her shoulder. Black stars danced in her vision. Blood flooded her mouth and her shoulder was numb with sick, hot agony.

Liris picked her up and slammed her into the wall, one hand around her lower jaw, grinding the back of her head into the wood. 'Bitch,' he breathed. 'While I normally enjoy our little games, I'm not in the mood for your spite tonight. You do not answer me back, you hear? You. Do. Not. Answer. Back.' Each word punctuated by a crack of her skull on the wall. 'You live because I will it, and you will die when I decide. Tonight, maybe, if you don't please me. Or on the altar to ensure our success in the war to come. Or after I give you to the war chiefs for sport. When I choose, understand? You belong to me. Now keep your fucking tongue behind your teeth and unclench those thighs. I've a need.'

The tears were coming and Rillirin willed them not to fall, glaring her soul-eating hatred at him instead. A wild, suicidal courage flooded her. 'Fuck you,' she wheezed.

Liris's mouth popped open and then he leant back to laugh, huge wobbling gasps of mirth. 'I'll break you, fox-bitch,' he promised and his free hand dragged at her skirts again.

Rillirin worked her fingers around the knife hilt digging into her side, slid it out of Liris's belt even as he forced her legs apart, and jammed it in the side of his neck. He looked at her in disbelief, hands falling slack, and Rillirin pumped her arm, the blade chewing through the fatty flesh and widening the hole in his neck.

Blood sprayed over her hand, her arm, her face and neck and chest, great warm lapping waves of it washing into the room until his knees buckled and he went down. She went with him, knife stabbing again and again, long past need, long past his last bubbling breath, until his face and neck and torso were a mass of gore and torn flesh.

Red with blood, red as vengeance, Rillirin spat on his corpse and waited for dark.

CORVUS

Eleventh moon, year 994 since the Exile of the Red Gods
Longhouse, Eagle Height, Gilgoras Mountains

Corvus, war chief of Crow Crag, paced below the dais. Lady Lanta, the Blessed One and the Voice of the Gods, sat in regal splendour beside the empty throne. The other war chiefs fidgeted on their stools and benches.

The Blessed One would not reveal more of the gods' plan until the king was present, and the king was not one for stirring himself unnecessarily. Still, the sun was high even this late in the year and Corvus would bet Lanta was as impatient as he. A full-scale invasion with only months to plan; an ally within Rilpor they could use to their advantage. The idea warmed his belly. Invasion. Conquest. A chance for glory such as there'd never been, for Corvus to put his name, and Crow Crag's, on the lips of every Mireces and Rilporian alive. And yet Liris lounged in his stinking pit like an animal.

The other end of the longhouse was crowded with warriors, complaining bitterly about the storm that had blown in. Slaves hunched and scurried to their chores, and Corvus's lip curled in disgust as an old man tripped and spilt his tray of bowls across the floor. Dogs lunged for the scraps, fighting around the man's feet and legs, scrabbling through the ragged furs piled up to keep off the chill.

Corvus kept pacing, fists clenched behind his back and face schooled to patience. He glanced at Lanta, sitting remote and inaccessible as the very mountains, and fought the urge to shake the information out of her, to slap it from her. *The Blessed One is not as other women,* he reminded himself. *She'll wind my guts out on a stick if I touch her.* Despite his own warning, he glanced at her with a mixture of irritation and hunger. She didn't deign to meet his eyes.

'The gods wait for no man. Not even a king.' Lanta's voice was honey and poison and Corvus noted how the other war chiefs froze at its sound. 'There is much to discuss.'

Edwin, Liris's second, jumped up. 'I'll go, Blessed One,' he said and scuttled down the longhouse to the king's quarters at the end, his relief palpable. They all wanted to settle this and get out from under the Blessed One's eye. Bana's death hung in the air like the scent of blood.

Corvus had completed two more circuits below the dais before the yelling began. By the time the others had struggled out of their chairs, he was at Lanta's side with drawn sword, ready to defend her.

'The king,' Edwin screeched as he shoved back into the longhouse. His hands were bloody. 'The king has been murdered. Liris is dead!'

For a moment Lanta's calm cracked, and Corvus would've missed it if he hadn't been looking at her instead of Edwin squawking like a chicken on the block. But then the mask was firmly back in place. Corvus's sword tip drooped on to the dais as Edwin's words sank in. Corvus opened his mouth, closed it again, and looked at the men gathered like a gaggle of frightened children below him, backs to the dais, eyes on the far door. They were bursting with questions for Edwin, but none seemed keen to approach him.

Lanta picked up her skirts and strode the length of the longhouse, bursting through the door to the king's quarters and slamming it behind her before anyone could see. Edwin stood outside it, staring at his hands in disbelief.

Liris is dead and the Blessed One is with the body. Eagle Height has no king. Eagle Height is vulnerable.

'Gosfath, God of Blood, Dark Lady of death, I thank you,' Corvus whispered. 'I swear to be worthy of this chance you have given me. All I do is in your honour.' One of the chiefs turned at the sound of his voice, his mouth an O of curiosity.

'My feet are on the Path,' Corvus said, completing the prayer. He took three steps forward, raised his sword, and started killing. The king was dead. Long live the king.

CRYS

*Eleventh moon, seventeenth year of the reign of King Rastoth
North Harbour docks, Rilporin, Wheat Lands*

'I will have you know I am the most trustworthy man in Rilporin. No, not just in the capital, in all of Rilpor. And these cards are brand new, picked up from a shop in the merchants' quarter a mere hour ago. Examine them, gentlemen, hold them, look closely. Not marked, not raised, even colouring, even weight. Now, shall we play? A flagon, wench.'

Crys clicked his fingers at the pretty girl hovering in his eyeline and plastered a wide grin across his face. He'd been watching this pair for the last hour, and now they were just drunk enough to be clay in his hands.

The men watched suspiciously as he cut and shuffled the cards, fingers blurring, and dealt them with a neat flick of the wrist only slightly marred by the fact the cards stuck in or skittered over the spilt beer. They'd be ruined, but he'd just buy more. What was the point in gambling if he didn't spend the money he won? He slapped the remains of the deck into the middle of the table, scooped up his cards, examined them, swallowed ale to hide his glee and breathed thanks to the Fox God, the Trickster, patron of gamblers, thieves and soldiers. He was all three, on and off.

The faces of his fellow players were so wooden Crys could have carved his name into them, but the man to his left was tapping his foot on the floor. Man to his right? No obvious tell. No, wait, spinning the brass ring on his thumb. Excellent, he'd dealt the cards right.

'Five, no, six knights.' Crys opened the betting and tinkled the coppers next to the deck. He smiled and drank.

'Six from me,' Foot-tapper said.

Ring-spinner matched him. 'And from me.'

Crys made a show of looking at his cards again, squinting at the table and his opponents. 'Um, two more.' He added to the pile with a show of bravado that sucked them right in. He leant back in his chair and scratched the stubble on his cheek, fingernails rasping. He'd better shave before tomorrow's meeting. He'd better win enough to buy a razor.

'So, you fresh in from a Rank, Captain? The West, perhaps?' Foot-tapper asked.

Crys hid a grimace behind his cup: always the West. City-folk were obsessed with the West, with tales of Mireces and Watchers and border skirmishes. The crazy Wolves – civilians no less – were Watchers who took up arms to guard the foothills from Raiders and protect the worshippers of the Gods of Light from the depradations of the bloody Red Gods.

Crys didn't reckon half the stories were true, and those that had been once were embellished with every telling until the Watchers and Wolves were more myth than men and every soldier of the West Rank was a hero. *They're soldiers watching a line on a map for two years, interrupted with brief bouts of fighting against a couple of hundred men. Yeah. Heroes.*

Crys snorted. 'The North, actually,' he said, swallowing his frustration. 'Finished my rotation there. Palace Rank next.'

'Palace, eh? Two comfy years for you, then, eh? Must be a relief. But I'm Poe and this is Jud.'

Crys nodded at them both. 'Captain Crys Tailorson.'

'Captain of the Palace Rank? I'm sure no one deserves it more. I imagine King Rastoth is in the very safest of hands now you're here, Captain.' Poe watched him closely, looking for tells. Crys made a show of thumbing one card repeatedly. Deserved? He'd be bored out of his mind for two years, more like. Still, there were likely a lot more idiots prepared to lose their money here than in the North Rank and its surrounding towns. Few men had dared gamble with him towards the end of that rotation. Not to mention Rilporin bred prettier lasses.

Jud brayed a laugh. 'You hear about those Watchers? Ever met one? I hear the men all stick each other up there. Ever see that?'

'I haven't served in the West Rank yet,' Crys said, uncomfortable. It was all anyone could talk about of late, the rumours coming from the west; General Mace Koridam, son of Durdil Koridam, the Commander of the Ranks, increasing patrols and stockpiling weapons and food. 'And that sort of business is against the king's laws,' he added belatedly.

'Strange people, those Watchers. Civilians, ain't they? Take it upon themselves to patrol the border. Why? They don't get paid to do it, do they? Why risk your life when the West's there to protect you?' Poe asked. He seemed in no hurry to get on with the game. 'I mean, West's best, or so they say,' he added with an unexpected touch of malice.

'I know why,' Jud said, laughing again. 'It's 'cause their women are all so fucking ugly. That's why they fight, and that's why they stick each other. Nothing else to do.'

'Wolves fight, Watchers don't,' Crys explained. Jud frowned. 'They're all from Watchtown, it's just they call their warrior caste Wolves and the Wolves have little or no regard for the laws of Rilpor. As you said, they take it upon themselves to fight. And there are Wolf women as well, I hear,' Crys said as he flicked his cards again, letting the happy drunk mask slip for a moment. *West is best? Maybe you don't need all that coin weighing you down, Poe.* 'Fierce and just as good as the men,' he added.

'She-bears. 'Bout as pretty too, they say.' Jud emptied his cup, helping himself to more as Crys eyed him. 'They're all touched with madness, those Watchers. Fighting for no pay, letting their women fight. Women! Can you imagine? What'd you do if you had to fight a woman, Captain?'

Crys licked his teeth. 'Try not to lose,' he said. 'It'd look awful on my record.'

Poe laughed and slapped the table, but Jud had lost his sense of humour all of a sudden. 'Look at his eyes,' he hissed, waggling a finger in Crys's direction and heaving on Poe's arm.

Fuck's sake, and it had all been going so well. Crys put his palms on the sticky table and leant forward, opening his eyes wide and staring them down in turn. 'One blue, one brown, yes. Very observant.'

He sat back and folded his arms, the soggy cards tucked carefully into his armpit where they couldn't be seen. Old habits. 'But I had thought you wealthy, sophisticated merchants of this city and as such not susceptible to the superstitions of countryside fools. Perhaps I was mistaken. Perhaps I've been wasting my time here tonight.'

Jud and Poe eyed each other, clearly uncomfortable. They were nothing of the sort and all of them knew it.

Poe's foot tapped and he managed a nonchalant grin. 'But of course. A topic of conversation only. You must hear it a lot in the Ranks, no?' He drained his mug and ordered a flagon. *About fucking time, too.*

Crys forced a mollified note into his voice, at odds with the irritation mention of his eyes always engendered. Splitsoul, cursed, unlucky. He knew them all. 'I do, sir. Men either stick to me like bindweed thinking I'm lucky, or they refuse to be anywhere near me. It's a real pain in the arse, has dogged me all my life.' Poe tutted in sympathy. 'Still, what can a man do?'

'Cut one of them out?' Jud honked and laughed into his cup, spraying Crys with froth. Crys unfolded his arms and watched him.

Poe thumped him in the arm. 'Forgive my friend, Captain. Too much ale. He's got a sword, you fucking idiot,' he hissed to Jud, who was clutching his arm and whining.

Crys drew out the moment, but decided against it. 'Come on then, let's play,' he said and Poe slumped in relief, thumping Jud again for good measure.

'You heard the good captain. Play.'

'Two,' Jud said sulkily.

Excellent. And about bloody time. 'I call,' Crys said and plopped his cards face up, watching the others reveal. He'd lost by a dozen, as expected. Poe had the winner and scooped coins and ale to his side of the table, baring yellow snaggle-teeth in something that might have been a smile. On a bear.

Crys groaned and drank; he topped up the cups of his companions with fatalistic good cheer. Poe collected the cards and Crys watched him shuffle: not even an attempt to separate the already played cards through the deck. He dealt and Crys knew he'd have a poor hand. No matter, he wasn't ready to win just yet.

Gods, that meal was heavy, he thought as he made his first bet, but it was doing its job of soaking up the ale. Jud was red in the face and giggling, superstitions forgotten against the prospect of winning Crys's money. He'd be the first to get sloppy and Crys and Poe could clean him out in a few hands. But then they'd need another third. No, better to bide a while longer and then take them both for a little too much instead of everything. Crys had no need of an enemy on his first day in Rilporin, and some men preferred to blame the man instead of their luck when it came to cards.

Plan decided, Crys sucked down some more ale and proceeded to lose another three hands.

Crys had found a lucky streak from somewhere. Strange, that, how his fortune had changed so suddenly. He'd won back most of what he'd lost but was still some way behind the others. Still, it was all running smooth—

'I've been watching you. You're a cheat.'

Crys lurched up from his chair and fumbled for his sword as Poe and Jud gawped, faces twisting with drunken outrage. The light fell on the speaker and Crys gasped, released the hilt and dropped to one knee. 'Sire. Forgive me, Your Highness. You startled me and I – I simply reacted. I beg your pardon.'

Poe and Jud grabbed their coins and fled, not looking back, leaving Crys to the mercy of the Crown and seeming glad about it.

'Shut up, stand up and pour me a drink.'

'Yes, Your Highness.'

'Sire or milord will do, soldier.' Crys straightened and Prince Rivil took the proffered mug and sipped, made a face and sipped again. 'Awful. I note you haven't denied my accusation.'

Crys's knee buckled again but he hoisted himself back up. 'Your High— Milord may say and think anything he wishes, Sire,' he said in a rush, staring anywhere but into Rivil's face and so looking at his crotch instead. He blushed, straightened and snapped into parade rest, staring over the prince's left shoulder and through the man behind him, one-eyed, well-dressed, a lord if Crys was any judge.

'Oh, for shit's sake, man, stop that. You think I'd be in a dockside tavern if I wanted pomp and ceremony? Sit the fuck down and have a drink. I'm here for relaxation, not to have my arse kissed.'

'I – yes, Your . . . Sire.'

Rivil folded long legs under the small table and leant forward, oblivious to the ale staining the elbows of his velvet coat. 'This is Galtas Morellis, Lord of Silent Water,' he said, jerking a thumb at the man seating himself beside him.

Crys's head swam. Galtas, Rivil's drinking companion and personal bodyguard. Crys was in it up to his neck and it didn't smell sweet.

'Teach me your version of cheating at cards,' Rivil said abruptly. 'I'm not familiar with it.'

Oh, holy fuck. A bed and a razor, that's all he'd wanted. All right, maybe a woman, but was that so much to ask when you'd been stationed in the North Rank for the last two years, negotiating border treaties?

Crys swallowed ale, wetting his throat, giving himself time to think, not that he could see a way out. 'It would be an honour, Sire. Would you care to use my cards?'

*

Crys's stack of coins was dwindling fast. At this rate he'd be sleeping in the gutter and shaving himself with his sword come morning. Or just using it to slit his own throat; the Commander didn't listen to excuses, even ones about meeting a prince in a grimy tavern.

'Oi, rich man. You're fuckin' cheatin'. I been watching you, you lanky bastard. You're doing our brave soldier out of his hard-earned coin. He risks his life on those wild borders and comes here for a bit of ease and rest, and you're fuckin' doin' him out of his money like you don't have enough of it already? Fuckin' nobility.'

Crys was suddenly and entirely sober. Galtas had swivelled in his chair and then risen to his feet. Rivil remained seated, his back to the speaker and his cool gaze resting on Crys. The message was clear: get off your arse and help, Crys Tailorson. Crys got off his arse.

'Sir, I assure you nothing untoward is occurring here. I am merely experiencing bad luck with the cards. It happens – a lesson from the Fox God. Your concern is touching—'

'Never fear, soldier, we'll have at him for you. Fuckin' lords comin' in here and screwin' over decent hard-workin' folk. Honestly, you're doin' us a favour if you let us have 'im.'

'Really, I don't—' Crys began into the heavy silence of dozens of men readying for a brawl.

The man was already swinging at Rivil's unprotected head and Crys could do nothing but bite off the words and make a desperate lunge over the table. Galtas caught the attacker's wrist, twisted it up and into an elbow lock, and threw him back into the press. He drew his sword, useless in the crowd but an effective deterrent to unarmed men.

'City guard's comin'. Scarper,' a voice called before anyone had a chance to react. Rivil's eyes snapped to Crys. The aggressors melted away and the rest of the patrons settled down, buzzing with conversation. Many slipped out, not eager to meet the Watch. Crys sat back down and emptied his mug.

Galtas remained on his feet, scanning the room for long moments, and then sat. Rivil jerked his head at Crys. 'You did that? Those words? How?'

'A knack,' Crys said. 'I can make my voice come from somewhere else.'

'Sounds like witchcraft. And with eyes like that, I'm not surprised,' Rivil teased. Galtas frowned, a dagger appearing in his hand.

'No. Just a knack, like I said.' Crys had both hands palm down on the table, as unthreatening as he could make himself. Rivil scraped all of his winnings, and Galtas's, over to Crys's side of the table.

'My thanks,' Rivil said, 'but why bother? I'm not exactly popular with the Ranks. Why not let that man kick the shit out of me?'

'You are my prince, Sire,' Crys said, dropping the coins into his pouch, 'even if you are a better cheat than me. No one kicks the shit out of the prince while I'm with him.'

'I'm glad to hear it. Come and find me when you're off-duty tomorrow. I might have a use for you.'

DURDIL

Eleventh moon, seventeenth year of the reign of King Rastoth
The palace, Rilporin, Wheat Lands

'Where is His Majesty?' Durdil asked. The throne room was empty but for guards, the audience chamber vacant too.

'The queen's wing, Commander Koridam,' Questrel Chamberlain said with an oily smile and the corners of Durdil's mouth turned down. *Third time this month.*

Durdil's breath steamed as he ducked out of the throne room and into a courtyard and took a shortcut through the servants' passages. Winter was coming early this year, and the preparations for Yule were increasing apace.

Servants flattened themselves against the rough stone walls as he passed, ducking their heads respectfully. He nodded at each in turn. Durdil knew every servant in the palace; it made it that much easier to identify outsiders, potential threats to his king.

A guard stood in silence outside the queen's chamber. Durdil slowed. He straightened his uniform and scraped his fingernails over the iron-grey stubble on his head.

'Lieutenant Weaverson, is the king inside?'

'Yes, sir.'

'Did he speak to you?'

Weaverson was impassive as only a guard can be. 'Not to me, sir. He was conversing with the queen.'

Durdil paused, chewing the inside of his cheek. Nicely phrased, no hint of mockery. 'Thank you, Lieutenant. As you were.'

'Sir,' Weaverson said and thumped the butt of his pike into the carpet.

Durdil moved past him and pushed open the door to the queen's private chambers. He hesitated on the threshold, bracing himself, and then stepped inside, closing the door behind him. Rastoth was in the queen's bedroom, staring at the empty bed in confusion.

'Your Majesty, you shouldn't be in here,' Durdil said quietly, and Rastoth looked over his shoulder, his eyes wide and watery. Durdil was struck by his gauntness. Where had that muscle and fat, that ruddy good humour, gone? This man was a shadow of himself.

'Where is Marisa, Durdil? Where is my queen?' Rastoth asked, his voice plaintive. 'I was just talking with her. She was right here.' He gestured vaguely and creases appeared between his brows. 'But that's not right, is it?' he whispered. His fingers smoothed the coverlet over and over, the material thin and cold in the freezing room. No fire burning, no tapestries on the walls any more. No rugs.

Durdil walked towards him. 'No, Sire, it's not right,' he said, his voice low. 'Marisa's gone, my old friend. Your queen's dead. Almost a year now.'

Rastoth mewed like a seagull from deep in his chest. He collapsed on to the bed and hid his face in palsied hands too weak to support the rings on each finger. 'No, that can't be. That can't be.'

He straightened suddenly, eyes bright with pain and coherence. 'Murdered. Disfigured. Defiled here in this very room,' he said, his voice harsh and broken and filling with rage. 'My queen. My wife. And her killers still at large. Are they not, Commander? Despite your promises. Despite your *every* promise?' He spat the words.

Durdil inhaled through flared nostrils and knelt before Rastoth, his knee protesting at the cold stone. No rugs because they'd been covered in blood. No tapestries because they'd been torn from the walls, covering the queen as her killers hacked through the material into her body. As though even the murderers couldn't bear to look on what they'd done before they killed her, the destruction they'd wrought on her body and face.

No shattered door bolt, remember? Marisa opened the door to her murderers, let them in. Her guards dead on the threshold, dead facing into the room, not out of it. It ran like a litany through Durdil's head. *The queen knew her killers. Her guards knew them, hadn't stopped them from entering, only engaged them when they were on their way out, the deed done.*

Durdil swallowed the thoughts. 'Yes, Sire. I have failed to find the killers of your queen. I have failed you.' He chanced a look up. 'But I have not stopped looking, my liege. I will never stop looking. I will find them. And we will bring them to justice.'

But Rastoth wasn't listening. 'Why, there she is. My little sparrow, hiding behind her loom.' He scrambled to his feet, tripping on the edge of his cloak and his knee catching Durdil's shoulder. He wobbled past and Durdil heaved himself to his feet, each of his fifty-six years an anvil on his back.

Rastoth had ducked behind the loom by the window.

'Where are you hiding now, my pretty?' he called. 'Marisa? Marisa, my love.'

Durdil winced. 'Your Majesty, we must return to your chambers. The hour grows late. Let us leave the queen to her rest. It has been a long day.'

Rastoth straightened and stared at Durdil through the strings of the loom, Marisa's half-completed tapestry collecting dust on its frame. He'd tried this before and Rastoth had flown into a fury. Durdil had no idea which way it would play this time.

'You're right, of course, Durdil. She's tired. I'm tired.' He glanced fondly at the bed. 'Sleep well, my beauty,' he said, and tiptoed to the door, hissing at Durdil to do the same when the heels of his boots rang on the flagstones.

Durdil grimaced and rose on to his toes and together they crept to the door of the empty room and squeezed through it. Weaverson didn't so much as glance in their direction, but Durdil stopped in surprise when he saw Prince Rivil.

'We must let her rest, Commander,' Rastoth murmured as he pulled shut the door. 'Perhaps tomorrow my wife will be well enough to be seen by the court again, do you think?'

Rivil stepped forward and Durdil relinquished his place at the king's side. 'I'm sure Mother will be well again soon,' he said, taking Rastoth's arm. 'For now it's you I'm worried about. You shouldn't be wandering around in the cold at this time of night.'

Durdil glanced at Weaverson and then followed his king and prince, listening to Rivil's careful voice, watching his hand firm on his father's elbow. 'Come, Father, you should be abed,' Rivil said with a nod to Durdil. Durdil nodded back and forced a smile for the prince.

Rastoth's fits were getting worse and there was nothing Durdil could do about it. His friend and king was losing his grip on reality; he was slowly becoming a laughing-stock. Durdil wasn't sure that even finding Marisa's killers could end Rastoth's illness now. Not that he had a single lead anyway. He knuckled his eyes hard and glanced again at Weaverson. Then he followed in the wake of his king.

DOM

Eleventh moon, seventeenth year of the reign of King Rastoth
Watcher village, Wolf Lands, Rilporian border

'I've got you this time, you old bugger,' Dom muttered. He was knee-deep in a stream that began high up in the Gilgoras Mountains and widened into the Gil, mightiest river of Rilpor. His bare feet were numb and the air smelt of snow, but the pike was cornered. Dom felt forward with his toes, the fishing spear up by his jaw.

The pike flicked its tail and Dom grinned as he edged closer. He'd laid the net behind him just in case, but this was becoming personal. A flicker again, and Dom lunged, stabbing down into the gloom.

The pike flashed past him, twisting out of the spear's path, and Dom spun, slipped on a rock and went to one knee. He gasped at the cold but the pike wasn't in the net, so he lunged back on to his feet and examined the pool.

'Come out, come out, little fishy,' he sang, 'I want you in my belly.'

26

Instead the sun came out and reflected off the water, blinding him, and Dom blinked. The brightness stayed in his vision, like an ember bursting into life, racing into a conflagration.

Dom groaned as the image of fire grew. He dropped the spear and splashed for the bank, panting. 'No,' he grunted through a thick tongue, 'no no no,' but it was too late. He was a stride away from land when the knowing came, and he hurled himself desperately towards dry ground before the images took him.

He felt his chest hit the mud as his surroundings vanished and then all that was left was the message from the Gods of Light, filling his mind with fire and pain and truth.

'You really are a shit fisherman, Templeson,' Sarilla laughed when he staggered back into camp at dusk. She pointed her bow at him. 'Why don't you just – ah, fuck. Lim! Lim, it's Dom.'

Sarilla slung Dom's arm over her shoulders and took his weight; she led him to the nearest fire and sat him so close the heat stung his face. He turned away, unwilling to look into the flames, and Sarilla chafed his hands between hers, and then dragged his jerkin off and threw her coat around his shoulders.

Lim arrived at a run and Dom held up a hand before he could speak. 'Just get me warm first,' he croaked. 'I've been belly up in that fucking stream all afternoon.' *It might not be what I think it is. Fox God, I hope it's not what I think it is.*

They stripped him, wrapped him in blankets and made him drink warm mead until the colour came back into his face and he finally stopped shivering. Feltith, their healer, pronounced him hale and an idiot. Dom didn't have the energy or inclination to disagree. He couldn't look at the fire, but he met the eyes of the others one by one.

'I have to go to the scout camp, and I have to go alone.' He waited out their protests, gaze turned inward as he fought to unravel the Dancer's meaning. His hand gestured vaguely west. 'It's coming from the mountains. I have to fetch it. Fetch the key. Message. Herald?'

Dom's face twitched and he spoke over Lim's fresh complaints. 'Don't know. Not yet. It's like – it's like a storm's brewing up there. There'll be a warning before it breaks, but only if I can get to it in time.' He grunted in frustration. 'I don't know. It doesn't make sense. Midsummer.'

'Midsummer? What about the message?' Sarilla said.

'That too. Shit, why is it so hard?' Dom grunted, knuckling at the vicious pain behind his right eye. Sarilla slapped his hand away. 'If the Dancer and the Fox God want me to know something, why don't They just tell me?'

'They are. We just don't have the capacity to understand,' Sarilla said, and for once her tone held no mockery. 'They're gods, Dom. You can't expect Them to be like us.'

'Sarilla's right, the knowings rarely make sense at first,' Lim soothed him. 'But midsummer? We're not even at Yule. We've got time, Dom. Don't push it; it'll come. There's no immediate threat?' he clarified.

'It's nearly a thousand years since the veil was cast,' Dom said suddenly. He had no idea where the words came from, but years of knowings had taught him to relax and let his voice tell him what he didn't yet understand. 'Now it weakens. The Red Gods wax and the Light wanes. Blood rises. Find the herald; staunch the flow.'

Dom focused on the mud between his boots, loamy and rich, his chest heaving as though he'd run down a deer. He swallowed bile. The pain crescendoed and then settled to a steady agony that made his vision pulse with colours around the edges. *This is it. I think it's starting. After all these years, it's coming.*

I need more time.

Lim, Sarilla and Feltith were silent, waiting for more. Dom squeezed his hands into his armpits to hide their trembling. No point scaring them before he had to. *Why not? I'm scared. I'm fucking terrified.* But he was the calestar, for good or ill, and with the knowings came duty. *Duty? Sacrifice, more like. My sacrifice.* Duty, he told himself sternly, silencing the inner voice.

'Everything's in flux, but there's always a threat,' he said, finally answering Lim's question. 'I'm going up there tonight.'

Lim didn't argue further. 'Rest a while longer and I'll pack provisions.'

'I have to go alone,' Dom insisted.

'You can't go alone,' Sarilla said quietly. 'If you have another knowing up there, in the Mireces' own territory, you'll be helpless. Even I don't want you frozen to death or eaten by bears. Or taken by Mireces.'

Lim glanced at Sarilla. 'Send a messenger to Watchtown and another to the West Rank. You know how much truth to tell to each. We don't know what we're preparing for yet, so let's not panic.' He pointed west, the way Dom had. 'But nothing good has ever come out of those mountains. Be alert.'

THE BLESSED ONE

Eleventh moon, year 994 since the Exile of the Red Gods
Longhouse, Eagle Height, Gilgoras Mountains

Lanta dealt regularly in blood and death in her exaltation of the gods, but what had been done to Liris . . . it was messy, wild. A frenzied, senseless attack, lacking in control, lacking in style.

Edwin had done a headcount and reported one missing slave as well as the various men out on business for the king or Lanta herself; then he'd taken a war band and hounds out in pursuit of the killer. The room stank of blood and fear, a scent easy enough for the dogs to follow in the clear mountain air.

Lanta's thoughts returned to her predicament. One missing slave was easy enough to replace. A killer easy enough to track down. One pliable king, however, would need careful consideration. Of the war chiefs, Mata would be—

She stopped halfway down the longhouse, trying to make sense of what she was seeing. 'What is this?'

Corvus, seated on the throne, looked up from inspecting

his boots. They were bloody, as were his hands. 'This, Blessed One, is a succession. I thought our people should have the smoothest transition after Liris's untimely death.' Corvus spared her a brief smile and picked drying blood from beneath a thumbnail.

He hasn't. He wouldn't, not without my approval. Her eyes flicked to the corpses at the base of the dais. *And yet he has.* She replayed his words as she fought for serenity. '*Our* people?' She arched a brow. 'May I remind you, Corvus of Crow Crag, that not too many years ago you were taken as slave from Rilpor? You were Madoc of Dancer's Lake then, born and raised a heathen. So these are *my* people, and *I* decide what is best for them.'

Corvus glared at her. 'Am I not a good son of the Dark Lady? I pay my blood debts, I raid in Her name, I worship Her and Her Brother, Holy Gosfath, God of Blood. I am Mireces, dedicated in blood and fire, war chief of Crow Crag and now King of the Mireces. That is all of my lineage you need to know.'

So quickly he challenges me. So quickly he eliminates any who would oppose him. And of course, there is Rillirin, who Liris dragged to his chamber after Bana's holy sacrifice. And Rillirin . . . interests me.

'Such a hurried transition, Corvus,' Lanta said in a low voice as she stalked through the silent audience, picking her way through the tangle of corpses below the dais. Slaves were wide-eyed with panic, huddled at the back of the long-house like a flock of chickens before the wolf. 'On whose authority do you claim the throne? I was not consulted.'

Corvus steepled his fingers before his lips. 'My own. But you can consult the other war chiefs if you'd prefer. Not sure how much talk you'll get out of them, though.'

Lanta paused in her stride and then continued, stately,

predatory. *So the challenge comes now, before his arse has even warmed the throne. Then let the gods decide.*

'As for authority, I claim it by right of conquest, as Liris did.' Corvus had pitched his voice to reach the end of the longhouse, drawing warriors to him. They crowded at Lanta's back.

'I stand beside the throne, my voice is second to the—' Lanta began as she stepped on to the dais. Corvus leapt from his seat and, firm but courteous, pushed her back down the wooden steps. Lanta wobbled, rigid and red with fury now, down on the floor with the rabble.

'I didn't invite you to approach,' Corvus said, his voice pitched loud. 'When I do, a seat will be made available for you behind me and I will ask for the *Dark Lady's*' – he stressed the honorific – 'counsel as and when I need it.'

'The Red Gods will not suffer me to be abused,' Lanta screeched, her fury a lightning bolt from a clear sky. *Insolent, arrogant child! He thinks stabbing men in the back gives him authority over the gods? Over me?*

Men shrank away from her anger, but Corvus's smile mocked. He returned to his throne before answering, stretching the moment long, forcing Lanta and the rest to wait.

'Where is your obeisance, Blessed One?'

Lanta gaped, disbelief etched across her face. 'What did you say?' she whispered.

'Liris was weak – you took advantage of that to seize more power than your station demanded. I'm restoring the balance. You may not have authorised a new king, but the Dark Lady did. So kneel. Or die. I don't much care either way.'

'I know the Lady's will,' Lanta shouted. 'I am the Blessed One. She talks to me, not you.' Her fists were clenched, face hot with outrage and anger. A challenge directed not just at her power, but that of the gods? *I'll see him writhing beneath my knife for this outrage.*

Corvus spread his red hands. 'Then you'll know it was Her will that I defeated my rivals. If She didn't want me on the throne, they would've killed me.'

There were murmurs and Lanta felt the shift in the room. He was right and everyone knew it; godsdamnit but she knew it. A change in tactic, then. 'King Corvus,' she said and he grinned, 'now is not the time for a change in administration. Perhaps—'

'Well, unless you can bring a man back from the dead, you're fucked,' he replied and there was muted laughter, quickly stilled.

Lanta bared her teeth. It had been years since anyone'd dared interrupt her. She remembered now how little she liked it. 'I simply meant, perhaps our people would prefer a united front until you settle into your new role. There are many things I can advise on. If you would allow it?'

'No.'

Lanta could feel her cheeks burning. The air fizzed between them as Corvus looked into her eyes, all cool detachment and deep amusement, daring her to look away.

She smiled. There were many ways to play this game and she had far more experience than he did. Still, he'd riled her. 'Perhaps men will be sent to Crow Crag for your consort,' she hissed, and heard the collective intake of breath. Had she really just threatened the king? Corvus flicked his fingers in dismissal, his face disinterested. As though she hadn't even spoken. Lanta inhaled hard.

'Perhaps you should focus on finding Liris's killer instead,' he said.

'Oh, don't you worry about that,' she said. 'They'll be

found and dragged before you for judgement. I wonder what sort of a king you'll be then, when you have before you the one who really granted you the throne.'

Lanta was never reckless; the gods had too many plans and she was too important to all of them. Yet that easy smile, those infuriating blue eyes, made her desperate to hurt him, but instead of her barbs finding his flesh, everything she said simply glanced off him, as though he was wearing that ridiculous Rilporian plate armour.

'Tread lightly, Blessed One,' Corvus said, his voice low with menace. 'You have no idea who you're dealing with.' He paused and smiled, friendly, open. 'But I can show you, if you ever threaten me or mine again.'

Perhaps that had been over-hasty, she conceded as she stared at Corvus and his bloody hands, his bloody boots. His strawberry-blond hair was wild and sweaty from the fight, and she dropped her gaze from his to examine the bodies. Wounds in the back. She snorted faintly. He hadn't even had the balls to do it properly.

But done it was. While she'd been examining the torn and bloody corpse of Liris in the room next door, she'd lost everything. The gods' desires subordinated to the desires and whims of a man. *No,* she vowed into the silence of her skull, *not during my lifetime. Not when I still have some power.*

'It is a comfort to hear you will not let Liris's killer escape. By all means conduct your own investigation; I shall entreat the Dark Lady's advice. Liris had taken a whore into his bedchamber before he was killed; she escaped during the confusion but I've already sent men after her. The chances are good she saw the killer and we can use her to identify the man,' Lanta said, deliberately keeping Rillirin's identity to herself. She needed every scrap of leverage she could find.

'Why don't you think it was the whore?' Corvus asked.

Lanta laughed. 'A slave and a whore? Impossible.' She turned away. *Even so, I'll have that cunt on the altar stone one way or another, belly open to the sky and soul food for the gods.*

'Blessed One,' Corvus said in a voice of honey, and she gritted her teeth and stopped. 'You still haven't made your obeisance.'

'I kneel only to the gods,' she grated over her shoulder, her eyes murderous slits.

Corvus tutted and shook his head. 'Not true. I hear you regularly knelt to Liris, mouth open and no doubt eyes closed. Who'd want to see that, after all?' He laughed and there was a ripple of shocked amusement through the hall, amusement at her expense.

Lanta could hear her teeth grinding and swallowed a roil of nausea. She stared at him in silence. The air grew thick with hate, but Corvus never lost that easy smile. She could level men with a glance but not, it appeared, this one. Not yet. So she curtseyed, low, deep, correct. *What does it mean, after all? Nothing. It is as empty as his supposed kingship and soon to be as distant a memory.*

In stunned silence, Lanta walked the length of the hall, proud and distant. She crooked a finger and her priest, Pask, held the door for her and then followed her through. It closed with a click and she sucked in a deep breath of mountain air. She had much to think about.

CRYS

Eleventh moon, seventeenth year of the reign of King Rastoth
Commander's quarters, the palace, Rilporin, Wheat Lands

'So, Captain Tailorson, it appears you have led a varied and interesting career in the last two years with the North Rank. Any particular reason for that?' Commander Durdil Koridam eyed him from behind his desk.

'No, sir.'

'Demoted to lieutenant for brawling with common soldiers, a month in the cells for smuggling a family over the border into Rilpor, promotion back to captain for outstanding gallantry under fire . . . Outstanding?'

'Major Bedras found himself surrounded by the Dead Legion. It seemed appropriate to save him.'

'From the Dead Legion? Alone?' Durdil's grey eyebrows rose a fraction.

'There were five of them, sir, youngsters on a blood hunt to prove their manhood.'

'And how did they manage to surround the major?'

'Couldn't say, sir.'

36

'No, though I note from General Tariq's subsequent report that the major is no longer a major.'

'As you say, sir.'

'And the family you allowed into our country?'

'A woman with three children, starving and filthy. Husband killed by the Dead, fleeing to save her children's lives. It was . . . it was the right thing to do.'

'You are a soldier, Tailorson. Right and wrong is for your superiors to decide.'

Crys met his eyes. 'Right and wrong is for every man to decide. Sir.'

Durdil leant back in his chair and pursed his lips. Crys stared past his left ear, palms clammy. 'There is a pattern here, Tailorson. You have talent, you have intelligence, you have flair. You could be an outstanding officer. And yet every time you reach captain you do something to get demoted. Are you afraid of being a leader?'

Crys's left eyelid flickered. 'Sir.'

'Was that a "yes, sir" or a "no, sir", Tailorson?'

'It was an "I don't know the answer to your question, sir", sir.'

'Well, you're honest, at least. You're to join the Palace Rank, Tailorson.' Durdil shuffled some papers. 'But because I'm curious about you, you're to be under my direct command.'

'Sir.'

The corner of Durdil's mouth twitched. 'Normally I'd assume the "Sir" was agreement, but with you I'm not so sure. South barracks. Report to Major Wheeler at dusk for the night shift. Dismissed.' Crys saluted, spun on his heel and marched to the door. 'And, Tailorson? Turn up hungover in my presence again and you won't be demoted; I'll flog the booze out of you myself. Off you go.'

How does he know? How can he possibly know? I've had a bath, a shave, a change of uniform. Crys was still pondering it when he exited the palace and was slapped in the face with a gust of rain. He shivered and hunched his shoulders against the wet. His scarf and cloak were in the barracks in the second circle of the city, a good half-hour's walk away. The palace crouched at the centre of the city, surrounded by walls like the heart of an onion.

He made his way through the gate into the fourth circle, walking fast and trying not to gawk. The palace in Fifth Circle was awe-inspiring and suitably royal, but Fourth Circle was home to the nobles. Real people lived here, albeit rich and powerful ones, in houses that were ridiculous confections of wood and stone and paint and carved plinths, all set in lavish grounds that could have accommodated three times the number of houses but seemed to serve no purpose except to look pretty.

Rich men and their rich fancies. Never mind the slums in First Circle and the beggars holed up in the tanneries or the slaughter district. Still, it was wide open and defensible and another layer of protection between the palace and any invaders.

Crys snorted and wiped rain from his face. Rumours of unrest were one thing, but Rilporin couldn't fall. Even the thought was impossible. He stood aside for a clatter of horses and their noble riders, peering up in case it was the Prince Rivil. Still couldn't quite believe that. When the prince'd run out of copper knights to bet with, he'd started using silver royals as if they were nothing, and he'd given Crys all his winnings at the end of the night. He hadn't counted it but he was pretty sure it was more than a month's pay.

Crys felt a stab of shame at how dismissive he'd just been of the nobility. Rivil wasn't like that and he was more than a lord. He was royalty and, yes, he gambled and drank, but he also rewarded those who served him and aided the king and the heir, Prince Janis, in running Rilpor. Rivil probably did more for the people than all the nobility put together.

Galtas, though. Galtas was as unpleasant as a runny shit, and the loathing was mutual. It had taken all of an hour for them to agree on that, and it was the only thing they did agree on. There was just something wrong about him, something inherently untrustworthy. Crys didn't think he should have so prominent a position close to the prince. But maybe that was Rivil's weakness? A certain blindness to the bad in people. It would be a shame if true. Crys found he didn't want to see Rivil get hurt.

He exited the fourth circle into the silk and spice quarter of the third, the scents wafting despite the rain. He bought dried mint for tea to settle his stomach and some massively overpriced pepper to spice up the standard-issue breakfast pottage. This might be Rilporin, but it seemed rations were the same wherever you were stationed.

Rilporin, fairest city in the world. He reckoned the whole of Three Beeches, his home town, would fit in Fourth Circle with room to spare. The shops and stalls stopped selling silks and spices and he was in the craft district, with wares of all kinds on display, from tiny polished metal mirrors to knives, cooking pots and jewellery side by side with carved wooden toys and fine beeswax candles. It was a warren of delights, from the pretty girls selling their goods to the gossip they let fall so easily from their painted mouths.

By the time he'd got through the craft district into the cloth district his purse was lighter and he'd had to buy a pack to carry his purchases. Still, the new knife for his brother Richard and the wooden horse for little Wenna were worth every copper and more. Just a shame he couldn't see their faces when they were delivered.

The sun was westering as he tucked the last of his purchases into his pack, and he slung it over his shoulder and hurried through the press towards the gate into Second Circle and the south barracks. Hungover was bad enough. If he was late as well, he may as well kiss his captaincy goodbye – again.

The south barracks were awash with the scent of fifteen hundred men living in close proximity. Feet and armpits and farts, mostly, the hint of sweat and blood souring the mixture further. Crys barely noticed; he'd been a soldier for twelve years and his nose had long since stopped recognising that particular odour.

The south barracks' captains shared a small room away from the main dormitories, a luxury he hadn't been expecting. He slid into it now, just as Kennett, his bunk-mate, was shrugging into his uniform.

Kennett whistled. 'Cutting it fine, aren't you?'

Crys flung the pack on to his bunk and tore at the buttons of his sodden uniform. He had one more, dry and mostly clean, which had been stuffed with packets of sweet-smelling herbs for the journey. He dragged it out of his chest and shook it out. 'Got lost,' he said.

Kennett eyed the pack and shook his head. 'Sure,' he said. 'Lost. Right.'

'What's this Wheeler like, anyway?' Crys asked as he towelled his hair and struggled into the dry uniform.

'An annoying little shit, mostly,' a voice said. Crys had his head stuck in his uniform and grunted in reply. 'Stickler for the rules, particularly for punctuality,' the voice continued.

'Sounds charming,' Crys said, his voice muffled. Kennett didn't answer. The voice didn't answer. *Shit.* Crys forced his head through the neck hole and looked over to the door. *Really shit.*

He snapped out a salute. 'Major Wheeler? Captain Crys Tailorson reporting for duty.'

'No, you're not,' Wheeler said. 'You're still getting dressed.'

'I got lost, sir. A thousand apologies, sir.' He buckled his sword belt, did up his buttons and dragged fingers through his hair.

'Did you?' Wheeler asked. 'I trust it won't happen again.'

'Absolutely not, sir,' Crys said and snapped into parade rest. Wheeler was taller than him, lean in the waist and broad in the shoulders. He stood with an easy grace that told Crys he knew exactly how to use the sword on his hip. His face was calm, his eyes curious and maybe, just maybe, the littlest bit amused.

'Are you an arse-licker, Tailorson?' Wheeler asked.

'No, sir, never could get used to the taste. Just keen to make a good first impression.'

Wheeler huffed. 'Well, you haven't, so stop trying to ingratiate yourself and fall in.' He gestured through the door and Crys saw his men. His Hundred. All listening to this little exchange with the greatest of enthusiasm. Crys saluted and marched past Wheeler into the corridor. He swept his gaze along the Hundred and found nothing to fault. What they thought was another matter entirely.

'Our post, Major?' he asked.

'East wing of the palace. The heir and His Highness Prince Rivil's quarters and surrounds. This is your lieutenant, Roger Weaverson. Rilporin born and bred. Take him with you next time you venture into the city, Captain. He'll see you don't get lost.'

'Thank you, Major,' Crys said, and nodded to Weaverson, a lanky youth with more spots than beard, but he too carried

41

a sword and carried it well. 'Lieutenant, Hundred, my name is Captain Crys Tailorson, late of the North Rank. I don't know you yet, but I'll come and speak to each of you during this shift. Any questions or concerns, please do speak up and I'll see what can be done.' He faced Wheeler again and saluted.

'You have command, Captain,' Wheeler said.

Crys nodded. 'Lieutenant Weaverson, fastest route to the palace,' he said.

They set out, his Hundred marching behind him, and Crys felt himself fall into the same rhythm, the movements as automatic as breathing. Weaverson took them on a circuitous route, and Crys had his earlier suspicion confirmed: the roads deliberately curved away from the gates in each circle to confuse and confound an enemy. Made it a bastard to do your shopping, but if this place was ever attacked, it'd be a blessing and no mistake.

'So, Lieutenant, what should I know about my Hundred?'

'Good men all, sir,' Weaverson said, as Crys had expected. Never mind, he'd find out soon enough. 'Can I ask a question, sir?' Crys nodded. 'Is it true about the Dead Legion and the Mireces, that they've allied to invade? You coming from the North, I thought you'd know the truth of it.'

'I know nothing of it, by which you can assume it's horse-shit, Lieutenant. My ear is always pressed most firmly to the ground, and I haven't heard it. The Dead have their own honour, their own code and their own gods. A version of our gods, really, when you get down to it. They're a small cult within Listre and even if they did join forces with the Raiders, there aren't enough of them to make much of a difference. So no, I wouldn't expect there to be verified news of an alliance.'

'So there isn't a Mireces invasion coming? Puck has a

brother in the West, and he said they're restless up there, causing all sorts of mischief.'

'Causing mischief and invading a country are two fairly different things, Lieutenant,' Crys said, and took the sting from his words with a grin and a slap on the boy's back. 'Soldiers talk. Gods, we gossip worse than women at the loom or men in their cups. But I might be wrong, so we should probably guard those princes really well, don't you think? In case the Mireces have made it into the palace? I want you using every ounce of your guarding muscles, all right? Let no inch of the blank stone wall opposite your face go unstudied during the endless, cold hours ahead. Concentrate really hard on the important stuff, like standing up straight and not farting when someone rich walks past.'

There were chuckles from the first couple of ranks behind him and a sheepish smile from Weaverson. 'It's an important job, lads,' he called, raising his voice, 'even if it isn't a complicated one. So if you cock it up, I'll know you're a complete imbecile and will treat you accordingly. This is my first shift as your captain. Don't make me look bad and I won't have to make you search for something I think I might have lost at the bottom of a deep and pungent cesspit.' More laughter, and Crys knew they were relaxing into his command, deciding he was all right, not a high-born, bought-his-commission, weak-chinned moron.

Crys took a deep breath of cold night air, sucking it in through his nose and exhaling through a broad grin. Greatest city, tallest walls, miles from a border that might get feisty at any moment. Even better, there was money in his purse and men under his command. Truly was it said that life could be worse than being a captain in His Majesty's Palace Rank.

RILLIRIN

Eleventh moon, year 994 since the Exile of the Red Gods
Sky Path, Gilgoras Mountains

She'd thought the storm a blessing when it rushed in, covering her tracks and blowing her scent downhill. She'd stumbled through the night, expecting every moment to be caught, for the Mireces' dogs to fasten their teeth in her and drag her into the snow. She'd made it on to the Sky Path and to the source of the Gil River before she'd heard the first howls on the wind. She'd made it so much further than she'd expected, a night and a morning and an afternoon.

Now, though, with the sky darkening to dusk again and her skin as blue as her gown where it wasn't rusty with dried blood, facing an angry mountain cat, Rillirin changed her mind. There were no more blessings left, not for the likes of her.

'I don't want your goat,' she hissed and the cat's yowl went up an octave. She edged back the way she'd come, back in the direction of her pursuers, wondering which way to die would be least painful. Probably the cat. But the cat's ears were better than hers and they pricked up, the rumble of threat dying in its throat. It'd heard those hunting her despite the howl of the wind. They were closer than she'd thought, then. She cursed and looked behind, catching flickers of torchlight further up the mountain, the faintest tang of smoke. Liris's blood was a beacon calling to the dogs, and she hadn't had the foresight to wash it off. Now it was too late.

Stay ahead of them, get down into the foothills, find someone who'll help. She shifted back towards the cat and its ears flattened, then pricked again. *Face it, no one's going to help a woman dressed in blue and covered in blood. You're dead whoever finds you first.* Rillirin swallowed tears and shoved her hair back out of her eyes. *Then fuck you all,* she thought, *I'll save myself. Somehow.*

Gripping the remains of the goat, the cat bounded lightly down the sheer rock face on to a ledge Rillirin hadn't noticed and vanished, its pelt as patchy white as its surroundings. Follow it or follow the path? Could the dogs handle the cat's path? Could she?

A faint howl on the wind made up her mind for her and she edged on to the steep rock, her boots scrabbling for purchase, the wind tearing at the remains of her skirt and throwing her off balance. She skidded, fell hard on her right hip and was sliding down the rock before she'd had a chance to suck in breath to scream.

She hit the cat's ledge, winded, and sailed on past, faster, stone burning the backs of her legs and arse until there was no more mountain and then she did scream, falling through space for long, endless seconds, eyes screwed shut, arms flailing uselessly through the air.

She hit water so cold it felt like knives stabbing into her. She'd thought herself cold before, but this was cold that burnt. Everything constricted and she hit the bottom. Fighting her way back up against the drag of her skirts, her head broke the surface and she warbled in a breath, lungs burning as well as her skin. She opened her eyes in time to see the rock the current slammed her into, crumpling her body and forcing her head back beneath the icy surface. She rebounded and the current swept her on, every breath a choking effort against the cold and the insidious lethargy creeping through her limbs.

She could hear the echo of men and dogs lost somewhere behind her, far above the river. If she survived the cold, survived the weight of her skirts dragging her down, survived the rocks, rapids and falls, she'd gladly pray daily for the rest of her life to any god who'd have her.

The river's voice changed, deeper and angrier, a full-throated roar. The cold, the pain: none of it mattered. There was a waterfall ahead, and Rillirin wasn't sure she'd survive this fall. She started to paddle, then to thrash, her limbs heavy and dull. The current picked up, swirling her with playful malevolence into the centre of the river, and then again, endlessly, she fell.

Rillirin must've gone another half-mile after the waterfall before the water slowed and she managed to haul herself on to the bank. She'd seen enough slaves die of cold in Eagle Height and so she stripped off her gown. She wrung out the worst of the water and then used the rough material to scrub hard at her skin, stimulating blood flow. *At least I don't smell of blood any more.* A giggle escaped through chattering teeth.

She staggered forward, fell to her hands and knees and stared blearily at the ground. Pine needles. She crawled forwards into the shadow of trees, a copse so small as to not be worth the name. The wind still howled through the trunks and gouged her skin but the softness under her knees brought tears to her eyes. She squirmed behind a trunk and the wind lessened. Rillirin curled on her side and dragged at the ground, piling needles up and over her, heaping them on to her thighs and flank and chest, against her shoulders and around the back of her head, draping the gown over the top. It cut the wind even further. A few minutes to restore some warmth and she'd look for some way to make a fire. Just a few minutes . . .

Rillirin blinked and stretched, felt an immediate bite of cold as the pine needles slithered away and the damp wool of her gown settled against her skin.

Daylight. Fuck, she'd slept all night. They could be right there, right behind her. Rillirin lay still, her eyes roaming between the trees and out on to the mountainside. The river chattered angrily behind her, swollen with snowmelt. There wasn't any movement, and she didn't expect the Mireces would wait for her to wake up before taking her captive. Had they passed her by, or missed her completely and taken the path she'd meant to take herself?

Rillirin slid to her feet and into her gown, torn and ragged now, one sleeve missing, but all she had against the cold. Checking for movement, she crept to the bank and splashed water into her mouth, wincing at the cold and the pain in her face and jaw, pain which started to spread throughout her body as her muscles woke.

A sharp wind carried the sounds of dogs and men, as though they were made of it, appearing every time it blew, allowing her no respite. With no time for thought or to plan a direction, Rillirin began to run again.

GALTAS

'Your highnesses, it is an honour.' The physician's bald head winked in the light from the window as he bowed. He gave a short nod to Galtas. Galtas managed a smile and looked back out through the window, bored already.

'Master Hallos, the honour is ours,' Prince Janis said. 'Thank you for coming; we know how busy you are.'

The honour is ours? Sanctimonious little prick. Galtas unsheathed his dagger and used the tip to clean beneath his nails. Busy? Busy failing to cure the king. Rastoth the Kind, they used to call him. Rastoth the Mad now. A smirk pulled at his lips and he bent his head so no one would see.

Hallos took a seat in the heir's small study and eyed the princes. He smoothed his beard, uncomfortable. 'King Rastoth's mind remains as sharp as ever, his intellect as great. These . . . confusions have nothing to do with age or infir-

48

mity, that much I am sure of now. I would venture they are the result of grief, Your Highnesses, a grief that has not lessened since your mother the queen's demise.'

Janis glanced at his brother, and Rivil's smile was wan. Galtas rolled his eyes. 'A grief we share with our father but, perhaps, are bearing a little better.'

Hallos sighed. 'Your mother's loss has destroyed the king's peace. He cannot conceive of a world without her by his side. It troubles him, disturbs his sleep, his equilibrium.'

'If we could only find those who took her from us,' Rivil said, voice coiled with anger. Janis put his hand over Rivil's clenched fist. 'I speak with Commander Koridam every week, read the reports he receives, and nothing. Still nothing. Almost a year has passed and still her killers roam free.'

'This failing is not yours, Rivil, nor mine, nor Koridam's. The culprits will be found eventually, found and brought to justice. We must trust in that.'

Galtas leant his shoulder against the wall by the window, his back to the group before the fire. Pious, pragmatic, devoted Janis. It was exhausting just listening to him. The man was as dull and pointless as an ugly woman. A clever, ugly woman. Galtas suppressed a shudder.

'Queen Marisa is with the Gods of Light now, Prince Rivil,' Hallos murmured. 'Be at peace knowing that. There is no more suffering for her.'

'Fuck the gods. I have prayed to the Dancer and the Fox God both, asking them to bring her killers to justice, and yet my father still suffers. They still remain free,' Rivil said, sullen with anger. 'My brother suffers. I—' His voice broke and he looked away, biting off the words.

Galtas glanced back, watched Hallos and Janis pause, awkward in the face of Rivil's grief.

'I have found a sleeping draught aids the king. Restful sleep does much to restore his strength. If you would like . . .?' asked Hallos delicately.

Rivil looked up and wiped at his eye with his thumb. He scrubbed his fingers through his dark gold hair. 'Thank you, but please, save all your efforts for my father. I fear our enemies may seek to take advantage of his illness soon.'

Janis frowned. 'Rivil, this is not the time.'

Rivil's eyes darkened, but Janis didn't notice. Janis never did. Galtas saw it, though, oh yes. Galtas always noticed.

Rivil focused on Hallos. 'And the visitations?'

'At present I have been unable to stem their flow. If anything, they are increasing in number and severity. It may be your father's way of coping, or working through his grief. In time I believe they will cease.'

'So you don't really think he sees my mother's spirit?' Rivil asked and Janis coughed, closing his eyes. Rivil ignored him again.

'I think he wishes to see her, wants it so hard that his brain tells him she's there,' Hallos said. He spread his hands. 'And yet her soul rests in the Dancer's Light now. Souls do not return from that.'

Janis pushed up out of his chair and Hallos and Rivil rose to their feet. Galtas pushed away from the wall and put away his knife. 'I think that's enough for now. Thank you, Master Hallos. We won't keep you any longer. Rivil, a moment, if you will. Galtas, you stay too.'

Galtas exhaled a deep breath, knowing what was coming. He stayed by the window, unwilling to attract Janis's attention more than necessary.

'What was that nonsense about spirits? I need you to grow up, Rivil. You cannot avoid your responsibilities – or the real world – forever. You may be the younger son, but you are also a prince of the blood with duties to Rilpor and the throne. So I'm asking you to act accordingly.' Janis stared at Rivil, lips pursed. 'Don't make me make it an order,' he added, and Galtas's eyebrows rose.

A muscle flexed in Rivil's jaw as he nodded, nostrils flared. 'You are right, of course, Janis. I forget myself.' He sounded sincere, at least.

I, on the other hand, forget nothing, Galtas said to himself, glaring at Janis's back.

'I know Mother's death hit you harder than you care to admit, brother. But it's taken something from all of us, don't forget. And yet we must keep going, stay strong. While the northern and southern borders are secure, General Koridam's latest report from the west indicates increased movement from the Mireces. They've made a couple of late raids, later than we would expect. The folk of the Cattle Lands and the Western Plain are afraid. They need strong direction from the throne, messages of support. You can aid in that.'

He clapped Rivil on the back while Galtas stifled a yawn. *Still in love with the sound of your own pompous voice echoing out of your arsehole. I've done farts that had more substance.*

'We cannot afford to fail, Rivil. We must make a responsible adult out of you,' Janis said and grinned to lighten the mood.

'Gods, I hope not.' Rivil laughed. 'I quite like being the rebellious prince.'

'A part you often play a little too well,' Janis said.

Rivil inclined his head. 'The burden of kingship will fall to you, not me. I can afford to have a little fun—'

Janis's face was hard. 'No, Rivil, you can't,' he interrupted, souring the mood once more. 'Not now, with Father so ill. Maybe not ever again, not in the way you mean. Understand that. Accept it. Royalty is a privilege and a burden, not a game.'

'You act as though you are already king,' Rivil said hotly. 'Our father still lives.'

'At least one of us is taking responsibility for his duties,' Janis said. He bit off whatever he was going to say next and strove for calm. 'Whatever the reports say, I do not believe our borders are as safe as we would like. We must be ready. We must—'

'I'm well aware of the monsters at our door, *Your Highness*,' Rivil said with icy formality. 'There's no need to keep reminding me all the time. I do my duty, and will continue to do it.'

'I know you will,' Janis said, and Galtas was surprised he couldn't hear the anger in Rivil's voice. Or maybe he just dismissed it. 'Which is why I need to you sit in the plains court this week. Galtas, keep an eye on him. The court, not the tavern, you hear?' Galtas inclined his head. 'Good. Then I'll see you for supper.'

They stood for a few seconds longer, but Janis was already at his desk and shuffling through reports. *And so easily are we dismissed, like boys to our rooms for a misdemeanour.*

Galtas followed Rivil into the corridor and closed the door with a gentle click. 'He does not—' he began with a hiss.

Rivil waved him to silence, but his face was white with anger. 'He is the heir. So he does. I must accept it.'

Galtas looked both ways along the corridor. 'You would make a better heir than him.'

Rivil held up his hand again. 'Don't.' He stretched the tension out of his shoulders. 'I'm to the plains court, then. I'll see you tonight.'

Galtas watched him walk away, and then stared hard at the door to Janis's study, fingers tapping on the pommel of his sword. Eventually, he left.

DOM

Eleventh moon, seventeenth year of the reign of King Rastoth
Scout camp, Final Falls, Wolf Lands, Rilporian border

They'd climbed out of the forests cloaking the foothills and
into snow and ice, isolated copses of stunted firs and pines
providing scant but welcome cover. There was nothing to
stop the wind up here and its constant keening set Dom's
nerves on edge, kept the pain in his head thrumming. It
would help if he knew what he was looking for, but that
hadn't been made any clearer over the last day.

The scout camp was perched just above the Final Falls
on the River Gil, a shelter cleverly disguised with snow and
rock so it was invisible from above. If the Mireces ventured
down the treacherous Gil-beside Road, the scouts would
spot them and run ahead to the village with the warning. It
was a miserable posting, but there hadn't been a surprise
attack in the years since they'd implemented it.

They were met with enthusiasm and Dom was grateful
for the distraction. Lim and Sarilla were soon absorbed into
the group and it took little effort to slip out when everyone

was occupied. Ash had the forward post, sitting a hundred strides further upriver, and Dom slapped his fur-covered shoulder as he passed.

'Where are you going?' Ash asked.

'Crossing over and a bit of a wander,' Dom said.

Ash stood up. 'On your own?'

'On my own,' Dom confirmed. 'Had a knowing. Said to come looking.'

Ash chewed his lip. 'That's not the best idea, and I've heard you come up with pretty bad ones over the years.' He hefted his bow. 'Let me come?'

Dom looked up at the white and black of the mountain. 'I'll only be a few hours,' he said. 'If I'm not back by then, come looking, all right? And keep an eye on the path,' he added as something tugged inside him.

'Stay safe,' Ash said and Dom could see his reluctance. Dom nodded and hopped from rock to rock across the river. His wolfskin jerkin cut much of the wind but it was still bitterly cold, and he hunched his shoulders and walked until he was out of sight and sound of the river.

'All right, then,' he muttered, closing his eyes. 'Where am I supposed to go? Whatever this key is, I could do with some help to find it.'

Nothing.

Dom huffed a plume of breath into the air and picked a direction at random, northeast uphill. The Dancer's messages were often obscure, but this was ridiculous. *Go and wander about in enemy territory looking for something, but I can't tell you what it is. You'll be fine.*

He had a sword, a short bow and quiver, and a knife. *Oh, and a tendency to fall down and commune with the gods at the most inopportune moments, don't forget.* He snorted, wiped his nose, and kept walking. No doubt Lim would be apoplectic when he returned, so he'd better make sure he found whatever it was he was looking for. Returning empty-handed would be even worse.

'If this goes wrong, I'll never live it down,' he breathed. His inner voice pointed out he might not live at all and he grimaced, but kept trudging. It was stupid, he knew, yet it felt right. The key was out here somewhere, the message that could confirm or deny the start of something that would change the world.

A squall blew in and ice crystals filled the air, making everything hazy and soft, so it took a few seconds to make sense of what he was seeing. A copse of pine, a movement of red like fox fur near the ground. But any foxes this high up would have turned white by now. Dom squinted and took a few more steps, and the thing moved, stood up, started to run. Red hair. Blue dress.

Mireces.

The wind dropped and the noises that had been concealed by it echoed across the mountain. She saw him and veered away, then jinked back again when men appeared from behind an outcrop. Mireces hunting Mireces.

'This is not helpful,' Dom muttered as he dropped into the snow and snatched an arrow, aimed low and took the first hunter in the belly. The second shaft hit the next hunter in the shoulder and he kept coming; the third was a mistake. The third took the man with the dogs in the throat and he let go of the leads as he died. Two dogs, big, with lots of teeth. One sprinted for the girl, the other came straight for him.

Two dead and one injured, but there were four more now and they had bows too, and Dom had no choice but to hunker down as arrows rained around him. The girl was screaming and the sound triggered a rush of light in his head. It was her. He was here for her. 'Balls,' he said as the dog barrelled into him and sent him over on to his back.

Dom jammed his right forearm into its mouth, the heavy leather armguard just about protecting his flesh. The dog shook him and Dom's punches missed. He thrashed, dragged his knife free and stabbed the dog's belly. It squealed, but didn't let go. He stabbed it again, trying not to look in its eyes. *Sorry. Not your fault. Sorry.*

The dog collapsed and Dom struggled from beneath it, scrabbling for his bow. The other dog had the girl by the calf and she was screaming louder as it shook her like a rabbit. The Mireces were closing in on them both when three were dropped in less than a second with arrows Dom hadn't fired. The man with the arrow in his shoulder turned and fled, and Ash popped up from behind a rock and killed the dog savaging the girl.

'Thanks,' Dom said. 'Good to see you ignored me.'

'Don't I always?' Ash asked, quartering the mountains with an arrow on the string.

'Let's get her.'

'Her?' Ash asked, frowning. The girl was dragging herself away, her blood a bright trail in the snow. 'Let the Wolves do for her. Mireces scum.'

'No,' Dom said, 'she's why I'm here. She's the key. The message.' *The harbinger.* He shook away the thought.

'Oh, gods,' Ash muttered. 'Are you sure? I mean, really sure? Because we're going to be leaving sign all the way back. We're bringing them right to us.' Dom spread his hands but didn't answer. Ash sighed. 'Fuck. Fine, then let's be quick about it. Who knows how many more are out there? Come on.'

They cornered the girl and she curled up small, hiding her face in her hands. 'Here to help,' Dom said soothingly. 'But we need to leave now, get you to safety.' She didn't move, didn't respond. 'All right, up you come,' he said and put his hand under her arm. She squealed and kicked and Dom felt a throb up his arm into his head. Definitely the key. 'Stop,' he said, making his voice hard. 'We're trying to save you.'

He dragged her to her feet and she shrieked as her torn leg took her weight. Dom and Ash slung her between them and made their way down the mountain and back towards the river and dubious safety.

They didn't go to the scout camp. Ash left Dom to drag her further downhill and went to fetch Lim and Sarilla.

Dom went a half-mile straight down, into thicker forest and patchy snow, and eased her down beneath a fir tree. He took off his wolfskin and wrapped her in it, hooked his bow and quiver on a low-hanging branch and loosened the long dagger in its sheath. She watched him with big grey eyes in a pinched face.

'You have got to be joking.' Lim didn't even look at him, just crouched opposite the girl and stared at her. The bites to her calf were bad, the blood the brightest, cleanest thing about her. The exposed flesh of her arms and legs was filthy, scratched and too pale with cold.

'You're safe, you're safe,' Dom said as Sarilla and Ash loomed above her. 'We're here to help, all right? Your pursuers are dead' – he glanced at Ash – 'mostly. There's nothing to fear.'

'What's your name, girl?' Lim asked. Dom pulled a roll of linen from the pouch on his belt, rubbed gently at the bite marks with snow, and then bandaged her leg. He shivered, saw her note it and glance at the wolfskin she was wearing. *Come on, two nice things I've just done for you, not including saving your life. So give us something in return.*

She was silent.

'She's your key? A Mireces?' Lim asked. Sarilla and Ash were eyeing the landscape as they listened and Dom knew the scout camp would be on high alert.

Dom licked his lips and squinted. 'She's the key,' he murmured, the words again coming from somewhere just a little outside of him, a touch beyond his control. 'But not Mireces.' She glanced at him at that, and then away. 'I'd say an escaped slave—'

'She's a spy,' Ash interrupted. 'What better way to infiltrate us? A young woman, cold and filthy and starving . . . they know we'd take her in. So we don't.'

'Send her on her way?' Lim asked.

'Knife in the throat'd do it,' Sarilla muttered.

Dom winced, but he couldn't blame either of them. Except that they were wrong.

'What's your name?' Lim asked again. Still nothing. 'We're trying to help here, lass, but you've got to help us too.'

'My name's Dom Templeson,' Dom tried with his most ingratiating smile. 'This is Lim. He's our chief. The scary woman is Sarilla and that's Ash. He's a hothead despite the cold.'

'Fuck off,' Ash said. 'I wish they'd finished her off. You do realise you've compromised the camp, and possibly the village, by taking her and killing the Mireces? And for what? Some fucking mute who'll likely murder us all in our sleep.'

'You don't wish that, because then she'd be dead and we wouldn't know anything,' Dom snapped as Lim snorted. *Best get it over then,* he thought. He reached for her face and she squirmed backwards, got her good leg under her and stood, cracking her head on a branch and sending a flurry of snow down on them all. Dom paused, secretly glad of the delay. The tremor he'd felt while carrying her had been strong, verging on painful. He wasn't all that keen on repeating it, but if she wouldn't talk, there was little choice. He needed to learn what she knew and he could probably force a knowing if he held on to her long enough.

'The Mireces are hunting you,' he said and saw her shudder, 'so we will protect you. But you need to help us do that.'

Lim looked at him, surprised, and Sarilla and Ash turned from their study of the terrain with identical expressions of disbelief. 'We're helping her,' Dom said firmly. He ignored the mutters and focused on her again. 'Are you Rilporian?'

The girl nodded and Dom felt a flicker of triumph. 'Were you captured by the Mireces?' Another nod. 'I need you to say something now, lass,' Dom murmured, taking a soft step forward. She wasn't fooled; she slid sideways out of his reach. He stopped moving and exhaled softly. 'I need you to tell me where you escaped from. Can you do that?'

As expected there was silence and Lim puffed out his cheeks. 'It's important, child. We need to know which village was tracking you, who it is we've killed on your behalf.'

'Eagle Height.' The girl's voice was rusty with disuse, her accent thick with Mireces harshness. 'Two days ago.' Lim's eyes narrowed, and Dom flinched.

'You're sure it was Eagle Height? Seat of Liris, King of the Mireces?' Lim asked and then grimaced. The girl's filthy robe darkened down the front, steaming piss streaking her legs and soaking into Dom's careful bandaging.

'Take her away, Ash, we need to talk,' Lim grunted in disgust. 'I'll fill you in later.'

Dom opened his mouth to protest but Lim gave a hard shake of his head and he waited until Ash had escorted her out of earshot. 'What's wrong with you?' Dom hissed then.

'I agree with Ash. She's likely a spy.'

'Really? You think she pissed herself on command?'

'Yes.'

Dom's eyebrows rose. 'She's Rilporian and she's managed to escape after who knows how many years serving the Mireces and you say she's a spy. She needs our help.' He flicked hair off his forehead and rubbed delicately at his right eye.

'Don't be taken in by a pretty face,' Lim said.

Dom scowled. 'Don't you be taken in by her accent,' he retorted. 'She's Rilporian.'

'So she says,' Sarilla interjected and Dom threw up his hands in frustration, staring from one to the other.

'It's more than that,' he insisted.

'This is really what you meant, then?' Lim asked. 'You said a message, or a messenger. She's it? What can *she* tell us?'

Dom bit his lip, shook his hair out of his eyes again and stared at the girl. She was looking around, backing off slowly. Ash grabbed her arm and pulled her to a halt. 'I'm not sure, but she's important. I just don't know how yet.'

'Then find out,' Lim said, 'one way or another. Either she's important or she's dead, but we need to know which and we don't have time. Gods,' he muttered and rubbed the back of his neck.

'You said there was no immediate danger,' Sarilla said in a tone that was nearly accusatory.

'I said there was always danger,' Dom contradicted her, but quietly. Last thing he needed was to start an argument.

Lim growled in frustration. 'Fine, take her back to the village and get her some decent clothes or she'll have her throat opened for her, Rilporian or not. I'll stay here for a day or two, make sure they don't come back with reinforcements. When I get back to the village, she'd better be ready to talk.'

'I'm staying too,' Sarilla said. 'You'll need my bow,' she added when Lim would have protested.

'Thank you,' Dom said.

'Just make sure you're right about this, and about her,' Sarilla muttered. 'We don't want to start a war over nothing.'

RILLIRIN

*Eleventh moon, seventeenth year of the reign of King Rastoth
Watcher village, Wolf Lands, Rilporian border*

Rillirin sat and watched. She was good at watching, and she
was very good at sitting still. Being unobtrusive had kept
her alive. It wasn't as cold as Eagle Height, so she didn't
allow herself to shiver, to move, barely to blink. Instead she
curled into the protective angle of the wall of Dom's house
and the woodpile, and she watched.

She watched the men do the chores alongside the women,
and she watched the women work with weapons alongside
the men. Mostly, though, she watched the short, spiky-haired
spearwoman who'd come to visit Dom and sat by the small
fire outside his door.

Her name was Dalli and she had a spear as long as
she was tall, plus the leaf-shaped blade at one end. Rillirin
watched her rub a fine layer of beeswax into the grain
of the wood, and then rub most of it back off again.
There was an expression of absolute concentration and
contentment on her face as she worked, oblivious to Dom

clanging the cooking pot or whistling through his teeth.

Rillirin had never touched a weapon, if you discounted the knives in the kitchens of Eagle Height. Her palms itched at the thought of picking up a spear and knowing how to use it. A prisoner in a Wolf village was much the same as a slave in a Mireces village, though, so she didn't move.

Dalli gave the spear one more rub-down and stood up, hefting it in one hand and then the other. Then she spun it and it hummed through the air. She smiled, shifting her hands and whirling its length through a series of figures of eight, spinning it around herself, spinning herself with it, feet dancing through the snow.

'Show off,' Dom called from inside, breaking the spell, and Rillirin blinked and exhaled; she'd been holding her breath. *I want to do that. I want to fight, to dance like that. To be strong.*

Dalli laughed, leapt at the door and stabbed through it into the gloom. Rillirin clapped a hand over her mouth and lurched to her feet. The movement alerted Dalli, who dropped into a crouch and spun, spear suddenly pointed at Rillirin's chest. Rillirin flattened herself against the woodpile, a branch digging hard into her kidney, and put both arms over her face.

'Hush, girl, I'm not going to hurt you,' Dalli said, and Rillirin chanced a look. Her heart was thudding high in her throat. Dalli had straightened and was cradling the spear in the crook of her arm, its butt resting on the top of her boot.

'Maybe I'll teach you one day,' she said and Rillirin's mouth formed an O of surprise. *How does she know?* 'Every woman should be able to protect herself,' Dalli added and Rillirin's face twisted with shame. The woman was mocking her weakness. She lowered her arms and stared at the snow, feeling her face heat up.

Dalli pursed her lips and then stepped forward and proferred the spear. 'I didn't mean anything by that,' she said quietly. 'Here, do you want to hold it?' she asked and from the corner of her eye Rillirin saw Dom appear in the doorway, knife in one hand.

It's a trap. They'll kill me if I take the spear. They can say I attacked them. But Rillirin looked at it, at the warm rich wood, the curves of the grain and the faint sheen of beeswax. She could just make out the hatchings carved into its middle for grip. It was beautiful.

Dalli ran her free hand through her short spiky hair. 'Go on if you want,' she said. 'It's up to you.'

Rillirin licked her lips, fingers twitching; then she shook her head and looked away, shoulders creeping up around her ears. *I remember this game. Drink the wine, wench, you've earned it, then a punch in the face if I did. Punch in the face if I didn't, sometimes.*

Dalli tucked the spear back under her arm. 'Another time maybe,' she said easily, with a smile Rillirin didn't – couldn't – trust. 'You just let me know and I'll be pleased to teach you. We all would, whatever weapon you fancy.'

Rillirin didn't reply. She slid down the wall on to the ground, arms around her knees. Still.

CORVUS

Eleventh moon, year 994 since the Exile of the Red Gods
Watcher village, Wolf Lands, Rilporian border

When Edwin had limped back into the longhouse and announced the slave had been taken by Wolves and his war band were all dead, Corvus had almost gutted the man there and then. One slave, one snivelling little bitch had managed to outsmart him and lead him into an ambush? And not only that, but she'd know all the secrets of the village, their weaknesses. If she talked, she'd give the Wolves all the information they could need to attack Eagle Height itself.

Corvus gathered all the available warriors in Eagle Height and set out without delay. They found tracks at the Final Falls fresh and only hours old, so Corvus led his men on as fast as they could go. If they could catch the Wolves in the open, he could slaughter them all, take back the wench and find out who'd killed Liris. Could be one of the men with him now, waiting for an opportunity to make a bid for the throne in much the same way he had.

Freezing sleet fell, marring the trail, and Corvus grimaced

and sped up even more. Lanta, in a knee-length gown and black leggings, ran easily at his side, as she had done for the last day and a half. He still didn't know why she'd insisted on coming, but despite his misgivings she hadn't held them up. She was faster than some of his men.

The sleet had plastered her hair to her skull, dulling its vibrant blonde to sand. He couldn't help but smile at her discomfort, though she hid it well. As war chief of Crow Crag, he'd run and fought through every kind of weather the mountains could throw at him. He was made for this. Sacrifice and communion no doubt had its strains, but she was in his world for a change and he intended to ensure she knew it.

Firelight. Corvus skidded to a halt and flung out an arm to stop Lanta running past. His warriors spread out in a skirmish line and hunkered down, and Corvus quartered the trees ahead. Campfires, more than one, and the smell of cooking.

'Gosfath's balls,' he muttered, 'we've found their fucking village.' He had a few hundred men, but there was no way of telling how many Wolves there were. Could be a hundred, could be a thousand. *The Lady's will. My feet are on the Path.*

'We're looking for the slave, remember. She's not a warrior, so capture any woman who can't fight. Kill everyone else.' He got the nod from Fost to his right, Valan to his left, and drew his sword. He heard the creak of bows being bent and strung. He gestured and they started the advance, a silent line in the wet, melding with the dark beneath the trees. 'Blessed One, stay here,' he said, not waiting for a response.

Pitch torches hissed and sputtered at intervals in the village, doing nothing to light the darkness. He signalled again and men began peeling off in pairs into the houses, pulling daggers as they slid through the doors. They'd entered all of three buildings before yelling put an end to their stealth.

Shouts of alarm went up and Corvus waved his men on. Wolves poured from the houses and arrows flickered in both directions; the clash of steel started up, shivering loud on his left flank. The empty village was suddenly full of Wolves, armed and armoured as if they'd known he was coming. About a hundred, maybe more; it was hard to tell in the sleet and flickering of torches. Fewer than he had, anyway.

An arrow stuck into the meat of his forearm and Corvus yelped, looked for the archer, saw him and charged. Bow and hand came up to block and Corvus's sword thunked home; the archer squealed and kicked, falling to his knees, the bow cracked, fingers pattering into the mud. Corvus stepped forward and mashed the severed digits beneath his boot. The archer's other hand came around in a blurred arc and a knife stabbed into his ankle. Corvus roared in pain and stumbled back, and then another Wolf leapt over his companion, hair flying, howling a wordless challenge as he swung his sword.

Corvus brought his blade up and they clattered together, screeching. The man was shorter, lighter than him, and Corvus bared his teeth and bore down, forcing the Wolf back, herding him into the archer so he'd trip. But somehow the archer wasn't there, and the Wolf managed to lash a boot into Corvus's knee, buckling it. He went down hard, twisting to the side, and felt a sword tip rake the bearskin on his back. *Motherfucker.*

And then Valan was there, hammering into his attacker, driving him back. Corvus swatted the arrow out of his arm and lurched to his feet, gasping, his attention snagged by one of his men clubbing a short Wolf in the face. He wrenched the spear from her hands and dumped her belly down across a wall. He kicked her legs apart and was fumbling with her trousers when a man glided out of the darkness and slipped a sickle-shaped blade around the Mireces' neck, jerked it in and across. Blood erupted across the woman's back and she lunged upright, turned and drove her elbow into his temple. She picked up her spear and lunged back into the fight, shrieking defiance. *Fuck, these women are tough. Pity they're faithless whores or I'd have one as queen.*

Still, the man was a fucking idiot, going for a rape when the battle's not won. If they hadn't killed him, Corvus would've taken great pleasure in doing it himself.

Flames were licking up from inside a few of the houses now, the smoke adding further to the chaos, and Corvus took the moments Valan had won him to turn in a circle and search. He stilled. There.

A tall warrior stood in a doorway, sword unsheathed. He made no move to engage any of the Mireces running rampant through his village, holding his position in front of a door. Corvus sucked blood out of the arrow hole in his arm and material of his sleeve and spat it on to the ground as an offering, then ran for him, stabbing a Wolf on his way past and leaving him to fall. The tall Wolf saw him coming and braced himself. Their swords met with a clatter and the Wolf parried and punched at the same time. Corvus gave ground, but the Wolf didn't follow and he knew the slave must be inside.

'Here,' he called, and heard Valan shout in acknowledgment.

'Wolves,' the man shouted in his turn, 'to me.'

Corvus attacked, shoving him back so he crunched into the door, and there was a scream from inside. 'Give us the girl,' he yelled as he trapped the Wolf's thrust on his guard and stepped close, drawing his dagger as he did. 'We just want what belongs to us.'

The Wolf snarled at that and attacked again.

'Come out or he dies, bitch. They all die,' Corvus shouted as he ducked a thrust. His dagger scraped over the Wolf's chainmail and the man spat in his face. 'Do as commanded, slave,' he added and the Wolf hacked at him again, fury clouding his eyes. The door opened and Corvus grinned. 'Good little bitch,' he muttered, and then he recognised her. 'Rillirin?'

His hesitation when he saw her nearly killed him. An archery string appeared around his throat from behind and someone dragged at his neck, sawing the string back and forth. 'Get her out of here,' his attacker shouted. 'Waypoint three. Fuck's sake, go!'

Corvus rammed his elbow back once, twice, and then the other one, half twisted and got his forearm under the back of his attacker's knee, yanked on his leg and flung them both backwards into the dirt. The archer had no response and landed hard, Corvus on top of him. The string slackened and Corvus struggled to his feet, kicked the man hard and then spun to the house. The door was open and empty. They were gone.

'Fuck,' he roared, and rounded on the archer, but the man was on his feet and backing off between the houses, hand axe in his right, long knife in his left. He reached the trees and fled, not looking back. The other Wolves were fighting a controlled retreat into the treeline north, south and east of the village, splitting up, turning tail and running, fading like smoke. In seconds the village was deserted.

Corpses littered the ground, most in the greens and browns of the Wolves, but there were scores in blue as well and his jaw tightened. *Treacherous, heathen bastards.*

'Valan, Fost,' he called. He swept his uninjured arm across the village. 'Burn it down. Every last fucking hovel.' He stared around in frustration and then let out a roar of pure disbelief. Rillirin? How?

Lanta prowled out of the darkness, predatory as she stared at the carnage, her hands extended in offering – the dead belonged to the gods now. Corvus grabbed her arm and squeezed, dragging her forwards and breaking off the prayer, ignoring the shocked mutters from his men. The wound in his forearm blazed and the pain made him squeeze harder. Her lips compressed but she made no sound and the triumph in her eyes made him want to beat her to death.

He shook her. 'You knew, didn't you?' he demanded, hoarse. 'How long have you known it was my sister we were hunting?'

DOM

*Eleventh moon, seventeenth year of the reign of King Rastoth
Waypoint three, Wolf Lands, Rilporian border*

Men and women trickled into the glade in the birch forest, the third of their many assembly points in the event of attack. Healer Feltith was already there, busy with those who'd arrived before Dom and the girl. Wolves huddled in tents, under shelters and around tiny fires.

Dom managed a smile when he saw Ash approaching. 'Thank the gods you saw them up at the Final Falls. That advance warning saved—'

'Where the fuck is she?' Ash snarled, grabbing Dom's shoulder and hurling him out of the way of the tent. He pushed through the flap and grabbed the girl by the hair, dragging her into the night. 'Who are you?' he roared into her face. 'What are you?'

'Ash, what the fuck are you doing? What—' Dom started; then he noticed the glow up in the foothills. They were burning the village.

Ash grabbed his arm with his other hand and hauled them

both towards a fire. Lim sat with Sarilla, her hand swaddled in a piece of shirt, face grey. Ash shoved them to a halt. 'They're fucking dead, Dom. Fucking scores of us, slaughtered. Because of her. I told you she was trouble, I told you we should've killed her. Did you even find out like Lim asked you to?' he added as Dom fought a riot of nausea. 'Who she is, why they want her? What have you learnt?'

'I haven't – It wasn't . . .' Dom started, but there was nothing to say. Ash's eyes burnt with the need to hurt and Dom swayed back from the violence. The girl was shaking at his side and Sarilla was staring at her with black hatred.

'Enough.' Lim stepped forward, limping badly but putting himself between the two men.

'Enough?' Ash gasped. 'Tansy's dead, so's Ross. Dalli nearly got herself raped and your wife's crippled.' He glared past Lim at Dom, pointing at Sarilla. 'She'll never use a bow again; fucking Raider cut off three of her fingers.' Ash spat. 'Because of you. Because of her.'

'You think I don't know that?' Lim snarled, and Ash subsided a little. Lim rounded on the girl. 'What did you do?' he asked. 'Enough of your silence. My people died for you this night. More will die if we don't know why they seek you.'

She whimpered, shook her head.

'Tell me,' Lim bellowed in her face and Dom flinched, reaching for him; Lim shook him off, not even glancing his way.

'I killed Liris,' she sobbed, hands up in a gesture of futile defence. 'I killed Liris, I'm sorry, I killed him.'

The clearing descended into stunned silence, and even Feltith paused in the act of bandaging Sarilla's hand to look at her.

Dom was staring at her; they were all staring at her. 'You

killed the King of the Mireces and didn't think to tell us?'
he managed, but she was too scared, crying too hard, to
hear him.

Ash moved first, shoved a sack and a folded tent into
Dom's slack arms. 'You could have told us that, not her. You
could have known days ago. But you didn't and this' – he
waved his arm – 'this is on you. So get the fuck out of here,
Calestar,' he hissed, 'and take your Mireces whore with you.'

Dom looked from Lim to Sarilla to Ash, his mind a whirl
of incomprehension, shame and simmering anger. 'Sarilla,
I—'

'Get her away from me before I slit the little cunt's throat,'
Sarilla growled and Lim helped him on his way with a shove
hard enough that he stumbled. He heard the girl squeal and
looked over in time to see Ash grab her throat and spit in
her face, before pushing her towards him.

'Lim,' Dom tried, but his adopted brother wouldn't meet
his eyes.

'Go to the temple and talk to Mother. You could use her
wisdom.' And they closed in around the wounded, their
backs an impenetrable wall and Dom on the wrong side.
Even Cam, the man who'd raised him like a son, the man
who'd never once pushed him to use his gift despite what
it might tell them, couldn't meet his eyes. They blamed him,
every one of them.

Dom's breath hitched in his throat and he backed away,
unable to turn from the sight of them ranged against him.
They were his people that had been killed, his friends and
neighbours. Theirs were the bodies littering the burning
village he called home. But they were right, weren't they?
This was on him. He could've stopped it if only he'd
pushed her. If only he'd used his gift, regardless of the
cost.

He didn't look away until he was inside the first line of trees, and then only because the girl touched his shoulder. He felt a tingle of understanding, a flicker from the knowing, and pushed it away. It was too late now. He didn't care if she was important, didn't care that such a momentary touch could ignite his gift. There wasn't anything worth learning from her now and no one to tell it to even if he did.

Too late for Sarilla, for the other wounded. Too fucking late for the dead.

'Go where you like, I won't stop you. I've lost family because of you, friends, lovers. Their deaths are my shame, do you understand?' Dom demanded, turning on her. He dropped the tent, grabbed her shoulders and shook, and then backhanded her so she fell into the mud. 'Maybe Ash is right. Maybe you are a fucking spy. You couldn't have done more damage if you'd fucking planned it.'

She rolled on to her back and wiped blood from her mouth and nose. 'You expect me to trust you, to tell you everything I know when I'm as much a prisoner here as I ever was in Eagle Height?' She stood up, shaky but tall. 'I spent nine years slaving for the Mireces. Nine years you will never begin to understand. And for nine years I listened to their stories about the Wolves. How could I possibly trust you? All I know is what they told me.'

Dom laughed, a wheezing giggle tinged with madness. 'What the fuck does it matter if you trust us? My people are dead because I didn't want to scare you. Because I trusted that if you had something to tell us about the Mireces you would, that you had some touch of being Rilporian left inside. That if you'd killed their fucking king you'd have let us know.' He bit off any more words. What was the point? Slumping, he picked up the tent again. 'Just go. Go on, go.'

'Go where?'

'Fuck do I care? To hell, maybe, to the Afterworld. You deserve it.' He hauled the tent on to his back and began walking southeast. She shifted from foot to foot, uncertain. Then she followed.

MACE

Eleventh moon, seventeenth year of the reign of King Rastoth
West Rank headquarters, Cattle Lands, Rilporian border

Mace Koridam, general of the West Rank, rested back in his chair and stretched his shoulders when Captain Tara Carter entered. 'Report?'

Tara saluted and stood at parade rest in front of his desk. 'There's a lot of movement up there. Some sort of raiding or tracking party, it looked like. Found what was left of some dead Raiders, gear and weapons mostly. Animals had been at the bodies, but most had Wolf arrows in them. We got within five miles of the Sky Path, but the number of Mireces patrols forced us back.'

Mace frowned and crossed his arms. 'Your orders were explicit, Captain.'

Tara met his gaze steadily. 'Yes, sir. I'm aware I went beyond my remit, but there was too much activity, so I made the call. Sir.'

'If this is about you proving yourself, Carter, I can assure you that you have singularly failed to impress me.'

'It isn't, sir. Word in the mountains is that Liris is dead, killed in his own bedchamber.'

Mace paused and eyed her. 'You're sure?' he asked, though Tara was already nodding. 'By the gods, this changes everything.' With Liris dead, they could have an opportunity to force a battle and break the Mireces once and for all, ending the constant border threat.

'My opposite number among the Wolves filled me in on that particular piece of intel,' Carter said as there was a knock at the door. It opened and she gestured. 'Dalli Shortspear. Turns out we weren't the only ones sneaking around the Sky Path.'

Dalli gave Carter and Mace a strained smile and Mace winced. 'Gods, woman, that's the most impressive black eye I've seen in a long while.'

Dalli fingered the bruising. 'Mireces spear butt, right in the eye. I will confess to a momentary confusion in the aftermath.'

Mace whistled. 'I'd confess to being unconscious if it was me. But you're otherwise well?'

Dalli gave a half-shrug, her usual energy missing. 'As well as can be expected. Mireces war party on the hunt for an escaped slave. She made it down to us and they followed her, attacked the village. Burnt the village. We lost nearly seventy.' She tapped her fingertips to her heart, commemorating the dead, and Mace and Tara copied her. 'We'd had a few hours' advance warning, but there were too few of us nearby to form an effective defence. We fought a holding action, then had to run.'

'My sympathies, Dalli, to you and yours. Any help you need rebuilding, please do ask. I'll increase our patrols in the meantime, give you a chance to recover.'

'Thank you, General, we'd appreciate that. We're stretched

thin. For now we've sent the girl to Watchtown with Dom, to keep her safe and . . . keep her away from the other Wolves. There's some bad feeling about what happened. The Mireces wouldn't have attacked if she wasn't there, and if she'd told us beforehand that she'd murdered Liris – well, let's just say we wouldn't have sent most of our warriors to winter in the smaller settlements.'

'She killed him?' Mace asked, incredulous. 'A slave?'

Dalli touched her face again. 'That she did, General. Or that's what she told us anyway, and we believe her.' She rested her hip against his desk and Mace was suddenly aware of her exhaustion. She was hurt and hurting, grieving, but she'd come to warn them anyway. *She puts half my men to shame.*

'At least that fat old bastard Liris is dead,' Dalli said. 'Even if too many of ours are as well.'

Mace stalked to the window and back again. 'You say there's bad feeling around the slave? We'd be happy to host her here,' he said, trying not to sound too eager. *Her knowledge of Eagle Height must be extensive. This could be the turning of the tide. But why did she have to make her way to the Wolves? I could do so much with that knowledge, so much.*

'She and Dom will stay at the temple. With luck there won't be trouble, but we'll bear it in mind.'

'Of course. If her presence in Watchtown becomes complicated, let me know and we'll send someone to fetch her. In the meantime, if you learn anything from her, please do share it with us.' He paused and Dalli dipped her head. 'Do we know who the new Mireces king is yet? Or if there even is one?'

Tara sighed. 'That we don't know. I can take a patrol—'

Mace held up a finger. 'You've done enough, Carter. Just

let me have your full report by this evening.' She opened her mouth to protest. 'I've told you before, being a reckless idiot is not going to get you promoted any faster. If anything, it'll make me more inclined to demote you. You are not the only captain with a Hundred in the West Forts. I appreciate your zeal, but I have other capable officers who can take out patrols. And I'm not sure your men would appreciate another run out so soon. Dismissed,' he added when Carter looked like protesting anyway.

She saluted and stalked to the door, closing it very firmly behind her. Mace suppressed a smile; Carter was going to be an outstanding general one day, if she managed to stay alive that long. And if she could actually bloody listen to orders.

'She's a good one,' Dalli said, breaking into his thoughts. 'You're lucky to have her.'

'I know, I just wish she didn't think she had to prove herself all the time.'

Dalli snorted. 'She's the only woman in the Rank, and she's an officer. Of course she has to prove herself all the time. She's fighting the instincts of five thousand soldiers.' Dalli poked at the bruise again. 'Your men aren't as enlightened as ours; most of them don't believe Tara should be wearing trousers, let alone wielding a sword. She'd probably be better off joining the Wolves.'

'Stop trying to steal my best officer, Dalli,' Mace said with a mock frown. 'You can't have her. Listen,' he said, moving back to the desk, 'how bad is the feeling about this woman?'

Dalli's brows drew together. 'Bad enough. Seventy is too many for a single skirmish on our own ground. Those four incursions we repelled over the summer cost us less than a hundred, plus your losses of course. To lose so many now, this late in the season . . .' She closed her eyes. 'It's been a hard year for us.'

'Then maybe she should stay at the forts,' Mace said. He squeezed her shoulder and she opened her eyes again. 'Think about it.'

'I've got to visit a few settlements in the foothills, tell them what's happened, then I'll be going to Watchtown. I'll see what the atmosphere's like. If necessary, I'll bring her here.' She stood up from his desk. 'But for now, General, with your permission I'll raid your kitchens and then find somewhere to get my head down for a few hours. Long way still to go.'

'Of course. Dancer's grace upon you.'

She gave him a crooked smile. 'And you, General.'

When Dalli had left, Mace wandered back to the window and looked down on the fort, then up at the mountains clawing the air, white and angry against a white sky. Change was coming: he could feel it. Maybe a king-killing slave from Eagle Height could help ensure that change was to their advantage.

CRYS

A couple of easy years, they said. A rest from the threat of
border patrols, they said. Crys stood in the audience chamber
and tried to keep his eyes open. He'd been here a few weeks
and was bored out of his mind. Most of his wages had gone
on drinking and gambling and he'd been threatened with a
flogging already for being late on duty. That was Rivil's fault,
though; the prince could drink like a horse. Though it wasn't
exactly the done thing to blame your superiors for your own
tardiness.

His Hundred were in charge of the king's honour guard
this week, and he'd thought that'd liven things up. So far
he'd stood and listened to the king mumble for four days.
He couldn't make out most of it, and what he could didn't
make much sense. And the court? Crys had never seen
such a bunch of expensively clothed arse-lickers in all his
life.

Only Rivil's endless supply of court gossip had kept him

going, and he'd discovered which of the twittering court ladies was not blind to a dashing young officer offering a supportive hand during a turn in the gardens.

He'd spent the morning amusing himself by examining their outfits, grateful for the fashion for low-cut necklines. He'd be asleep if there wasn't an army of well-endowed bosoms parading in front of his face.

The doors opened and the princes entered together. Crys snapped to attention, thumping his pike on to the marble, the sudden movement sending a rush of blood to his numb feet. Rivil winked as he walked past and Crys fought to remain stoic as the prince flicked him the finger for good measure.

Galtas followed a few paces behind, as always. The bastard's single eye blazed a challenge at him. Crys really was going to have to give the little prick a beating at some point. He was bigger, but Crys would bet he was faster – he'd just stay on the side without the eye.

The princes bowed to the king and Rastoth beamed at them. 'My boys,' he boomed cheerfully, 'my good boys. You are well?'

'Very well, your majesty,' Prince Janis said with another bow, 'and how is your health?'

'Excellent,' Rastoth said, though Crys noted that Rivil glanced to the physician for confirmation. Hallos inclined his head. Janis stepped forward and offered Rastoth his arm as he rose, and the three of them made their way about the throne room, courtiers simpering and smiling like a flock of birds around them.

Crys followed, his knee stiff from standing still for hours.

Rivil dropped back to walk at Crys's side. 'Bit of a limp there,' he whispered.

Crys glanced at Janis, then back to Rivil. 'It's the size of my cock,' he whispered, 'drags me to the right. What's a man to do?'

Rivil burst out laughing and Crys grinned. Janis looked back and frowned. 'I'm not sure our wise and devoted heir approves of our friendship,' Rivil joked, giving Janis a little wave.

'He's just fuming because the king's stopped next to Lord Hardoc. Or is it Lord Haddock? His breath smells like a week-dead fish, anyway.'

Crys kept a wary eye on Commander Koridam as Rivil sniggered. 'His daughter, though,' the prince said and whistled. 'Have you seen the tits on her? Face like a cow's, but with tits like that I'd – Commander, what a pleasure.'

'Your Highness, if you are finished with my captain, may I have a word with him?' Durdil asked.

Gods, what now? Crys saluted, bowed to Rivil, and gestured to Weaverson to take his place. He followed Durdil out of the audience chamber and down the long corridors to the commander's study. *Whatever it is, it can't be more boring than guard duty.*

Durdil sat at his desk and stared at Crys. He cleared his throat. 'Captain Tailorson, Prince Rivil has requested you to lead his honour guard when he and Prince Janis travel west. They're going to visit the West Rank before winter sets in.' Durdil's eyes were narrow with calculation, so Crys kept his face neutral, as though this was only to be expected. 'I understand you've become quite the prince's boon companion lately.'

Crys's elation died rapidly. 'I – It is difficult to refuse a prince, sir, when he gives an order.'

'I see. And drinking until dawn with him, that's because he orders you to, is it?'

Damn. 'Well, no, sir, but when I'm off-duty—'

'An officer is never off-duty, Captain Tailorson. Especially not an officer serving within the Palace Rank. One who is under my direct command.'

Shit. 'If my actions have been improper, sir, then I apologise. I will decline the prince's request.'

Durdil huffed. 'You'll do no such thing, Captain. As I noted on your first day, you have the potential to be an outstanding officer. You are not embracing that potential. Captain of the princes' honour guard will necessitate you performing at the highest level for an extended period of time. The safety of the princes is paramount, so I expect regular reports and thorough examinations of everything the king wishes examined. And I have asked the heir to keep an eye on you – I have mentioned I am considering you for promotion and would value his opinion on his return.'

He grinned, though Crys felt no desire to smile in return. 'I may also have mentioned that in your desire to achieve that promotion, you will be taking your duties extremely seriously and will have little time for carousing.'

Godsdamn shitting shit. 'I am indeed honoured, sir. I will serve to the best of my ability.' Crys wondered if it rang as hollow in Durdil's ears as it did in his own.

'It will be a testing of your mettle, captain.' Durdil leant forward and put his palms flat on his desk. 'Do not let me down.'

'Of course not, sir,' Crys said in his blandest voice. He snapped out a salute, spun on his heel, and exited the office.

Careful what you wish for, imbecile. Sometimes you actually get it.

TARA

Eleventh moon, seventeenth year of the reign of King Rastoth
West Rank headquarters, Cattle Lands, Rilporian border

'Correspondence from the king, General,' Tara said and handed it over.

Mace looked up from his letters and frowned. 'What now? We can't have a reply to the report about the raid and Liris's death already. The throne doesn't move that fast.' He arched his back until his spine clicked.

This was one of the best things about being Mace's adjutant, being here when he read his correspondence. Tara knew what the common soldiers thought they did up here, but at least they didn't say it in front of her any more. *Not since I broke that big git's arm in two places.* She grinned as Mace checked the name and seal on the envelope and then broke the wax.

His mouth opened as he read and then the colour drained from his face. Tara stepped forward, alarmed, and Mace swallowed and straightened in his chair.

'It seems we are to be graced with royalty,' he said. 'The

princes Janis and Rivil are coming to inspect the Rank, the forts, the supplies, the trade routes and anything else they can think of.'

Tara raised her eyebrows. 'The princes? Why?'

Mace sighed. 'The king's health is not as robust as it once was,' he said.

Tara kept her face neutral. *That's an understatement.*

'This may be the start of the princes assuming more control to ease the king's burdens. Janis is capable, more than capable, but distant. It's hard for men to be inspired to die in his name if he's an enigma to them. Rastoth in his day could inspire anyone to do anything. Janis needs to learn to do the same.'

'The West's definitely the right place to start then,' Tara said, ignoring the churning in her stomach. 'We're more loyal than the other Ranks as it is. West is best, after all,' she added with a grin. Everyone said it.

'I think that will be up to the princes to decide,' Mace said and Tara's smile faded. 'They're the future of this kingdom, Captain. Janis will be king and Rivil the Commander of the Ranks, so they need to see us at our absolute best.'

'Future commander?' Tara asked. 'Surely that will be you, General.'

Mace folded his hands on the desk. 'Me, Captain? While I admire your loyalty, I have no desire to be Commander of the Ranks. I am content with my position as general of the West. Which of course is entirely dependent on the princes' assessment of my command. They'll be here in a week. They'll have my quarters, so I want you in charge of making sure they're fitted out as best we can and my stuff is moved into the barracks.'

'Colonel Abbas's room—' Tara began.

'You know what would happen if I turfed Abbas out of his quarters?' Mace asked.

'Good point, sir. Well, my quarters then.' Despite her words, Tara didn't much want a repeat of the fourteen months she'd spent in the barracks with the rest of the soldiers, even if they had made her one of the dirtiest fighters in the Rank. There wasn't anything Tara wouldn't use as a weapon, and there wasn't a body part Tara wouldn't target if it'd get a fat fucker with rape on his mind off her. Still, Mace was the general and she was a captain.

'The barracks, please, Captain. If it's good enough for the men, it's good enough for me.'

'As you say, General.' *Best get it said, then.* 'Sir, about the princes, would you prefer it if I took out a long recon?'

Mace stared at her for a second. 'Captain Carter, you are a bloody good officer first, if a little . . . hasty, and a woman second. You didn't get this far by hiding from your superiors, or hiding your' – he gestured vaguely and Tara's face warmed – 'female attributes. You're up for rotation in two years: better get used to strangers having an opinion on you soldiering. Until then, I'll vouch for you personally.'

Tara's face warmed again, with gratitude this time. 'Thank you, sir.'

'How many Hundreds are patrolling?' he said and Tara pictured the barracks, the kitchens, the drill grounds inside and outside the forts.

She grimaced. 'Seven, sir, with the Wolves out of action. It'll put a stretch on us to get all four forts inspection-ready with that many men out.'

'Best get busy then, eh, Captain?' He jerked a thumb at the door. 'Get your arse on to the wallwalk and flag the news to the other forts. I want this place hopping in an hour.

Spick and span, Carter, spick and span. We've royalty coming.'

'Yes, sir,' Tara said and saluted. *Princes Janis and Rivil. Do I even have a dress I can fit into these days? Do I even know how to wear one?*

GALTAS

Eleventh moon, seventeenth year of the reign of King Rastoth
South Harbour dock, Rilporin, Wheat Lands

Galtas watched the loading of the royal barge with little interest, his mind on other things. He'd argued against Crys's inclusion in the trip, especially against him leading the honour guard, offering to do it himself in the end. Rivil had helpfully pointed out Galtas held no formal rank. Galtas had equally helpfully pointed out they could hire a private guard as so many other nobles did, and he could lead that. Last thing he needed was that inquisitive little shit poking his nose in.

Then Janis broke in and said Palace Rank was the only appropriate guard for princes. Galtas hawked and spat into the calm waters of the harbour at the memory, at Janis's utter dismissal of him. *Appropriate.* Oh, Janis was all about that, wasn't he? Appearance was everything. He wondered what went on underneath that dour, faithful, self-righteous exterior. What perversions Janis must keep hidden to protect his reputation. Galtas didn't doubt he had them, but years of prying had never revealed so much as a whore or a bastard or an unexplained death. It was impossible.

'Careful with that,' a voice snapped and Galtas jerked back into the real world and scowled down the dock. Tailorson was directing the loading. The captain waved his arm, then leapt from the dock into the barge to catch the swinging cargo and help lower it to the deck.

Galtas fingered the pouch of poison hanging from his belt and spat again. Quite the little hero. Gods, he was almost as insufferable as Janis, and significantly closer to Rivil than the heir would ever be, despite outward appearances.

There were plans to be safeguarded and an inquisitive soldier was an unnecessary risk. Galtas touched the poison pouch again, checked the position of the sun, and then made his way to the Ship Tavern on the edge of the water outside the city.

Many plans, and many ways they could go wrong already, without Rivil being distracted by his new pet soldier. He took a table in a quiet corner and put his back to the wall, sipping at the ale the girl brought. If those plans came to fruition, he'd never have to bow and scrape to the likes of Janis again, or put up with shits like Tailorson.

He drank and waited, eyeing each new customer and wondering if his contact would be on time. Waiting was the hard part.

THE BLESSED ONE

Eleventh moon, year 994 since the Exile of the Red Gods
Longhouse, Eagle Height, Gilgoras Mountains

Lanta seethed. She'd felt Rillirin's presence, she'd seen into their stinking excuse for a village, and then Corvus had slaughtered all he could find and the rest had fled. Her humiliation cut deep and she knew the Red Gods were displeased. She was displeased.

'We are no closer to finding Liris's killer,' Lanta hissed. Corvus twitched, but had no answer. She could hear the enamel squeaking on her teeth, they were so tightly clenched. He'd left a band of five led by Edwin and Valan scouring the forests for Rillirin and ordered the rest back to Eagle Height, and when she'd argued against it, he'd suggested she stay and search herself. The mockery in his face when she'd declined had been plain. 'Rillirin could be anywhere by now.'

'We'll find my sister when the gods will it,' he said, 'and then we'll learn everything she has to say.' He'd a fondness for quoting the gods' will at her, as if he even knew what that was. A fondness for ignoring her, for ignoring the gods too when it suited him.

Lanta feared nothing, not even death – death would simply bring her into the gods' very presence, to sit with the Dark Lady as Her Blessed One for all eternity. But the thought of that little cunt slipping through her fingers filled her with something akin to fear. Fear and bright, pure rage.

'She was right there, Corvus, and you didn't take her. You let her escape. Is your sense of family—'

'You will address me correctly, Blessed One,' he said smoothly, 'as "Sire" or "your Majesty". I give you that courtesy and you will do the same for me. As for my sense of family, Rillirin is a heathen and so she is dead to me. You think I would have allowed her to be a mere bed-slave to be used by any man who could claim her if I felt anything for her?'

'*Sire*,' she managed, swallowing bile, 'be that as it may, Rillirin knows who killed Liris, but she also knows many of our secrets. Secrets we have just handed to the Wolves. The invasion, maybe even the ongoing negotiations with the Rilporian, may all be spilt. She is a weakness we cannot afford.'

'And yet the gods will it otherwise,' Corvus said and Lanta's teeth squeaked again. 'As for the Wolves, we sowed bloody confusion in their very fucking homes, killed them while they slept. The survivors won't be able to stand against us for long.' He waved a hand in dismissal. 'Commune with the gods, ask them for direction. Leave Rillirin and the war to me.'

Lanta sought for calm. 'I shall pray and seek guidance. For our cause and for you, that you may have your eyes opened.'

'Oh, I see clearly, Blessed One. Very clearly.'

His arrogance made her want to spit in his face, to draw

her sacred hammer and put it through his temple. Instead she curtseyed and went to the door leading down into the cave-temple, controlling her temper until she was out of sight.

'I will have that little bitch under my knife for this,' she whispered, the sibilants echoing back to her. 'Corvus's arrogance, his ignorance, may destroy us all. I will not let that happen. The gods *will* triumph. They *will* have Rilpor. I have sworn it and I need no king to bring it about.'

In the temple, Lanta took a deep breath and stilled her mind and heart. To step into the circle unprepared was to have your soul torn to pieces. She lit the candles and threw bunches of dried sage on to the brazier and smoke rose, thick with visions. She knelt, palms on thighs, eyes closed and breathing steadily, until she felt the pathway to the gods break open and she rushed along it into the presence of her mistress.

In the stillness of the temple Lanta's body twitched and bent, shuddering with pain that was indistinguishable from pleasure.

'I am here, my child,' the Dark Lady said and Lanta's mind thrilled with awe and terror. Sweat darkened her dress. 'You are distressed?'

The Dark Lady was a voice in Lanta's head, a voice of fear and blood and orgasm, and Lanta opened herself like a flower to its owner. 'My goddess, I fear Your will may not be done. I fear Corvus is not strong in his faith, that he will fail to accomplish Your desires. Will you guide me, tell me what must be done? Should I remove him?'

The Dark Lady was silent and Lanta waited, muscles tensing in waves through her body as the Goddess rifled through her mind and memories, her desires and plans. Lanta didn't fight it, didn't try and hide anything from Her. Not that she could have. All her ambitions and secret wants she put on view, and the Dark Lady pondered them, turned them over like trinkets, and discarded them.

'Corvus does my will,' the Dark Lady said abruptly, and Lanta sucked in a breath. 'He is one of many instruments I command. You are another. The Rilporian is a third. The calestar the fourth. When all those pieces come together in one place, then will my victory be complete.'

'The calestar? I did not know.'

'You did not need to,' the Dark Lady said and Her voice hurt. Lanta submitted. She could feel Her amusement. 'You do not like Corvus, do you? Or is it that you do not like that he has stripped you of power?' Lanta's mind was crushed suddenly in a vice and she screamed, clutching her head. She fell to the stone as the Dark Lady tore open her skull.

'You do my will, child, as does Corvus. Your petty ambitions mean nothing to me. If you hinder my plans with this feud with him, you will regret it. Never forget you could be replaced as easily as he could, as Liris was.'

'Your will, Lady,' Lanta gasped. 'I will not fail you.'

The pain was gone and instead she felt the touch of fingertips, stroking along her skin, caressing, soothing, exciting. Lanta forced herself back on to her knees, shaking with the echoes of pain and the Dark Lady's sudden arousal.

'See that you do not fail me, child. Rilpor will belong to Blood again and, after it has fallen, all the world will know my wrath.'

DURDIL

Eleventh moon, seventeenth year of the reign of King Rastoth
Physician's quarters, the palace, Rilporin, Wheat Lands

'I will no doubt regret asking this, but how do you keep the cadavers so fresh?' Durdil asked.

Hallos tapped the side of his nose and sat forward in his chair, putting his glass to the side. 'You have your secrets, my old friend, and I have mine. I've had a few of your recruits assisting me with my research.'

Durdil eyed him dubiously. 'You haven't made any of them into cadavers, have you?' Hallos laughed and waved a hand. 'How many recruits?'

'Three, and they're all fine, before you ask. They had a few days' leave and wanted to make some extra coin. They'll be well enough to return to the barracks tomorrow.'

'Hallos!' Durdil snapped. 'My soldiers are not your personal playthings. You know I had four drop out last year after you got your hands on them. One of them still has a limp.'

'It's vital research, Commander. The king himself gave me permission.'

'I'm not sure he was aware of what you'd be doing to them. You're a physician, not a soldier. What did you learn this time?'

'Not much, unfortunately. I'm trying to find a way to swiftly elicit unconsciousness so that wounded men can be treated. A blood choke, you call it. Only they keep waking up when the pressure on the neck is released.'

'You are not to keep pressure on indefinitely,' Durdil almost shrieked.

Hallos patted the air. 'I know, I know. I am a physician, after all. The brain would be compromised if the choke were applied for a sustained period. I tried it on some dogs before I moved to humans.'

'You tried it on . . .' Durdil trailed off and then drained his glass. 'Remind me never to bring my hounds to the palace.' He paused and replayed Hallos's words. 'Wait, you said they'll be well enough to return to the barracks tomorrow. Where are they now?'

Hallos shifted in his seat. 'Hospital,' he muttered, and then patted the air again. 'Precautionary only, I promise. I am making progress on ascertaining how long a healthy man can hold his breath in a variety of situations, though. Under water, in toxic smoke, while under stress, while running. All fascinating.'

'And how is this of use?' Durdil asked.

'Well, say the palace caught fire, gods forbid. The king is trapped in his quarters with a fire raging its way towards him. You're at the other end of the corridor. Now I'm confident that a fit man, as you undoubtedly are, could sprint that hundred yards while holding your breath in around twenty seconds. Meaning you know how long it will take you to reach the king and escort him to safety.'

Durdil choked slightly on his drink. 'Twenty seconds? You have a lot of faith in an old man, Hallos. But let's go along with the scenario. I heroically hold my breath and sprint the length of the corridor, full of toxic smoke, and burst into the king's quarters. Now, once I've got my wind back, which I imagine would take several minutes and perhaps a small lie-down, how do I get his majesty out? With all due respect, I do not think him capable of sprinting a hundred yards while breathing, let alone while not.'

'Ah, but this is where the research really comes into its own,' Hallos said excitedly. 'One of my volunteers breathed in toxic smoke for eleven minutes by the sand clock before finally passing out. Now, it wouldn't take eleven minutes to walk a hundred yards, would it? And even if Rastoth were somehow incapacitated and you had to carry or drag him, it wouldn't take you more than a minute, two at the outside. And we can tell from my research that your body would be able to withstand that much smoke without long-term adverse effects.'

'You poisoned one of my recruits for eleven minutes?'

'Durdil, you're missing the point. The human body is resilient: there's so much it can absorb, endure, before it starts to break down.'

'Well, we know I wouldn't need to sprint the hundred yards if I could walk it without dying.'

'Yes, but these were simply two experiments conducted under similar conditions. It's not meant to be taken as a training manual.'

'Truly, your research astonishes,' Durdil said, deciding not to point out that any man who'd ever burnt his dinner could tell you surviving a smoke-filled room for two minutes was easy, though surviving your wife's withering scorn afterwards took a little more grit.

'Oh, this is minor stuff, really. I'm taking a man's appendix out tomorrow. It's causing him terrible pain. Would you care to assist?'

Durdil smiled. 'I think I'll leave that to you. I would rather how it's done remained a mystery. Though I feel that there are too many mysteries for me of late. This is a young man's game, and I don't think anyone would mistake me for one of those any more.' Durdil rotated his glass, staring at the firelight winking through the red of the wine. Like the colours inside your eyelids when you turned your face up to the sun.

'Speaking of young men, how is Mace faring? Wolves and Mireces keeping him busy?'

Durdil's expression was grave. 'More mystery. I had word only today that the Wolf village was attacked by Mireces hunting an escaped slave. Turns out the slave killed King Liris before fleeing. But they can't find out who's taken the throne.'

Hallos whistled. 'Have you told Rastoth?'

Durdil wouldn't meet his eyes. 'Yes. He's still sending the princes west. Both of them. Despite the danger. And then he forgot I'd told him.' He rubbed his face, weary beyond words.

'The princes can look after themselves, and Mace will ensure they're kept safe. I spoke to them, you know, about Rastoth.'

'And?'

Hallos shrugged. 'They're still grieving for the queen. They want their father back. The kingdom needs a king, Durdil. Perhaps it's time for Janis to be crowned. I know it's been suggested already.'

Durdil stiffened. 'Rastoth still lives.'

'Barely. And you've made no progress on Marisa's death.

I can't imagine he will begin to recover until that chapter is closed.'

'So it's my fault?' Durdil demanded, and then apologised. 'Forgive me, Hallos. I am tired. But Rastoth is my king. I cannot countenance deposing him, not even in favour of Janis.'

'The killers know the court; they knew the queen. Even the guards knew them. Galtas said they were dead facing the door, so they were killed when the assassins came back out. So they must have known them or they'd never have let them into the queen's presence in the first place.'

Durdil sat forward. 'Galtas said that? Those details are confidential. Not even the princes know that.' He drained his glass and thumped it on the table, and then raked his fingers across his scalp. *Galtas? How did he know? Unless . . .*

He stared into the fire. He could still taste the blood in the air from that night, the thick stench of it and the sight of it daubed in bright swathes on the walls. Stepping over the dead guards with his sword drawn into that red room and seeing a slender arm sticking out from under a pile of torn tapestry. An arm that, when he crouched beside it, he saw wasn't attached to a body. He felt an echo of the nausea that had risen in him then and swallowed hard. She'd been in pieces. Not just killed, but dismembered. His throat was tight; he took the glass Hallos refilled for him and drank.

'As you say, they must have known us intimately. Which is why I've started investigating the court. The nobles, the nobles' wives, the clothiers, the queen's jeweller, her bathing attendants, her dressers, even her chambermaid. There's nothing.' He met Hallos's eyes. 'I even investigated you, my friend. I'm sorry, I had to. It was my duty.'

'I hope I passed,' Hallos said, a little unsteadily.

'You did, of course, Hallos. Of course.' Durdil paused. 'I even looked into the whereabouts of the princes, you know,' and he heard Hallos gasp. He spread his hands. 'What else could I do? Someone she knew, Hallos, a friend, acquaintance or servant. Why not a son?'

'And what did you find?' Hallos hissed, leaning forward.

'Nothing, of course. The heir was in his chambers, accounted for by a dozen separate, reliable witnesses, and Rivil was with Galtas in that posh inn in the cloth district. Innkeeper himself told me.'

'Isn't he dead now, that innkeeper?' Hallos asked and Durdil was glad for the change in subject.

'Aye, stabbed by his wife of all things. She found out he was sleeping with his daughter by marriage. Suppose you can't blame the poor woman.'

'People, eh?' Hallos said. 'The more you learn about them, the less you understand.'

Durdil huffed and reached for his drink; then he paused, hand extended. *So the innkeeper who vouched for Galtas is mysteriously dead. And Galtas knew the placement of the bodies. But no, because Rivil was there with him. But then, they often drink in the Gilded Cup: the innkeeper could have got his days mixed up. And now I can't ask him. But I can ask Galtas where he was the night the queen died.*

Brooding, he drank. He didn't notice Hallos leave.

DOM

Eleventh moon, seventeenth year of the reign of King Rastoth
Wolf Lands, Rilporian border

The air had the silent weight of snow when Dom half woke
and rolled over. He snuggled into the warmth of a neck and
back and drifted back to sleep, dreams flitting behind his
eyelids like swallows. The images became clearer, and then
stranger, darker, tugging at him until he gasped and jerked
awake. He flailed and broke contact with the girl, and the
images vanished. She moved too, rolling over and pressing
her back against the freezing canvas, her breathing harsh.

The knowing swelled and burnt its way through his skin
where he'd touched her, worming its way towards his skull.
He stretched out a foot and kicked at the tent flap, allowing
a spear of daylight and a blast of freezing air into the gloom.
They stared at each other by its light, Dom turning over the
images he'd seen, probing at them like a tongue at a rotten
tooth.

The tent was so small they were still practically touching,
even when they were both straining away from each other.

He caught a whiff of old sweat and rain from the ragged plait of her hair that lay across the space between them, but he didn't move it. Right now he didn't know if even that much would bring on another knowing and he wasn't risking that here, with only her for help and company.

Normally I can't tell when a knowing will happen. Why is it with her I know one's coming? Why is everything twisted around her? She's like an oak and the world is ivy, climbing her, revolving around her. He scrubbed at his face. *So what happens to the ivy if she falls?*

He forced the images to the cage at the back of his mind. 'I'll kindle the fire. Pack up,' he growled and wriggled out into the snow. He reached back in for his jerkin and coat and brushed her arm. She yelped and he huffed in irritation, at her and at the tingle that shot through his fingertips. 'Hurry up,' he snapped, anxiety and grief and anger making him sharp, 'we should reach the plain by noon if we don't dawdle.'

Dom squatted by the embers of the fire and laid more wood on it until it blazed and he could melt snow for tea. He threw some dried rosehips into the bowls and went to piss while it heated.

I'm afraid of her, that's what the problem is. She's going to change everything. 'No,' he said aloud, 'she's going to set in motion old plans I thought I'd escaped.' He stared unseeing at the melting yellow snow, then shook himself like a dog and returned to the camp.

Rillirin had collapsed the tent and screwed it into a bundle three times its proper size and was struggling to tie the leather thongs around its bulk. Her face was red with the effort and he watched her in silence, the echo of the glimpse he'd seen through her throbbing behind his right eye.

'You're making a mess of that, aren't you?' he said when

he couldn't bear to watch any longer. Sharp again, when he shouldn't be. Couldn't help it. She squeaked in alarm and spun to face him, the bundle dropping from her arms and unfurling again.

'Forgive me, honoured,' she whispered. 'I'll do better, I promise.'

'This is the third time I've shown you how to do it, isn't it?' he said. He didn't wait for an answer, but spread out the tent and showed her how to roll it. 'Got it this time?' he asked. She bobbed her head. 'Good. Check the tea.'

She'd made the bowls from pine bark and resin their first day out from the village, when Dom had been too numb to do anything but stumble through the woods. Crude but effective and lightweight, they slipped easily into the tent folds for carrying and had come in handy every day since.

'You ready?' he asked when he'd finished his tea, and she drank the rest of hers and stowed the bowls. She hefted the tent on to her shoulders and Dom adjusted it, teasing one corner out of the ties to hang down to her calves and keep off the worst of the wind. They hadn't even had time to find her a coat before they'd left. Before they'd been banished. He killed the fire, buckled on his sword and headed east. Rillirin limped along behind him, bent slightly beneath the tent but unprotesting, dogging his heels like a whipped cur.

They walked all day, reaching the edge of the Western Plain by late afternoon. The sun was already fading when they made camp. Rillirin was pinched with cold and Dom built up the fire, then put out a hand to stay her. 'Get warm, lass, I'll do the rest.'

He could see her instinct to obey warring with her fear that he would punish her for laziness, so he threw her the pigeons he'd brought down with his sling. 'Pluck these, will you?'

She hunched by the fire, working quickly and piling the feathers in her lap. When she was done and the tent was up, she held up the handfuls of down. Dom raised an eyebrow. 'No thanks.' He put his head on one side, curious. 'You keep them,' he said.

Her eyes flickered to his face and away; then she carefully separated the feathers in half, took off her boots and stuffed her socks with them. He could see the tiniest smile graze her lips as her toes warmed up.

'Clever,' he said approvingly. The silence stretched between them as the pigeons roasted in the top flames and chestnuts cooked in the coals. Dom turned his back to the fire and looked up at the sky, tracing the constellations sprayed across the velvet of the night. His fingers tapped against his vambrace and he hummed softly. 'Would you like to talk?' he asked.

There was no response so he turned back and she looked away hurriedly. 'Of course, honoured. What do you want to talk about?'

'No,' he said as he poked his knife into a pigeon, 'do you *want* to talk? You have the choice.'

'Of course, honoured,' she said again.

'All right. What do you want to talk about?' he pressed.

'Whatever you desire, honoured.'

'Please stop calling me that, lass. It's a Mireces term and neither of us is Mireces.' He pulled the pigeons off the spit and put one in her bowl, juggled chestnuts from the fire and split them evenly. 'Here you are. All right, can you tell me your name?'

She was quiet, staring at the food, and for a second he thought she was praying. *Who to?* Had she fooled them all? Was she praying to the Red Gods? Then she looked up and there was a wet sheen to her eyes. 'Rillirin Fisher,' she whis-

pered and he knew it had been a long time since anyone
had asked or cared.

'Rillirin Fisher,' he repeated. 'That's a beautiful name.
Rillirin. Rill.'

'Not Rill,' she snapped; then she cringed. 'Forgive me,
honoured, I spoke wrong.'

The vehemence, the sudden sick expression, told him that
Rill was associated with some bad memories. 'I apologise,'
he said formally, 'Rillirin. And I'm Dom Templeson. I know
I've told you that before, but now we're properly introduced.
We'll be at Watchtown tomorrow. Stay close to me, all right?
It's our town, a Watcher and Wolf town. People might be a
little . . . hostile.'

She paused with the pigeon's leg in one hand, her eyes
wide, fingers suddenly white.

'But you're under my protection and I'll keep you safe,'
he told her. 'We're going to visit my mother – my adopted
mother. She's high priestess at the temple of the Dancer and
Fox God. She can cleanse you, if you want it.'

He concentrated on eating, pretending he couldn't hear
the muffled hitches in her breathing, the sniffs as she fought
tears. *How desperate for cleansing would I be after nine
years in the hands of Mireces?* His eyes drifted to the
vambrace on his right arm and what it concealed, and then
he turned his thoughts carefully in another direction, like a
parent steering a recalcitrant toddler away from danger.

'And Liris? Can you tell me why you killed him?' he asked
as he sucked the meat from the last of the bones.

The silence stretched even longer this time and she dropped
the chestnut she was holding back into her bowl. 'He was'
– Rillirin's hand rose to her throat, fell back into her lap
– 'he was going to rape me. He still had his dagger in his
belt, so I, you know . . .' She made vague stabbing gestures

and then stuck her hands in her armpits and hunched over, nostrils flaring.

Dom wiped grease from his mouth and studied her. 'That took real courage, Rillirin,' he said, 'to resist him like that. To keep yourself safe.' Her mouth twisted and he knew that it was probably the only time she'd managed to fend him off. Still, it was the last time he'd ever try, she'd made sure of that.

Yes, and her actions led to dozens of Wolf deaths.

She wasn't to know that.

But I could've. I could've known that, if I'd pushed, if I hadn't wasted those two days in the village on feeding her, making her feel safe, I could have saved us all.

Dom stared into the flames, almost daring the knowing to come. *Do I want to be that man?* he asked himself. *Someone who'd frighten a woman for his own gain? Wouldn't that make me another Liris to her?*

Dom grunted, blinked, looked away. He finished the pigeon.

CRYS

Twelfth moon, the seventeenth year of the reign of King Rastoth
The road to the West Rank Forts, Cattle Lands

Godsdamn fucking winter wind, Crys thought as he unloaded the princes' tent from the wagon. *Will it ever stop?*

As if in answer, a finger of cold slid beneath his scarf and tickled his neck. He shuddered, pulling it tighter. Even the north had been warmer than this.

Tacking up the River Gil for days on end against the current and wind had been a misery despite the plushness of the royal barge, the weather worsening every day until they were all at each other's throats. Crys'd been relieved when they made it to the Rank harbour and could get back on land. He knew what he was doing on land.

But then they'd commandeered horses and a wagon and struck out into the Cattle Lands where the wind seemed to come straight off Mount Gil itself, carving into any exposed flesh in an unrelenting attack.

Crys shivered again and the grey mule stretched its neck

towards him. Crys skipped sideways out of range of its yellow teeth. 'Bastard animal,' he grunted, 'you think pulling a wagon for a couple of days is tough, try riding alongside your stinky hide the whole way and still having a night watch to stand. I swear, you bite me one more time and I'll knock your teeth out.'

'He doesn't understand you, you know.'

Crys whipped his head around to see Galtas leaning against the back of the wagon. 'Lord Morellis, I beg your pardon, but that bloody animal understands every word I say. He's a devil sent by the Red Gods.'

'All because he tried to bite your cock off. Some men pay for that sort of thing.'

You probably would. 'From a wench, aye, not from something with teeth as long as my finger,' Crys said instead.

'Shame you weren't able to put it to good use at that whorehouse in Yew Cove,' Galtas said, a sly smirk in his eye. 'Your cock, I mean, not your finger. Though if your finger's bigger . . .' He trailed off, smiling again. 'But you weren't interested, were you?'

Crys reckoned Galtas had been the author of that particular piece of gossip. Crys's lack of needs; Crys preferring to spend the evening with Prince Janis. Were Prince Janis and Crys . . .

He'd put three men on a warning for repeating that one. Janis's reputation had to be beyond reproach, and Crys wasn't particularly impressed that his name was being dragged into it either. An evening of chess with Janis hadn't been high on his list of ways to pass the time, but as he'd explained to Commander Koridam back in Rilporin, you don't refuse a prince.

'I've got my hand if all else fails,' he said, aware Galtas was awaiting a response.

Galtas smiled, the effect much like the mule's baring of teeth. 'Just not on watch, eh, Captain?'

Crys hauled the tent on to his shoulder. 'You take the fun out of everything, milord.'

'One of the privileges of rank, soldier. On you go.'

Crys flicked a salute and marched past Galtas; he dumped the tent in a dip in the landscape that did fuck all to cut out the wind. Privileges of rank? Gods, he was an arse. At this pace, they had two more days to reach the forts, though if the weather carried on like this they'd all freeze to death well in advance. Didn't all have ermine and wolfskin cloaks like the princes. *Maybe I could win one of Rivil's next time we play cards.*

The thought cheered him and he set about laying out the tent frame as he imagined swaggering through the honour guard dressed like a prince. But no. Word of that would definitely find its way back to Durdil.

Godsdamnit, he thought again. *Godsdamn winter and commanders and bloody soldiering too.* The wind blew wet snow in his face. 'You motherfuc— Your Highness. Er, we'll have the tent up in no time, Sire. The men are lighting a fire just over there if you'd care to warm yourself.'

Janis nodded. 'Need a hand?' he asked instead, and before Crys could fumble a reply, took an end of the tent and shook it open, held it against the wind while Crys put the frame together. They slung the material over the top and started pegging it down. 'It's bloody freezing, isn't it?' Janis said when they were done. 'Bit of exercise warms the blood, eh?'

'Yes, Your Highness,' Crys said. 'Allow me to get the rugs and bedding from the wagon.'

'Come on, Rivil,' Janis called, breaking the intense conversation his brother was having with Galtas. They both looked over, identical expressions of guilt quickly masked. 'Lend us a hand and we can all get warm that much quicker.'

Flustered, Crys led Janis to the wagon and jumped inside. He began handing the prince the rugs to lay on the tent floor against the chill. Rivil and Galtas wandered over a moment later and Crys noticed Rivil's unconcealed irritation, but he took the proffered bedding and carried it to the pavilion, dropping it inside. The pair disappeared soon after and Crys called a few men to spread the rugs out and fetch the three cots for the princes and Galtas. He lit the brazier and set it in the centre, beneath the smoke hole; then he laid out the bedding.

'Thank you, Captain,' Janis said as he sat on his cot with his portable writing desk. 'Let me know when supper's ready.'

'Yes, Your Highness,' Crys said and made his escape. The wind tugged at him as soon as he was outside, but Crys ignored it now. They might still be in the Cattle Lands, but the mountains loomed black in the blackness, feet covered with thick, concealing forest. Just because an attack by men or wild beasts was unlikely didn't mean Crys wouldn't prepare for it. He did the rounds of the sentries already walking the perimeter in pairs.

The princes had an honour guard of twenty men, men he hadn't known well before this assignment. They were amiable enough, he supposed, but there was a clear division between those who served Janis and those with Rivil. *Am I Rivil's, too? Or am I captain of the honour guard and without bias, as I should be?* He followed the perimeter trail silently, looking for fault and unable to answer his own question.

Mac and Joe were bickering again. He ghosted out of the darkness and got within two paces before Mac spun, startled, his hand dropping to his sword. 'Too late for a sword now, Mac,' Crys said, making his voice harsh. 'By the time you've drawn it your guts'll be tangling around your knees. You should have dropped me with an arrow twenty paces back.'

Mac licked his teeth and scuffed at the snow, silent.

'Mac doesn't like first watch,' Joe supplied with friendly malice.

Crys eyed the pair of them. 'That so?' he said, and Joe realised his mistake. 'Then you can have the third watch.' Third watch was the darkest, coldest and most miserable of the watches, in the small hours before dawn when it was hardest to wake and to stay alert. 'But that leaves me short of a pair of guards now, doesn't it? So you should probably take first watch as well. The others are already settling down with supper and some warm blankets, after all. I wouldn't want to disturb them.'

Mac was still silent, but Joe's mouth opened in protest. Crys stepped very close. 'Yes, soldier?'

'I, ah, so that means a pair gets the night off?'

Crys winked. 'Well done, soldier, yes it does. Who do you think that pair will be? Well, I can tell you, one of them will be me,' he added before Joe could speak. 'I plan on sleeping all night long, warm and cosy and full of supper. My first full night's sleep since we set out. Ah, lads, I can't wait,' he said, slinging his arms around both of them and steering them along the perimeter. 'And it's not even one of the privileges of rank. It's a privilege of not being a silly twat like you two.'

He dragged them to a sudden halt and turned them to face him. 'If I hear one more argument or angry word between you, I'll have General Koridam flog you both when we get to the West Forts. We have charge of the safety of the princes of this land. They are our only concern. I don't care if one of you screwed the other's wife, daughter, mistress, sister or mother. I don't care if you owe money, stole or killed someone's grandma. Do I make myself clear? Whatever this disagreement is, it is done. Understand? Done. Now do your fucking jobs or I will make you live to regret the honour of being chosen for this posting.'

'He said Prince Janis was—' Mac blurted and Crys's fist buried itself in his gut. Mac doubled over, gagging.

'What did I just say?' Crys demanded. He glanced at the rest of the camp, scanning the perimeter, trying to see through the darkness for threat. 'You are endangering the princes. I'm an easy-going sort, but I will not stand for that. I will not.' He paused to make sure they got the message.

'Now, I don't give a runny shit for who said what. Next man to say anything at all gets a beating now and a flogging at the forts. Do not test me on this.'

Joe's mouth closed on whatever retort he had, and Mac pushed against his knees and forced himself to stand straight. He glared into the darkness, wheezing.

Looks like my warm and cosy bed will have to wait, despite the boast, Crys told himself. Lead by example, Durdil had said, don't make them do anything you wouldn't do yourself. He pulled his cloak tighter around himself and took a single pace back, leaving the pair ostensibly in charge of the perimeter, but staying close enough to make them uncomfortable, backs of their necks prickling with his gaze. He counted off the seconds until one of them would cast him an anxious glance, betting on it being Mac. *Still, I'd love to know what it was Joe said about Janis.*

RILLIRIN

Twelfth moon, seventeenth year of the reign of King Rastoth
Watchtown, Western Plain

Dom and Rillirin approached Watchtown's main gate across
a vast white plain and Rillirin slowed. High wooden walls,
thick gates barred with iron, and the scents of woodsmoke
and cooking.

The nest of vipers, Liris had called it, home of their enemies.
Watchers and Wolves and devils, prophets and killers,
Watchtown was the centre of all that was evil. According to
the Mireces.

But Rillirin had shared a tent with a Wolf, walked with
a Wolf, for five days and nights now. She'd listened to him
breathe in the dark, had woken from nightmares of Liris's
corpse coming to claim her and Dom had been there, asking
if she was all right. Seeming to care.

Liris lied about so much. Of course he lied about this too.
But still Rillirin stopped and Dom left her behind, oblivious,
his stride eager. *Walk into the nest of vipers, or wait for*
Corvus to find me. She looked across the blanket of snow.

113

She could see the temple grounds a mile or so from the town, and a copse of trees. Everything else was white, as far as she could see, under a sky as blue as a robin's egg.

'I'm not a slave any more,' she whispered fiercely. 'I don't have to do what they tell me. I don't.' She faltered and turned to stare northeast, as best she could reckon it. 'I could go home.'

Rillirin had heard the others talking about her before the village was attacked, heard Dom refer to her as a messenger, but whatever message she was supposed to give was hidden from her. Unless it was death – if so she'd delivered that one already. Maybe that was why Dom watched her all the time, not with lust, or hate even, which she deserved for the catastrophe she'd brought on him, but with an intense curiosity and something she'd swear was fear.

Liris is dead too, though, she reminded herself. *I did that. I killed him and I did it on purpose this time. I wanted him dead and he is. And I'd have killed the Blessed One too if she'd been there.*

That was bravado, though, and Rillirin knew it. The Blessed One terrified her in a way Liris never had. The Blessed One could condemn her soul to the Afterworld as easily as look at her. Raising a hand against the Voice of the Gods was the surest way she knew to forfeit her soul and her life.

'Are you all right?'

Rillirin jumped. Dom was standing a few paces away. She had no idea how long he'd been there. 'Forgive me, honoured,' she whispered.

Dom clicked his tongue. 'Come on, let's get into town. There's a storeroom just past the gate; we can leave the gear there.' He led off and then slowed his pace to match hers.

'Watchtown is the home of my people, the birthplace of

the Wolves. We've been here for a thousand years, you know, descended from the warriors who defeated the walkers on the Dark Path and freed all Gilgoras from the tyranny of the Red Gods. Full of history, full of strength, this place. If there's anywhere you can be safe from Their hateful influence, it's here.'

It was the cleanest-smelling town she'd ever been in. Just smoke and food, and the hint of hops when they passed a tavern. The wide roads were packed earth cleared of snow, river stones forming paths along the shop fronts where customers stamped their boots free of mud. In the centre of the street was a long mound of snow, shovelled there to keep the rest of the road clear for wagons and horses. Rillirin watched a group of children on the mound, running up and down it, shrieking laughter and hurling snowballs.

Her mouth curved in an approximation of a smile and then she saw the crowds of Watchers strolling the streets, talking, shopping. She gulped, her stomach clenching. But Dom walked at her side, pointing out alehouses and fletchers, butchers and tailors, with such enthusiasm and pride Rillirin began to relax. *It's pretty. And everyone's so friendly with each other.*

They passed a shop squeezed in between a wool-seller and a wood-carver, the table in the window stacked with golden loaves of all sizes. The baker, an old woman who leant on a spear in the doorway, smiled and gestured. 'Fresh baked today, my dear, still warm from the oven. Only a copper for two.'

Rillirin's mouth flooded with saliva, but she'd no money. She shook her head and stepped back, bumped into someone and turned. 'Forgive me, honoured,' she said automatically and the stranger's face hardened. He squinted down at her and she looked away fast, heart leaping like a salmon.

'Say that again,' he demanded.

'Forgive me, honoured,' she whispered as the baker grabbed her spear, all hint of welcome gone from her features.

'Mireces,' the man said loudly and everyone on the street turned to look. 'Listen to her. Uses that fucking "honoured" thing to address people. Mireces, I tell you, right in fucking town.' He grabbed her by the shoulder and wrapped his other hand in her hair.

Rillirin thrashed and then fell still, a rabbit before a stoat, waiting for the end. *Time to die.*

'Morning, everyone, and isn't it grand to be back in town?' Dom strolled into the gathering mob and pulled Rillirin out of the man's hands, draping an arm across her shoulders. The man was so shocked he let her go. The muscles in Dom's neck tensed but his smile was easy.

'Hello, Stott. I'd like you all to meet Rillirin Fisher of Rilpor, a young lady who escaped from slavery in Eagle Height itself and made her way alone down the Sky Path to our scout camp. We took her in and I've brought her here to speak to the council of elders and be cleansed in the temple.'

There was a rustle of noise, a few smiles sent in her direction. He was making her sound clever and resourceful, as though she'd planned it all. She darted a glance at him, confused. Wasn't this his opportunity for revenge?

'You vouch for her, Dom Calestar?' Stott asked and Dom turned a hard grin in his direction.

'I do, yes. Rillirin is no threat.' His fingers tightened on her shoulder, digging hard into the muscle. 'Lydya, two loaves for our guest, please,' Dom said and flipped a copper through the air. The old woman caught it and selected the bread, passing it back to him with a wary glare.

Dom had one arm around her and the bread in the crook

of the other, but Rillirin sensed the danger lurking beneath his skin. Stott must have seen it too, for he grunted and moved out of their way. Dom smiled for the crowd a last time. 'Dancer's grace upon you all.'

That seemed to do it; the men and women began to disperse, muttering and huddling into knots, casting hostile glares at her despite Dom's words. *They hate me because I was a slave, because I aided the Mireces. They'll never trust me; I'll never be welcome. And once the news about the village reaches them . . .* She swallowed past the constriction in her throat, feeling as though she was breathing through a reed, not enough air, her head light, stomach heavy.

Dom's arm slipped from her shoulders and he shook himself like a dog. 'Here, eat some of this while it's still warm,' he said and tore a chunk from a loaf, his voice strained. 'Give Lydya another copper – here you are – and you can smear that with as much honey as you want.' Rillirin did as she was told. The old woman gave her another smile, and if this one wasn't so genuine Rillirin didn't blame her. She couldn't taste the bread, the honey thick as hate in her throat.

'We'll see Elder Rachelle now. She'll have questions for you, and I'd advise you to answer them well. After that I have a few things to buy, and then I think we need a cup or two of ale, don't you?' Dom said as they resumed their walk. She didn't answer, watching as he flexed the fingers of the arm that had been around her shoulders.

'Thank you for saving me. I know it must have been hard to go against your people for the sake of a Mireces. Here and – and back at the village.' Rillirin didn't want to talk, didn't like talking, talking was dangerous, but he deserved her thanks.

She gulped ale. She'd answered Rachelle the way she did the Blessed One, eyes down and with absolute honesty. Anything else and she could tell the woman would sense it and kill her. Afterwards, they'd left her alone in Rachelle's big kitchen while Dom gave the names of the dead.

When he came out he was hollow and he hadn't spoken a word as he led her through town to buy what he needed. They'd all stared at her, everywhere she went eyes on her and all of them hostile. *At least in Eagle Height they ignored me when they didn't need anything. I didn't exist to them.*

Dom looked up from rubbing his hand and gave her a brief smile, his eyes preoccupied. 'My pleasure,' he said and she felt a loosening in her chest. Was forgiveness that easy with these people? Or with him, anyway? 'Though you shouldn't name yourself Mireces. It's not your fault you were captured.'

She exhaled a tiny snort and stirred the froth on her ale with a fingertip. 'It took them three years to make me stop calling myself Rilporian. I suppose now I have to relearn it all over again.'

'How did they make you stop?' he asked and Rillirin cursed, but it was too late: his question dredged up the memory and before she could distract herself it flooded over her.

Liris's hand on the back of her head, his awful strength as he forced her face into the barrel of water. Fresh from a mountain stream and cold as knives, cold enough to scorch as it flooded into her eyes and nose. Lungs burning as above her they chanted the count and laughed at her struggles until she started to drown. Then they'd pulled her out, given her a couple of seconds, and back in she'd gone. Again. And again.

Rillirin took another swig of ale. Her hand shook. 'Every time I said I was Rilporian they beat me and held my head under the water 'til I thought I'd die. Some days it went on for hours, even after I'd said I was Mireces. It was a sport. They used to bet on me, on when I'd break. When I'd start to beg.' Her mug was empty and she pushed it away, wiping her hand over her mouth.

'Another?' He pointed and signalled before she could respond. 'Two,' he called. 'How old were you?'

She swallowed. 'Eleven.' *Though by fourteen, they had other uses for me.*

'I'm sorry they did that to you, Rillirin.'

'You don't need to be sorry, you weren't the one who did it.' She dared to look him in the eye. 'I'm the one who's sorry. So sorry for everything that happened, all those deaths. You should hate me – everyone else does. You should never have saved me.'

Dom watched her over the rim of his cup as he drank. 'I will always save you,' he said and then cleared his throat, spoke on before she could ask what he meant. 'The scouts up by the Final Falls gave us a few hours' warning of the attack. That meant we could decide what to do. We decided to fight, though most of us were already here or in our small family settlements throughout the foothills. It was our decision. We could have scattered; we could have fled. We could have given you back to them.'

He put his cup down to rub his right hand and then shake out his arm. 'But we fought. Yes, it was a battle we hadn't expected to fight, but that changes little. I could've let you run, and they'd have hunted you down. Maybe you'd have got as far as the plain, and then there are hamlets and farmhouses in danger. Better to fight them on our ground, contain them there, force them back rather than let them in.'

'But you lost,' she whispered.

Dom's mouth turned down and he plucked at the week-old beard on his cheek. 'They lost more than we did, and they lost you too. That's enough.' He looked away and his voice dropped to a whisper. 'It has to be enough. And it'll be Yule soon. Lim and the others will come from the village; the whole town will try and squeeze into the temple. It'll be a new year, a new start. For us all.'

She scratched a dirty fingernail into the knife grooves on the table top, flicking looks out into the tavern. The glares she received were mainly hostile, but the tavern's bustle unwound another knot in her chest. The noise and movement were comforting somehow. And the colours. In Eagle Height they wore blue and black, or blue and brown. But here there were men and women in shirts of red, yellow, green, orange. Grey trousers, green trousers, brown jerkins over pink shirts. One woman in a scarlet gown with a black shawl over it.

The place was so alive, so full of laughter. Rillirin couldn't remember the last time she'd heard so many people laughing without it sounding cruel or being directed at another's suffering.

She turned back to the table and watched Dom out of the corner of her eye. His gaze was turned inward, his mouth tense. *Sarilla will be here in a few days, then. Crippled, angry, hating Sarilla.* She gulped and drank ale, trying not to think about it.

'Does your hand hurt? You keep rubbing it,' she asked. The malty warmth of the ale lined her tongue.

'Hmm?' Dom looked up from his hands, his right eyelid flickering. He pressed delicate fingers against it. 'No, just a headache.'

'In your hand?' Rillirin smiled, feeling foolish.

Dom frowned. 'Are you drunk? On two cups of ale?'

'I've never had ale before. It's nice. Fuzzy.'

'Fuzzy? Shitting hell, you are drunk.' Dom drained his cup and signalled for a refill. 'I've got some catching up to do then, haven't I? I mean, who knows what sort of monster you'll turn into on two cups of ale? Best if we skip straight past the two-cup beast and discover the third.' He waved and the tavern girl appeared again with a sly grin. She bent down and whispered in Dom's ear and he chuckled, patting her arse affectionately. Rillirin's cup was topped up a third time, Dom's a fourth. Or was it a fifth? This time the woman left the pitcher on their table.

'I can't pay for any of this,' Rillirin hissed as Dom raised his cup and clinked it with hers.

Dom winked. 'That's all right, we'll find some way for you to make it up to me.'

She felt the blood drain from her face, her head suddenly light. *Fuck*. It was so obvious, so fucking obvious that she hadn't even considered it. She was in his debt now and she had nothing to pay with. He'd been so slick she hadn't spotted what he was doing.

'I – I think you should have this cup as well,' she said and pushed it across the table. Dom's brows rose. 'I owe you for two loaves and two cups of ale. I don't want to increase the debt any more.'

'Don't forget the honey,' he said, the corner of his mouth turning up.

The ale churned in her gut, sour in her mouth. Had she forgotten every lesson slavery had taught her in the scant handful of days since she'd escaped it? Now he would think she was trying to cheat him. 'Of course. Forgive me. The honey too.' She swallowed and looked at the faces blurring through the room. 'When will you take payment?' she managed, but despite everything her voice cracked on the last word and she saw, from the corner of her eye, his frown.

'Payment? What are you talking about?' He rubbed his right palm against the edge of the table.

'You have bought me,' she said, her voice barely above a whisper. The alcohol roiled in her stomach and washed into her head with every beat of her speeding heart. *He might not be cruel. Please, gods, don't let him be cruel.*

Dom coughed ale across the table and stared at her. Then he wiped his chin and leant forward. She squirmed back, her body a flinch. 'We do not buy and sell human lives in Rilpor. Yes, there are women who sell their bodies for money and yes, even Wolves take advantage of it. I didn't think you a whore.'

'I'm not,' she snarled before she could bite back the words. 'A whore at least is willing. But payment is payment, and I have nothing else to give.'

'You'd give yourself to me for a loaf of bread?' Dom's eyes were wide and his voice low. 'That's what you think you're worth?'

Rillirin's face was hot with shame but she managed a mirthless laugh. 'I've been worth far less.'

'It's a gift, Rillirin, no payment is due, I swear by the Dancer. A gift,' Dom repeated. He coughed again and rubbed the back of his neck. 'We need to get drunk. Really drunk. And then pretend that conversation never happened.'

He was revolted and she didn't blame him. 'I have to go,' Rillirin said, lurching up and banging into the table.

'Don't go, Rillirin. Please. I'm sorry.' Dom reached for her hand and she snatched it away. She looked towards the door.

Go where? They'll kill me if I leave his side; they know what I am. But he can't even look at me. Misery swamped her and she couldn't bear to see the disgust in Dom's face.

She stared at the table and tears dripped from her nose on to the wood.

He stood and put both hands on her shoulders, warm and strong. 'Sit and drink with me. Please. Please,' he said again when she hesitated, 'and forgive me for the name-calling. Please sit. It would be my honour to buy you as much ale as you can stomach.'

Rillirin let him push her gently back into her chair. 'But the price,' she protested, grasping on to the only thing she could understand. *Everything has a price.*

Dom flicked his fingers, dismissing the comment and then flexing both hands. 'Not much call for spending coin in the forests. I can afford it. And it's a gift, Rillirin, do you understand? I expect nothing from you except the pleasure of your company as we drink. Not that sort of company, either,' he added in a rush and a faint blush stained his cheeks.

'You're a free woman, Rillirin Fisher of Rilpor,' he continued, pushing her cup gently back across the table, 'and free women can accept drinks from free men without it requiring payment of any sort.'

Rillirin found she was staring into his eyes, so brown they were almost black and earnest, and honest.

'You're a free woman, Rillirin,' he repeated, the words sending a delicate shiver through her. 'Will you drink with me?'

Her head was spinning. *Free.* 'Your will, honour— Yes, Dom,' she managed, even finding a crooked smile to go with it.

Dom banged his fist on the table. 'Yes. That's my girl,' he said and grinned. 'Right, do you know any Mireces drinking games?'

'I do, actually,' she said and paused. 'But they usually end with vomiting.'

Dom banged his fist again and laughed, and the sick tension in Rillirin's chest loosened, loosened and fell away.

'Excellent,' he said. 'That's exactly the level of drunkenness we're aiming for. Teach me.'

GALTAS

*Twelfth moon, seventeenth year of the reign of King Rastoth
West Rank headquarters, Cattle Lands, Rilporian border*

'Your Highnesses, may I present my staff? Colonels Abbas,
Dorcas and Bors of the sub-forts. Majors Costas, Caspar,
Shepherd and Potter. And the most promising captain from
each of the forts: Pike, Salter, Wainwright and Carter.'

'That one's a woman,' Rivil pointed out.

'Captain Tara Carter, yes, Your Highness. As I said, one
of our most promising captains and my adjutant.'

'Well, that is . . . unusual. Don't think I've ever heard of
a woman Ranker. Parents bought your commission, did they?'
Rivil enquired with a smile.

Tara looked to Mace; he nodded. 'Worked my way up
through the ranks, Your Highness,' she said. 'Joined up at
seventeen, but only General Koridam was prepared to give
me a place in his Rank.' She bowed, then blushed and made
an awkward attempt at a curtsey, which looked ridiculous
in trousers.

Galtas was bored of the lengthy welcome already, but a

female soldier might provide an interesting interlude. And aside from the cooks and washerwomen she was the only woman here. And not completely unattractive, though he didn't like the short hair one bit. *Still, looks like she's got a decent pair of tits under that uniform.*

He drummed his fingers on his sword hilt as the audience dragged on, yawning ostentatiously when the subject shifted to the fort, the Mireces, the supply lines, as though none of it interested him. He noted Colonel Abbas's grimace of distaste, and Janis's narrow-eyed stare.

Galtas glanced sideways at his honour guard. The Palace Rank uniforms were smarter than the shabby West's, he was pleased to note, but other than that a soldier was a soldier. Unless she was also a woman.

He looked back at Carter, waited until she glanced at him and gave her a rakish smile even as his ears sucked in the information Mace let slip so easily. Carter didn't react. Still, they'd be here a few days, more than enough time to talk her round despite his other duties. She probably couldn't fuck the soldiers without getting into trouble. She was probably hornier than the Fox God Himself.

The audience over, the Rank came to attention, saluted and separated to form two columns. The soldiers stationed in Forts Two, Three and Four marched past the royal party and out through the gates.

'. . . care for a tour of the armouries?' Mace was saying and Galtas pricked up his ears.

'Of course,' Janis said with what appeared to be genuine enthusiasm. Rivil echoed the sentiment and then requested Crys accompany them while the rest of the men headed for the barracks. Galtas sucked his teeth. Seemed Rivil couldn't go anywhere without that obsequious little shit these days.

'Ooh, look, swords,' Galtas enthused as they entered the

armoury. 'And over there, those are spears. And shields too. Why, anyone would think this was an armoury. What fun. Where's the wine?'

'Enough,' Janis hissed and Galtas smirked. It really was too easy. He slid forward until he was standing at Carter's elbow. 'Hello,' he said. 'Lord Galtas Morellis, adviser to Prince Rivil. We haven't been properly introduced, which is a terrible shame.'

'Captain Carter, West Rank,' she said, not at all impressed by his nobility, it seemed.

'I'd love a tour of the fort, Captain,' he tried.

She looked at him for a brief moment, and then away again. 'That's what this is, my lord,' she said, 'a tour. Excuse me,' she added and walked after the general.

Crys made a noise that might have been a smothered laugh and Galtas glared at him. 'Captains,' he muttered. 'Thick-as-shit jumped-up cunts, every one of them.'

'As you say, milord,' Crys said blandly, his blue eye shining in the gloom, the brown one invisible. 'And not susceptible to your charms, either,' he added with a touch of malice.

Galtas bit back a retort and shoulder-barged Crys out of his way as he caught up with the others. He had more important things to do than bandy words with that little prick.

CRYS

Twelfth moon, seventeenth year of the reign of King Rastoth West Rank headquarters, Cattle Lands, Rilporian border

Crys decided he liked Tara. Then again, he'd like a scabby bear as long as it had an aversion to Galtas godsdamned Morellis.

'The tunnels that connect the forts begin here, I see,' Rivil was saying. 'It really is ingenious, General.'

They stood by a small iron-banded door at the back of the armoury. It looked exactly the same as the ones Crys had seen in the North and East Ranks. He'd run those tunnels in full armour in the pitch black during drills in the North Rank. He shivered at the memory.

'Thank you, sire,' Mace said, 'though the credit goes to the designers of the forts. The tunnel allows us to reinforce a sub-fort in danger of falling, or evacuate one that cannot be saved, all without sending men over the walls. You could get from here to Fort Four a mile away without coming above ground if you needed to.' He bowed and gestured, letting Janis precede him back out of the armoury.

Crys glanced at Rivil and got the nod to carry on. He followed Mace and Janis, ears straining behind him. *Probably shouldn't have stirred Galtas up,* he thought, but couldn't quite bring himself to regret the comment.

'Not sure I believe the "West is best" hype,' Galtas said, 'not when they've got a woman commanding men. How well d'you reckon a bunch of pussy-whipped soldiers'd fight?'

'She says she worked her way up through the ranks,' Rivil replied. 'She'd have earned their respect.'

Galtas snorted. 'Worked her way through them, more like. Slept her way to an officer's rank, you can bet on it. "General Koridam was the only one to give me a place,"' he squeaked. 'Course he did. In his bed.'

Crys shook his head slightly. Galtas's reputation as a fighter was well known and well earned, from everything Crys had heard, yet he dismissed Tara without thought. Crys studied her as she strode at Mace's side. Sword familiar and easy on her hip, eyes on the roam looking for danger, thighs that'd probably crack Galtas in half if she wrapped them around him. Mace didn't suffer fools. If Tara was a captain, she deserved the rank and could hold her own in a scrap.

'Everything I've heard says Mace Koridam is as honourable and unbending as his father,' Rivil said.

'The only reason Durdil can't bend is arthritis. The man's a relic. No, this Tara shagged her way to her captaincy. Tailorson probably did the same,' Galtas added, and Rivil heaved an impatient sigh. Crys smiled without humour. *Eavesdroppers rarely hear compliments,* his mother had always told him.

'Oh come on, Sire,' Galtas insisted. 'One minute he's caught cheating at cards, the next you're buying him drinks and making him head of your honour guard. You think that's all a coincidence? You're trusting your life to a known gambler and thief.'

Crys glanced back at that, but the pair had stopped and weren't paying him any attention. He faded into the shadows to listen.

'I tire of this rivalry, Galtas,' Rivil said, his voice as cold as the snow. 'I believe Crys is destined to be one of my advisers. Make your peace with him.'

One of his advisers? Crys blinked. *Well, that's unexpected.* He jumped as Janis strode back past him.

'Rivil, Galtas, hurry up. What are you gossiping about back here?'

'Nothing, brother,' Rivil said. 'Galtas and I were merely having a difference of opinion.'

Janis stared at Galtas. 'My brother has, for reasons unknown to me, befriended you despite your background and despite your many shortcomings. While my father allowed him to give you land and title out of his own inherited estates, I would remind you that when I am king, I may not be so lenient. You owe everything you are to my brother and, while it would pain him, I will send you back where you came from should your loyalty prove wanting. Sheep farm in the Grazing Lands, wasn't it?'

'Potter's shop in Shingle, Sire,' Galtas grated and Crys could hear barely contained fury in his voice. His mouth popped open. *He's a fucking commoner! Lord Galtas Morellis is a potter and a peasant.* Crys put his hand over his mouth to stop the laughter bubbling out.

'That's right. Galtas Potterson,' Janis said. 'Well, it's a trade you can always fall back on should your luck run out.' He crooked a finger and Rivil trailed him out of the armoury.

Crys watched them go; then he looked back at Galtas and froze, the smile sliding from his face. Galtas's one eye blazed with naked hatred as he glared at the princes standing in the open space between the armoury and the granary. 'I may not be noble,' he muttered, 'but you'll never be king.'

A chill settled in Crys's bones. *If you plan treachery, what better way to insinuate yourself into the heir's inner circle than to befriend his younger brother? Has Rivil's blindness allowed a threat into the very heart of power?* Sweat prickled across Crys's brow as Galtas smoothed out his expression and stalked past him. *Are you a traitor, Galtas Potterson?*

GILDA

Twelfth moon, seventeenth year of the reign of King Rastoth
Dancer's temple, Watchtown, Western Plain

Gilda had spent years bringing the gods' Light to her people. Midwife, priestess, counsellor, she'd seen much and done more in her long life on the plain and in the hills.

She'd never met anyone as broken as Rillirin Fisher.

With Dom's help she held Rillirin under the water, pale against the blackness of the godpool's basin, and Gilda could feel her terror. Dom had told her what the Mireces had done to her, but a cleansing was a cleansing and there was only one way to do it. She could see Rillirin watching her through the veil of water and smiled, nodding.

'Holy Dancer, Lady clothed in sunlight, this child comes to you with open heart and begs for cleansing. Fox God, Lord of wit and ingenuity, great Trickster, this child comes to you with open mind and begs for wisdom. She has been befouled, tainted by the Mireces and their bloody gods. Cleanse her, that she may be whole.'

Gilda felt the fight building in Rillirin's body as her lungs began to burn, felt her tensing to thrash. She met Dom's eyes and he nodded, ready. 'Sweet Dancer, Lady of Light. Fox God, bringer of truth and justice, free her soul and clear her mind. Rillirin Fisher is a true child of the Light; welcome her.'

Rillirin gave a single great convulsion and then Gilda and Dom were pulling her up out of the water, holding her steady as she dragged in lungfuls of air. Dom wrapped a blanket around her shoulders and lifted her over the lip of the pool, swinging her into his arms and pressing a kiss to her forehead. 'Welcome back to the Light, Rillirin Fisher. I give you my hearth and home, my food and roof. I welcome you as family and will always protect you.'

Rillirin was shuddering with cold but she turned huge grey eyes on Dom, astonished. 'What?' she whispered.

He smiled. 'As Gilda and Cam welcomed me as theirs when I came to the temple as a boy, so I welcome you. You will always find in me a friend.'

The gods were doing more than cleansing the girl, Gilda thought as she wrapped another blanket around Rillirin. With luck they were cleansing Dom and bringing him some much-needed peace. Her fingers brushed Dom's arm and she could feel its tension. 'You are cleansed,' she murmured to Rillirin, 'and you are safe in the Light of the gods. There is no more to fear for you here.'

'Cleansed before Yule, so you can start the year in peace and freedom,' Dom added.

Rillirin looked up from the circle of his arms. 'I'm clean?' she asked and Gilda nodded, taking her hand. Rillirin's face was slack with wonder. 'Not . . . damned? Truly?'

'No, my sweet, not damned, not dirty, and not bad,' Gilda said and nodded again when Rillirin began to cry, great heaving sobs that confirmed all Gilda's suspicions. She reached out and Dom passed her into Gilda's embrace; then he shook the water from his hands and arms, grimacing.

'Doesn't matter what they said to you, Rillirin. Doesn't matter what they did to you. You are cleansed. They are a bad memory and a series of scars on your skin.' Gilda met Dom's eyes. 'Many of us carry scars we wish we did not, memories we would like to forget. Each of us has to decide whether those scars and memories will control us, or whether we can be free of them.'

Dom's mouth turned down and he blinked, breaking eye contact. Rillirin looked up at Gilda, sensing the words weren't just for her. 'I want to be free,' she whispered, 'but I don't know how.'

'You'll remember soon enough, child, and if you don't, then we'll teach you. For now, let's get you dry and dressed and warm, Rillirin Fisher, child of Light.'

Dom reached out to pull the blanket higher around her shoulders, but Rillirin gasped and jerked away, pulling Gilda in front of her. 'Blood oath. T-t-traitor,' she stuttered, pointing over Gilda's shoulder. Dom had rolled up his sleeves for the cleansing and the circle of scars around his right forearm were clearly visible above the wolf head inked into the inside of his wrist.

'Let us explain,' Gilda said soothingly. 'Hush now and listen. It's not what you think.'

Rillirin retreated. 'He wears the mark of the Dark Path. I've seen men make those marks on their arms, swearing blood oaths of vengeance. He worships the Blood, is bound to the Dark Lady Herself. He can't be trusted, can't be here in this temple.' Her face was a mask of horror and betrayal. 'You said you'd cleansed me—'

'We have,' Dom interrupted softly, 'and the marks on my arm need not concern you. They were made a long time ago in a moment of grief, of madness and youth. I do not walk the Dark Path and I never will. These are . . . a reminder of something I must never forget. But I stand in the Light, I swear it.'

'But you swore to Them too,' Rillirin whispered. 'You cannot undo an oath sworn in blood.'

Pain flashed across Dom's face, but he said nothing else and even Gilda didn't know how much truth he was telling. She never had, not from the moment they'd found him with the cuts fresh in his arm and his wife dead in his lap. But as high priestess of the Dancer and Fox God, she trusted utterly that Dom was safe in Their grace. The Red Gods hadn't touched her boy and she would swear on her own soul that he was clean.

Her hand found an amulet and she squeezed it hard, then slipped it from around her neck and put it over Rillirin's head. 'Here, child, a blessing from the gods now you are cleansed. Dom wears one the same – show her, Dom. See? An amulet of the gods pressed against his skin. He stands in the Light, not in the Blood.' She squinted at him in the gloom, trying to see through the layers of protection he wove around himself, to see the truth through the shadows and the secrets. 'He stands in the Light,' she repeated, her voice firm.

Rillirin sniffed and looked at the amulet, at its twin shining on Dom's chest. There was a line between her brows, but she didn't say any more.

He's the calestar – who can guess all the things he sees and knows? I don't know why he did it, but I trust him. I do. Gilda watched Dom stand up from the side of the pool and roll down his sleeve, covering the bracelet of scars. His fingers were clumsy as he tied the vambrace on over the material and slung his coat on. Rillirin's hand held hers and she squeezed it; she led her away from the pool towards the exit, Dom following. Gilda glanced over her shoulder at him. *He's my boy. I do trust him.*

I do.

MACE

Twelfth moon, seventeenth year of the reign of
King Rastoth
West Rank headquarters, Cattle Lands, Rilporian border

'Your Highnesses, it has been an honour and a privilege to host you at the West Forts.' Mace steepled his fingertips and pressed them to his lips. *Oh, gods.* 'Before you leave us, there is a, ah, a delicate matter I feel bound to discuss with you.'

Rivil let out a peal of laughter. 'Galtas and Captain Carter?' he asked. 'He didn't, did he? I was sure she'd knock him back. Don't worry, I'll make sure he claims any bastard she ends up with.'

'Rivil,' Janis snapped, 'this isn't a laughing matter.'

'Er, no, Your Highness, this has nothing to do with Tara, though the matter does concern the lord.' Mace hesitated, awkward, and Rivil's humour became suspicion. 'There's no easy way to say this, Your Highnesses. A concern has been raised about the . . . loyalty of Lord Morellis. He was overheard making what sounded very much like threats against you, Prince Janis. It is my duty as a soldier to make you aware of this, should you wish to take any action.'

Janis and Rivil exchanged glances, and Mace could see anger in Rivil's eyes.

'And who has been telling tales about Galtas?' Rivil asked in icy tones.

'Someone I trust,' Mace said. *Damn you, Crys Tailorson, you'd better be right about this.*

'Someone who doesn't have the courage to make such outrageous claims in person?' Rivil demanded. Mace spread his hands helplessly. 'This is disgusting. I would trust Galtas with my life. I *have* trusted him with my life, with my safety. He's been nothing but loyal for years.'

'What do you propose, General?' Janis asked.

'That depends on you, Sire. You are the one he has spoken unwisely about. I am happy to host him here for as long as you wish, or to escort him to the West Rank harbour and see him safely onboard ship back to Rilporin.'

Rivil exploded out of his chair. 'This is outrageous and I will not listen to any more of it. Galtas is my friend.' He rounded on Janis. 'If you want to send him home, then you'll have to send me home, too.'

Janis stood and so Mace did too, more uncomfortable than ever. He mentally directed some colourful curses at Crys and schooled his face to blandness.

'Calm down, Rivil, you're behaving like a child. General, thank you for bringing this to our attention, but Rivil trusts Galtas.' He looked at Rivil, who had bristled at Janis's first words and now subsided. 'And I trust my brother. If Rivil vouches for him, then that is good enough for me.'

Mace inclined his head. 'Of course, Your Highness. Prince Rivil, I apologise if this has caused any distress.'

Rivil forced a smile. 'I understand, General. Your dedication to duty is what has made you such a force to be reckoned with. The Mireces no doubt fear your name, let alone your presence.'

'Well, I wouldn't go that far,' Mace murmured, 'but thank you for the kind words. I trust your journey will be as pleasant as we can hope for out here in the west. Again, it has been my honour. Dancer's grace upon you.'

Janis reached out and shook his hand. 'And upon you, General. Your hospitality has been most welcome.'

Thank the gods for that, Mace thought as he led them down to their horses as far from each other as they could get. Hope blazed on Crys's face and Mace gave a tiny shake of his head. Crys's expression solidified and he stared without blinking at Galtas.

He really believes this, Mace thought as the princes mounted. He saluted. 'Protect Their Highnesses with your life,' he said.

'I will, General,' Crys said before anyone else could speak. 'I swear.'

CORVUS

Twelfth moon, year 994 since the Exile of the Red Gods
Blood Pass Valley, Mount Gil foothills, Rilporian border

Corvus hadn't realised just how close they were to the valley before they walked out of a stand of birch and were in it.

'And you're sure we can trust him?' he asked Lanta for the third time.

The repetition did nothing to disturb her tranquillity. 'I am sure, Sire. Gull's report is clear, and he doesn't trust lightly. The Rilporian's kept his promises and done all that has been asked of him.'

'The Lady's will,' Corvus acknowledged, but there was still a flutter of nerves in his gut. The risk was great, but he'd never heard that Mace Koridam of the West had enough guile for so elaborate or long-running a subterfuge. Their Rilporian ally was genuine. He had to be genuine. *My feet are on the Path. And if this is a trap, I'm taking them all with me.*

Lanta touched his arm and pointed. Mata was labouring up the slope, waving as though he was drowning. 'Riders,' he panted, 'around twenty. Armed.'

'Shit,' Corvus swore. 'Under cover, now, all of you.'

'No. Of course he brings guards. He's a man of position, nobility. He will have ensured the men are loyal. And three dozen? That's not so many more than we have.'

Corvus pressed his lips together. *Not so many more? It's twice our number, even if we do have the high ground.* 'Can we be sure they're who we're here to meet?' he demanded.

Mata wiped sweat from his face. 'There's a man in black with an eye patch,' he said, 'as you specified. The rest are soldiers and nobles.'

'Soldiers and princes, not nobles,' Lanta said with a small smile. Corvus saw her fingers skate over the hilt of her knife. 'Exactly as promised.'

'Then let us greet our . . . guests,' Corvus said. He gestured and his men fell in behind him. He held out a hand and Lanta took it, and they began walking down the slope towards the valley floor.

'My feet are on the Path,' Lanta murmured and Corvus suppressed both a smile and a huff of relief.

Not as confident as you'd have us all believe, are you, Blessed One? He looked at the group again and pushed away the smugness. As war chief of Crow Crag, he'd been privy to the broad plans cooked up by Lanta and the priesthood, but it was only as king that he'd learnt their scope and audacity, the careful years of nurturing, the agents secreted throughout Rilpor. Lanta's ambition took his breath away.

'If this works,' he whispered and glanced at her.

Lanta's eyes were alive with excitement and for once she made no effort to conceal her emotions behind cool detachment. 'If this works,' she replied, 'they will give us Rilpor.' Her hand tightened on his. 'And we will give it back to the gods. Blood rises, my king.'

And I shall rise with it, Corvus thought.

CRYS

'Form up around the princes. Your Highnesses, those are
Mireces and we are a day's ride from the West Forts. Mount
up; we're leaving.'

Janis was already kicking snow over the fire and Crys
looked away from them and up the slope of the valley. A
dozen men and one woman, the blue of their shirts and her
dress startling against the snow, swords and spearheads
glinting in the low sun.

*Gods, this can't be happening. I should've argued harder;
I should've insisted we didn't come. I should never have
agreed to this mad idea.*

Blood Pass Valley was wide open, a half-mile between its
gently sloping sides and the trees that covered them, and the
princes and their guards were too far into it, too far from
the regular patrol routes or fort lookout posts. And who
knew how many more Mireces were in those trees? Hundreds,
thousands even.

142

If I survive this Durdil'll demote me down to private and have me cleaning out shit pits for the rest of my life. And I'll deserve it.

If I survive this.

Crys had backed three steps towards the line of horses before all hell broke out behind him. His stomach lurched and he spun, dragging out his sword and expecting to see Mireces pouring from the trees flanking them. Instead, the majority of his men turned on the rest and cut them down, swords winking silver and then red. Galtas had a dagger at Janis's throat and the heir was on his knees in the snow.

'Fuck me, I was right,' Crys breathed and charged, not needing to see any more. He ducked a swing from Joe and punched his sword into the man's flank, ripped it free and kept running, weaving and dodging, focusing on one thing only: protect the princes.

'I'd stop there if I was you,' Galtas called and Crys skidded to a halt in a spray of snow, Janis's sudden flinch and the trickle of red into his collar all the evidence Crys needed that Galtas meant what he said.

Crys dropped his sword and raised both hands. 'My lord Morellis – Galtas, please. You can't do this. You mustn't. It's treason.' He chanced a glance at Rivil, frozen at Janis's side, his eyes wide. *Close enough to reach Galtas before I can. Look at me, Rivil. Look at me. You can do this. Come on, come on, look at me. Look!*

'Treason?' Galtas said and brayed a laugh. Janis twitched.

Crys felt men approaching his back and prayed to the Fox God his chainmail would hold when they stabbed him in it. His guts were turning to water and adrenaline pumped through him so hard his hands were shaking, vision blurring.

Janis and Rivil are decent swordsmen. Get them to their horses and we can get out of this mess while Galtas and his traitors are being torn to pieces by the Mireces. Gods, I never thought I'd be grateful to see those blue-clad heathens, but they might just save our skins. Enough of a head start and we'll be back at the forts by midnight.

Crys felt himself steady a little. The wind cut at the sweat on his face, but his heartbeat was slowing now, the world coming into focus so sharp it hurt.

'This isn't treason,' Galtas went on, 'this is a return to the old ways, where might is right. And here and now, I have all the might, so to speak.' He grinned. 'Look around you, Captain. Look at who these men are answering to. Not you. Certainly not Janis here.' He shook the heir by his collar.

'What is it you want, milord?' Crys asked, stepping closer. A hand on his shoulder from behind pulled him to a halt and he stopped. *Let them think they're in control and they might let me close enough.* 'Why now? Why here?'

Galtas laughed again and clubbed Janis across the back of the head. As the heir fell forward with a shout Crys lunged, hand reaching for his own knife. *Close quarters, stay on his blind side. Kill him and get them to the horses. Easy.*

But men on either side tripped Crys and forced him on to his knees and Rivil still wasn't moving. Crys grunted as his arms were twisted up behind his back, but the pain didn't matter when Galtas ripped open his coat and the shirt he wore beneath it was as blue as a summer's afternoon.

'Here's why, you snivelling little shit-fuck,' Galtas crowed and clubbed Janis again as he got to his hands and knees, sending him back into the snow.

Galtas walks the Dark Path. He worships the Red Gods.

The corpses of the men loyal to Janis and Rivil were cooling in the snow, and Crys could hear the crump of feet as the Mireces got closer. He was out of options.

Cold, Rivil. Be cold as ice. He's not your friend. He was never your friend.

'Sire? Rivil,' Crys hissed, 'get his knife. Rivil, get the bastard's knife now.' He jerked his head at Galtas, who looked between them and chuckled, waving the knife in Rivil's face as though daring him to make a grab for it. It was back at Janis's throat before Rivil could react.

Crys struggled, but the hands and the rope around his wrists held him tight. 'Fucking do something,' Crys yelled in desperation, trying to jerk Rivil from his paralysis. 'Rivil, you cunt, *do* something!'

It worked. Rivil looked at him, took a step back to give himself space and then kicked Janis hard in the face.

There was a moment of frozen stillness as Janis arced back into the snow and lay still.

'No!' Crys shouted, horror sluicing his gut. 'What are you—'

'My feet are on the Path,' Rivil said. There was nothing in his expression that Crys recognised from the man he'd come to know and trust, and then Rivil walked past him towards the Mireces. 'Welcome to Rilpor, my friends.'

GALTAS

Twelfth moon, seventeenth year of the reign of King Rastoth
Blood Pass Valley, Mount Gil foothills, Rilporian border

There'll be no turning back after this.

But there had never been any turning back, not for Galtas. His future was indelibly tied to Rivil's, and that meant Rivil needed to be king if Galtas was to have everything he wanted. *And I will. Especially now that Crys is proven as disloyal to his prince as I always knew him to be. Rivil's chief adviser? I think not.*

Galtas knelt in the snow next to Rivil and Corvus. Rilporians and Mireces mingled in the semi-circle around the scaffold. Mac had his knife poking into Crys's kidney, and Galtas knew it was the only thing keeping him still and even that might not be enough. Not once the ritual began. He said a brief prayer that Crys would resist and they could string him up next to Janis.

'My high priest Gull, your tutor in Rilporin, has spoken highly of your devotion over the last few years, Prince Rivil. He was particularly proud of the way your mother met her

146

end. That first step on to the Dark Path was taken well, but now it is time to further your journey and deepen your connection to the gods.' The Blessed One studied Rivil's face and eyes, then turned her attention to Galtas, seeking, calculating. 'Once we have done this, there is no revoking your oath. Your souls will belong to the Dark Lady and Gosfath, God of Blood. Your feet will walk the Path forever.'

'I long for it,' Rivil said and Galtas echoed him. Most of the honour guard made the same pledge, and of those who didn't, their loyalty to Rivil was absolute; they wouldn't betray him.

Crys, though, was grey with shock, slumped on his knees with his arms bound behind him and bleeding from the nose and mouth. His dual-coloured eyes, which had always fascinated Rivil and disturbed Galtas, were blank with incomprehension and iced with fear.

Janis was babbling again, and his voice went up an octave when the Mireces hauled him up the scaffold feet first and tied his ankles to the cross beam, his wrists to the post. He hung there, upside down and naked, the wind off the mountains whipping his skin into blue goose bumps.

'It took us years to perfect the sacrifice to please the gods,' Lanta said as she undid the buttons holding her sleeves to the shoulders of her dress, peeling them off to expose slender, muscular arms. 'The Dark Lady and Gosfath, God of Blood, deal in death and mutilation. Their coin is pain and fear. When do you pray most fervently? In battle, no? Or when the knife slips and you're suddenly looking at the inside of your own body? Fear and pain bring our minds into alignment with the Afterworld, and so our gods demand fear and pain during worship. If you aren't shitting yourself at a sacrifice, you don't know the gods.'

Galtas blinked at the sudden profanity coming from those

perfect lips, but he couldn't deny she spoke truly. She was the Blessed One, the Voice of the Gods, her power even stronger than Gull's. His stomach flipped as she pulled the sacred hammer from the belt loop beside her spine.

'Rivil – brother, you don't need to do this,' Janis's voice was thick, panicked. 'I'll renounce my claim to the throne, go into exile in Listre or Krike, I swear by the Dancer. You can have the throne. Just don't sell your soul to evil. Please.'

Lanta tilted her head to study his upside-down face. 'The Dancer? You know, don't you, that the Dancer is sister to the Red Gods? That She went to war against Her own siblings, Her and Her bastard Trickster Son? And you think of Her as peaceful, as just.' She chuckled and caressed Janis's face. 'The Dancer slaughtered millions of the true faith and cast my gods into the void. They would have died for all eternity if the first Mireces hadn't followed them into the wastes and sustained them with their own blood and belief.'

'You remember your history differently to us then,' Janis managed. 'As I recall, you didn't so much voluntarily exile yourselves as you were run off the land like peasant thieves. And it didn't take much to make you turn tail, either. You're descended from cowards and kin-killers, and you think blood magic and human sacrifice make you holy. I pity you.'

'Save your pity, prince,' Lanta sneered, the caress becoming a stinging slap, 'you'll need it all for yourself in about twenty seconds.'

'Holy Dancer, Lady clothed in sunlight, bringer of peace to the lands and hearts of all people, shine Your grace on these men and teach them the errors of their ways,' Janis recited. His face was red with the blood running into his head, slick with clammy sweat despite the cold.

Even now his piety is sickening, Galtas thought, shifting on his knees, the snow soaking through his trousers. *Even now he seeks to undermine us, to take away our glory with his feeble attempt at martyrdom.*

'Every drop of blood spilt in Their name helps the Red Gods draw closer. Every scream of sacrifice thins the veil that keeps our Bloody Mother, our Red Father, from this world.' Lanta drew a nail the length of her palm from a pouch on her belt. 'Without death and sacrifice, we will never see the gods return. Thousands must die to tear the veil asunder. Are you willing to spend the lives of thousands?'

'We are,' Rivil and Galtas said together.

'And if one of those lives is your own?'

'The Lady's will.'

'Then let us begin,' she said, facing Janis and pressing the nail against his instep. Galtas couldn't feel the cold any more. He rocked on his knees with every thud of his heart. *My feet are on the Path. My feet are on the Path.*

'Shining Lady, bring me into Your Light, and teach me patience and fortitude through this trial. Fox God, in your resourceful—' Janis's prayer bubbled into a scream as Lanta drove the nail through the top of his left foot and into the beam behind.

'Dark Lady, beautiful goddess of fear and death, we offer You this man. Take his body one part at a time. God of Blood, of war and mutilation, we offer You this man. Take his life an ounce at a time. Red Gods, we worship You. Dark Lady, beautiful goddess . . .'

Lanta drove the second nail into Janis's right foot. Janis screamed louder. The third nail went into his left ankle and Galtas blinked at the genius of it, the artistry as she worked, left then right, left then right, along his legs. He chanted the prayer with the others and felt the gathering presence of the gods. *This is power. This is glory. The gods will return and They will be well pleased.*

Sweat darkened Lanta's blonde hair and stained the collar of her dress as she nailed Janis's legs to the oak. It looked difficult, finding the proper space between the leg bones so the nail went in cleanly, a regular, uniform line of dull grey heads creeping along his legs like flat, metal ticks sucking on the running blood.

When Janis passed out, Lanta knelt by his head and rubbed his chest with handfuls of snow until he woke. 'What would be the point in nailing him when he can't feel it?' she asked. 'His pain, the purity of it, is what draws the gods to us.'

The nails went in all the way to the knees, and then one in each kneecap, the crunch as they went through the bone echoing in Galtas's head. The nailing took lifetimes and he lived every one of them, his voice gaining strength as the prayer and the power washed through him, transported him along the Dark Path and maybe, if he was lucky, into the presence of the gods Themselves.

Lanta raised the last nail to the sky and they fell silent, the prayer ending as suddenly as it had begun. Galtas's throat was tight with fear and sore with chanting, his back wet with sweat.

That's Janis Evendoom, Heir to the throne of Rilpor, hanging upside down and dying for the glory of the Red Gods. Look at this that I have done.

In the echoing quiet, the Blessed One stretched Janis's scrotum out and positioned a testicle over his anus. She placed the nail on it and pressed down hard, raising the hammer high.

Janis was delirious, but still Galtas watched through slitted eyes, hands clapped firmly over his groin. The hammer flashed in the dull light and Lanta smashed the nail through the bollock and into Janis's rectum.

Janis's scream burst the blood vessels in his eyes and

snapped his vocal cords. He sucked in a breath as the second strike drove the point out of the side wall of his alimentary canal and into the wood. The third stroke thumped his balls into paste and Janis vomited, the puke trickling down into his eyes and nose.

Lanta wiped it away with a gesture that was almost tender. 'He mustn't choke to death. He must live long enough to take our messages to the gods. Do you feel Their presence now?'

Galtas nodded. There was a crackling in the air, a greasy feel to his skin, the hairs on his arms standing up. He was glad to see Rivil's face was as ashen as his own must be. Even Corvus was pale, his eyes fixed on the nailed prince. The Dark Lady was watching, the God of Blood drinking. Galtas knew it in his brain and balls and belly and fear tightened his throat.

'Then make your oath and your request.'

'The throne of Rilpor,' Rivil breathed, sweat trickling down his face. Opposite in the half-circle, Crys leant forward and vomited, tears running down his face. 'The conquest of Rilpor. Glory. Our souls in return.'

'Our souls in return,' Galtas repeated.

'Granted.' Janis's voice was guttural and more breath than sound. Rivil yelped and Galtas felt his scalp tighten. Janis's tongue, swollen purple and twice its normal size, flicked out and around, and then he smiled. 'Granted. You have the throne, and I have you.'

Lanta and the Mireces bowed to Janis, to whatever was speaking through Janis, and Rivil dropped forward like a puppet with its strings cut, hands thumping into the snow. He pressed his face into its cold.

'We feel Your presences and we thank You for Your words. We are Yours to command.' Lanta's voice was high, enraptured. She leant forward and kissed Janis's swollen, puke-stained face.

'Rivil,' Janis said and Rivil shuddered at being singled out. Galtas watched from beneath his brows. 'You have allies in the east. Bring them. Corvus, prepare for war.'

'Your will, Red Ones,' Lanta said. They waited for more, but there was nothing. Lanta brushed the snow from her knees, rose and carefully returned the hammer to her belt. Now, in the aftermath, her hands shook. 'Your feet are on the Path, Prince Rivil, Lord Galtas. And we are your allies in the overthrow of your king.'

'Let us discuss the war to come,' Corvus said, rising, and Rivil scrambled to his feet, swaying slightly.

Galtas couldn't tear his eyes from Janis. *We've done it. Bound ourselves to the Red Gods and the path of power and glory. Our victory is beyond doubt.*

'We thank you and the gods for this alliance,' Rivil said, clasping Corvus's forearm. 'Together we will see Them return.'

'We will have little chance to communicate once you return east. We should plan our movements now, the timing and direction we will take.' Corvus was jubilant, expansive in the aftermath of the Dark Lady's pronouncement.

I like him, Galtas thought. *He'll betray us once the war is won, of course, but I still like him.* He stood, shaking out his legs.

'I have a basket of carrier pigeons,' Rivil said. 'We'll leave them with you in case of emergencies.'

'We'll need Janis, of course, if it is permitted?' Galtas interrupted.

'Need him?' Lanta asked. 'His body is of no more use and the Dark Lady has his soul.'

'Galtas is right,' Rivil said. 'We must take the body back

for the king to weep over. But the nails in his legs may cause some comment.'

'If you insist.' Lanta sighed, flicking back her hair and smearing her cheek with blood. 'Mata, lend the Lord Morellis your axe, will you?'

DOM

*Twelfth moon, seventeenth year of the reign of
King Rastoth
Dancer's temple, Watchtown, Western Plain*

Dom nearly took off his own foot with the axe when it happened, the image of red and white and silver slamming into his mind just as he swung at the wood on the chopping block. The blade thudded into the hard ground and a second later he followed. He jerked forward, smacked his head off the block and toppled sideways into the snow. Upside down, silver dots and red lines adorning his legs, dark shapes kneeling in a semi-circle. And one other, bright not dark, shining with godlight from within. Chosen.

'Dom? Dom! Gilda, Gilda!' Hands on his face, hands that burnt and twisted the images into something else. Dom heard himself scream and the hands vanished, replaced seconds later by others, warm and soothing and safe.

'Dom, it's Gilda. You're in the temple in Watchtown. You're safe; you're safe. There's nothing to hurt you. Tell me what you're seeing.'

154

'Man in the snow. Silver dots, upside down. And the godlight. Shining with it. Shining . . .'

'Where, Dom. Dom? Calestar,' snapped the voice and Dom jerked, fought towards the surface. 'Where?'

'Inside the veil. Inside. Silver dots. Godlight.'

Gilda swore. 'Rillirin, help me get him inside. Come on or he'll freeze. Now, girl.'

'I can't touch him. It's not that I don't want to help, but – look.' There was a pause and then Dom felt it again, a touch followed by fire. He screeched and wormed away, his eyes still filled with the pattern of dots and lines. Couldn't see anything else. Bile flooded his mouth and he gagged, coughed, squirmed away again. Get safe, somewhere safe, wait until he could see again.

'Gods. Fine, get the barrow. Dom, you're on your way to being the least dignified calestar we've ever had. I hope you're pleased.' There was a hint of humour in her voice that steadied him.

His vision was clearing by the time Gilda had draped him over the barrow. He caught glimpses of Rillirin, wide-eyed and trembling as she wheeled him along to the temple house where they slept, her face reddening with effort. Gilda was at her side, lips pursed and her hand on Dom's arm, fingers pressed to his pulse.

'Is this because of his blood oath?' Rillirin panted.

'No, being the calestar is a gift of the Gods of Light. He sees bits of the future, warnings and suchlike.'

'The shit bits,' Dom grunted and then groaned. 'I can walk,' he muttered. 'Stop, I can walk.'

'Good, because we'd be upending this over the doorstep otherwise. Come on, out you come.' She hauled him upright and they staggered together through the door, Rillirin hovering around them like a frightened bird. Dom fell on to the nearest cot and turned his face into the pillow, groaning.

'Hurts,' he grunted.

'I'm not surprised; you nearly brained yourself.'

'No. Inside,' he said, rolling back over and clutching his skull. 'Fucking shitting gods, Gilda. Hurts.'

'Hush. I know it does. Sleep and it'll fade. Sleep, boy. Sleep.' She stroked his temples, her voice slipping into the sing-song she'd used when he was a boy first brought here and the nightmares and the knowings had threatened to tear him apart. When his parents had realised what his gift was and given him to the temple, Gilda had been the only safe place in a world swamped with misery. Even now her voice could soothe him. The pain thudded along with his heartbeat, but that was slowing now, the exhaustion pulling him towards its depths.

'And that was him seeing the future?' he heard Rillirin whisper.

'It was a knowing. Just a small one – he didn't lose consciousness. We'll learn what he saw in more detail when he wakes. Now fetch me a needle and thread, and make sure you boil them first. We need to sort out that cut.'

Dom heard her leave; then he dragged his eyes open when Gilda shook him. 'Wha'?'

'Why can't she touch you?' Gilda whispered.

'I've no idea,' Dom mumbled, 'and I don't want to know. Leave it.'

'You held her at the cleansing.'

'Barely,' he said and turned his face away. He rubbed his knuckles hard into his right eye. She was there again, the woman. He'd been seeing her on and off ever since Rillirin arrived in the village, as though she'd brought a ghost with her. She was there in the quiet, unguarded moments between sleep and waking, watching him with a curious tilt to her head. Never spoke, never did anything. Just watched him. Always watching. A stranger.

Dom grunted and squeezed his eyes tighter. *Liar. I know exactly who She is, and what She wants. I just have to decide when to give it to Her. What price I'm willing to pay to keep my secrets that little bit longer.*

Keeping secrets from the gods. Keeping secrets from kin. And the girl with the burning touch. Dom had a feeling she'd lay bare every secret he had, given the chance. And wouldn't they all be fucked then? Sleep rose to claim him and he let it. It was easier than thinking about what was coming.

'They're here,' Gilda called and Dom slunk from the house like a dog who'd eaten the beef while his owner was out. He was both hopeful and hopeless that the anger and hurt would have cooled, but it was obvious from their stances and expressions that the weeks of separation had done nothing but allowed the rage to scab over; it was still raw beneath. Dom could see the expression of betrayal on Lim's face when he saw Gilda standing with her arm around Rillirin's shoulders. Cam's face was closed, his expression hidden behind his salt-and-pepper beard.

Of them all, it was Rillirin who had changed the most, and every day she changed a little more. The cleansing had taken something from her, and left something else in its place. These days it was Dom flinching at her presence and not the other way around as the knowing grew in strength.

Dom had hoped the last one, the silver dots and red lines, would have taken the edge off. Didn't seem to be working so far. He swallowed his anxiety and made his way to Gilda's side just in time for her to give Rillirin a squeeze and run forward into Cam's arms.

'Where have you been, you old dog?' Gilda murmured after he'd pressed a deep, long kiss to her mouth. He patted her rump affectionately. 'It's been months. You love the woods more than me?'

Cam jerked his head at their son. 'Had to keep an eye on Lim,' he said, 'stop him doing anything reckless.'

Lim's face was sour as he moved into Gilda's arms and he glared at Rillirin and Dom over her shoulder.

'Where has your smile gone, son?' Gilda asked when she let him go. He ran his tongue over his teeth and didn't reply.

Dom felt Rillirin shift closer to him when Gilda hugged Sarilla and he reached out, putting his arm around her like Gilda had. The knowing she carried swelled again, faster than ever before, and he fought against it as it gathered, pregnant with the promise of pain, a sword waiting to fall. It wouldn't be long now. Not long at all.

Rillirin noticed his grimace and ducked from beneath his arm. She nudged him towards his family.

'Welcome to the Dancer's temple.' Gilda spoke the traditional words as Dom greeted the others with mumbles. There were no hugs or smiles for him. 'In three days we welcome midwinter and the turn to spring. A time of healing for us all. There is much to prepare, so unpack and then there'll be work for you all,' she finished as she always did, but this year there were no groans and protestations of old war wounds, merely more silence.

'Where's the girl staying?' Lim grunted into the void. 'We'll not stop under the same roof as her.'

'Her name is Rillirin.'

'She could be the Dancer Herself, for all I care,' Sarilla snarled, holding up her hand and ripping the bandages from it. 'She did this.' Gilda winced and so did Dom; it was the first time he'd seen the wound properly.

Rillirin took a step forward, her face pale. 'I have a tent. I'll keep out of your way.'

Dom looked at her but she shook her head once and walked away from the group, leaving him in a circle of silence and accusation. He was tempted to run after her so they could be miserable together.

Lim spat; then he led Sarilla and Ash into the guest quarters, jostling Dom out of his way as he went.

Cam followed more slowly, his arm around Gilda. He clapped his free hand on Dom's shoulder. 'Sort it out, boy,' he said, and left Dom to stare after them.

Sort it out? How exactly? He ran his hands through his hair and straightened his jerkin. *Shit. Fine, if Rillirin can talk to them, so can I – and the sooner the better. I'm going to need them for this knowing, and it's coming.* Despite his resolution, his feet dragged as he followed them into the house next to the temple.

RILLIRIN

Yule eve, seventeenth year of the reign of King Rastoth
Dancer's temple, Watchtown, Western Plain

People trickled in from Watchtown throughout the day, bringing firewood and food, ale and wine. Elder Rachelle smiled at Rillirin as she set up the trestles and began organising the jugs and bottles and barrels, though she was one of the few who did. Once news of the attack on the village had reached Watchtown, any ground Rillirin had gained with them was lost.

Rillirin might not be able to heal the rift with the townsfolk, but there was one thing she could do. She'd spent days working on it in her hiding place around the back of the temple, where she spent most of her time to keep out of the way of the others. She'd known the first time she'd seen Sarilla's hand what to do. Now, she screwed up all the courage she'd learnt in the last few weeks, every kind word Gilda and Dom had had for her, and headed into the crowd, searching.

Sarilla's fiery ginger hair was too easy to spot, and Rillirin

160

faltered for a second. 'Come on, come on, give it to her and run,' she muttered. She followed Sarilla and Lim towards the temple; they heard footsteps and looked back to see who it was. Lim's eyes narrowed and he planted himself between the two women.

'Please, this is for you,' Rillirin said, looking past Lim and into green eyes blazing with hate. 'Sarilla Archer.'

Sarilla's eyes flared with pain. 'You use my warrior name when it's your fault I'm no more than a cripple?' she demanded. 'You make fucking mock of me?'

'No,' Rillirin croaked as sweat dribbled down her ribs, 'you're still a warrior. Just take it. Please.'

Lim snatched the fabric-wrapped package from Rillirin's hand and passed it to Sarilla. As soon as she had it, Rillirin backed away to the temple door and stood in its shadow. *Holy Dancer, let me have done it right. Please let it work.* The rest of the townsfolk were oblivious, snatches of song drifting from all corners of the temple grounds, children running and squealing around the bonfire, boars and sheep roasting over spits.

The sun was setting in a blaze of pinks and oranges, surely a good omen for the coming year. 'Lady clothed in sunlight,' Rillirin whispered, and the words steadied her heart.

Sarilla unwrapped the gift: a contraption of wood and leather straps, it crouched in her palm like a spider. They bent close to examine it and Sarilla turned it over, scowling, and then placed it against the stumps of her missing fingers. She gasped and her expression melted into wonder. Three pieces of curved wood became fingers curled just enough to draw a bowstring.

Sarilla held out her hands to her husband and he fitted the leather loops over her thumb and forefinger, tied the thongs securely around her wrist and threaded them between the wooden fingers, pulling it tight. She hissed as they pressed into the raw flesh, but tossed her head when he would have stopped.

'Where's Ash?' she demanded when it was secure.

'Your hand is still—'

'Don't even try,' she warned and Lim subsided.

'Ash,' Lim called when he spotted the tall archer in the throng. 'May Sarilla borrow your bow?'

Ash paused, uncomfortable, and Rillirin held her breath. Sarilla raised her right hand and the bowman's eyes widened. Wordlessly, he unslung it from his back and passed it over. 'The draw's heavy,' he warned.

'Good.' Sarilla flexed meaty shoulders and the men took a couple of steps back. She found clear space and took her stance, placing her forefinger and the carved wooden fingers on the string. If Rillirin had done it right, their curve was shallow enough to slip free when Sarilla's forefinger released the string.

Eyes narrow with concentration, Sarilla aimed the empty bow at Rillirin and began to draw. Her breath hissed, but the bow bent and she brought the string to her lips for a second before releasing. Rillirin flinched but the others stood still, listening as the bowstring thrummed, and then Dalli approached and held out a long bundle covered in oilskin.

'You left your bow in camp,' she murmured. 'I brought it along, just in case. You'll have to look at the crack in the stock, though. Won't last long without repair.'

'How did you—' Lim began.

'I didn't. But a warrior should never be unarmed.' She grinned. 'Happy Yule.'

Sarilla gave Ash back his bow and unwrapped her own. She wept, clutching it to her chest, and Ash handed Lim his quiver and pointed out through the gate.

'There's a target set up there already. Go on, lass, go and work on your aim before you lose the light.'

Rillirin shuddered out the breath she'd been holding as the pair wove through the crowd towards the gate. She followed them with her eyes, and when they'd gone she noticed Dalli was watching her and so was Ash. They nodded, and Dalli grinned.

Rillirin nodded back, tentatively, and Dalli beckoned her with one hand, miming drinking with the other. Rillirin nodded again, more firmly this time. *A drink. Gods yes, a drink*. She took a deep breath and left the protective shelter of the temple.

Dalli slung her arm around her. 'Well done,' she said. 'Sarilla scares the life out of me, so just watching you do that made me thirsty. In which case, you must be parched. Ale or wine?'

TARA

Tara slid between the trees, stepping in the footprints left by the man she was following. He didn't form part of her orders, but he was heading her way and Tara was curious. She felt a momentary flash of guilt at disobeying the general again, but only momentary. Mace hadn't sent any couriers from the forts to the river, and it was unlikely to be a farmer out on his own this close to Yule and this far from habitation.

No patrols out this way, and Wolves don't normally come this far into the plain. So who are you?

Distracted, it took her precious seconds to realise the prints led her in a circle around a dense stand of holly a hundred strides from the river, and then he was leaping out from behind her.

Tara got halfway round and her sword drawn before he slammed into her and they both hit the snow. Flat of her blade between them and the tip practically up her fucking nostril, Tara went straight for his eyes, fingers hooked. Instead of lunging back like she wanted, he whipped his head side-ways and forwards. She caught an ear with her little finger and nearly dislocated it, and then he had his head in the crook of her neck and she couldn't bite, gouge or punch he was so close. The sword was cold and sharp against her cheek.

'Ranker, Ranker, Ranker,' he panted in her ear. 'Palace Rank. Captain. Please stop trying to kill me.'

That voice. And she'd noticed something about his eyes just before she tried to pull them out. 'Captain Tailorson? *Crys?*'

He'd managed to grab one of her wrists in the fight and she noted he didn't release the pressure at her words. Instead he jammed his free hand under her jaw and his index finger into the pressure point just below her ear. She squealed and let him push her face up and sideways, trying to relieve the pain.

What the fuck is going on here? He knows me; we spent the better part of a week answering our respective masters' calls in the fort. Went hunting together. Drilled together.

Crys was studying her eyes as though he'd never seen her before.

'You're not in uniform,' Tara grunted through the pain in her jaw and ear, 'but I am. West Rank insignia, captain's stripes. Tara Carter, adjutant to General Mace Koridam. You last saw me less than a week ago.' Nothing. 'Care to let go? Captain?'

'Who's with you?' he demanded, his voice hoarse.

'Nobody. I'm taking Yuletide greetings to our friends in Watchtown and requesting a report on the slave girl they captured. Who's with you?'

Crys shook his head hard and then stared around the copse with open fear. 'No one, I hope.'

'What do you mean, no one? Where are the princes?'

Some of the wildness left Crys's eyes, to be replaced with sudden grief, and finally he let her go, sliding to the side so she could get out from under him. Tara rolled once, came to one knee, levelled her sword at his throat and then stood. 'What have you done?'

'I haven't done anything,' Crys said, uncaring of the blade inches from his flesh. He was whiter than the scuffed snow around them. 'But Prince Janis is dead.'

Tara's sword tip drooped and then steadied. She swallowed. 'Is this a joke?'

'Does it sound like it? Prince Janis Evendoom walks into a bar and gets killed. Ha-motherfucking-ha.'

'All right, calm down.' He was twitching, his eyes roving the landscape behind her, barely aware of what he was saying. 'Are you in danger?'

'You could say that,' Crys said. 'Seeing as I had to fake my own death to escape. I have no idea if they're tracking me, but they can't let me live. If they suspect I'm alive, then yes, they're coming. They can't risk me telling the king what I've seen.'

'Who can't?' she asked, a sick feeling in the pit of her stomach. *He's not with his men. He's not with Prince Rivil. But he can't be running from them. Why would he be?*

Crys snorted without a hint of humour. 'You won't believe me when I tell you,' he said.

Tara stepped back and then lowered her sword. 'I'll take you back to the fort. You can report to the general.'

Crys lurched to his feet, both hands out, imploring. 'No! Please, Tara, please – not the fort. If they are looking for me, that's the first place they'll check. I'm going to Watchtown and then to Rilporin.'

Tara shifted from foot to foot, working her jaw to loosen

the pain while she thought. 'No, we go to the fort. If what you say is true—'

'I'm sorry,' Crys said and drew his sword. Tara gaped, bringing her own weapon up to guard even as her mind fought the evidence of her eyes. 'I can't go back that way. I won't. But I can tell you what I know and you can tell Koridam, all right?'

There was nothing but utter sincerity in Crys's face and Tara knew it'd be a fight to the death if she insisted. *No point me dragging a corpse back to the forts. And second-hand news is better than no news.*

Tara held up her left hand and sheathed her sword with her right. 'All right,' she said. 'Tell me. And then make sure you go to Watchtown and bloody well stay there until Mace decides what to do.'

DOM

She was nearby. He could feel her, an itch in his brain that flared to pain. It had been getting worse all day, all this most sacred of days. He could be thirty paces away from her and still feel it.

'You should go with Lim and Sarilla,' Ash said and passed him the jug. Dom drank. 'You need to clear the air.'

'Do we need to clear the air, Ash?'

'No. I don't like the stance you took, but I respect you taking it. What's done is done, and we've all made mistakes.' He slung an arm around Dom's shoulders and ruffled his hair. 'I mean really, how could you know they'd be chasing her? We all thought she was just an escaped slave.'

Dom felt a softening of the hard ball of tension in his belly and found a smile for the taller man. 'You thought she was a spy, if I remember correctly.'

'Pfft, a mere whim. A spy? Impossible. I don't know why you even thought it.' He gestured at Rillirin, sitting with

168

Dalli and laughing, and pain shot through Dom's head. *She's laughing. I think that's the first time I've seen her laugh, and it hurts.* He screwed shut his right eye.

'Your gift?' Ash asked, noting the grimace.

'It's getting stronger. Just being near her hurts. And the dreams are getting worse. She's pulling something – or someone – through.'

Ash stopped, pulling Dom to a halt with him. Snow dusted his curly hair, and despite the haze of ale in his eyes, his words were clear. 'You've never been able to delay a knowing before. Why this one?'

'It only comes when I touch her, I don't know why, and it wasn't like this when we found her. And then everything happened and you sent us away, and I didn't think there was any point doing it then. I thought the Mireces coming for her was the knowing and I'd missed it. By the time we got here I knew there was something else.' He rubbed his face with both hands. 'It's going to be bad. This one's going to be really bad.' He hesitated and then looked up at Ash. 'I'm scared.'

'We're all here now,' Ash said. 'And we'll be right there with you. Lim and Sarilla will come around, don't worry about that, and we'll all make an effort to welcome her if you need us to. Do it tomorrow, first day of the new year. Do it then, when the Dancer's still close.'

Easy for you to say, Dom thought. He heaved a breath. 'All right, tomorrow. But for now, I think I'm going to get drunk. Horribly, hideously drunk.'

'Too fucking right. And I'll help.'

Dom staggered from the guest quarters, groaning at the horror of being upright. The noon sun stung tears from his eyes. They'd been up all night, celebrating the turn to the light, the young and the old woken in time for the sunrise. *A new year.*

He weaved towards Rillirin's small tent and gave the side a hearty kick, cursed as he overbalanced and flailed wild arms to stay on his feet. If he was up and feeling like shit, someone else should be too. He heard a grunt from inside, but the tent flaps remained shut.

'Hey,' he hissed, slapping the canvas, 'come out. It's me.'

'No.'

'Come on, I want to talk to you.'

'Talk to someone else.'

'It's important.'

Rillirin groaned and dragged herself from the tent, shivering beneath a blanket. Snow drifted around her tired face and settled in her hair.

'Do you know any good hangover cures?' Dom asked.

'Is that why you woke me up?' she demanded in a voice groggy with exhaustion.

He shrugged. 'One of the reasons,' he conceded. 'I remember mixing Father's whisky with Ash's elderberry wine, and I know there was ale at some point, and now I think I'm going to die.' He noted the glint of amusement in her face.

'Only cure I know is to roll naked in the snow,' she said and then yawned wide enough to swallow a chicken.

'All right,' Dom said and began pulling at his boot. 'Well, are you coming too or just watching?'

Rillirin's mouth opened in shock and then curved into a smile. She giggled.

'Now that,' Dom said without a hint of insobriety, 'makes me feel much better. Come on, breakfast's cooking.'

The smile vanished. 'I'm not going in there,' she whispered, backing away and tripping over the tent pole. It collapsed with a soft whoosh of air and they stared at it in silence.

'Have to now. Come on, lass, it's going to be different. I promise,' he added, smiling his most winning smile. The knowing pressed at his mind like a fist.

'I – I can't,' she whispered, and Dom reached out to put an arm around her. She flinched. He flinched.

'You must. It's the day of my knowing. You're needed.'

'What does that mean?' she asked, voice panicky. Dom's smile cracked but he gestured again, unspeaking, and this time she moved towards the house.

Rillirin balked again at the door, but Dom pushed her in the back and she moved into the long, low room. Lim and Sarilla were sitting on a cot, heads close together as they whispered. Ash was lying beneath a mound of furs on the opposite side. He deigned to raise a finger in greeting.

'Rillirin's here,' Dom said, stilling the conversation. Lim and Sarilla stood, fast, awkwardly. The girl tried to run but Dom blocked the exit, more by accident than design. She trod heavily on his foot and he grunted. She froze, a rabbit confronted with a stoat, and then tensed as Sarilla approached. Dom could hear her breathing, shallow pants as though she'd run miles or was preparing for pain.

'Rillirin, we won't lie – your coming has been difficult for us, marred with violence and death. But Gilda has told us some of your story, and – and that you have been cleansed and claimed as family.' Sarilla's eyes met Dom's with a promise that they would discuss that later.

Shit.

'I will not pretend that we can be friends,' Sarilla added, 'but your fear is something we can understand. We made no pretence of trusting you, yet expected you to tell us what you knew. In hindsight, that was foolish.' She raised her right hand. 'Whatever else you have done, your gift has given me back to myself, and for that I thank you.'

Rillirin chewed her lip, her face unreadable, flushed. 'I know you do not trust me,' she said, low and clear and in a rush as Ash sat up in bed to listen, 'and that I do not deserve your friendship or to be a part of your family. I'm grateful that Dom made that promise, more than I can say, but it was wrong of him. I know how much death I have caused.'

She hesitated and Dom could sense her fear, and the kernel of determination that had forced so many words out of her. 'I accept punishment that it might prove my loyalty to you. But I do not know how it is done in your tribe.' She dropped her blanket and pulled back the sleeve on her right arm. 'You saved my life at the expense of too many of your own. It belongs to you now. The Mireces flay or brand.' She swallowed hard. 'If you find me unfit to trust afterwards, I will leave. I will leave anyway, if you desire. Your will, honoured.'

Lim reached out and Rillirin inhaled through flared nostrils. He pulled her sleeve back down and gripped her fist. 'While my feelings are the same as my wife's, I also trust that Dom had his reasons for saying what he did. He knows things the rest of us can't, and while it would ease my heart for a moment if I hurt you, it would not last and guilt would soon take its place. So there will be no brands or knives. And my name is Lim, not honoured and not chief – not to you. You're not a Wolf, so I'm not your chief. Understand?'

Rillirin nodded and Lim looked around the room, his eyes sharpening on Dom, and Dom knew that whatever gulf existed between them and Rillirin, he was stuck on the same side as her.

'Here, we learn to trust one another through talking, and then through training, and then through love, and then through fighting. Friends, warriors, family, war-kin. We will start with friends, I think. With talking. Yes?' Lim let go of her wrist and stepped back, gesturing her to a seat on a cot.

Rillirin sagged and Dom put his hands on her waist to support her. She startled at the unexpected touch and he snatched away, blinking back the pain of contact. It wouldn't be long now.

'Food!' he said instead, forcing a cheery note into his voice and making them all jump. 'I promised Rillirin breakfast. So come on, share.'

Some of the tension leaked from the room as they all looked at Ash, who stared back with wide, innocent eyes. 'What?' he asked.

'Hand it over, boy,' Lim growled and Ash sighed.

'Boy? Still he calls me boy. I've thirty summers, am older than that one.' He flung a hand in Dom's direction. 'And far better looking,' he added, grinning. Still, he rummaged beneath the bed furs and produced a bundle wrapped in linen. Inside were a whole roast duck and a handful of cooked onions. Rillirin's mouth dropped open in surprise, and then sagged further when he pulled three stoppered clay jugs from beneath the bed and a hunk of cheese and some apples from a sack.

'Ale, anyone?' he asked and Cam burst into laughter. Gilda murmured a small prayer as the others found their pilfered goods and put them in the middle and they began to eat.

'Aren't you hungry?' Dom asked, noting Rillirin's stillness.

'I don't have any food to contribute,' she said and reddened.

'Here, have mine,' Dom said, passing his portion over. Rillirin stared at it. 'Honestly, I can't eat any more anyway,' he lied smoothly. 'Go on, stuff yourself silly. It's Yuletide.'

'Yes, seeing as you're family,' Sarilla muttered and Gilda hushed her.

Rillirin hesitated, staring at the other woman with dismay, but Gilda gestured and she took the bread and cheese from Dom. 'Thank you.'

Dom watched her, drinking steadily to dull the pain, dull the anticipation. Not long now. Not long at all.

'Rillirin, we could do with you answering some questions for us now,' Lim said. 'It is important.'

Rillirin looked up at the mention of her name, then down at her fingers. She knotted them together and nodded.

'Before you start, there was a knowing a few days before you arrived,' Dom interrupted. Lim frowned. 'Small and still unclear, or I would've told you sooner. A man hanging upside down, a pattern of silver dots and red lines – what?'

Rillirin's hands were over her mouth, her pupils wide and black. 'Silver dots? In a line?' Dom nodded. 'With red coming out of them?' He nodded again. Every eye was intent on her now. 'I know what it means now. I couldn't work it out before. It's a sacrifice. It sounds like a sacrifice to welcome new converts on to the Dark Path. They tie the victim upside down on a scaffold and nail his legs to the beam. It brings the . . .' Her voice dropped further and she mouthed 'Dark Lady' without actually saying it.

Dom's heart began pounding and sweat prickled on his scalp and armpits.

'How do you know?' Lim demanded, suspicion blooming like mould.

'I've seen it done. My brother Madoc, he was taken at the same time as me. He slaved in Crow Crag but was brought to Eagle Height when he asked to convert. Only the Blessed One can perform that type of sacrifice. She killed a man and made Madoc a Mireces.'

Dom wanted to point out how valuable Rillirin was, he wanted to say I told you so, but the pain in his head was growing, linking that knowing to the one that was coming. He stifled a whimper.

'So your brother is now Mireces?' Lim demanded, oblivious.

'Yes. He took the name Corvus. He's war chief of Crow Crag now.' She met Lim's eyes. 'I am Rillirin Fisher of Dancer's Lake. I've twenty summers and was taken by force nine years ago with the other children when the Mireces destroyed our village. They slaughtered everyone else.'

'Corvus,' Dom repeated. He grunted and stretched his neck. 'Corvus Madoc Corvus Crow Crag Eagle Height king.' His tongue was thick in his mouth and his vision blurred, stretching the firelight around Rillirin, smearing her features with light and blood. His stomach rolled and he belched, heaving.

'Dom?' he heard Lim say, then, 'It's starting.'

'Shit.' Ash and the sound of dragging furniture, space being cleared behind him. *Mireces. Mountains. Dancer's Lake. The Dancer.*

The bitch.

'Watch him with the fire.'

'What's happening?' Panic in Rillirin's voice, flooding his mind, intensifying his fear. He was looking at the ceiling, head thrown back, cracks and clicks through his spine. *Just breathe. Accept the fear, the pain. Let the knowledge come. Breathe. Please breathe.* Dom dragged in a breath, held it, grunted it out. *Better. Again.*

The room faded into a million buzzing black dots. 'Take my hands,' he slurred, voice tangling in his throat. 'Rillirin, take them. Quickly.' His arms were as heavy as tree trunks and he fought to reach her, fought back the terror. Always fighting. *Always fight.*

'Get ready to catch him,' Lim warned as Rillirin reached out and put her hands in his.

RILLIRIN

Yuletide, seventeenth year of the reign of King Rastoth
Dancer's temple, Watchtown, Western Plain

For a long second nothing happened and then Dom's eyes rolled up in his head. He fell sideways off the cot, dragging Rillirin on to her knees, and then the convulsions began.

'What is this?' Rillirin's voice was shrill and she strained to pull her hands away. Dom released her and she tumbled backwards into Sarilla's legs. 'What is it?' she repeated, horrified, as she scrambled to her feet.

'Dom's gift,' Sarilla said. Rillirin stared at the thrashing man, at Lim cupping his head so that it didn't batter into the ground or the cot. Gilda prayed steadily, her eyes fixed on Dom's writhing face.

'Gift?' *This is no gift, this is evil. A punishment. A punishment for his blood oath, probably.*

'The knowing,' Sarilla insisted. 'Dom's learning why you're important to us, what it is you're meant to do.'

'We already know that. I herald the war.' *But why me? I'm nobody. I'm nothing.*

'There's more,' Sarilla said grimly, 'or this wouldn't be happening.'

The big room was too small all of a sudden, oppressive. Something drew near, something watched, though whether of good or evil she couldn't tell. Rillirin was crouching slightly, as though the roof were sinking.

The convulsions continued. Blood mingled with the foam splattering from Dom's mouth, blood from a bitten tongue and lip. 'Sweet Dancer,' Lim breathed as blood began leaking from his nose as well.

Without warning, Dom's back arched impossibly until he was resting on only his heels and the back of his skull, belly straining for the sky.

'Fuck,' Ash squawked and jerked back, falling on to his arse. 'Get the healer,' he croaked and Sarilla bolted from the room.

'Little brother, little brother, come back now,' Lim chanted, thumbs stroking Dom's forehead. Rillirin couldn't breathe as she watched him teeter like a bent bow, sweat misting his face and cords standing out in his neck and arms. Finally, he collapsed, and Gilda pressed fingers to his throat.

'Too rapid, far too rapid. Get the opium.'

Dom's eyes opened to slits. 'No,' he breathed and smiled like a corpse. His eyes flickered to Rillirin and there was awe and fear in his face. 'Who are you?' he whispered and then retched. Lim turned him on to his side, his knuckles bleeding from cushioning Dom's head. Dom puked and then flopped back, staring at her through a tangle of black hair, his head in Lim's lap. 'I know who you are,' he said and his voice was slick with horrified glee.

Rillirin shrank away from him, found Ash hovering at her side: protecting or guarding, she wasn't sure. 'Who?' she managed, swallowing hard. *This is madness, and they're all infected with it. He's ill; he doesn't see anything, not anything real.*

Dom laughed, the sound raw. 'The Red Gods are coming. Gilgoras will soak up gore and vomit black smoke. Her forests will burn. Mountains will fall and rise; kingdoms will crumble. Rilpor will die. Fox and Wolf stand in the way; the Dancer fights. Lost. All lost.'

Dom closed his eyes, squeezing tears down his cheeks. 'The herald will bring death to love, and love to death.'

Rillirin felt her jaw hanging loose. *Death to love? What sick game is this?* Her eyes slid sideways to Ash, who was intent on Dom. She took a step back and Ash's hand found her upper arm. He didn't look, just squeezed. Hard. She fell still.

Gilda wiped Dom's face with a damp cloth, smearing blood across his jaw. His eyes were blank. 'Enough,' she whispered. 'My poor boy, no more.'

'Tell us about Corvus,' Lim said, his eyes full of apology as Gilda turned on him. 'We need to know.'

'I don't . . . please . . . I don't want to,' Dom gasped, eyes wild as they searched the faces above him, skittering over Rillirin's as though they couldn't bear to rest there.

'Easy, little brother, easy. Tell us about Corvus.'

'Rillirin.'

'Yes, Rillirin is Corvus's sister. What else? What does he plan?'

'Corvus, King of the Mireces.'

They all turned to look at her. 'Corvus took the throne? Madoc is king?' Rillirin's ears were roaring. '*Madoc* is King of the Mireces?'

Dom held out a hand to Rillirin and Ash nudged her forward. 'Your blood is royal, herald,' Dom said. 'How much of it needs spilling to get the taint out?' His laughter was on the far side of madness. Grey-faced, he grabbed Rillirin's hand again.

Rillirin shrieked and tried to pull free, her bones grinding in his grip. The room was silent but for the crackle of the fire and Dom's harsh breathing, the tattoo of his boot heels on the wooden floor, Rillirin's whimpering.

He didn't arch this time. The convulsions slowed, lessened to twitches, and then he lay still. Rillirin pulled her crushed fingers from his limp hand and held them to her chest. *Get away. I have to get away, just get away.*

'He's not breathing,' Lim said.

'Give him time,' Cam said but his voice was steel wound to breaking point.

'He's never gone under twice before,' Ash said. 'What if he can't come back?'

'Shut up,' Gilda snapped. 'Of course he'll come back. He has to.' But none of them looked convinced and Rillirin wasn't surprised.

'Death to love,' she muttered. It made no sense. None of this made sense and her hand was hurting and no one was watching her. She thought again about running. *Now, while they're distracted with the madman.* She looked at his face, slack in unconsciousness but gaunt, the bones of his face clear beneath his skin. *He vouched for me, he kept me safe, spoke the words at my cleansing. I can't go. I can't leave him.*

Dom choked, dribbled blood on to the floor, and inhaled a ragged, bubbling breath. 'What did I miss?' he whispered and passed out.

It was snowing hard and everyone was asleep when Rillirin returned from the latrine, brushing flakes from her hair and shoulders. She threaded her way to the fire and squatted, shivering. Dom hadn't woken, not once since his knowing hours before. He slept uneasily, his face beaded with sweat, eyelids flickering.

'Hush, now, hush,' she said, imitating Gilda's sing-song. ''Twill be all right.' His eyelids flickered and then opened. There was an instant of emotion in his black eyes when he saw her, there and gone. 'Here,' she said, pressing a cup to his lips.

'Thank you,' he mouthed, voice less than a whisper.

'Do you want food? Are you hot? Cold?'

He turned his head away and slept. Rillirin tucked the furs around him, careful not to touch his skin with hers, with whatever curse she'd brought with her. Tears gathered on her lashes.

'I should never have come here.' She whispered it into her hands, forehead pressed to her knees. 'I should have just let Liris do what he wanted, let him kill me.' The guilt she'd thought washed away at the cleansing surged up yet again. Sarilla's grudging thanks meant nothing, not if Dom died, madman or not. *Death to love.*

'I'm glad you fought Liris.' Rillirin flinched at the croaky whisper. 'I'm glad he didn't take anything more from you, and I'm glad you killed him. This was always going to happen.'

Rillirin kept her head down. 'But not this badly. That's true, isn't it? You wouldn't feel like this, if not for me. I made it worse.'

A ghost of a smile crossed Dom's lips. 'I wouldn't feel a lot of things if not for you, Rillirin. But not all of them are bad.'

'Stop trying to make me feel better,' Rillirin said, sniffing. 'I'm the herald of the end of the world. Liris's whore is a better fate than that.'

'You weren't a whore; you were a victim,' Dom said, breathy with exhaustion. His eyelids flickered and then he focused on her again. 'Do you want to tell me about it?'

Not a fucking chance. She looked for his pity, his disgust, but all she could see was sadness and it melted a little more of the ice around her soul. 'I was fourteen the first time, had no idea what he wanted. I was too scared to fight him. I was a slave and he was the king. I was a fucking child, Dom. And then afterwards he gave me the dirty plates I'd gone in to collect and told me to do my job, like it hadn't even happened. But it had, and it kept on happening. And then I started fighting back, but he liked that even more.'

'It made it worse,' Dom whispered.

Rillirin shrugged and sat back, watching the glowing coals. 'Only physically. They'd already killed the good in me by then. Pain's just pain.' She coughed and gagged. 'Even that pain.'

Dom reached out and laid a trembling hand on her head. 'No one will ever force you again, Rillirin,' he said and his voice was solemn, like he was pronouncing sentence. 'No Watcher, no Wolf would dare. And I will kill any man or woman who tries, I swear that to you.

'You used my name,' he added. 'I think that's the first time you've called me Dom without having to think about it. I like my name in your mouth.'

'I like it, too,' she said, surprising herself. 'And whatever I'm the herald of, I'm going to help you fight it. I'm going to help all of you. No more secrets, I swear.'

'No more secrets,' he said and his hand dropped from her hair. 'So I should probably tell you about the scars on my arm.'

'You don't,' she began.

'I do. I owe it to you.' He drifted for a moment then, and Rillirin didn't mind. She wasn't sure she wanted to know.

'I was married once,' he said, so low she had to shift closer to hear. 'Her name was Hazel Shortspear. She was carrying my child when she was killed. They raped her first, then cut open her belly to kill the babe.'

Gods, no wonder he went mad. 'It was the Mireces?' she asked, because of course something so awful would be the Mireces.

'It was men dressed in blue. But I don't think they were. I'll know them when I see them again.'

Rillirin gasped, hands over her mouth. 'You were there?' she whispered.

'I came back to see the end of it. She got three before they overpowered her. She was a killer, my Hazel, and damn good at it. But there were just too many. The others beat me senseless and left us. She died alone.'

'She died knowing you would live,' Rillirin tried, wanting to touch him, not quite daring to.

'She died knowing our child would not,' he contradicted her and there was nothing to say to that, so she didn't.

'Hazel Shortspear? Dalli's sister?'

'No, Shortspear was her warrior name, like Sarilla Archer. War-kin.'

'But you're a Wolf,' Rillirin said. 'You don't have a warrior name.'

Dom grunted. 'No. I don't. I prefer Templeson to Calestar, but I'd give them both up in a heartbeat to be a proper Wolf.'

Rillirin brushed her fingertips across his knuckles and then she slid her palm on to his. They both waited, tense and fearful, but nothing happened. She tightened her grip and made herself look him in the eye. 'These visions save lives, don't they?' she asked and he nodded. 'Then that makes you

182

a warrior. Besides, you were pretty good at saving me up in the mountains.'

The corner of Dom's mouth twitched, and he started to speak, but his eyelids flickered and instead he slept, his hand in hers.

CORVUS

First moon, year 995 since the Exile of the Red Gods
Blood Pass, shoulder of Mount Gil, Mireces territory

They'd reached the pass between Mount Gil and White Peak by Yule, Corvus and Lanta and their guards. The only update on Rillirin's whereabouts had come from Rivil himself. The West Rank knew the Wolves had captured a Mireces slave, and that they were holding her in Watchtown to see if she would be useful.

Corvus had sent Mata to find Edwin and Valan and their five men, who were still combing the forests looking for Rillirin. They'd been out here ever since the attack on the Wolf village when his sister had slipped through his hands. Truly the gods were helping them, for Rivil to have known about her. The men would never get into Watchtown, but they could at least keep it under surveillance and seize the opportunity the next time she was moved. *And then we'll finally get some answers, find out which of my men is a king-killer.* It would be good to have the bastard dead. He might be able to relax then.

His thoughts returned again to Rillirin, as they did more and more these days. It was her stubborn refusal to acknowledge the Red Gods as the only true gods that had kept her as a bed-slave. If she'd converted, Liris would have honoured her with rights and position and slaves of her own. King's consort was only one step down from queen, after all.

It'll be different when she's with me, he thought. *She'll see the truth; she'll set her feet on the Path and be a good child of the gods. Lanta won't touch her then, not once she converts.*

The shelter in the pass was finally complete, and they'd even managed to coax a fire into life despite the howling wind, and Corvus crowded into it alongside the others – no kingly propriety if you wanted to survive in the mountains. Lanta pressed against his side, her thigh along his, her head on his shoulder.

'The men are well drilled,' Corvus said, 'but now we must focus on crafting them into a Rank. There will be no victory in a pitched battle without discipline, and I think there are many battles to come.'

Corvus stared at the blowing snow and the last of the sun, pink and peach on the drifts below them. Born on the plains, but made in the mountains, he could see the beauty in its promise of death to the unwary. He took some salted fish out of his pack and shared it with Lanta. 'That's the thing about Rivil,' he mused, 'he thinks we're a rabble, that we lack discipline. He intends to use us as shock troops, to cripple the West Rank and then get wiped out by the survivors. In the meantime, he marches his own army to Rilporin to depose his father.' He chewed patiently at a hard mouthful of fish.

'He's an arrogant fool,' Lanta agreed. 'Both that he thinks we will lose, and that he will win unaided.'

'I'm looking forward to seeing his expression when we take Rilporin from him,' Corvus said. The last of the light faded and night swept up the pass, stranding them in a tiny circle of orange firelight. The darkness pressed in.

'Then you do not plan on settling for the terms offered?' Lanta asked and he could hear her smile. 'The whole of the Western Plain between Krike and the River Gil isn't enough for you?'

He swallowed the fish and wrapped his arms around himself. 'I think something a little more regal would suit me better, don't you?' he murmured.

'The throne of Rilpor?'

'The throne of Rilpor,' he confirmed. 'Rivil's arse won't even have time to warm it.'

DOM

*First moon, eighteenth year of the reign of King Rastoth
Dancer's temple, Watchtown, Western Plain*

What? Where am I? What is this?

It was some sort of cavern, black and echoing and vast. Dom turned in a circle, boots scraping on stone, a cold finger of air trailing across his skin.

How did I get here? A flickering of flame cut through his panic and a figure approached, torch held high in a slender hand and the flames highlighting a face astounding in its perfection.

'Who are you? Where am I?' Dom tried as his brain threw up several possibilities, none of them pleasant.

'So you're the new calestar?' she asked, her voice bouncing and clattering from the stone until it was a roar in his ears. Calestar, calestar, star, star, star . . . 'The one born to oppose me?' She tutted. 'I expected more.'

She stepped closer, head on one side, predatory, and swept the torch before his face, so close the heat stirred his sweaty hair. She put her free hand on his chest over his frantic heart.

187

'Who are you?' he asked again. He saw her smile and run her tongue over her upper teeth. She pressed closer, her cheek against his.

'I'm coming to find you, Calestar,' she murmured into his ear, hand trailing down to his belly and lower. 'You have something I want.'

'What?' he gasped, shuddering. Her touch was a snake sliding against naked skin, both repellent and alluring.

'A promise.'

'What promise? Who are you?'

'Come and find me. I'll explain everything, my love.' She reared back to look him in the eye. 'And stop pretending. You know who I am. And you know that you belong to me.'

Dom's heart gave a single sudden lurch. He did know. 'Dark Lady,' he whispered, and Her eyes widened with delight. Then She struck, Her lips sending a bolt of lightning through his body, fusing their mouths together in a kiss that tasted of ozone and blood and sent fizzes of feeling streaking through his body.

'My love, my love.' Her voice echoed without and within despite Her mouth being locked to his, and it stirred a heat in him that hurt his heart. His hands were on Her shoulders and he pushed, straining away, filled with horror and sudden, unquenchable lust. His body was responding despite himself. There were other hands touching him beneath his clothes, multiple hands teasing, stroking, caressing, and he moaned, and then turned the sound into a growl and shoved at Her as hard as he could.

The Dark Lady broke the kiss and Dom gasped, rubbing his mouth and backing away, putting distance between him and that silky skin. He spat on the cavern's floor and shuddered. 'Stay the fuck away from me,' he panted, hands out in front of him. 'Don't you fucking touch me.'

'Not bad for your first try,' She said with a small, cruel smile, 'both at kissing me and at turning me away.' She laughed low in her throat. 'But we both know you can't resist me.' She swept the torch between them, the tattered flames filling his vision. 'Off you go, my love. But don't worry, we'll meet again soon.' She licked her lips. 'I can't wait to do this again.'

The flames burnt into Dom's head, searing, engulfing his brain, and with a jerk and a whooping inhalation, he woke. In his bed. In the dark.

Alone.

GILDA

First moon, eighteenth year of the reign of King Rastoth
Dancer's temple, Watchtown, Western Plain

Dalli was teaching Rillirin the spear, the pair having selected and carved one for her from the copse. It didn't have a blade yet, but they'd sharpened the end and hardened it in the ashes of a fire so it would penetrate the target.

Gilda leant on the paddock gate and smiled at Dalli's impatience, smiled more that Rillirin didn't shrivel up because of it. She'd seen in a new year free from the Mireces. A new start, new beginnings.

'All right, lighter on your feet, that's it, tense the belly, tense I said, and lunge,' Dalli said. The spear juddered across the target and went in a few inches. A goat stared at it.

'Not bad,' Dalli said yet again and Rillirin snorted.

'I didn't even scare the goat.'

Movement caught her eye and Gilda watched Dom walk slowly from the temple house, stooped like an old man. He flinched when the cockerel crowed, pulled the blanket tighter around his shoulders, and shuffled into the temple. *He's been*

190

spending a lot of time in there the last couple of days. And his sleep is never normally this broken.

Cam crept up behind her and pounced, wrapping her arms around his waist and kissing the side of her jaw. She squeaked and then laughed, slapped his hand when it began to wander. 'You want that business, you should try visiting more regularly,' she scolded, but she turned her head so his kiss landed on the corner of her mouth.

Cam rested his head on her shoulder. 'How's the lass doing?'

Gilda gestured and they watched Rillirin attempt an unauthorised figure of eight, the spear's point raking across Dalli's scalp and making her duck.

'Oh, sorry,' Rillirin said as Dalli spouted curses at her. Cam snorted, but the next time she lunged feet, hips and spear moved as one and the tip struck the butt and sank in deep.

Dalli thumped her on the back. 'Good. Much better,' she said, grinning. 'Now we'll try it with a grown-up's spear.'

'Ouch,' Cam murmured.

'You're just as bad when you teach the sword,' Gilda reminded him. 'What's going on with Dom?'

Cam shifted. 'You've noticed it too, then.' He sighed and kissed her earlobe. 'No idea. I tried to get him to open up this morning, but he won't talk about it. Says he's tired from the knowing.'

Gilda watched Rillirin and Dalli as they examined the torn skin on Rillirin's palms. She could see her pride in the wounds, caused from learning to fight back, see her relishing the pain.

The sun poked through a crack in the cloud and outlined them in pale gold. Rillirin turned her face up to the light, eyes closed, a faint smile on her face. 'She looks so innocent,'

Gilda murmured. She turned in Cam's arms. 'The boy's keeping something from us,' she said. 'He's learnt something in the knowing he isn't sharing, I'm sure of it.'

Cam rubbed at the bristles on his chin. 'Then we'll winkle it out of him, one way or the other. Corner him and force him to tell us the truth. We can't help him if he doesn't.'

Gilda took a deep breath and closed her eyes for a second. 'That's why I love you, Cam old man,' she said. 'You don't argue with me.'

Cam laughed and slipped his fingers in the neckline of her dress. 'What would be the point in that?' he asked, and made a spirited attempt to get his tongue in her ear.

'You're incorrigible,' she said even as she felt herself blushing. *After all these years he still makes me feel like a girl.* They kissed, and Gilda was debating whether they could slip away for an hour when Watchtown's horn blew a triple blast.

Cam dropped her, Dalli shoved the spear back into Rillirin's hands, and together they jogged for the temple gate while Rillirin shrank to Gilda's side, face pinched with sudden fear. Lim and Ash came out of the stables and, a long moment later, Dom hobbled from the temple.

'What's happening?'

'Triple blast means someone's approaching the town. It's not an alarm as such, more of a make-ready. Cam, love, what is it?' she called as the horn sounded twice, standing down the alert. They'd recognised whoever it was.

'Sarilla's bringing in a stranger,' Cam said, 'a Ranker.'

They all crowded to the gate and watched the pair approaching. 'Coming to the temple, not the town,' Gilda noted.

Lim grunted and waved; Sarilla waved back. Gilda looked behind her, sensing space where someone should be. Dom stood with his back pressed to the temple wall, his gaze locked on the stranger coming in through the gates. His eyes were as big as goose eggs and even from here Gilda could see his chest heaving. Whatever he was hiding, this man was a part of it.

CRYS

First moon, eighteenth year of the reign of
King Rastoth
Dancer's temple, Watchtown, Western Plain

'What's going on, Sarilla?' the Wolf chief asked. Crys stood by the godpool, where it was said a man could tell no lies, and the Wolves stood in a line between him and the exit. *Fine by me,* Crys thought, *I don't want to go back out there anyway. Possibly not ever.*

'This is Captain Crys Tailorson, head of the princes' personal guard on their journey to the West Forts. Found him a mile from the treeline when I was checking snares. He knew Captain Carter's name.' She shrugged. 'Then he asked for sanctuary.'

The Wolves stared at him, one harder than the rest. It was as though he was trying to dig the secrets out of Crys's head with his eyes. They'd made him give up his weapons and his palm itched for his sword.

'Sanctuary?' asked the tall, scarred archer.

Crys nodded. 'Yes. Protection, cleansing, food if you can

spare it.' He was babbling and he knew it, couldn't stop. 'Anything, really, to keep me safe.'

'Safe from who?' the chief asked again. 'Who are you?'

'He's the Trickster,' said the staring one.

Crys shifted, uncomfortable. 'I'm a soldier, like your friend said. Crys Tailorson of Three Beeches. Joined up when I was seventeen, spent my qualifying years in the East Rank before beginning my rotation. Over the years I lost a couple of promotions, earned them back, then came to the attention of Prince Rivil when I joined the Palace Rank a couple of months ago.'

His face twisted. *I trusted him, I admired him. He was my friend. And all the time a traitor – to the Crown, the country, the gods. To me.*

He sat suddenly on the bench beside him and the movement made them all twitch. All except the starer, who hadn't shifted his gaze from Crys once. Crys wasn't sure the man had even blinked.

He rubbed the sweat from his cheek on to his shoulder. 'The schedule was for us to sail up the River Gil, visit the forts and then travel across country to the harbour below Dancer's Lake and charter a boat down the Tears back to Rilporin. Instead, after we'd visited the Forts, Prince Rivil expressed a desire to visit the Blood Pass Valley – to see the site of so many famous victories, he said. We had twenty men and General Koridam had swept the area a few days before; it was empty. So, like a fool, I agreed. We were ahead of schedule, after all. When we got there we found a party of Mireces waiting for us.'

The Wolf chief swore. 'And that's who you're running from?'

Crys forced a laugh. 'If only it were that simple, sir.' He put his head in his hands for a second, swallowing nausea, throat stinging with bile. 'Prince Janis is dead. Rivil, Galtas Morellis and nearly all the soldiers under my command took part in his sacrifice to sanctify their conversion to the Red Joy.'

Tears gathered in the corners of his eyes as the Wolves watched him in uncomprehending silence. Then a babble of voices rose. Crys clutched the Fox God's amulet he wore at his throat and spoke over them. 'Janis is dead and Rivil is a traitor. What they did was . . . It was the worst thing I've ever seen in my life.'

'What did they do?' the chief asked in a hoarse voice. The pretty redhead beside him had her eyes closed and both hands over her mouth.

'They called her the Blessed One. She'd come with the Mireces and she nailed Janis to a beam, dozens of nails through his legs. And the Dark Lady spoke through the prince before he died, told Rivil he would be King of Rilpor if Rivil pledged himself to Her. And he did.'

'She spoke through him?' the starer asked. 'How? What did She do?'

'The woman asked Janis questions, but it wasn't Janis answering. Her voice – the Dark Lady's voice – came from his mouth.'

The high priestess stepped forward and placed her hands on Crys's shoulders. 'Tell them everything you can think of,' she said, 'and then we will talk of your soul and whether you need – or would like – to be cleansed.'

Crys found he was gripping her forearms hard, and concentrated on letting go. 'Thank you, priestess,' he mumbled past the lump in his throat.

She nodded and patted the side of his face, and then drew a circle on his brow. 'I am Gilda, and left to right is Dom, Dalli, Lim our chief, Rillirin, Ash and Cam. And Sarilla who found you.'

'What else, Captain?' Lim asked. 'How are they going to communicate? Is Rivil going to fund a private army? I can't imagine Corvus will be happy to do all the fighting only for Rivil to get the throne.' He glanced at Sarilla. 'Mace'll need to know this.'

She nodded. 'The king needs to know too. If Rivil's on his way back there, his feet newly nailed to the Dark Path, then Rastoth's a hog tied ready for slaughter and doesn't even know it.'

'General Koridam should already know,' Crys said. 'I met Captain Carter a few days ago, other side of the river. She wanted me to go back to the fort with her, but I refused. I' – he blushed – 'I threatened her. But there was no way I could go back there; it's the first place they'd look. I'd faked my own death in order to get away from Rivil and the others, you see, but I've got no idea if they fell for it. I killed two soldiers during a snowstorm, dragged them away as far as I could get, made it look like they'd been cut down while tracking someone. Then I legged it. Anyway, I told the captain, and she was going straight to the fort to tell Koridam.'

Lim was nodding. 'Sensible. Dalli, when we've finished questioning him, take a horse and get to Mace fast as you can. Fill him in on any blanks and ask him what he wants to do next.'

Good, this is good. They believe me, they're preparing for the worst, and I'm going to get cleansed. I'm safe here and the West Rank can prepare. Crys's heart rate began to slow and he started to relax.

His eye was caught by a sudden lunge of motion. The starer, Dom, stumbled forward, stretched tall and then hunched over, saliva stringing from his chin. 'War will come soon,' he said, his right eyelid flickering as he stared in Crys's direction with blank, empty eyes. 'The Mireces will break the West Rank, raid the Western Plain and the Cattle Lands, destroying and burning. Burning Watchtown. But Corvus won't stop once Rivil is king. He will take Rivil and sacrifice him. And the Red Joy will be ascendant. Corvus, King of Rilpor.'

Crys's mouth was hanging open but he snapped it shut and darted forward as Dom stumbled; he caught him beneath the armpit just as Ash reached him on the other side.

Dom seized Crys around the neck, squeezing. 'Why do you shine?' he demanded in a thick voice. 'You shine with godlight. Why? Who are you?'

'What? No one,' Crys wheezed as Ash prised at Dom's hands. 'I'm no one. I'm a soldier, just a soldier. That's all. A soldier.'

'Godlight. God's eyes. Splitsoul.' Dom shook him and there were spots fizzing at the corners of Crys's vision.

'Crys Tailorson, just Crys Tailorson, son of John and Mara, and a poor captain in the Ranks. Please, I'm nothing.'

Dom grunted and released him, his knees buckling, and Ash dragged him on to a bench. He sat still, head bowed, hands dangling between his thighs.

'What is this?' Crys asked. His back was against the wall, the width of the godpool between them and no idea how he'd got there. 'How does he know all that? What does he mean, shining? Who is he?' They were all staring at him, calculation in their eyes.

'Dom's the calestar,' Gilda said. 'He sees the future. Not always, and not well. Your information has revealed a little more of the pattern to him. He'll sleep now.'

Dom's face was that of a week-dead corpse as he scanned the room. 'You have much to do, Rillirin Fisher of Dancer's Lake, herald of the end,' he whispered and the redhead twitched, taking an involuntary step back. The dead stare moved on, settling on Crys, and Crys felt the hairs stand up on the nape of his neck.

'And the godlight will lead us all, to death and beyond.'

DURDIL

First moon, eighteenth year of the reign of King Rastoth
The palace, Rilporin, Wheat Lands

'You want how much?' Rastoth asked. Questrel bowed low, strands of his long oiled hair unsticking from his bald pate to wave at the ground. *I'll have to be careful,* Durdil thought. *At my age if I slip in that shit, I'll break a hip.* Despite years of military discipline, the corner of his mouth twitched.

'It really is very little, Your Majesty,' Questrel said, straightening and smoothing his hair deliberately across his head. 'Compared with the Crown's income.'

'Very little? It's six hundred gold kings only days after Yule. I recall that cost me enough.'

'Sire, that was a religious festival. This is the return of your sons from the west. An opportunity to show the heir to the people, for them to hear him speak.'

'Let us say I agree to this mad scheme. What does it involve?'

'There is little for you to do,' Questrel said with a delicate twitch of his pale lips. 'I have taken the liberty of designing

200

the programme myself. You will simply receive your sons home with a little more pomp than normal.' Durdil watched him pat his hair again. *I'm not shaking that hand later.*

'Durdil?' Rastoth snapped and Durdil dragged his thoughts together and stepped forward, boot heels ringing on the marble.

'It is certainly an idea that will be met with approval from the citizens, Your Majesty. They always enjoy an opportunity to see the royal family.'

'Prettily said, Commander,' Rastoth said in a wash of sour breath, 'but you're not the one paying, are you?'

Durdil inclined his head. *No, I'm not, and Questrel knows full well that money could be better spent on a thousand other things. Building works in the south. A new hospital in the fish quarter. Cheap housing in the slums so they're not really slums any more. A pay rise for a hard-working Commander of the Ranks wouldn't go amiss, now that I think about it.* Questrel bowed again and produced a scroll from a table at his side. The king's private study was overly hot and Questrel's upper lip glistened. *Like a slug crawled over your face in the night,* Durdil's inner voice noted.

'The programme for the day, Your Majesty. The circle of praise led by our most senior priests, food and drink for the commoners, of course, a parade along the King's Way, new uniforms for the Palace Rank officers and some palace dignitaries.'

'New uniforms?' Rastoth said, baffled. 'Why do they need new uniforms?'

'These will have a special badge sewn on to the arm to commemorate the princes' mission to the west,' Questrel said, venturing a small smile.

Durdil burst out laughing and Rastoth pressed his lips together. Questrel swallowed, his throat bobbing like an apple. 'They have not been to war, chamberlain,' Durdil said. 'Their Highnesses have been to view the forts and check the supply lines. They have not bravely repelled an invasion nor saved the life of a plucky farm girl from the ravishings of the Mireces. They have inspected troops and read reports, patted some shoulders, perhaps. I'm not sure it merits a commemorative badge.'

'Koridam's right,' Rastoth said, giving in to chuckles. 'No uniforms.'

'As you wish, Your Majesty,' the chamberlain squeaked, and Durdil suddenly realised that Questrel would probably have had his own court uniform remade at the same time. *A nice shiny new jacket, Questrel, that's what you wanted, eh? A few hundred silver royals spent just so you could have some new brass buttons?*

'The rest meets with your approval, though, I hope,' he said and Rastoth grunted.

'Do it,' the king sighed and Questrel bowed and practically ran for the exit before they took anything else away from him and his big day. *Don't slip on your way out,* Durdil thought. *Please, slip on your way out. I haven't had a laugh in weeks.*

Rastoth passed a hand over his face and blew bad breath into his collar. When he beckoned, Durdil dropped into a stiff crouch, one hand on Rastoth's chair for balance. 'I'm tired, Koridam,' he said. 'In truth, I'll be glad to have the boys back. The palace is empty without them and Marisa. She'll sail with them, won't she? She'll come back home to me?'

Oh gods. 'Queen Marisa is dead, Your Majesty. Over a year now. She died in her chambers, if you remember.'

'What?' Rastoth's voice quavered. 'My little nightingale, dead? But yes, yes she is. I remember now. It's all so vague,

Koridam, everything's so distant these days. I need my boys. I need Janis. He's nearly ready now, isn't he?'

'Your Majesty, Prince Janis is ready. But you have many years left in you yet,' he added with forced good cheer.

Rastoth patted his hand. 'You're a loyal soldier and an excellent commander, Durdil my friend,' he said. 'But you're a terrible liar. The Dancer's waiting and so is my Marisa. Don't think I should make them wait too much longer.' He leant forward until his face was nearly touching Durdil's. 'You'll serve Janis as well as you've served me?'

'It will be my honour, Your Majesty. I will give such aid as I can for as long as Prince Janis requires it.'

Rastoth gripped Durdil's hand tightly. 'And you'll find Marisa's killers?'

'Of course, Sire,' he said. *When the princes return, Galtas Morellis will be with them. And I have some questions for that slimy little one-eyed bastard.*

Rastoth grunted and let go of his hand, sinking back into the chair, staring moodily into the fire. Durdil rose and winced as his knees popped, rubbing a hand over his brow. He bowed low and signalled the guards at the door. 'His Majesty will rest now,' he said absently, his mind occupied with Galtas and his unexpected knowledge of the queen's demise.

Durdil watched him go and then limped to the window, stared out at the mud and slush of a typical Rilporin winter's day. *Hard to believe Yule is over and we're turning towards the Light*, he thought. *Hard to believe I still can't prove who killed the queen.* He focused on the scene below, grabbed the latch and swung open the window.

'Oi,' he yelled, 'Hallos! Leave my bloody recruits alone, you old buzzard.'

Hallos looked up and so did the soldiers, two lying in the

mud, two more kneeling on their chests. They slid off and on to their feet and even from here Durdil could see their guilt.

'I'm not doing—' Hallos tried.

'Just bloody don't,' Durdil yelled and slammed the window. 'Gods alive, that man will be the death of me,' he muttered. His eye fell on the report Rastoth hadn't read yet and he picked it back up, leafing through the pages. Durdil puffed out his cheeks, snatched up the quill and crossed out 'persons unknown'. He hesitated a second longer, then scratched 'query Lord Galtas Morellis' in the space above.

'It's just a theory,' he muttered. 'What's Galtas going to do? Kill me?'

Durdil put the report carefully back on Rastoth's desk, checked the fire was banked, and left the king's study, heart and step suddenly lighter.

THE BLESSED ONE

First moon, year 995 since the Exile of the
Red Gods
Longhouse, Eagle Height, Gilgoras Mountains

'Gull did his work well,' Lanta said as she sat with her priests
in the corner of the longhouse she had taken for her own.
'Most of the men pledged themselves and took part, as Rivil
had promised. The gods have their souls now.' She took the
cup Pask offered and sipped, chasing out the chill from the
long trek home.

'And you think this Rivil will honour his alliance with
Corvus?' Pask asked. As Lanta's senior priest, he'd had charge
of ensuring the faith was not neglected in her absence. Lanta
glanced around the longhouse before she replied. She'd been
away too long, but Pask had kept their interests alive. The
warriors had turned to him in the absence of herself and
Corvus, and that pleased her. The warmth of their reception
had pleased her more.

'For a time. Corvus and Rivil will use the drop caches in
the foothills to co-ordinate the attack and Rivil left a basket

of carrier pigeons with us. If we need to send a swift message, we can.'

'And if he needs to send a swift message to us?' Pask pressed.

'That is not so simple. It seems he believes we are the only ones who might make a mistake.' Pask and her other priests frowned and she held up a hand. 'His terms: worship of the Gods of Light will be outlawed in Rilpor. Only the true faith will rule there. In addition, we will be given the Western Plain, from the foothills all the way to the Krike border. Everything south of the River Gil will be ours in return for giving Rivil the throne.'

Pask tapped his fingertips on his knee. 'Then he is a true son of the Red Gods. I had doubted it.'

I doubt it still, but the Dark Lady has Her plans and will take Her revenge when She sees fit.

'And Corvus has agreed to this tithe of farmland as our reward?' Pask continued. 'Will we have slaves to tend this paradise for us or will that remain outlawed too? It does not seem such a decent bargain.'

Lanta clapped softly. 'Well done. Rivil thinks we are so desperate to leave the mountains that a swathe of poor grassland will satisfy us. But of course, once the country is subjugated under the rightful rule of the Red Gods, Corvus will take the throne. Rivil's a fool; he has no idea of our intentions. We will rule Rilpor first, and then all Gilgoras, for the gods.'

Pask watched her quietly as the other priests murmured their approval. 'And you would be happy for Corvus to be King of Rilpor?'

'Do you have an alternative?' Lanta asked.

Pask leant in to speak into her ear. 'A new land could require new rules, new traditions. Corvus's focus is power in this world, where yours is to bring about the gods' return and ensure Their dominion. Your position could be strengthened.'

Lanta looked at him out of the corner of her eye, silent.

'Why a king in Rilporin?' Pask breathed. 'Why not a queen?' He leant back and gestured to the other priests. 'My brothers and I have spoken. We would support the claim. It would be to the gods' glory.'

Lanta kept her face neutral. Seeds planted years before were beginning to bear fruit. *Corvus has brought this on himself. He seized the throne with little thought for what comes next.*

'I seek no power over men and women,' she said. 'My purpose is simply to be the humble vessel of the gods.'

'And you would remain so,' Pask murmured. 'But by taking the throne, you could ensure that every soul in Rilpor was dedicated to the gods. As queen you could ensure ritual and sacrifice were conducted properly, that the Gods of Light were truly dead.' He spread his hands. 'But perhaps it is something to think about?'

Lanta pursed her lips. 'Perhaps,' she said. 'For now, with Edwin and Valan still hunting Rillirin, the king is all alone. He has no seconds in whom to confide. He may require the gods' guidance. I shall go to him.'

Pask and the others bowed. 'Of course, Blessed One. We will prepare the sacrifices to honour your return and the king's.'

'Thank you, Pask. Thank you all for your efforts here in my absence. The gods have been well tended.'

Pask swelled with pride as Lanta rose to her feet, suppressing a groan at the pain in her feet. She would bathe, choose a gown carefully, unbind her hair. She'd seen how Corvus looked at her.

She paced the length of the longhouse, Mireces nodding in respect, slaves cowering from her path. No Blessed One ever became consort, but these were different times. If Lanta could stand Corvus's touch for long enough to bind him to her, it might be an easy way to share the throne. And after that . . . well, being king was such a dangerous business.

MACE

'Elder Rachelle, Chief, thank you for receiving me. Captain Carter related the intelligence gathered from Captain Tailorson. I am here to verify its truth.'

I am here to have repeated to me the worst thing I can possibly imagine, and then try and work out what to do next.

They sat around Rachelle's kitchen table, the fire in the corner baking Mace's legs and back: Lim, Tara, Rachelle, Captain Crys Tailorson pale but composed, a clutch of amulets around his neck as if he'd decided to join the priesthood all of a sudden. *Or his faith's been shaken.* His uniform jacket had been washed and repaired, but it was shabby and he looked uncomfortable in it, the shoulder with the insignia stitched on it pressed into the chair back.

Well, it is the uniform of the heir's personal guard. If what he claims is true, and I cannot imagine any scenario where fabricating such a tale could do any possible good, then I

209

imagine wearing that is similar to having a target painted on your chest.

Rachelle gestured at Crys. 'The captain told his story to the Wolf chief, and he has told it to me. He has told it while standing beside the godpool, and we do not doubt it. But of course, such a claim should be heard first-hand.' She reached over and touched Crys's sleeve. 'Would you like us to stay?'

Crys's face softened. 'No, thank you, Elder. The offer is appreciated, but if we could beg the use of your kitchen for an hour, it would be appreciated.'

Mace grunted. He still had his charm, even if he did look haunted. Rachelle and Lim stood, Lim inclining his head to Mace. Mace nodded back. 'Thank you both. The West extends its gratitude and friendship, as always.'

Rachelle swung the big kettle back over the fire before she left. 'Help yourselves to tea.'

When the door had closed, Mace rose from his chair, leant on his knuckles on the table and stared Crys out. 'Tell me this is a lie,' he said softly.

Crys picked up a sheathed sword from beside his chair and put it on the table. 'I can't do that, sir. I wish I could.'

Mace stared at the weapon and his breakfast tried to fight its way back up his throat. 'Janis's sword?'

'Janis's sword, General. I took it from his corpse when I made my escape. It was the only weapon in the wagon, laid in honour upon his chest in case we were stopped.' Crys coughed and wiped his mouth. 'I can take you to the place it happened if you need further verification. He was sacrificed in the most brutal manner I've ever seen, and I've seen some things in the North, things the Dead Legion has done. But there should still be some evidence at the site.'

'Evidence? Such as?'

210

'They nailed Janis to a scaffold and . . . well, they couldn't take him back like that, so they cut his legs off to hide the evidence. Left them attached to the scaffold. Far as I know, they're still there. Animals will have been at them, but there should be something.'

Tara made a noise as though she was swallowing a mouthful of puke. *Deep breaths, Mace. Deep bloody breaths.* 'Explain your escape.'

'They kept me tied in the back of the wagon with Janis's body. We were on the way to Dancer's Lake when it started snowing so hard we were forced to stop. Then the wind got up and it was a full-on winter storm. The wagon, the tents, the sentries were all being lashed with snow. I cut the rope on the sword, took it and ran. My sentries came after me, as I knew they would, and I doubled back, got halfway up Trickster's Mount before they caught up with me. I killed them, dragged them to a crevasse and arranged the bodies to look like we'd fought there, then tore my cloak and left it hanging half in the crevasse, threw my gloves and scarf in there. Anything to make it look like I'd fallen in. Then I ran.'

He paused and Mace straightened up, folded his arms and studied Crys's face. *It's clever, but is it too clever? Is this an elaborate double bluff?* Crys met his eyes steadily, and Mace was struck again with their oddness. The brown one sucked in the light and gave nothing away; the blue one blazed with emotion. 'Then what?'

'Headed here.' He gestured. 'Captain Carter found me near Watch Ford and, well, I'm afraid I threatened her when she insisted I return to give you my report in person. I knew Rivil would check the forts if he suspected I was still alive. I thought getting my news to someone they wouldn't think of was safest.'

Mace clicked his tongue and looked from Crys to Tara. Tara's face was stony, and Crys's story matched hers. *They cut his legs off. That's something I can use in my report. It'll verify Crys was there, if nothing else.*

'Tell me what Rivil and Corvus are planning.'

'Drop cache communications both ways and carrier pigeons from the Mireces to Rivil if they need it; a spring invasion; Mireces get the Western Plain in return for aid. The outlawing of the worship of the Gods of Light. The fall of Rilpor. The return of the Red Gods.'

The words were so blunt they shocked Mace all over again. 'And how do you propose we stop it?' he found himself asking.

'Their high priestess said that the more blood spilt, the easier it'll be for the Red Gods to return. If it's true, then the more we fight, the more we invite Them back. So instead, we arrest Prince Rivil and execute him for treason. That's one death, nowhere near enough to tear the veil. If we do that before the Mireces invade – if we can prove to them their ally is dead – they might not try anything. They'll know they'd be wiped out if they did.'

Mace pulled the kettle off the fire and poured hot water into three cups of ground mint leaves. He passed them around.

'And if they come anyway?' Tara asked.

'Then we exterminate them and pray the veil holds.'

They sat in silence and Mace stared out through the window. Watchtown was awash in pre-storm grey light, clouds the colour of lead sweeping in from the mountains. A sky weeping for Janis Evendoom.

'You've never served in the West, Captain. Why not?' Mace asked eventually.

Crys blinked at the change in subject but answered readily

enough. 'Never deemed suitable, sir. Bit of a reputation. Earned a couple of promotions, lost them, spent a little time in the cells. Not a model soldier, sir.'

And yet you've just paraphrased my exact thoughts on how to win this war. We have to kill Rivil. And then Rastoth is left without an heir.

'Captains, neither of you are to discuss this with anyone – soldier, Watcher, Wolf, civilian. No one, is that clear? The commander and the king must be informed.'

'I expect they would both want to question the only eyewitness we have,' Tara said, and Mace clearly saw the pulse jump in Crys's throat.

'Carter's right. It doesn't matter how detailed my report, it doesn't matter if you write the report for me, the commander and the king will have questions. Dozens of questions that only you can answer.' Mace tapped his finger-nails on the cup and then drank, wincing at the heat. 'I'll write my report today and you can leave tomorrow. Carter will accompany you.'

Tara's expression solidified further. Crys recognised a dismissal when he heard one and stood. 'Yes, sir,' he said, his emotions firmly under control. He saluted, nodded to Tara, and spun on his heel.

'Send in the girl, Rillirin Fisher,' Mace said as Crys reached the door. 'I've questions for her too if we're to defeat our enemies.'

The word was bitter on his tongue. *Since when has a prince of the blood been an enemy? A heathen enemy?* Mace shook his head. 'The world's fucked,' he muttered. 'We're fucked.'

'Sir?' Tara started and Mace held up his hand, already knowing what she was going to say.

'Because you're the one who first found him and you can

check for differences in the story he gave you, has just given us, and is going to give my father. Because I am a suspicious bastard and yet a soft-hearted one who doesn't want to believe Rivil murdered his own brother. Because, gods preserve us, if this tale is true, he's going to need help getting in front of my father and, possibly, someone to defend him in case of assassination attempts. And because I want someone to report direct to me on how the news was received and what happened when Rivil was arrested. Good enough?'

'Yes, sir.'

The door opened again and Dalli popped her head in. 'Can we come in? This is Rillirin and she'd very much like to spill every Mireces secret she knows.'

RILLIRIN

First moon, eighteenth year of the reign of King Rastoth
Dancer's temple, Watchtown, Western Plain

'Come on then. Time to see if you can make a kill.'

Rillirin looked up from where she was fletching arrows. Dom was dressed for the cold, bow and quiver on his back. He held out a coat and cloak.

'Kill?' she said. 'Only by accident.'

Dom smirked. 'That's not the point, though. It's my turn to hunt, and we don't go out alone, so you're my second.'

Rillirin climbed to her feet and picked up the spear she'd been learning with. It was small even compared with Dalli's, but it was still a weapon. Her weapon. 'So I'm your protector, then?' she asked.

The corner of Dom's mouth curved up. 'Yes, Rillirin, you're my protector,' he said with a theatrical sigh. 'You coming or not?'

'Where?'

'Treeline. The deer'll be on to the plain but they like to have cover to run to, so we go to them.'

'What? That's miles,' Rillirin protested and Dom's smile got bigger and more mischievous. It was good to see him smile; it'd been missing too much lately.

'I know,' he said. 'That's why we're riding.'

'Oh. Good,' Rillirin said without a hint of enthusiasm. Dom sniggered and led her to the paddock outside the temple. Rillirin threw on the coat and cloak and followed him. It hadn't snowed in days and there were patches of pale green grass and mud showing on the track to Watchtown.

Ash drifted in their wake and Rillirin groaned. 'Don't you have something else to do?' she asked. Ash and Dalli were the only two who'd thawed towards her, and she enjoyed their company – most of the time.

'I'm standing for Crys at his cleansing later, but for now' – Ash spread his hands – 'there's nowhere I'd rather be than watching you try to ride a horse.'

'Great.' Rillirin took a deep breath and clambered on to the horse, the spear banging into her eyebrow. She grimaced at Ash's snort of laughter behind her.

'Ready?' Dom asked as he mounted moments later.

Oh gods, I've forgotten again. 'Not in the least,' she squeaked, already trying to get her feet out of the stirrups.

'Because?'

'Because I didn't check the girth and you left it loose,' she said and then squealed as the saddle slipped sideways. She clung to the mare's mane and freed one foot from the stirrups, landed on her back with a thump as the animal sidestepped, snorting its disapproval and threatening to drag her. Dom roared with laughter even as he urged his horse close enough to grab her mare's cheek strap and hold her still.

Ash was whooping and clapping and Rillirin found herself laughing as she untangled herself and stood, flicking snow from her hair. 'You bastard,' she said and then cringed. 'I'm sorry—'

'Why? I can be a bastard,' Dom replied with a shrug. 'Don't worry about it. Now, before I freeze to death, can we please get going?'

Rillirin straightened the saddle and tightened the girth. She checked it twice before mounting, managed to get the spear butt sited on her boot, and then wheeled the mare with one awkward hand. 'Race you!' she shouted, surprising them both, and spurred her mount out through the temple gate. It wasn't pretty, elbows all over the place and teeth rattling in her head, but she kept her seat and didn't drop the spear.

'Oh no you don't,' Dom yelled. His gelding reared and launched into a gallop and the pair raced away across the patchwork expanse of snow and grey grass towards the smudge of trees. And Rillirin was laughing.

DOM

First moon, eighteenth year of the reign of King Rastoth
Edge of the Wolf Lands, Western Plain, Rilporian border

'How far are we from Dancer's Lake?' Rillirin broke the silence and Dom dropped his head into his hands as the doe startled, ears flicking, and then bounded away into the trees.

'Oh. Sorry,' she said over the alarm calls of birds and the doe's grunting cough.

'We've been here an hour, silently waiting for dinner to trot into view, and when it does all you can think to do is start talking?'

'I was just wondering, that's all.'

'And that's what you'll tell the others when we return without supper, is it? That you were wondering and you're sorry they're going to have to eat rabbit. Again. You have seen Lim's face when you serve him rabbit, yes?'

'I said sorry. We can wait for another.'

Dom grunted and stood up, stretching stiff muscles. The cured horsehide kept them off the snow but did nothing to warm them and he stamped his feet and hopped about.

'Nothing'll come this way for a good while now and it'll be dark by the time we get back as it is. And you can't daydream every time you get bored. And you shouldn't have been bored, anyway.'

'I wasn't bored,' Rillirin protested as she stood up. 'Well, not all the time. Why don't we just go into town and buy dinner? We can say we caught it.'

Dom closed his eyes for a second and then opened them and looked up at the sky. He raised his hands. 'Dancer, please, if this is some sort of punishment, haven't I suffered enough? Can't you inflict her on someone else for a while?'

'Hey, you promised to look after me,' she retorted, hands on her hips. 'You didn't say for how long, so you're stuck with me. Forever.'

She was smiling and he had to smile back. Damn those bottomless eyes of hers, but forever didn't sound too bad, despite the lack of venison. The roses in her cheeks told him she'd realised what she'd said, but she didn't deny it. Or look away.

'Yes, well, I was obviously delirious. I was ill, hadn't eaten in days. Much like how I'll be feeling later.' He wagged a finger under her nose and she made a grab for it. He snatched his hand away and when she overbalanced he let her fall against his chest. She gave an exaggerated shiver and he wrapped his arms around her.

'You know your trouble? You're trouble. And I've had enough of trouble. You can be someone else's problem from now on. If anyone'll have you,' he said.

Rillirin shoved him hard in the chest, breaking out of his arms, and he stood there stunned. 'I'm not a slave,' she growled, her eyes hurt and angry and bewildered. 'You don't just *give* me away.' She snatched up her spear and headed into the trees in the doe's wake.

What? What've I said?

'Rillirin,' he called after her, but she broke into a run. 'Ah, fuck,' he muttered, grabbed his bow and hurried to catch her up. 'I didn't mean it like that,' he shouted ahead into the trees, but she kept going. 'More damn prickly than a hedgehog,' he grunted, feeling the muscles in his legs twinge at the unexpected exercise.

Her trail was easy to see and went on for a damn mile. She was a fleet hedgehog, anyway. Dom burst into a glade where a giant beech had fallen and brought down several smaller trees. He was winded and cursing himself and her in equal measure, disgusted at the stabbing pain in his lower back, a hangover from the knowing. He skidded to a halt in a spray of leaves. Rillirin, pressed against the fallen trunk, her chest heaving for breath. Pinned by a fair-haired man with a sword to her throat.

What the—

Dom reached up and back and pulled out an arrow, nocked and loosed. The shaft pierced the man's back and lodged in his liver, blood staining his blue tunic purple. He coughed in surprise and collapsed. From behind the trunks emerged half a dozen more.

'Ah, fuck,' he muttered again, pulse beating in his eyes and mixing with the sweat to cloud his vision. He saw swords and one spear as Mireces ran for him and for Rillirin, who was clambering over the dead man and fumbling to set her spear.

Dom pointed his bow at the spearman, inviting the attack, and the Raider obliged. He dodged the throw – just – heard the hum of it passing and shot back, missed. Fucker was too close for a second shot, charging in the wake of his spear, dagger in his fist. Dom flung his bow, missed again, dragged his sword from its sheath, set his feet and let the

Mireces run on to three feet of sharp, folded steel. The man grunted, looked down, puzzled, and Dom twisted the hilt, opening the wound and freeing his blade. Blood, entrails and stink followed it out.

Spinning in a circle, sword extended, looking for his next opponent and trying not to puke. Heart thudding, a liquid hammering too high and too fast. Adrenaline would take him so far and guts further, but sooner or later those guts'd be tangling his feet.

From the corner of his eye he saw a Raider club Rillirin to the ground, but then a muscular woman with mud-brown hair stepped forward and engaged him. Not many female Mireces took up weapons so she'd have to be good to have made it this far. The clang of metal hurt his ears and shivered up his left hand all the way to the shoulder. He stepped, ducked, watching her shoulders and eyes and hips as she struck again and again, parrying her power, learning her.

She leant too far into a thrust and he grabbed her sword hand and pulled her off balance, punched her in the face and felt her teeth and nose give. She dropped like a sack of shit and, as he turned to face a third attacker, acting on the prickle up the back of his neck, Dom stomped the heel of his boot through her temple. She twitched, flopped and he stomped again, didn't have time for more.

Behind him a scream, hoarse, and he hoped it was a Raider and not Rillirin. This one was good, weaving his sword tip in complicated patterns to disguise his lunges. Dom side-stepped twice before realising he was being herded into the woman's corpse. Or not-corpse, as she made a feeble grab at his leg. He leapt right, gasping as the Mireces' sword opened the flesh of his forearm.

But the man was over-extended and facing the wrong way and Dom rammed his blade up under his ribs and into his heart. He collapsed and this time Dom made sure, stabbing them both in the throat. He left them, searching for more Mireces, his bloodlust driving his muscles now, the only thing he had left.

Thrum of a bowstring and he dived for the dirt, the arrow skimming overhead. The next took him in the back of the right thigh as he scrabbled upright and he yelled in pain, began a limping run for cover. A third laid open his scalp before he could put a trunk between himself and the enemy.

Fucking shitting bastard shits. Arm, leg, head. What, do they want me a piece at a time? Do it or fuck off. He breathed deep and snapped the tail from the arrow sticking out of his ham. *Just rest a while, breathe. Breathe.*

A shrill scream and he was leaping out of cover again. He ducked to avoid the expected shower of arrows, but none came. Rillirin was on a man's back, legs around his waist, left arm around his throat and hand grasping her right biceps, right hand pushing the back of his head down into a chokehold. She didn't have it yet and the man she rode thrashed his head, fighting to break her grip. At his feet another, the archer, had hold of her leg and was fumbling for his dagger, his quiver mercifully empty.

Shit like this never fucking worked, but Dom threw his sword anyway. It hummed through the air and struck the archer hilt-first; he slammed face down into the mulch. Dom sprinted after his blade, mildly astonished at his own heroics.

Rillirin's man was on his knees now and her face was a mask of hate and strain, cords standing out in her neck. He clawed weakly at her forearm, trying to hook fingers in to gain some breathing space. Dom reached the man he had flattened, put a boot between his shoulder blades and grasped his face. Shoulders straining, he wrenched the Mireces' neck up and around until it crunched. Gasping, weaving, hamstring screaming, he picked up his sword. 'I'll finish him,' he panted.

'No.' Her voice was stretched with effort and hissed between her teeth, but there was no denying her venom. Dom took an unsteady step back and watched as the man's face, already red, darkened to purple, whites of his eyes starred with burst blood vessels.

'I'll leave you to your business then,' Dom mumbled. He checked the corpses, and then checked them again. Five and the one Rillirin was taking her sweet time killing. But there'd been seven, hadn't there? He was sure he'd seen seven. With his nauseating adrenaline comedown, he just had to hope the survivor didn't come back for more. Dom wasn't sure he had another kill in him.

The man was dead. Rillirin's face was bruised and bloody and she was crying, but her eyes glittered with more than tears.

Good for you. Hope you're not expecting a fucking title.

'Drag them over there,' he sighed, wiping blood from his right eye and flapping his sword in the general direction. For a moment she looked crushed, but then she dragged herself to her feet and grabbed the dead man's arm. Grunting, she began heaving on it, but she was done now, as little energy left in her as in him. He grabbed the other arm and hauled, his wounded leg shuddering, threatening to buckle.

Finally it was done, six corpses piled together in a flail of twisted limbs and a stench of opened bowels.

'As the forest feeds us, so we feed the forest. Dancer, take these bodies and give them back to the earth. Fox God, Trickster, we thank You for guiding our hands. Do you want a trophy?' he asked and handed Rillirin a dagger with a bound-leather handle. 'This belonged to your enemy. Now it belongs to you. You have killed for the Watchers in company with a Wolf.' He put his hand on her shoulder; both of them were shaking. 'We are war-kin now, Rillirin, closer than blood. Closer even than family, some say.'

Her smile was radiant through the mud and bruising and she hugged the knife to her chest like a babe. *Gods, she's beautiful.* He wrenched his thoughts away from what was under her clothes. 'Now, are you going to help an old man with a shot leg back to the horses to be treated at the hospital?' he asked.

'You're not that old,' Rillirin said and wobbled away to retrieve her spear, leaving him floundering behind her. He stooped, hissing, to pick up his own bow and then a Mireces spear to take his weight. The shakes were bad and he began to wonder if he really would make it back to his horse without help. Gods, he needed to piss.

Rillirin slowed and then stopped, waiting for him to catch up. She put an arm around his back and Dom felt a surge of emotion at her touch. Not a knowing – not this time. He looked down at her bloody face and pressed a kiss to her hair. When she looked up he chanced it; he kissed her mouth. She held it for a second and then slid her face away, but she squeezed his waist, a cautious, non-committal sort of squeeze. But still a squeeze. Dom decided not to cheer and concentrated on walking.

'I'm sorry,' he said as they finally came into view of the horses. 'What I said before was a thoughtless joke. But if I could advise not running head first into an ambush next time, I'm sure we can talk things through.'

'Next time? You're planning on being a giant cock again then?' she asked and pushed him away. He squawked as his injured leg took his weight, flapping like a chicken to regain his balance.

Astonished and furious he stabbed a finger in her direction, saw her smile, mischievous and oh-so fucking amused. He narrowed his eyes and mustered his dignity. 'Why, you little—' he began and she pressed a finger to his lips.

'Careful. Don't say anything you might regret.' She stretched up on to her toes and replaced her finger with her lips, a grazing kiss he almost didn't feel. But a kiss. She'd kissed him. Voluntarily.

Dom ran his tongue around his gums. 'Now I'm worried.'

She shrugged a shoulder. 'Don't be. I'm happy.'

'Happy? I've been shot,' he protested, waving a hand at his leg and head, thrusting his bloody sleeve under her nose. 'You've got nothing more than a couple of bruises.'

She grinned and untied the horses. 'Maybe I'm better at this than you. Come on, we should get back to town.' She looked behind her and shivered. 'Just in case.'

Dom nodded and eyed the saddle. 'Have to leave that here,' he said. 'Can't sit a horse with an arrow in the back of my thigh.' His leg was shuddering constantly and he was dizzy with pain and blood loss.

Rillirin unsaddled his gelding and gave him a leg-up, and Dom lay face down over the horse's back. 'Take it slow, all right?' he muttered. 'Really slow.'

Rillirin mounted, gathered up the gelding's leading rein, and clucked her mare into a walk. Dom grabbed the reins and a handful of mane and did his best not to slide off as they made their way on to the plain.

DURDIL

First moon, eighteenth year of the reign of King Rastoth
North Harbour docks, Rilporin, Wheat Lands

Durdil watched the ship approach on the current, the harbourmaster himself flagging them to their berth close to where Durdil waited with the carriage and a hundred of Rastoth's Personal Guards. His heart lightened at the thought of the princes' return and that they'd have Galtas with them.

'Time for some answers, *Lord* Morellis,' he muttered. 'Guard! Attention!' he snapped and the Hundred snapped erect, spear tips winking in the weak winter sun.

The ship didn't slow, didn't turn for the harbour. Instead it carried straight on, past the cheering crowds, down the side of the city towards the private jetty by East Tower. The cheering faltered and Durdil squinted at the ship's mast – Janis's insignia flew, but there was something wrong with it. The wind unfurled it and he saw the scarlet slash across the crest. His stomach lurched.

'What the fuck?' he breathed. 'Personals, with me,' he

226

barked and quick-marched off the dockside towards the gatehouse. Once in the city he broke into a jog down the King's Way, sentries waving him through the gates with puzzled expressions.

Never going to reach East Tower in time. Have to meet them in the palace; they'll take the tunnel. Why is Janis in mourning? A wave of cold prickled up his spine and across his scalp. *Not Mace. Please, gods, anyone but my boy.* Durdil tried to convince himself Janis wouldn't proclaim mourning for a man he barely knew, but this was Janis. Of course he would, especially if he was bringing the news to the newly bereaved himself.

'Move,' he roared as a carter struggled with his horse. The animal took one look at the running, metal-clad soldiers and panicked, dragging the cart along the road. Durdil dodged it and ran on, faster now, breath whistling in his throat. The blood pounded in his ears, calling his son's name with every beat.

'Your Highness,' Durdil managed, 'what has happened? The mourning colours – You didn't stop at the harbour . . .'

The words dried up as Rivil's honour guard carried the bier out of the gloom of the tunnel that ran from the palace to East Tower. Durdil looked from it to Rivil, the scarlet of his mourning sash bright against the green velvet of his coat. Durdil's throat clicked as he swallowed. 'Where is His Highness Prince Janis?' he croaked.

'My brother has left this world, Commander,' Rivil said, resting his hand on the rough wood of the open casket. 'Janis is dead.'

Durdil stared at him, bewildered, relieved, horrified. His eyes moved slowly across the guards standing at attention behind the prince and the coffin. The room the tunnel emptied into was sparse and cold and Rivil's pronouncement seemed swallowed up by the blank stone walls.

Lord Galtas slouched at the back, the red of his sash stark against his black coat and trousers. He sported a scarlet eye patch too, an affectation that made Durdil want to rip it off his head and ram it down his throat.

He looked at the guards again. 'You are missing men,' he said, clinging to the comprehensible. 'Were they caught up in this tragedy?'

'Some of the men died with . . .' Rivil trailed off, a mute gesture more eloquent than words.

Durdil had no choice now; he had to look. He crept to the casket. Janis was pale and still, no visible injuries, though his open eyes spoke of terror-filled final moments. Durdil tapped his fingertips to his heart. 'My prince,' he whispered. 'Sleep now in the Light.'

He was turning away before his brain processed the corpse's odd foreshortening. His fingers twitched the silk sheet from Janis's lower half and he cried out, stumbled back. Janis's legs were missing.

He sucked in a deep breath and studied the body, then Rivil. The prince was solemn but not as grief-stricken as Durdil would expect. He gazed at the space where Janis's legs should be without emotion. *He's had longer to process this, of course, but this – this mutilation . . . How can he be so calm?*

'What happened?' he asked.

'I should tell my father first,' Rivil said. 'He has lost his son and heir.'

Rivil went to brush past him and Durdil stopped him. 'His Majesty is fragile, Your Highness. Break it gently, what-ever it is.' Rivil nodded; then he arched a brow when Durdil didn't stand aside. 'And you, Your Highness? How are you?'

Rivil gusted a sigh and stared up for a second. 'Broken,' he said, but it was forced. Durdil stood aside.

'Take my brother to the temple,' Rivil said to his men. 'With me please, Commander. Galtas, you too.'

Durdil followed Rivil up the stone stairs into the palace proper, then through corridors and chambers to the king's private study. Galtas dogged his heels, oppressive as a summer storm, yet nothing compared with the thoughts swirling treacherously through Durdil's head.

GALTAS

First moon, eighteenth year of the reign of King Rastoth
The palace, Rilporin, Wheat Lands

If Crys lives, this is where we get arrested for treason. A thrill of nerves shivered through Galtas. *The Lady's will.*

'Father, there has been a tragic accident.'

Rastoth's brow furrowed and his welcoming smile faded. 'Where is Janis?' he asked, and Galtas noted how he turned to Durdil for reassurance. Durdil was silent.

Rivil bowed his head, every inch the grieving brother. 'Gone, Sire. We were riding to Dancer's Lake to charter a boat when a storm blew down from the mountains. Snow, ice, hail, winds so strong we could barely stand up in them. We made it to a small copse, looking for some shelter. We'd just set up camp when a branch fell and pinned some of the men, Captain Tailorson included. Janis ran to their aid. He was pulling at the branch, trying to free the trapped men.'

Rivil stopped and adjusted his sash. Rastoth's eyes were huge and watery and misting with pain. Durdil's face was blank, calculating, the muscles around his mouth tight with suspicion. *Come on, Rivil, convince them. Or at least Durdil.*

'I should have realised the danger,' Rivil said and Galtas ventured a shake of the head and a heavy sigh. 'I should have seen it coming. If the branch could come down, then the whole tree . . . and it did. Before I had a chance to react, the tree fell. It crushed Janis, crushed his legs, killed the men he was trying to save. The rest of us, we tried everything we could, but we couldn't free him. I'm sorry, Father, but Janis is dead.'

Not bad. Look at Rastoth. With luck the shock will kill him. Go on, drop dead. Die, you fuck, just die.

Rastoth didn't die, but he did crumple like parchment curling in a fire. Boneless, he slid from his chair, a high wailing shriek dragging from his chest. Durdil had one hand on the wall to steady himself, the other to his brow hiding his eyes.

Galtas opened the door. 'Get the physician instantly,' he snapped and one of the guards saluted and ran off down the corridor.

'How? How?' Rastoth said, over and over. Rivil tried to pull him back into his chair, but Rastoth wasn't moving.

Rivil knelt opposite him. 'I stayed with him until the end, Father, prayed with him, did what I could to ease him into the Light. He didn't die alone, at least.'

'Who else witnessed the death of the heir?' Durdil asked.

'All of us, of course,' Galtas said. 'We were trying to free him and the others – Crys, Joe and Mac. We were all there with him. But the cold, the wind – it was impossible.'

'Come now, Father,' Rivil murmured, 'come on, let's get you into a chair. You shouldn't be sitting on this cold floor. Durdil, help me with him.' Together they lifted Rastoth and bundled him into his seat. He was still mewling like a crippled cat, but then Hallos arrived with a sedative and forced it down his throat. Slowly, he quietened.

'What is going on?' Hallos asked, and then he saw the mourning sashes. Wordlessly, he turned back to the king.

'Where exactly were you when the storm blew in?' Durdil asked.

'Does it matter?' Rivil snapped, showing a flash of anger.

'I'm afraid so, Your Highness,' Durdil said.

The room was quiet but for the crackle of the fire, Rastoth's whimpering. Durdil lit several more candles, shining the light of suspicion on Galtas and Rivil. Not even pretending to believe them.

'On the road to Dancer's Lake, as His Highness said,' Galtas put in, clenching clammy fists. 'A few days out from the West Rank.'

Durdil's gaze was steady and penetrating. 'I don't recall there being a copse anywhere after Trickster's Mount,' he said.

'It was before the mount,' Galtas said. 'Wasn't it, Sire? Didn't we pass the mount the day after?'

'I think so,' Rivil said absently, watching Rastoth and Hallos fluttering around him.

'I understand this is difficult, Your Highness,' Durdil said, 'but any information you can give me is invaluable.'

Rivil turned at that. 'Why? Janis is dead, isn't he? What difference does it make?' His tone was brutal and Rastoth jerked at it. Hallos winced and suspicion hardened in Durdil's face.

'Commander, the prince is devastated and his memory of the . . . tragedy is hazy,' Galtas said, smooth as silk. 'It happened before we reached Trickster's Mount. But why is the location so important?'

'I would have thought that was obvious,' Durdil said in

a low voice. He turned his shoulder to the king. 'Prince Janis's body is not intact. We must send a recovery party out to bring back the rest of his remains so that he can be interred beside his mother.'

What? Sweat slid down Galtas's ribs, gathering in the socket under his eye patch, itching.

'Commander, we did everything we could to retrieve the heir's body intact,' he said, 'and, as His Highness has already told you, it was impossible. It will be impossible for someone else.'

'You were in shock, you'd lost your prince and your captain, and it was imperative you got back here to tell the king. I understand that . . . sacrifices had to be made,' Durdil said.

Oh, Commander, you have no idea. Galtas fought the nervous urge to giggle at Durdil's choice of words.

'But now, of course, we simply must do better. I expect General Mace Koridam will have men there already?'

Rivil and Galtas exchanged a glance. 'Your son, Commander?' Rivil asked in careful tones. 'Why would that be?'

Durdil looked surprised. 'Well, if you hadn't even reached the mount, then obviously you sent someone back to inform the general of the accident. You were only a day or two out.'

'I am afraid our grief clouded our thinking,' Rivil said, spreading his hands. 'You understand.'

Durdil was silent. Apparently he didn't understand. 'You were closer to the West Forts than the Tears, and still you continued to the Tears?' He scratched his cheek. 'I would expect your honour guard to have advised differently.'

'Captain Tailorson is dead,' Rivil said. 'The men were as much at a loss as the rest of us. He was a popular man, after all.'

'Ah,' Durdil said, 'of course. That explains it. Hallos, how is His Majesty?'

'The king sleeps,' Hallos said. 'I will stay with him.'

'Thank you, Hallos,' Durdil said. 'Your Highness, milord, with respect you look exhausted. Grief can do that. Perhaps we should leave His Majesty alone for a while? I'll have private quarters readied for your guard – I think it would be wise to keep them separate from the rest of the Rank until we have decided how to break the news.'

So you can question them, you mean, Galtas mused as Rivil thanked Hallos, *not that they'll say anything to compromise us.* Gold and treachery sealed many a mouth.

'Galtas, let us retire to the temple. There are torches to burn and prayers to say,' Rivil murmured. Galtas bowed to the drooling figure of the king and followed Rivil from the study, his shoulder blades tingling under the heat of Durdil's glare.

DURDIL

'Lies, lies and more lies, gentlemen. And one of them at least
I can prove.' Durdil slapped his palm on the table. 'Their
location. Lord Galtas said they were between the West Forts
and the mount in a copse when the accident happened.'

'There isn't a copse on that road, not until a day out from
Dancer's Lake,' Major Wheeler of the Palace Rank said.

Durdil's smile was grim. 'Exactly.'

Hallos cleared his throat. 'They were in the middle of a
snowstorm, Commander. It's quite possible they got turned
around, wandered into the treeline.'

Wheeler was already shaking his head and Durdil gestured
for him to explain. 'Treeline's half a day from the road. Too
dangerous to be any closer – wild animals, Mireces. There's
no freestanding forest around that area.'

'So they weren't in a copse when Janis was killed by a
falling tree,' Durdil said. 'So is it their location that's a lie,
or the nature of the heir's death?'

Hallos grunted and tugged at his beard. 'About that.'

Durdil's head swivelled towards the physician. 'You have examined the body, then?' Hallos nodded. 'Wheeler, check the door.'

They waited while Wheeler opened the door and peered both ways along the corridor. The Commander of the Ranks had his own suite of rooms, and Durdil had ordered that there be no guards stationed there for this meeting. That in itself would cause rumour, but with Hallos there they'd assume it had to do with the king's health. *Rather gossip that the king is ill than gossip the heir is dead and his brother is under suspicion for killing him.*

'Clear, sir,' Wheeler said.

Hallos stood and led them from Durdil's study into his planning room. Wheeler skidded to a halt when he saw the body on the table.

'Yes, Hallos and I brought him from the temple,' Durdil said before Wheeler could speak. 'Prince Rivil and Galtas are with the king again; we have some time. Hallos, tell us.'

Hallos slid the red silk coverlet from Janis's corpse, exposing his naked flesh and the raw, splintered ends of his legs, hacked off above the knee. Wheeler put his hand to his mouth.

'Nothing from the waist up. Not a scratch, not a bruise. No impact bruising from branches anywhere on his body. Yet the bruising on the face is consistent with a blow, and I found a couple of lumps on the back of his skull as though he'd been hit there too.' He leant closer and beckoned. 'But that's not what's significant. See the discolouration of the face, the stars of broken veins in his eyes?'

Durdil peered into Janis's face. 'The colour isn't due to decomposition? He's been dead nearly two weeks.'

'Much of it is, yes, but look at his fingers, too. Again

swollen, discoloured. And here, there are faint restraint marks on his wrists.'

Durdil's head snapped up. 'Restraints?'

Wheeler gave a strangled yelp and they both looked where he was pointing.

'Ah yes, and then there's the state of the prince's genitals,' Hallos said.

Durdil swayed on his feet and grabbed at the edge of the table. 'His genitals?'

'Specifically the trauma to the testicles.' Hallos reached out and lifted Janis's cock out of the way and prodded carefully at the scrotum. It was flat and torn. He pulled Janis's legs apart. 'The arsehole too, ripped open.'

'I'm going to be sick,' Wheeler muttered.

'Control yourself, Major,' Durdil snapped. 'Hallos, what are you saying?' he asked over the rushing of blood in his ears.

'If a tree pinned Janis's lower legs, we'd expect to see more evidence. Scratches, bruising, abrasions from branches up his thighs and across the abdomen. Abraded palms where he pushed at the wood. Instead, his body is entirely unhurt except for his genitals and his head.'

'He'd have hit his head when he fell,' Wheeler said. His face was greasy with sweat.

'Perhaps.'

'And a branch could have skewered him through the groin,' Durdil added. His mouth watered and acid burnt his throat.

'Again, perhaps,' Hallos said. 'And yet, there is no evidence a branch did this. No flakes of bark left in the wounds, no abrasions to such delicate skin. Whatever did this, it was driven into him with great force but did not splinter or break, and leaves no part of itself behind.' He met Durdil's eyes. 'Whatever caused this, great care has been taken to remove it afterwards.'

237

'What are you saying?'

Hallos ran a palm over his bald head; his big shoulders slumped. 'I think Janis was tortured.'

'Cover him up,' Durdil said and headed back to his study. They sat at the table and stared at each other. 'You're saying Janis was murdered.'

'I'm saying he didn't die under a tree,' Hallos said, 'and that his injuries are consistent with torture.'

Durdil shifted his gaze to Wheeler. 'Who wins, Major? With Janis dead, who wins?'

'Prince Rivil, sir. He becomes heir.'

Durdil shoved himself out of his chair. 'Wheeler, the king is never to be left alone. Two guards at all times, when he eats, when he bathes, when he shits, when he sleeps. More when Rivil or Galtas are present. Hallos, is there enough evidence to accuse the prince?'

'No, sir. We can question his story, but we can't prove torture or anything else. The most we can do is cast doubt.'

'And if we do that, Rivil will know we suspect him. We need evidence. Leave that to me. In the meantime, I want your oaths you'll speak to no one of this. Rastoth will have to announce Janis's death to the court later today, it simply can't be kept secret. The three of us must appear to accept Rivil's story, that Janis died a hero in a tragic accident trying to rescue his men.' Durdil rubbed at the ache in his knee, always sharper when he was under stress. 'You two, get the body back to the temple and then keep your mouths shut.'

'And you, sir?' Wheeler asked, standing.

Durdil ran his tongue over his teeth. 'I'm going to send a courier west, and then I'm going to have a little chat with Rivil's honour guard. After that, Lord Galtas Morellis and I have some unfinished business regarding the queen's death. Let's see what else he spills at the same time.'

TARA

'Let me get this straight. You're scared of the man who stood for you at your cleansing and spoke the words of protection and family because you found out he's crooked? You know how many people speak words of family at a stranger's cleansing? You should be honoured.'

Crys's face was hot. 'You don't understand,' he hissed, peering over Tara's shoulder to where Ash sat at the tiller, guiding the boat past Shingle's harbour. He gave a gaggle of children on the dock a friendly wave. 'He kissed me!'

'He kissed you on the brow, you idiot. Happens at every cleansing. He didn't stick his tongue in your mouth.'

Crys grimaced. 'Don't.'

Tara laughed. 'You men are so terrified of having your masculinity called into question. Here was I thinking you'd resent me accompanying you because I've got tits, and it turns out the man who likes other men is your concern.'

Crys crossed his arms over his chest.

'Look, d'you want me to talk to him?' Tara tried. *Though gods know what I'm going to say. Crys is an idiot, most likely.*

'What? No. There's nothing to talk about. I just don't want him getting any . . . ideas.'

Tara put her head on one side. 'You know how you feel right now?' she asked in a low, intense voice. Crys shrugged. 'Well, that's how most women feel on a daily basis around soldiers and rich men and strangers and even friends. Afraid of being attacked, or being raped. Every day. Try and remember that.'

She walked aft before he could reply and sat on the rail by the tiller. Crys looked back, at her and at Ash, and then away again. It'd been like this ever since they'd set out. Crys had taken Ash out drinking as a thank you for the cleansing, and he'd learnt his new friend was something unexpected. He'd been like a cat around a sleeping dog ever since.

'He still angry?' Ash asked. There was no shame in his blue eyes and Tara admired that. Ash knew who he was and embraced it.

'I think so. He's probably met dozens of crooked-backs in the Ranks, you know, but he just doesn't know it.'

'Please don't call us that,' Ash said without looking at her and Tara felt a blush creep into her face.

'Sorry. I think he's worried it's catching.'

Ash snorted. 'Most men are. Gods, it's like they think we automatically fancy any man we're fewer than ten strides from. We're attracted to certain types in the same way they are. But put one of them in a room with one of us, and they think all we want to do is fuck 'em. Crys wouldn't rape a woman he was attracted to, but he thinks I'd rape him.'

Tara squinted in a sudden gust of wind. 'I don't think he

thinks you'd do that. Honestly, I don't know what he thinks. Besides, you do fancy him, don't you?' she added.

Ash tongued at a shred of meat stuck in his back tooth and spat it over the rail. 'Yep,' he muttered. 'A lot.'

Tara puffed out her cheeks and then laughed. 'This is brilliant. For once it's not me fighting off unwanted attention. I can just sit back and watch someone else squirm instead.'

Ash's eyebrows disappeared under his curls. 'And here's me thinking the West Rank was full of heroes, not rapists. Anyway, I'm not chasing him. He's made his position extremely clear, in simple, colourful language and accompanied with a drawn dagger. To be honest, I'd be happy if he just relaxed enough to talk to me.'

'Well, that's something we all need to do tonight,' Tara said. 'We'll be at Rilporin tomorrow and we still don't have a viable plan to reach the Commander.' She punched him in the arm. 'And you two need to sort this out. We're here to protect Crys and make sure he gets to Durdil with his story. That means he needs to trust that you'll look after him if he needs it. He can't be wondering what your motivation is all the time.'

Ash locked the tiller and stretched. 'My motivation is the same as yours: to get Durdil to arrest Rivil. But how do I convince him of that? Swear an oath I'll never touch him?'

'That won't be necessary.'

Crys's voice was hesitant, but it still made them jump. *He's quieter than a cat when he wants to be. How long has he been listening?*

'I've been an idiot and I apologise, Ash. You and yours have been nothing but good to me since I arrived in Watchtown. You stood for me at my cleansing. You've been a friend and you're risking your life to come to Rilporin with me.' He raised a hand to his face. 'I've been treated differently since I was a boy because of my eyes. Seems to me I shouldn't do the same because you're . . . different.'

Tara looked between the pair of them and then threw out her arms, dragging them both to her. 'Ah, you boys,' she said, 'all friends together. Hooray.' She shoved them away as Ash grinned and Crys scowled. 'Now that that's settled, how do we tell Durdil Koridam that Prince Rivil is a heretic and a murderer and has allied with our greatest enemies to overthrow our king and our gods? Hmm?' She put her hands on her hips. 'Don't you think it's time we focused on that instead of who wants to get into whose linens?'

CRYS

*First moon, eighteenth year of the reign of King Rastoth
South Harbour, Rilporin, Wheat Lands*

'Here we go,' Crys breathed. He was both relieved and frightened to be at Rilporin's docks, especially as his chances of surviving an encounter with the prince were exactly zero. *Please don't be here. Please don't be here.*

'Um, Crys,' Tara hissed. 'There's a lot of scarlet flying.'

Crys looked up at First Bastion, the closest tower. A red pennant flew from its top and there was one on First Tower as well. He looked east around the curve of the city, and South Tower One was flying red.

'Fucking shit. They know.'

'So Rivil's here,' Ash muttered, dragging his gaze from the city walls, higher than any he'd ever seen.

'Must be.'

'All right, nobody panic,' Tara said. 'No one's giving you a second look. Let's just get to the palace.'

Crys touched the bandage they'd wrapped around his head and over one eye; then he tongued at the split lip Tara had

243

given him as an added disguise. Though she'd taken a little too much pleasure in it for his liking.

Ash was gawping at the walls again. 'Stinks,' he pronounced sagely, wrinkling his nose as they wandered along the docks to the main road leading to the gatehouse. In the distance, around the long curve of the western wall, they could just make out the north harbour and the Tears. Rilporin sat at the confluence of the two great rivers, surrounded on three sides by water and the fourth by the wall.

'Stinks? Rilporin is the greatest city in the world. This is the smell of success, of money and jewels and big dinners,' Crys said.

'Big shits more like,' Ash complained and Crys laughed despite himself, the banter calming some of his nerves. 'Impressive though,' Ash added. 'Enemy'd have a time getting in here.' They walked through the gatehouse, an echoing tunnel of stone burrowed through the thickness of the wall. Ash whistled and listened to its echo.

'Right, where do you want me?' he asked as they emerged into the market built on the killing field beneath the wall. It was a riot of noise and colour, brightly dyed awnings and gaudy traders clamouring for their attention.

'Away from the barracks and the gates. This is First Circle, so if you head along there you'll reach the merchants' quarter. It's probably best for gossip. There're some decent taverns too. See what you can learn: when Rivil got back; the story that's been told to the court and the people; anything about me. Tara, we'll head straight for Durdil's quarters at the palace. Once I'm safely in, come back and find Ash, pool your knowledge. And keep a low profile. If anything happens to me, find Durdil. Make him listen.' Crys shook his head at an old man holding up an even older dead fish, and then flipped a copper to a beggar girl.

'Dancer's grace and Trickster's luck go with you,' Ash said and vanished into the crowd, gawking like a child at his first Yuletide celebration. He was taller than most, and Crys tracked his progress through the market until he was lost from view.

'Straight down the King's Way?' Tara asked, adjusting her uniform. She was attracting attention, but that was the point; while everyone was staring at a woman in uniform, they weren't paying attention to the bruised and bandaged soldier by her side.

'No, I'm likely to know too many men on the main gates. We'll go roundabout.'

A half-hour's brisk walk got them to the palace. Crys grinned when he saw who was on door duty. 'I must see the Commander, Lieutenant. I have vital information regarding the security of the realm,' he said.

'West Rank?' the soldier asked. 'I'll need your names.'

Crys stepped close and lifted the bandage from his eye. 'Hello, Roger, how's the guarding going?'

Weaverson's eyes widened. 'Captain? What – word is you're dead,' he said in a low voice, eyes darting through the crowds thronging the assembly place in front of the palace. 'Prince Rivil himself told the Commander.' He spotted Tara and his eyes popped out of his head.

'Well, you can see I'm not. Let us in, will you?'

Roger shifted from foot to foot. 'I'm sorry, sir, I can't do that.'

'You don't trust me?' Crys asked, putting as much affronted dignity into his voice as he could. Tara was watching the approaches but his neck was prickling.

'Prince Rivil said you died along with the heir. Now you turn up here. What'm I supposed to think?'

You're a lieutenant. No one cares what you think.

'You're an excellent young officer, Roger,' Tara said, stepping around Crys and smiling into Roger's eyes. 'A real asset to the Palace Rank, I can see. I'm Captain Tara Carter of the West. This is a report from General Mace Koridam. It's addressed to the Commander of the Ranks and I have been instructed to put into his hands directly. Captain Tailorson has a verbal report for the Commander as well. So you're going to let us in, because if you don't, you will be impeding two officers in their duty. Do you understand?'

Roger's face was a study in pimply misery. 'Yes, sir, er, ma'am,' he said and stepped aside. 'But—'

They slid past him into the gloom of the palace, ignoring his final protests.

'He's going to be off-duty in less than an hour and chances are he'll tell his new captain about us.'

'Then we've got less than an hour to locate Durdil and get you safely under cover,' Tara said. 'Speaking of which, pull that bloody bandage back over your eye.'

Crys walked faster, head up, shoulders back and Mace's report in his hand. Tara marched at his side. One thing he'd learnt guarding this place was no one questioned the confident people with pieces of paper. They cut through the corridors and counting rooms, slid into a servants' corridor and trotted along it, exited into an antechamber and hurried for Koridam's office.

'Captain Tara Carter of the West Rank with urgent correspondence for the Commander of the Ranks.'

The under-secretary pursed his lips and stared Tara up and down with deliberate disdain. His eyes flicked to Crys. 'And you?'

'I have information for the Commander regarding the prince.'

'I meant your name.'

'You don't need to know his name. I vouch for him,' Tara said. She stared past the man as though he didn't exist. Crys was impressed.

The under-secretary's pale eyebrows rose fractionally. He pointed at the rug. 'Wait.' He rose from behind his opulent desk and scuttled to a set of doors, slid through and vanished from sight. Crys breathed a soft prayer to the Dancer that no one he knew decided to pop in. They stood at parade rest and waited.

Eventually the under-secretary poked his head back through the door and beckoned. 'Over there.' He pointed, exited the larger room and closed the door behind him.

Crys spotted a desk. He approached with Tara and saluted. 'I am here with vital information for the Commander of the Ranks. I must see him at once.'

'The Commander is not available.' The secretary gave a small smile that made his mouth look like a puckered arse.

Crys scratched his neck. 'Commander Koridam is always available.'

'He is not available,' the secretary repeated as he shuffled papers into exact alignment. 'Your name?'

'Who is available then? And who are you?' Crys countered. *What the fuck? Godsdamn pissing functionaries.*

The man sighed. 'I cannot reveal that information without identification.'

'Really? I could go to the docks and find out in three seconds just by asking around. Who's the prick in the yellow velvet hat who thinks he's the fucking King of Rilpor?'

'Then do not let me detain you from the docks, sir,' the secretary said with prudish malevolence. 'Your appearance would suggest it is where you belong, after all.'

Tara spoke before Crys lunged over the desk and throttled

him. 'I have a report here from the general of the West to be placed directly into the Commander's hands,' she said. 'Captain Tara Carter, West Rank.'

'Then you may see the Commander. As for you,' the secretary sneered at Crys, 'you can leave the palace. Guard!'

Heavy footsteps the other side of the door and Crys panicked and drew his sword, making the secretary squeak and dive behind his desk. Tara swore at him and unsheathed her blade.

If Rivil or Galtas or any of the honour guard comes through that door they're dead, no time for pleasantries. His mouth tasted of copper and he couldn't swallow. *Gods? Anyone? A little help?*

The door handle turned and Crys threw off his cloak, pulled a dagger with his free hand and crouched. Tara took two steps forward. 'If this goes bad, get out and don't wait for me,' she said. The door opened before Crys could argue, and Durdil Koridam strode into the room with three guards.

'What is this? Who are you?' Durdil snapped, his hand raised to order the attack.

'My lord? Commander?' Crys threw his sword and dagger behind him, raised his hands and dropped to his knees. Tara copied him. 'Commander, I'm Captain Crys Tailorson. You may remember me; we met before Yule when I first entered the Palace Rank. Shortly afterwards I was recruited by Prince Rivil into his personal guard?' He ripped the bandage off his head.

Durdil studied him and his eyes widened and then slitted in confusion. He signalled to his guards and they sheathed their swords. 'Come with me, both of you,' Durdil grunted. 'You.' He pointed at the secretary and then the soldiers. 'You never saw this man. You never heard this conversation. Understand?'

The secretary nodded frantically, looking as though he would never speak of anything to anyone ever again. Durdil looked back at Crys and then at the doors. 'Fetch your blades and follow me,' he said, 'and put that bandage back on.'

CORVUS

First moon, year 995 since the Exile of the Red Gods
Crow Crag, Sky Path, Gilgoras Mountains

They'd lose men on the way down to the plains. It was too early in the season, the weather too unpredictable; the weak and the sick would be culled. *Meaning the strongest and fiercest will be left to face the West Rank and the Wolves. The Lady's will.*

Corvus found he hadn't missed his home village. Compared with Eagle Height it was small and poor, but the men it bred were the toughest he'd ever known. 'Will you be ready?'

'Aye, Sire, we will,' Fost said and let out a piercing whistle. The warriors of the village moved through the drill, a little ragged, a few missed steps, but on the whole they were a small, deadly little army, well armed and armoured. More armour than the Rilporians would ever have seen them in. A nice little surprise.

'This isn't a raid, Fost, this is invasion, war, and the glory of the gods. Don't lie to me.'

250

'We're ready, Sire. You can wind out my guts on a stick if we're not.'

Corvus turned his cheek to a blast of wind full of needles of ice and watched as the warriors continued their man-oeuvres, oblivious to the weather. A group of archers adjusted for the wind and loosed at targets fifty paces away. Most hit.

Corvus's skin itched with excitement. 'Good. Discipline maintained, the village in good order, the slaves compliant. You are war chief of Crow Crag in my place.' He looked at Valan as he made the pronouncement, saw his dismay. He'd been Corvus's second at Crow Crag, so the village should be his by right now Corvus was king. But Valan was just returned from Rilpor with news that his patrol was dead and Rillirin was still in Wolf hands. That Rillirin had killed for the Wolves, no less. Valan had a lot of trust to earn back. Best keep him close for that.

'Your will, honoured,' Fost said, grinning.

'And are you ready to move out?' Corvus continued as they strolled into the longhouse, the gaggle of chiefs and priests trailing after them, Lanta moving smooth as silk in their midst.

'We are, Sire. We want only the date.'

'First day of third moon, so keep preparing. Take the Sky Path and meet me and the others at the head of the Gil-beside Road. We'll take it down into Rilpor.'

There were murmurs as servants brought in platters of roasted mountain goat in bloody gravy, along with hot bread and boiled turnips and jugs of ale and liquor.

'Third moon is only a few weeks away, Sire, and the Gil-beside is treacherous even at midsummer. Would the Blood Pass not be an easier route?' Fost asked as he passed the platter to Corvus. 'We risk the snowmelt.'

In answer, Corvus set aside the platter and took the skin Lanta proffered. He cleared a space on the table and Fost, his second, and the war chiefs from the other villages he'd brought with him clustered close.

'The Gil-beside, Blood Pass, the West Forts, Watchtown, the River Gil, Rilporin.' He tapped each point in turn. 'The Rilporian intends for us to die in the first battle, here,' he said, indicating on the map, 'and while we will spill as much blood as necessary to tear the veil, I don't intend to win Prince Rivil's war for him and then go quietly to the Afterworld. The promise of the warm lands is one you have waited for over generations. This year, the year of the gods' return, I intend that you get what you have been promised. So this is what's going to happen . . .'

Dust shivered from the rafters at the cheering and stamping of feet as the warriors understood the plan and made sense of the map. Corvus stood and raised his cup. The longhouse's occupants did the same. 'Drink your ale and fuck your women,' he shouted. 'Soon enough we go to war.'

DURDIL

'Captains, this is Major Wheeler – Tailorson, I assume you remember your commanding officer? – and the court physician, Hallos. They both know everything I know, and I trust them without reservation. There are some anomalies in the report Prince Rivil gave us, and we're hoping you can help clear those up.'

Durdil couldn't decide what would be better, for Crys to prove or disprove Rivil's story. *Maybe if I'd never asked Hallos to examine the body, I could've just pretended everything was normal. A tragic accident.*

'The report from General Mace Koridam supports Captain Tailorson's story inasmuch as it can. We recovered evidence at the scene of the heir's death,' Tara said and swallowed. 'It's probably best for me to explain after Crys has told you what he witnessed.'

Durdil looked between them, and then he gestured for Crys to speak. It took a long time, and there were many

253

interruptions, and by the end Durdil was fervently wishing he'd never decided to look into it.

'You're aware this is the worst possible thing you could have told me?' he said eventually, slumping in his seat. 'And I don't even mean the details of the torture.'

'Sacrifice, sir, not torture. Well, torture in the form of sacrifice,' Crys pointed out. 'This was all done to consolidate Rivil's and Galtas's journey on to the Dark Path. The only good thing to come out of it is I was able to overhear some of their plans. The Mireces will attack within weeks, and try to wipe out the West Rank. Your son already knows this, is doubling patrols and stockpiling weapons and food. The Wolves are aware too. In fact, we brought one with us.'

'A Wolf in Rilporin,' Wheeler muttered. 'Wonder if he's started a fight yet.'

'Probably,' Tara said. 'Commander, about the evidence I said we'd recovered. It's – I don't really know how to phrase this delicately – it's a pair of severed legs, cut just above the knee and nailed to a scaffold. Crys's story was so outrageous that the general sent a patrol to the location he'd given us.'

'Theoretically, we can't prove they belong to the prince,' Crys began.

'Oh, I could do that if I had them here,' Hallos interjected. 'I made a thorough study of the cut marks on Janis's legs, produced some drawings. I'm sure I could match the splintering of the bones.' He frowned at the grimaces around the table.

'I think it's safe to assume they're a match,' Durdil said heavily. 'The question is what we do now.'

'Rivil is arrested and tried for treason, heresy and regicide,' Crys said. 'Commander, speak to the council, present your evidence, get a bill or a motion or whatever to put to the king, and get Rivil locked up. We don't have much time.'

Durdil leant his chin on his hand and studied Crys. 'It's not that simple,' he said. 'First we must tell the king, make him understand his son is not fit to rule. Then we must try him and while we do that we must find a new heir to the throne.'

Hallos was shaking his head. 'Durdil, I don't think Rastoth would understand, let alone believe you, if you told him what Rivil's done. The chances of him remarrying and getting another heir are negligible, and his health is deteriorating fast. I'd have given him a year or two at most before this. Now, seeing his fragility in the wake of Janis's death, I fear telling him of Rivil will kill him on the spot.'

'A sick king, a traitorous heir and a Mireces invasion,' Wheeler pronounced. 'We've already lost.'

'Then name someone on the council,' Crys said, his voice tinged with desperation. 'Someone respected, someone strong . . . What?'

Durdil stifled his laughter. 'The nobles on the council are sycophants and morons to a man. Lord Hardoc? Lord Silais? Lord Galtas Morellis, perhaps?'

'Why do we have to tell the king?' Tara said. The others turned shocked faces in her direction. 'What? Come on, why? You're Commander of the Ranks, charged with the safety of the realm. You know this is the best and only option we have. Arrest Rivil, have him quietly executed, and tell the king and the court he's gone away somewhere, to manage his estates or put his brother's affairs in order. Anything. Then we take the body west and put it on display for the Mireces king. They cancel the invasion: job done.'

'He doesn't even have to be dead,' Crys added. 'Take him west as a prisoner, show him to Corvus, tell him there are no reinforcements coming and all the Ranks are ranged against him. Once the war is over – or better still, has never begun – we can work out what to do with Rivil.'

Durdil pursed his lips and met Wheeler's eyes. The major lifted one shoulder and gave a slight nod. 'Him being alive is better than him being dead, at least for now,' he said.

'Hallos?'

'If we could keep the circumstances of his travel west secret from the king, we might be able to manage His Majesty's health long enough to find an alternate heir.'

'About that,' Tara said and Durdil held up a finger.

'Aren't you full of ideas?' he said and Tara shut her mouth, dropping her gaze. Durdil huffed. 'Go on then.'

'I was going to suggest you, sir,' Tara said quietly. Durdil's eyebrows shot up his head. 'You're young enough, a proven warrior, a proven negotiator; you have an heir in place already who is also young and a proven warrior. The dedication of the Koridams to Rilpor is well established. Your good name goes back generations and you have extensive lands and holdings. You're a nobleman. If Rastoth were to honour anyone, you're the obvious choice. In my opinion.'

Durdil raised his finger again and then pushed away from the table and stalked to the windows. Cold radiated from the glass on to his hot face and he stared unseeing out on to a small courtyard. Pear trees grew in stone troughs around the perimeter, their twisted branches stark against a cloudy sky. It was Durdil's secret vice that he enjoyed cultivating them, whiling away many an afternoon while he dictated his reports to a scribe.

Now their branches were knuckly fingers accusing him, lamenting his hubris while the hairs stood up on his arms. His mouth was dry as Tara's words ran around inside his skull, banging excitedly on his brain while the rational rest of him dismissed them as fantasy.

'Captain Tailorson,' he croaked, 'a room will be made available to you down the corridor. You are to stay in there at all times, do you understand? If Prince Rivil gets word you're in the palace, I will not be able to vouch for your safety. Captain Carter, find your Wolf friend and make sure he doesn't spill any secrets. Keep a low profile. Wheeler, Hallos, about your duties, please. We'll reconvene tomorrow.' He faced into the room and swept it with a stern glare. 'I will draw up a list of potential heirs to Rastoth's throne,' he said. 'I will not be on it.'

DOM

Dom tried. With every ounce of will he had left he forced his eyelids apart, and then had to blink to convince himself they were open. It was black. Unremitting black. The echo of his breathing told him where he was and he tensed, tried to roll over, failed. Red torchlight flickered into existence, its source invisible, and he made out the stalactites poised above him, dagger tips pointing at his heart.

'Hello, my love,' She whispered. 'Hello, my young calestar.'

'Lady Dancer, sweet and true, bless me with Your guiding hand, let Your Light shine on me,' Dom recited, stumbling over the words in his haste to get them out. *Please, no, not again.*

The Dark Lady's lips curled into a sneer.

'Lady Dancer, bountiful Goddess, Whose Light is eternal dawn and endless noon and infinite sunset, Who brings us the seasons and the birthing and the dying times, I ask for Your aid,' he tried again.

258

The Dark Lady paused, one hand cupped to Her ear. 'Maybe She's out,' She mocked. 'Or maybe She doesn't believe in you. But I do, my love, I believe in you, and it pains me that I have to come to you each time. When will you come to me?'

'Never,' Dom grated, jerking at the bonds he couldn't see that held him on the slab.

The Dark Lady laughed. 'You tease,' She said and then Her eyes flashed with fury. 'I don't like being teased. Tell me, my love, have you met my brother, Gosfath?' A shape loomed behind Her, its deformed head weaving amongst the stalactites. It reached down a hand of immense proportions and stroked a finger across the Goddess's belly. She shuddered.

'Later, my love,' She murmured. 'For now, slake yourself on this man. Show him a small taste of what we will do if he continues to refuse to comply.'

Dom lifted his head from the stone. 'You should be careful, you know,' he said, reckless with fear. 'All these little visits teach me about you, too. I know your plans now, and I'll tell them. I'll tell everything. I know about the veil, about how you're *trapped* behind it like a rabbit in a snare. And—'

Gosfath, God of Blood, roared, the sound so huge it made Dom's eardrums flutter. The words died inside him and his breath froze in his chest. With a wet organic sound Gosfath shrank in on Himself until He was a mere foot taller than His Sister, and then He leapt like a cat on to the slab and crouched between Dom's feet. A long black tongue flicked out and around and was gone.

Sweat stung Dom's eyes as Gosfath stretched forth a red hand tipped with black talons and placed it on his stomach. He sucked in his belly and strained away as Gosfath began

259

to press, talons digging, burrowing, leaning into His task, into Dom.

'Hush, my love,' the Dark Lady said as She leant her hip on the slab and watched Her Brother work. 'Everything you know I allow you to know.'

'I'll tell,' Dom crowed, laughing madly. 'I'll still tell.' Then the talons punched through his belly and he screamed.

And woke in his cot in the temple house, the first light of dawn peeking through the shutters.

'What's wrong? Bad dream?' Lim asked, his voice slack with sleep.

'What? What?' Dom's hands were feverish over his skin, looking for the wounds the god had inflicted. There was nothing, his skin smooth and unbroken. But the muscles still shuddered with the memory of pain, and Dom's mouth tasted of blood.

'Did you have a bad dream?' Lim asked again from the next cot over.

Dom swung his legs from under the blankets and sat up; he ran his hands through his hair. 'Yeah,' he muttered, 'bad dream. Go back to sleep.'

CRYS

It was a pleasant incarceration, but it was incarceration
nonetheless. For his own good, of course. He wandered from
the fireplace to the window for what felt like the thousandth
time and sighed, letting his breath steam the glass. Tara had
sent word through Durdil that she and Ash were safe and
sharing a room in a tavern in the silk and spice quarter. Crys
snorted to think of that pair in bed together, then curled his
lip and thought about something else.

*All right, I admit it. I'd kill for the company of either of
them right now.*

Crys shuffled the cards through his fingers without looking,
forehead pressed to the glass so he could just make out the
drill ground for the Palace Rank. A cavalry Hundred was
practising, horses cantering through complex patterns so
close that collision looked inevitable and was always
narrowly avoided.

His gaze slid over the walls to the city, shining white in

261

the sun, the streets swept clean. The plains were brown and white and stretched into the distance beyond the limit of vision. Somewhere out there, too far to see, the mountains bucked into the sky with angry heaves, shoulder upon shoulder, to pierce the sun himself. And in them, the Mireces prepared for war.

Crys heard the door click open and leapt to attention, in case it was Durdil. It wasn't.

'Captain, Commander Koridam extends his gratitude for all you've done and has asked me to assist you in leaving the city.'

'He doesn't need anything more of me?' Crys asked. 'So there'll be no trial, then?' Major Wheeler shook his head. 'I have to admit, part of me's relieved,' Crys added, moving to the bed and collecting his coat. 'I'd be the only one swearing to my version of events, after all. The rest of the honour guard would all back Rivil and Galtas.'

Crys still had Janis's sword and he pulled it from under the coat and turned with it in both hands to present it to Wheeler. It was only luck that the sheathed blade deflected Wheeler's dagger, knocking the man's arm down so the tip of the knife sliced down the front of Crys's hip instead of lodging in his chest. *Or my spine. He was going to stab me in the back.*

Crys reacted despite the shocked babbling of his brain. He dragged Janis's sword free, used the scabbard to poke Wheeler back a step, and slid sideways along the bed until he was in open space.

Wheeler's long blade came out and flicked for his head. He parried and riposted, felt his sword trap on Wheeler's guard and twisted it free.

'Fuck's sake,' Crys snapped, launching a flurry of blows at the major, 'I am getting really fucking sick of men I trust being traitors. Commander!' he yelled. Durdil's study was only down the corridor. There was no comforting answer and Crys saved his breath for the fight.

The room was small and in his boredom Crys had explored every inch of it, but Wheeler was good. Wheeler might even be better than him and Janis's sword was slightly too big for ease. His hip throbbed hot and sticky and his foot squelched in the blood running into his boot, and Crys knew the only way he was getting out of this alive was if Wheeler was dead.

'How long?' he gasped, ducking a wild slash and nearly losing an eye to the major's dagger.

'Who do you think introduced Rivil to Gull, our high priest here in Rilporin?' Wheeler laughed, and then grunted as Crys's sword battered his down to ring loud on the stone of the floor. Surely someone would have heard that?

Apparently no one did because as the fight dragged on and they both began to tire, no one came. Crys was slowing, his lunges shortening as his leg refused to take his weight.

Wheeler sensed the weakness and pressed, forcing him back, herding him into the bed. Crys made a wild attempt at leaping backwards on to it and failed spectacularly, his heels clipping the edge of the mattress and flinging him flat.

It saved his life. Wheeler thrust at the place Crys's chest had been, encountered no resistance, and fell on top of him. Dagger and sword went into Wheeler's ribs on either side, while the major's sword ended up somewhere above Crys's head on the mattress. His dagger, though, ended up in Crys's shoulder, ripping into and back out of the side of his upper arm, leaving a grotesque flap of flesh hanging.

Crys howled and his dagger went into Wheeler again, and the man stiffened and gurgled on his chest. Crys kicked him off, slapped his hand to his injured arm and then rolled

Wheeler on to his back. The major was bubbling, his mouth opening and closing, before he choked on a rush of blood.

Crys sat on the edge of the bed and stared at the corpse for a while. Then he staggered to the desk, found a piece of paper and quill, and scratched 'Heretic. Trust no one', on to it. He pinned it to Wheeler's chest by stabbing the dagger through it, then ripped a strip from the bed hangings with shaking hands and tied it around his arm.

He slid into his coat, a stream of curses pouring from his mouth, buckled Janis's sword to his belt, and crept out of the room on legs no stronger than a newborn fawn's. Tara and Ash were in danger and it was high time Crys got out of the city.

GILDA

In the end they cornered Dom in the temple, his family and
Rachelle, Dalli and Rillirin too. They listened to his weak
excuses, and then Gilda pushed him towards the godpool
and they got to the truth.

'The Red Gods visit me, before and after knowings and
when I'm asleep,' Dom said, his voice little more than a
whisper. Gilda's hand rose to her throat of its own volition,
but Dom looked embarrassed more than anything else. As
though being visited by the Dark Lady was a weakness, a
failing on his part.

'How is that possible?' Rachelle asked.

'How long has this been going on?' Gilda demanded at
the same time.

Dom raised his hands, palm up. 'They've discovered the
. . . the pathway in my head – the godspace – that the Dancer
uses to send me Her knowings, and They've realised They
can use it, too. As for how long, since before Yule.' He patted

265

the air. 'I could handle it; it wasn't bad before. You didn't need to know.'

'Is this the secret you've been keeping?' Lim asked and Dom nodded quickly. Gilda's eyes narrowed. *A little too keen there, my lad, a little too happy to agree. I'd say this is one of the many secrets you keep from us.*

The drip of melting snow pattered outside and sun bright enough to hurt came through the cracks in the walls and cast an oblong of pale gold through the doorway.

'Is this my fault?' Rillirin whispered, chewing her thumbnail. 'This is because of me, isn't it?'

Dom beckoned and she went to him reluctantly. 'Not at all,' he said, pulling her to his side and wrapping his arm around her waist. 'It is not,' he added. 'Worry about everything else that's happening, not about this. This is just entertainment.'

'Entertainment? What do you mean?' Gilda asked. He was so calm about it, accepting of it, as if it was normal. *Or as if he thinks he deserves it.*

Dom stared into the pool at his side, his face bitter. Maybe not so accepting after all. 'They do it because They can. Because it amuses Them while They wait for Rivil and the Mireces to tear the veil and release Them back into Gilgoras.'

Gilda eyed him closely, her skin crawling at the thought that They would torture him just for fun. 'What else?' she asked, because she knew him and because she couldn't see the catharsis of confession in his face.

Dom squeezed Rillirin tighter and pressed a quick kiss to her hair; then he let go and sat on the edge of the pool. He looked tired as he rubbed his eyes. 'The Dark Lady knows me, knows who I am, the . . . things I've done.' His left hand covered his right forearm and the scars it bore. 'She says I'll go to Her willingly in the end, that I belong to Her. She wants my soul and She's convinced She'll get it. Perhaps She might. But She's a little too keen, if that makes sense. It worries me that if I ever break, if They break me, that it'll do more than just add a soul to Her collection. It's like there's more to it than that, but I don't know what.'

There was suspicion and fear in Rachelle's face, and Gilda forced her own expression not to reflect the same emotions.

'That stupid bastard blood oath,' Sarilla growled, 'why did you—'

'Enough,' Gilda snapped. 'That conversation has been had many times over the years. What's done is done. Dom, tell us how we can help you.'

His laugh was bitter and Rillirin sat beside him and took his hand in hers. He stared at the ceiling. 'You can't. This is my task, my burden. Don't,' he said when Lim looked ready to protest, 'believe me, if anyone could help, could stop it happening, I'd bite their hand off. But you can't. It's not too bad. It'll probably get worse but, for now, I can handle it. So how about we stop focusing on me and start focusing on winning the war, eh?'

His defences were back up and they'd get nothing more from him now. As one, they formed a circle and Gilda led them in prayer – for victory, for those they'd lost, and for all those they were going to lose. Gilda watched Dom as she chanted, wondering whether he would be one of the ones they'd lose. Or whether it would just be his soul that was taken. She wasn't sure which of those would be worse.

CRYS

First moon, eighteenth year of the reign of King Rastoth
The Gilded Cup, silk and spice quarter,
Rilporin, Wheat Lands

'Fuck the gods! What happened to you?' Ash demanded when he opened the door to Crys's persistent hammering. He slung Crys's unhurt arm over his shoulder and half carried him in, lowering him on to the bed.

'Tara, get Durdil now,' Crys gasped, 'don't care how you do it.'

Tara snapped her fingers. 'Easy, I saw him heading into Second Circle this morning.'

Crys groaned as Ash tugged his coat over his slashed arm. 'He's probably in North Barracks then. If they won't let you see him, get them to tell him sorry for the mess in his quarters and if he wants answers, to visit the courier from his son. That should be enough to get him here.'

'Got it,' Tara said. She paused at the door. 'Are you going to die? Because if you are, do you want to tell me what's happened?'

268

'Get out. I'll tell Ash if it looks like I won't survive the hour,' Crys said with as much sarcasm as he had left. He listened to her clattering down the stairs. 'Lovely bedside manner,' he managed.

Ash worked in silence, sliding Crys's shirt off and muttering at the state of his arm.

'That good?' Crys hissed as Ash swore.

'How?' asked Ash instead of answering him.

'Turns out Major Wheeler, one of Durdil's most trusted officers, is in it up to his arsehole with Rivil. Or was, until I stuck my sword through him.'

'You do like to make a mess wherever you go, don't you? All right, hold still, I need to stitch.' He disappeared to the dresser and came back with a bowl with thread floating on the water. 'You're losing a lot of blood and I don't have time to sterilise this needle and thread properly.' He fished the needle out of the water. 'So this is salt water.'

'Oh, you are shitting me,' Crys mumbled. 'Feel . . . dizzy,' he added as the room spun gently around him.

'That's a good thing,' Ash said as he threaded the needle. 'Feel free to pass out, because this is really going to hurt.'

It was, of all things, the thirst that woke him, but it turned out to be the most pleasant of his body's ailments. Crys groaned and, unsticking one eyelid, blinked slowly at the fuzzy outlines above him until they resolved into faces. Tara, Durdil, Ash.

Tara lifted his head and shoulders and pressed a cup to his lips. It was ale and it tasted like nectar. He swallowed most of the cupful before settling back against the pillow.

'Not too much of that,' Tara said, putting the back of her hand against his forehead. 'You're running a temperature.'

'I know, I've been in a fight. I remember nearly all of it,' Crys mumbled. 'Commander, Major Wheeler—'

'Is dead in my quarters, apparently. A message reached me shortly after Captain Carter.' He reached down and checked the bandage around Crys's arm and shoulder and grunted approval. 'Nicely done. Wheeler's death is most fortuitous, however,' he continued.

Crys wondered whether he'd hit his head during the fight. 'It is?' he managed.

'Very. Lord Galtas Morellis has disappeared. Prince Rivil says he believes Galtas had business to attend to, but doesn't know where he was going or how long he'll be. With an officer murdered in the palace itself, and Galtas mysteriously vanished, I can legitimately order a Hundred to track him down and arrest him.' Durdil assumed an innocent expression. 'After all, who else would have cause to murder Major Wheeler? Obviously the man discovered something Galtas preferred to keep hidden.'

'And Rivil can't do a damn thing about it,' Tara said, her admiration plain, 'because then he'd have to admit he'd sent Wheeler to kill Crys.'

Crys drank more ale, managing to hold the cup himself this time, hissing as the cut on his hip tugged against stitches. 'So Wheeler told Rivil I was still alive and everything we discussed in front of him. He knows we know, and he knows his assassin failed. So he's still after me.'

'Oh, he's after you all right,' Durdil said and to Crys's dismay he sounded almost cheerful. 'Which is why I'm sending you back west. With a death in the palace and Galtas under suspicion, neither Rivil nor the king can argue with me shutting down the city and keeping them both under extremely close surveillance. Any messengers Galtas tries to send back we'll intercept. We've cut the prince off from his allies, Captain. Rivil can't get to you and he can't leave the palace. He can't reinforce the Mireces.'

'You mean we've won?' Crys asked, his head swimming with ale and blood loss and a tidal wave of relief.

Durdil rocked his hand from side to side. 'Let's not count our chickens before they hatch, Captain,' he said and grinned, looking much younger and more alive than Crys had ever seen him, 'but as long as we can get our hands on Galtas and keep Rivil under lock and key, it certainly looks that way. The Mireces might still force a fight, but that's one battle my son can win.'

Crys managed a thumbs up before he slept again, and when he woke Durdil was gone and the bed was swaying with a sickening motion that wouldn't stop. Eventually he rolled to the edge of the cot and threw up, aiming vaguely for the bowl on the floor. Some of it went in.

'Disgusting,' Ash said from his seat at the other end of the narrow room and Crys yelped in surprise, and then yelped again as his shoulder protested his sudden movement.

'Uh, this may sound strange,' Crys said slowly as he took in his surroundings, 'but I don't remember your room at the inn looking like this.'

Ash laughed and came to collect the bowl. He wrinkled his nose and laid a cloth over it, putting it to one side. 'We're on board,' he said. 'You slept through the whole thing. Durdil sent us in a wool wagon to the south harbour and bundled us on to a boat of supplies for the West Rank. We're heading home.'

'Thank the gods,' Crys said and patted the amulets on his chest. His bare chest. His free hand slid beneath the blanket and Ash laughed again.

'Yes, you're naked,' he said. 'I couldn't get to the cut on your hip after you passed out and I didn't know how bad it was. Your arse was in the breeze the whole way to the docks, it was truly disgusting. Besides, I didn't think you'd want to be wearing that uniform much longer. We've got some fresh clothes for when you're up and about.'

Crys's face was so hot his hair nearly caught fire. 'You undressed me?'

'You would have preferred Tara?'

'What? No!'

Ash winked and threw him a pair of linens. 'I can say this with perfect honesty, Captain. You are not the first naked man I have seen in my life.' He chuckled. 'Nor the most well endowed.'

'Hey,' Crys protested, but for some reason he was laughing.

RILLIRIN

Second moon, eighteenth year of the reign of King Rastoth
Watch Ford, the River Gil, Cattle Lands

It was wrong to be happy in such circumstances, but Rillirin hadn't been happy for as long as she could remember, so she wasn't going to let anything stop her now. She rode a piebald mare with a sweet temperament and a pink muzzle, her spear in her right hand, reins in her left. Her thighs were burning from hours in the saddle, her hands blistered and shoulders aching from working the new, heavier spear with its leaf-blade at one end and its counterweight ball of iron at the other. None of it mattered.

Dom rode on one side of her and Dalli on the other, and all around hundreds of Wolves rode with them. They were going to base themselves in their main summer village in the foothills between the River Gil and the Blood Pass Valley, and from there they'd sweep for movement and be ready to aid the West Rank in battle.

Rillirin's palm threatened to slip on her spear and she tightened her grip. *Dom said I probably wouldn't have to*

273

fight. Not enough training. Her stomach fluttered with relief even as her head rebelled at being left behind.

Dalli's cousin, Seth Lightfoot, ran easily at the head of the column, checking the trail and looking for ambush, even out here on the plain. They had archers to the fore, led by Sarilla, and more at the rear. Wherever they went, Wolves took no chances.

Dalli was relating a ridiculous story about a Ranker she'd slept with a few winters before, the telling of it graphic enough to make Rillirin blush and squirm in the saddle. Dalli kept laughing at her expression.

'Gods, girl, the man who finally tumbles you is going to have a task and a half. Sex is supposed to be fun, remember?'

Rillirin's face was hot and her laughter was forced, but she liked that Dalli was talking to her as though she was normal. 'Yeah, I can't see that happening,' Rillirin said. 'I sort of made a promise that no man would ever touch me.'

She could sense Dom's sudden interest and squeezed her knees together in reflex, but then pulled back on the reins when the mare lengthened stride. The horse snorted and dropped back to a walk.

'Pfft.' Dalli waved her hand airily. 'I make oaths like that all the time. Swearing off sex is the same as swearing off drinking,' she said and looked over to Dom.

'Never lasts,' they said together and laughed.

'If you say so,' Rillirin said, trying for nonchalance and falling short. She wanted to join in but had nothing she could share; stories of Liris didn't exactly make people laugh. She fumbled for another topic, an amusing story of her life, and came up blank. *Gods, I'm pathetic.*

Still, she was riding with the Wolves, almost as if she was one of them, and second moon was being kind so far. There'd been a brief thaw and the fug raised by the horses surrounded their riders in a pungent cloud of warmth.

'Heels down,' Dom reminded her and she grimaced and adjusted her position.

'Ow. How many times are you going to say that?' she complained as her calves protested.

'Until you don't need reminding,' he said, and leant over to punch her lightly in the thigh. 'Next step is to tie lead weights to your boot heels.'

Rillirin opened her mouth to reply when Dom stiffened in the saddle and then tumbled out, making no effort to catch himself. His gelding reared and whinnied, hooves flashing as Dom's weight dragged it in a circle.

'Dom? Dom!'

Horses were pulling up all around them and Rillirin dropped her spear and threw herself from the saddle, Dalli a step behind. He was thrashing in the grass like a dog with a rabbit, sounds juddering from his mouth, eyes rolled up in his head.

'Lim,' Dalli screamed and then, 'get the horses back.' Wolves guided their skittsh mounts away, leaving Dom in the mud and slush. Dalli and Rillirin knelt either side of him, trying to still his limbs.

'Leave him,' Lim ordered, arriving at a run. 'You'll do more damage if you try and control it.' They let him go, sliding out of range of his arms, waiting for him to quiet.

'Little brother,' Lim said, his hand on Dom's chest, 'easy now, little brother. There you go. Ssh, now, ssh.'

'Beware the east,' Dom stuttered, his eyes opening on to a landscape only he could see, one blasted and desolate and reflected in his face. 'Beware the east and the poison of love. Poison,' he repeated. 'Enough to kill us all. Just one drop and the fire rages. Everything burns.'

Rillirin took Dom's mud-splattered hand and pressed it to her cheek. 'I'm here,' she whispered, 'I'm here, just breathe.' The man lying before her, mud smeared across his mouth and the tip of his nose, had nothing in him of the Dom she knew. His brown eyes were shards of pottery sunk in his head, broken and crazed and couldn't be put back together. But he clung to her hand as though it was a raft on a raging river, nostrils flaring as he sucked in air.

'Breathe, love,' she whispered, and bent down to press a kiss to his cheek, his lips. He tasted of metal and winter and rich earth, and he smelt of horses and fear and death. 'You're all right, I'm right here. I'm here.' She barely listened to the conversation going on above them.

'East, he said. Rivil's plans were to find allies in the east, remember?'

'Poison,' Sarilla said. 'Assassination, maybe?'

Rillirin looked up at that, met Lim's eyes for a second, and then Lim swore. 'Fucking hell. Rivil's going to kill the king.'

MACE

'Come on, you bastards. What are you up to?' Mace stood on the topmost level of the watchtower and raised his fist to the mountains looming over him as though he could shake the Mireces out of them. And yet nothing. Not a whisper, not a flicker of blue beneath the trees. Instead, the winter mocked him from its home in the rocks, blowing the scent of snow and cold stone into his face despite the dawning green of the plains behind him. He shivered.

'Sir? Captain Carter's back.'

'Excellent, excellent. Send her straight up.'

'Yes, sir.'

Mace had reached his office and tidied some papers before there was a knock on the door and Tara came in, leading Crys and Ash. Crys had a limp, a sling and an almost healed split lip. Mace gestured them to a seat and Crys sank into his gratefully, his free hand pressed to his hip.

'Report,' Mace said and braced himself. A variety of

277

emotions chased across his face as Tara spoke, with occasional interjections from Crys and Ash.

When they were done, he relaxed into his chair with a whoosh of expelled breath. 'I like it, I like it a lot,' he said. 'All except the part about Galtas being missing. No one's heard anything?'

'Not by the time we'd left. With luck the slimy little shit has been found and hanged.' Mace raised an eyebrow and Tara's lip curled. 'His behaviour was improper when he was here.'

Mace banged his fist on the table. 'I have told you to let me know if that happens, Captain,' he growled.

'I handled it. You had enough to worry about with the princes.'

Mace fought the urge to tear out his hair. *Will the woman ever bloody listen to a single godsdamn bloody order in her life?*

'Sir? I find myself without a Rank or formal instructions,' Crys said. 'I was sent here to keep out of Rivil's way, but I'd still like to do whatever I can to help. The Mireces are probably stupid enough to attack even when they know Rivil isn't coming. Do you think you'd be able to find a place for me?'

'Congratulations, Captain,' Mace said without hesitation. 'You're now a member of His Majesty's West Rank, the finest fighting force in all the world. Thank you for volunteering.'

Crys exchanged grins with Tara and Ash and managed a painful salute for Mace. 'Thank you, sir. I also still have Prince Janis's sword. What with one thing and another I never got to give it back, and if Rivil recognised it, he'd know I still lived.' He levered himself back out of his seat and unbuckled his belt. 'I think you should have it, sir.'

Mace's mouth dropped open. 'Me? I couldn't – that's a royal sword, Captain. I'll . . . I'll keep it safe somewhere. It'll have to be passed to the new king, when the court or Rastoth chooses one.' He laid the sword on his desk with great reverence. 'You're sniggering, Carter. Care to explain?'

'Your father's name came up during the discussion of a new heir,' Tara said. 'It occurred to me that you might be given that sword for real one day.'

Mace's stare was blank and went on for too long until Tara blushed and looked away. He sat back down. 'Captain Tailorson, visit the armoury when we're done here and find yourself a suitable replacement blade.'

'Yes, sir.'

'Ash, your assistance to the captains is recognised and appreciated. My father's correspondence authorises you to relate everything that happened in the capital to your people so they're aware. Please tell your chief we'll continue to sweep north of the Blood Pass Valley into Blackgate Woods. I understand your people will be south of the valley, between it and the River Gil. Please send word if any movement is spotted.'

Ash nodded, shook hands with Tara and Crys, and then rose. 'Of course, General. We'll stay in touch. Tara, Crys, a pleasure travelling with you. Stay out of trouble.'

Tara shooed him away. 'You first,' she said.

When he'd left, Mace rounded his desk and approached them both. He waved them back into their chairs. 'Sit, sit. Captain Tailorson, I had my doubts when I first met you, doubts about the story you were telling. But not any more. You've done a great service for this country by coming forward and telling us what you saw, by being prepared to testify against Rivil. Now, while I'm happy to recruit you into my Rank, a trial and your testimony may still be required, so I'll do my best to keep you out of trouble. However, I will need your written statement, signed and witnessed by myself and our priest, before the end of tomorrow.'

'Of course, sir, whatever you need. I've already provided one for your father, but it makes sense that you keep another here in case anything should happen.' He shifted in his chair, trying to get comfortable. 'I heard the priestess and the Mireces king, sir. They're in this for their gods, and the land and the glory are just an added bonus. My gut tells me they'll still come no matter what happens with Rivil and his alleged reinforcements. I'd be surprised if there wasn't at least one scrap between us and them.'

Mace rubbed his hands together. 'I'm counting on it,' he said grimly. 'A pitched battle is the one thing we've never managed to draw them into. Let's break the bastards once and for all.'

GALTAS

Second moon, eighteenth year of the reign of King Rastoth
East Rank Forts, Grazing Lands, Listran border

'Well, this is most unexpected. Most unexpected indeed.' General Skerris of the East Rank examined the document again, checked the prince's seal again, and then squinted at Galtas. Galtas gave him an easy smile.

The two thousand men of the main fort were drawn up in parade lines to welcome their noble visitor. No one had yet questioned why Galtas came alone, or without prior warning.

'His Highness will by now have been announced as heir to the throne of Rilpor,' he said, tapping his fingertips to his heart for Janis, 'and this knowledge has changed the man he is forever. Rivil is to be king, General. Gone is the prankster, the affable prince whiling away his time with soldiers and merchants. Prince Rivil is determined to do justice to his brother's memory and his father's legacy. And so he has asked me to inspect the Ranks on his behalf, and acquire personal assurances of loyalty from them. No doubt the

Crown's announcement of Prince Janis's tragic demise mentioned the king's ongoing health?'

Galtas leant closer and Skerris did likewise, pulling worriedly at his enormous moustache, all three of his chins wobbling with concern. 'Between you and me, General, Janis's death has broken our king. The royal physician fears for his health.' Galtas lowered his voice further. 'His sanity, even. Who knows what orders he may give? And Prince Rivil fears he is not ready to lead, that he will never be ready. But he knows that the time may come, sooner than any of us would wish, when he may have to act to curb the king's . . . wilder impulses. He is keen to reassure the Ranks that he will never act in anything but Rilpor's best interests. Also, he would dearly like to know that he has the support of the greatest men of this country should that unfortunate time ever arrive.'

Skerris's piggy eyes widened when he realised the prince counted him among such men. 'But of course, of course,' he wheezed, adjusting the wide leather belt over his considerable gut.

Galtas glanced down again, reassuring himself it was still there. Skerris had two belt pouches. Two. The skin on Galtas's face felt tight, as though he'd been burnt, and his heart was thundering. *Now or never.*

'We must do all we can to aid the prince in his duty to the gods,' Galtas said and tapped his fingernails on the buckle of his own belt. Skerris looked. Galtas wore two belt pouches.

The fat man stilled, only his fingers twitching, and then he met Galtas's eye with an expression of polite interest. 'We all serve the gods,' he said.

Shit. 'We all have a path to tread,' Galtas tried, 'and His Highness has set himself a mighty task.' *Well, if he doesn't get that, he isn't what I think he is.* The weather was mild but Galtas shivered. He pulled the pouch off his belt and clinked it idly in his hand, outwardly a bored nobleman doing his master's duty. The nails it contained tinkled together, a deeper chiming than you got from coin.

Skerris heaved out a breath and glanced around, beckoning to his senior staff. Galtas took a step back, dropping the pouch and grabbing for his sword. 'My feet are on the Path,' Skerris said, and bent down to pick up the pouch. He passed it reverently back.

'My feet are on the Path,' recited every one of his officers.

'Thank the gods,' Galtas said, his voice shaky. 'My feet are on the Path as well, and so are the prince's. The gods have a task for the East Rank, General, if you've a mind to listen.'

'We live to serve, my lord,' Skerris rumbled, 'and if the task is what I think it is, then the Rank belongs to the prince and we'll march where he commands.'

Galtas adjusted his eye patch, impressed. 'That is welcome news, General. All your men are believers?'

'Oh, no. But leave that to me. When the time comes, they will be, reluctantly.' He tapped the side of his nose. 'But reluctant or not, a soul once given cannot be ungiven. They will serve.'

Galtas stared past the officers at the men standing at attention. 'How?' he murmured.

Skerris gave him an evil little grin at odds with the bumbling, blubbery facade he cultivated and jerked a thumb at himself. 'Born and raised on the Path, milord. I'm an anointed priest of the Dark Lady.' Galtas's mouth dropped open and then he scanned the officers around him. Skerris nodded. 'Converted and blessed them all myself,' he confirmed. 'Sanctified in blood, sacrifices performed. Loyal to the gods, loyal to me, and now, without reservation, loyal to Prince Rivil.'

Galtas clapped him on one immense shoulder and grinned at the others. 'Let's retire somewhere more private, General,' he said. 'We have much to discuss and a short timeline. The Mireces will be invading soon.' He laughed at the expressions on their faces. 'Much has happened in the last months, my good General. More than you know.'

DURDIL

*Second moon, eighteenth year of the reign of King Rastoth
The palace, Rilporin, Wheat Lands*

'You are looking well today, Your Majesty,' Durdil lied. Rastoth was slumped in a chair in his private audience chamber, his mourning sash stained with soup and three days' growth of grey beard straggling like lichen across the crags of his face. He looked awful and everyone knew it, including, probably, Rastoth himself.

The scarlet of the sashes they all wore was a note of unruly cheer in the general gloom of the chamber and the atmosphere it contained. It hinted at a spring that two of the occupants, at least, dreaded.

'Where's the traitor?' Rastoth snapped and Durdil saw Rivil flinch.

'Lord Galtas Morellis?' the Commander clarified and Rivil's lips turned white. The prince was seated at Rastoth's desk, ostensibly checking his correspondence. Durdil had already been through it and removed anything he thought Rivil shouldn't see. Which was most of it. He'd left a

285

particular report in there, though. Baiting the hook and, perhaps, taking a risk he shouldn't.

Hallos was seated at another table in the window, grinding herbs in a small mortar. Another concoction to bolster the king's failing body, no doubt. Durdil wasn't sure there were any herbs left in all Gilgoras that could heal the king now.

'Are there any other traitors?' Rastoth demanded and Durdil blinked. *He's having a rational day? Thank the gods.*

'None that we know of yet,' Durdil said. 'The latest report from Major Renik, who is leading the hunt, confirms the man hasn't been seen in any of the towns or villages of the Wheat Lands.' Durdil put his hands behind his back and shifted slightly to get a better view of the room. 'They're heading east to see if they can pick up a trail on the Tears or into the Grazing Lands.'

Rivil was ready this time and gave no indication of alarm. A moment later, however, he raised a sheaf of papers and squinted at them; then he placed them carefully back on the desk. He tapped the topmost page. 'What is this, Commander?' he asked in a friendly tone.

Durdil moved to stand behind him and looked over his shoulder. 'What is what, Your Highness?' *Gods, I hate subterfuge. I'm no good at it and there's no honour in it. The world has changed since I was young.*

'This report,' Rivil said, picking it up again, 'regarding my mother the queen's murder. You wrote it?'

'I did, Your Highness. That investigation remains ongoing, as you know, and His Majesty receives regular updates.'

'I see. You have written, and I quote, "query Lord Galtas Morellis" where you discuss suspects. His is the only name, in fact, on what is then a very short list.' Rivil swivelled in his chair; his face had the faintest hint of red in it. His eyes were very cold. Other than that, he oozed calm detachment.

He was a better actor than Durdil, but then, he needed to be.

'Ah, that's where that report got to,' Durdil said as Rastoth's head rose from his chest. 'I'd thought it was still in my chambers. Must have got mixed up with some other papers.' The lie slid cool and easy from his tongue and his rigid honour creaked in protest. He held out his hand for it but Rivil didn't let go.

'You think my friend killed my mother?' Rivil asked and now there was a tremor in his voice. Anger? Fear? Guilt, perhaps? 'Why in the gods' names would you think that? Galtas has never been anything but loyal.'

'Of course,' Hallos put in and Rivil twitched, 'he knew of the placement of the soldiers' bodies, didn't he, Durdil? And you said that information was confidential. You said nobody knew that, not even the princes. Most strange.'

Rivil stood, forcing Durdil back a pace. 'This is ridiculous. Soldiers talk. Galtas spends time in their company. I imagine most of the Palace Rank knows the details of Mother's death.'

'Galtas killed my Marisa?' Rastoth asked, and the madness in his voice had been replaced by icy rage. His fingers were claws on the arms of the chair, and while his eyes were still watery, they pierced Rivil like a sword.

'No, Father, he did not! Galtas was with me in the tavern, don't you remember, that's where we'd been all evening. I told you. So did he.' He pointed an accusatory finger at Durdil. 'The Commander questioned us, like we were common fucking criminals! Like he doubted us even then. And now, all this time later, he still suspects us. It's an outrage.'

Rastoth waved him away so he could focus on Durdil. 'Galtas killed Marisa and you suspected him, so he went to your chambers searching for the report and Wheeler disturbed him and he killed him, then fled.'

'No!' Rivil shouted.

'That is a very interesting theory, Your Majesty,' Durdil said. 'It would appear to fit with the facts of both cases, at least for now.'

Rivil stared between them, wild and furious. *Come on, make a mistake, Rivil, give me something, anything I can work with. Even a hint.*

'Lord Morellis is my friend,' the prince said, smoothing his coat, his sash. 'He has served me well and faithfully. I do not for one second believe he could kill my mother, or Major Wheeler. You are mistaken in this, all of you.'

'Would you swear by the gods he had nothing to do with it?' Durdil pushed, knowing he was showing some of his hand, that Rivil would see his suspicions stretched to more than just Galtas. It'd be worth it, though. He wouldn't swear on the gods if he knew the words were lies.

Rivil stared at him for a second and then put the crumpled report back on the desk. 'You have offended me, Commander,' he said, 'and you have questioned the honour of my friend. I do not need to swear on the gods because I know you are wrong and that you will be proved so when we find Wheeler's killer.' He shook his head. 'You have all offended me.' He tugged at his sash. 'Here, now, when we should be united in grief, you seek to drive a wedge between my father and me.' He lowered his voice. 'How could you?'

Rivil made for the door and Rastoth half rose from his chair, one hand out to his son.

Durdil could have applauded the performance. Instead he spoke. 'I apologise, Your Highness. But for now, Lord Morellis must remain our chief suspect in both cases until we can definitively prove otherwise. A murder has taken place in the palace itself. As we did after the queen's death, I have ordered Fifth Circle to be shut to all comings and goings. The king's Personals are in control and all nobles, functionaries and Palace Rankers have been ejected. We are all required to stay within the palace walls until such time as Lord Morellis is brought before the king for questioning. But be assured, we will continue to pursue all inquiries in case your friend is indeed innocent.'

Rivil's fingers tightened on the door latch and then he spun back into the room. 'We are your prisoners?' he demanded, striding towards Durdil. 'You would lock us up?'

Durdil plastered polite concern on to his face. 'You are heir to the Throne of Rilpor now, Your Highness. Your safety and that of the king is my only concern. I fear you would not be adequately protected should you wander the city. Or travel further afield.'

'Be calm, Rivil,' Rastoth said, 'Durdil has my full support in this. We will do as you say, Commander, until Galtas is found and tried. Or any other suspect,' the old man added as Rivil's mouth opened to complain.

'And what are we to do while we are incarcerated?' Rivil asked in icy tones.

Durdil inclined his head. 'I would not presume to say, Your Highness.' *But with the Personal Guards in charge, your heretical honour guard won't be visiting, that I can promise you.*

Rivil's nostrils flared, but he held his tongue, bowed to Rastoth and exited the room.

And now we wait, Durdil thought, wiping the sweat from his palms on to his trousers. Hallos gave him a tiny nod of approval. *And we see who blinks first.*

THE BLESSED ONE

'These are the last days of the life we have known. Soon, we will all leave these mountains that have both culled us and nurtured us. Until then, you have a sacred duty. Every warrior, every boy and every old man goes to war. Only the cripples and the slaves will be left, along with Pask, my priest, to tend to your souls.'

He'd do more than that, of course, but the women must feel this was their chance at freedom. Secrets would spill when they thought there were no ears to hear. It was an easy way to discover the loyalty of the war chiefs, the warriors, when what they confessed to their women in the dark was repeated in the light.

Lanta surveyed the women of the village gathered before her, the life consorts secure in their power and position, the rest eyeing each other already. She'd given the same speech to the women in Cat Valley, Falcon's Landing and Crow Crag on the way back along the Sky Path. She'd ensured

290

the priest at each village understood his duty. When the men marched to war, old grudges would be settled and some of the women would die. It was their way. It was the Lady's will.

'We cannot say how long it will be before we send for you, but never doubt that we will. Preserve the children – whatever feuds fester among yourselves, the children are not to be harmed, for they are our future. Pask will know and Pask will inform me if any die. Those responsible will follow them into the Afterworld, and not gloriously.'

The threat was effective and Lanta, her point made, relaxed and gifted them with a smile, a rare indulgence. 'We march to glory, women. Many will fall, their deaths wetting our path, washing the veil until it vanishes like mist in the sun. We are the ice that cracks rocks. We are the wind that fells trees and the storm that batters all life.' She raised her arms and the women copied her, swept up in her passion. 'We are the Mireces, chosen of the gods, and our feet are on the Path.'

'Our feet are on the Path,' the women shouted.

Lanta lowered her arms and then raised one hand in supplication. 'Do not let our victorious warriors return to claim their women and find only slaughter. Do not let your slaves rise against your rule. Do not kill each other to be consort to a man who may not return.'

The longhouse was silent now and Lanta knew the men listened as well as the women. The dogs had slunk beneath the tables, unwilling to attract her ire, and the slaves had melted from her view. Smoke from the central fire wended its way towards them and tickled the back of her throat. Lanta ignored it.

'If you are unsure of the subjugation of any slave, bring them to me before we leave and I will sacrifice them to aid our war. Do not spare the lash or the club once we are gone, and do not let them rise.'

They all knew the stories of villages going on raids and returning to find their women and children dead and their slaves vanished into the mountains. It hadn't happened in decades, but the threat remained.

Lanta gave them another smile and the women smiled back, reassured. 'The gods are with us in war, and they are with you, who secure our future through your children. We go to claim what is ours that they may live in the warm lands. We go to claim what is the gods' and ensure Their return. We will live reflected in Their glory and we will die sure in the knowledge that the Afterworld awaits us. What have we to fear? The Dark Path is our journey, the Red Joy is our ending.' She raised her arms once more. 'And the return of the gods is our holy purpose.'

The cheers came from behind as well as in front and Lanta turned and extended her arms to include the warriors in her blessing. Throughout the longhouse, men and women fell to their knees like wheat before the scythe.

The gods demanded victory. Lanta would give it to Them.

DOM

Second moon, eighteenth year of the reign of King Rastoth
Watcher village, northern Wolf Lands, Gilgoras foothills,
Rilporian border

It was good to be back under trees, despite the circumstances.
The nagging ache behind Dom's right eye was becoming an
old friend, never really gone, and he'd swear sometimes it
saw things the left didn't. But that was impossible, wasn't
it? It was just flickers of light through the tree branches
swaying above, the sudden dart of birds.

Dom sat on a horsehide on a rock outside a ramshackle
dwelling. They normally spent the winters south of the River
Gil and summers north of it. They weren't supposed to be
here yet and no one had come to repair the houses before
they arrived. Still, it wouldn't much matter once the war
started.

He stared around the village, crammed with almost every
Wolf they had who wasn't on patrol or sentry duty. All were
busy with weapons or supplies, an air of quiet industry and
grim-faced necessity surrounding them. A breeze tore the

flames of his fire into rags of yellow, flinging them at the sky.

'Rillirin's the herald, bringing the war to us,' he muttered, tapping his fingers against the ragged knees of his trousers. 'But more than that. Death to love and love to death. Don't know. There's poison in Rilporin, maybe the poison of words in the wrong ear. Lies and deceit. Or maybe the poison is in the blood – is Rivil killing his father and seizing the throne?' He pursed his lips. 'But then why ally with the Mireces? Why fight a battle you can win with assassination? Killing Janis brought the throne one step closer. Killing Rastoth hands it to him.'

'But it doesn't bring us back, does it, my love?'

Dom started to his feet and dragged a knife out of his belt. 'Who spoke?' he demanded, lurching in a circle and startling a blackbird out of the leaf litter. A few faces turned to him but none looked alarmed. He was alone.

'Oh, you're never alone, my love. Not truly.'

He recognised it this time, both the voice and where it came from, and sheathed his dagger. 'Great. Now I'm hearing things,' he said, trying to make light of it.

The Dark Lady laughed, low and inviting. 'You've heard things all your life, little Calestar, heard and seen. Now you're just hearing them more clearly, waking and sleeping. Besides, you enjoy my visits, don't you?'

There was a patch of darkness stealing through the trees to the north. *Just cloud shadow, that's all.* He refused to look into the sky to see if he was right. *Just a cloud.* Dom sat back down and stretched his hands to the fire, ignoring Her last comment, Her presence in his skull and against his skin.

'Right. Rillirin brings us the war and Rivil allies with the Mireces to spill enough blood to tear the veil and bring back the brother-fucking Dark Lady and Her pet idiot.' He paused. 'What, no laughter this time? I thought it was funny. But blood alone isn't enough to tear the veil, it can't be. Blood's been spilt for centuries and the veil has remained intact. So why this war? Why now?'

Dom wasn't sure if he was asking Her or thinking aloud, but he got more than he was expecting with Her response. Pain seared up his right arm and into his shoulder, neck and chest. He bent double, gasping, clenching his arm between his thighs. Pale flames licked along his wrist, almost invisible in the sunlight, touching nothing but his arm, burning and burrowing into the bone. He could smell cooking meat.

'Because of you,' hissed a voice right into his ear. 'Because a calestar swore a blood oath of vengeance and thinned the veil for us, his treachery to his gods the ultimate heresy. You did this, my love. It's all you. When you break, the veil breaks, and then you'll have no one to blame but yourself.'

'No,' Dom gasped. 'No, that's not right. That's not why—'

The voice, presence and flames flickered and vanished, leaving Dom huddled into himself, stunned and racked with pain. 'Not true. It's not true,' he whispered. There was laughter on the wind.

'I'm back. Look what – Are you all right?'

Dom forced himself to sit up and smile. 'Fine, just a bit of cramp. It's the cold. So come on, what have you got?'

Rillirin held up a brace of fat ducks. 'Dinner,' she announced and patted the sling at her belt. 'Who needs bows and arrows?' she added smugly. 'Oh, I saw Lim. Ash is back from the West Forts and the general and Lim agree it'll probably be soon. While that soldier, Crys, didn't hear the exact date Corvus and Rivil agreed, he said there was a sense of urgency about everything they did after Janis.'

'I'm glad Mace agrees,' Dom said absently. 'That ties in

with my own . . . understanding. And at least we don't have to try and convince the West Rank to move on the word of a calestar.'

'Maybe if they knew it was you, they'd be more likely to believe the knowings,' Rillirin ventured, propping her spear against the rock.

Dom snorted. 'No thanks. The fewer people who know I'm the freak with the visions, the better. What else did Lim say?' he asked before she could protest.

'That we'll be in the party setting out in the morning to take watch at Blood Pass Valley.'

'Good. Finally get to do something useful.'

She dropped the ducks in the snow and bent to graze a kiss on his cheek; Dom turned at the last second and their mouths met. Rillirin jerked back in surprise, but then giggled. 'Every time,' she muttered, shaking her head.

'You should stop letting me then if you don't want me to,' Dom said, waggling his eyebrows.

Rillirin waved a hand in dismissal. 'Oh, I didn't say that,' she said, cheeks red, then surprised him with another kiss, a little longer this time and tasting like snow. Butterflies made their way through his belly.

Death to love? he thought as Rillirin settled beside him and passed him a duck. They plucked in silence. *Please don't let it be this she kills.* He pressed his thigh to hers, relishing her warmth as the pain in his arm subsided into a ferocious itching that made his fingers twitch.

He was losing himself in the pleasure of her company when fingers stroked down his back and a laugh sounded low in his ear. 'She'll never compete with me, my love,' a voice whispered. 'And you know it.'

Dom blinked and closed his right eye, fingers spasming in the feathers. Rillirin didn't notice. He counted to ten and forced the eyelid open, breathing deep through the pain, pushing back the dread, trying his hardest to forget what he knew, what he'd seen. What he had to do.

Don't break, Dom. Don't ever break.

TARA

*Third moon, eighteenth year of the reign of King Rastoth
Final Falls, the Gil-beside Road, Gilgoras foothills,
Rilporian border*

Tara felt sorry for Major Costas as the sentries stationed at the Final Falls and Costas's Hundred mingled. The sentries were from Fort Four and Costas operated out of Two, so the gossip mills were running overtime.

'Costas? What kind of a name is that? Sounds Mireces to me,' one sentry whispered, casting covert glances at him. Costas sat his horse in silence, letting it drink from the frothing, icy Gil spurting the taste of winter out of the mountains into the early spring air.

'He says his mother was Listran.'

'And mine's the Dancer!'

'Enough,' Tara snapped and the men shut up. She'd be the next topic of conversation, no doubt. Mace Koridam's pet project, his secret lover who pretended to be an officer to stay at his side. She knew them all.

She glanced at the major again, sitting painfully erect in

298

his saddle. He looked up the steep, rocky riverbed and then urged his horse into the pool and across to the other bank. Tara frowned and followed his gaze, scanning the steep, twisting path next to the river.

Tara turned to glare briefly at the men making coarse jokes about Costas and his horse; then she urged her own into the river and across. 'Something wrong, Major?' she asked and noticed Costas's lips tighten. He had such a painful inferiority complex that he thought having a woman assigned his second in command for this recon was an insult. More the other way around. She was twice the officer he was. What did he have to worry about? So what if his parents weren't noble, if they'd saved up for years to buy him a commission? He should be bloody proud of that.

'Up there. I saw a movement around those three rocks by the lip, the ones leaning together like an old man hunched over. Do you see?'

Tara squinted up the steep-sided ravine. 'I see three boulders piled together,' she said doubtfully. 'But nothing else.'

'Well, I definitely saw movement, like someone ducking out of sight. And you can get all the way up into Mireces territory along here.'

'Yes, sir, but it'd be difficult to move a large force down along the river.'

'I didn't say it would be easy,' Costas said, gazing upwards. 'Get a couple of men to go up to the three stones and scout around, please.'

'Yes, sir,' Tara said and wheeled her horse, plunging back into the pool. 'You and you' – she picked the ones who'd been most vocal about the major – 'take a wander up to the lip where the river becomes the falls. Suspicion of movement.'

The two men didn't dare grumble until they were out of her earshot, but she could sense their hostility as they waded into the Gil up to their waists. *Bet that's chilly.* They slogged past Costas and started gingerly over the spray-slick rocks on to the foot of the Road. Tara watched them for a second, and then slid her gaze up. Her eyes widened. Shit. Costas was right.

'Come back,' Tara hissed, her fists clenched on the reins. 'Get your arses back here.' *Issue the order, damn you.* It was pathetic and petty but, regardless of the circumstances, Costas would have her flogged if she gave an order in his stead.

But he'd seen it too, thank the gods. The major managed a 'Hey!' before his stallion coughed and stumbled. It grunted, staggered again, and went to its knees on the far side of the river. Tara caught a glimpse of blue fletching sticking from its chest.

Arrows. Mireces. Oh shit.

Above them, men in blue came leaping down the rocks, scrambling, falling, screaming in their haste.

'Move,' Tara yelled, a flogging be fucked, and then they were all shouting, lining the bank and screaming for their men. Costas's face was a picture of pure, baffled astonishment as he struggled up from his horse, nearly taking a hoof to the skull as it kicked. The soldiers Tara had sent over showed no such confusion, leaping over the stones and rocks and leaving Costas gaping behind them.

One of them fell, arrows in his back like spines, and then the other at the edge of the pool, landing with a splash before bobbing jauntily back up to the surface. Costas stared at the body, his mouth open, and Tara urged her horse into the river. 'Major? Major, move your shitting arse,' she screamed.

He turned as though he were in a dream and she waved frantically at him. A second later reality kicked in and his face drained of blood.

'Fuck,' he squeaked and plunged forward into the Gil, went to his knees in the battering water, drank a mouthful as an arrow whickered overhead, lurched up, gasped and flailed on. 'Take cover,' he roared in a voice Tara had never heard from him before.

His Hundred and the sentries scattered behind boulders, shrubs and trees. 'Return fire,' he commanded as Tara urged her mount deeper into the river. She rode for him, reaching down to take his hand, and a giggle burst from her lips when she saw the wet wool of his breeches sagging from his arse. *Mooning the Mireces. One way to make a name for yourself.*

Costas grabbed her stirrup and she turned for the bank, head hunched between her shoulder blades and her horse providing Costas with cover. It screamed and she looked back to see an arrow embedded deep in its haunch. It was slowing, limping through the water, hooves slipping on the rocks, and Tara kicked free of the stirrups and threw herself from the saddle, grabbing Costas by a fistful of tunic and splashing through the water to the dubious safety of the rocks.

They crouched behind a boulder with a raw recruit, who was crying, and a sentry coolly stringing his bow. Tara's own bow and quiver were on the saddle of her horse, and Costas only had his sword. She put a hand on the recruit's shoulder while Costas, hopefully, assessed their position. 'What's your name, lad?' she asked as though they were out at drill and the boy had missed his step in the march.

'Poll,' the boy squeaked, grey beneath his freckles.

'Well, Poll, what say you string that bow and make these bastards pay, eh?' she said and swallowed sour spit. Costas looked seconds away from puking too. 'Come on, now, I know you're a fine shot, and I've heard tell you're a hell of a boar-hunter. Everyone reacts the same to an arrow in the guts, lad, so how about you start shooting?'

Poll nodded convulsively and grabbed an arrow to hold it shaking on the string. He whooped in a breath and his eyes narrowed, and then he drew smoothly and evenly to his lips, held, and released. Costas's head darted around his side of the boulder and a Mireces collapsed screaming, the arrow through his right eye. He pounded Poll on the back and gave Tara a single nod of acknowledgement.

'That's it,' he shouted, 'now keep it up.' Poll managed a grin as he drew again, sighted, and let fly. Costas grabbed Tara's shoulder, hauled her back to give Poll and the sentry room.

'Carter, we're isolated and spread out. I need a defensive wedge or we'll be picked off one at a time.' He eyed the landscape. 'There, that half-circle of stones. That's where we'll make our stand. You signal those men' – he pointed – 'and I'll tell these. We'll draw fire when we start moving, so the men already over there will need to provide covering fire. Do you understand?'

'Yes, sir,' Tara said and half saluted, relief swamping her guts that he was taking charge. That he was giving the right orders.

At the signal, the men furthest away moved first, sprinting and weaving from one side of the clearing to the other. The Mireces were too far away to do more than fire a few hasty arrows. This time. When the runners were settled, they nocked and waited for the next wave, started loosing as soon as four men broke from cover and began sprinting. They lost one that time, an arrow in his spine that took his legs from him. He fell face down and screaming and Costas started to move. Tara dragged him back.

'You can't save him. Save the others. Save the boy here'

– she indicated Poll, whose face had paled at the screams but who was still managing to loose – 'and for fuck's sake save me. Him you can't.'

'Fuck!' Costas yelled and then risked a look again. The enemy was crossing the water; they were out of time. 'Right, go now,' he shouted. Poll and the sentry had time for one more shot each and then the foursome burst from behind the boulder and began to run. Arrows bounced off the ground around them and one parted Tara's hair, but then they were diving head first into the shelter of the stones, heedless of the bruises or the men they fell on to.

'Archers to the fore, two ranks, one kneeling, one standing. Those without bows give them shield cover. Loose in waves on my command. Get a rhythm going and keep it going until they stop, reach us, or you run out of shafts. When they do reach us, it'll be hand-to-hand but we fight in rank the way we've been trained. Every man supports his comrade. If a gap appears in the front rank, second rank moves to fill it.'

It's what Tara would have ordered. She drew her sword and eyed the oncoming mass of men. This wasn't a raid; this wasn't a scouting party. Costas had a hundred men and the sentries numbered twenty. The Mireces came in their thousands.

This was the godsdamned invasion they'd expected to come down the Blood Pass. Only reason Mace had sent so few of them out here was because this was the route the Mireces weren't supposed to be taking.

Costas took a deep breath and met the eyes of as many of the men as he could manage. 'There's a lot of them, lads,' he said and got a wry chuckle. 'But we hold them here for as long as we can. Tara, you're taking word to the Rank. Go now, and Dancer go with you.'

What? 'Major, I can fight.'

'No, you're going. We'll give you as much time as we can, time you're already wasting.'

'If this is because I'm a wom—' she started, fear making her furious.

Costas glared her into silence. 'This is because you're the fastest runner I have and you know the route. Now bloody well run.' Costas pushed her out of the front rank and took her shield, holding it for young Poll. The others stared at her and then shuffled into place, cutting her out.

'Dancer's grace,' Tara said. She spun on her heel and crept off through the scrub, her throat strangely tight.

'All right, lads,' she heard Costas say almost cheerfully, 'we're here for one reason only.'

'King and country?' a soldier asked and Costas laughed.

'Fuck King Rastoth,' he shouted, 'we're here to ensure Carter gets back home. Now, the Dancer's watching, and She's waiting for us, but I say let's make Her wait a little longer, because Carter's running like a scared hare right now, and if we give her the chance, she's going to bring the Wolves and the rest of the West Rank back here and they're going to carve this bunch of motherfuckers' – his voice rose into a scream – 'into bloody ribbons.'

'Cos-tas! Cos-tas! Cos-tas!' they yelled as Tara made it to the treeline. She looked back and the Hundred were clashing their swords on their shields in time to the chant. She could see even more Mireces from here and knew they'd all be dead inside an hour.

'Heroes of the West Rank,' she heard Costas's voice, faint on the wind, 'it's been a pleasure, you bastards.'

Tara wasted – or didn't, depending on your view – a few seconds saluting the almost-fallen, then she ducked into the trees and started to run.

RILLIRIN

Third moon, eighteenth year of the reign of King Rastoth
Blood Pass Valley, Gilgoras Mountains, Rilporian border

'Still no movement?'

'Nothing. It's empty, Chief. They're not coming.' Ash scratched his back, stretching. Long time sitting watching. 'We've been here for days. Maybe Dom got it wrong.'

'Dom didn't get it wrong,' Dom said without rancour, not shifting his gaze from the pale slash of the valley.

'They're coming,' Lim agreed. 'There's Crys's testimony too.'

'And you couldn't possibly disbelieve anything pretty-boy has to say, could you, Ash?' Dom said, and now he did look at Ash. Ash grinned and gave him the finger.

'Have we heard anything from the West Rank?' Lim asked, worry etching lines into his forehead.

'Only that they continue to patrol the plain and Blackgate Woods. No movement there either. Haven't found anyone using the drop caches. Haven't found the damn caches either.'

Lim grunted. 'Neither have we. Your opinion?' he asked

and Rillirin looked away from the pass and at the men watching her.

Her? She flushed, and then lifted her chin. She knew the Mireces better than they did, better than anyone. And she'd fucked up once. She wouldn't let anyone else die because she was too cowardly to speak. 'They're coming. If Dom says they're on their way, I believe him. But not just that,' she added as Ash rolled his eyes, 'it's third moon. The weather's mild enough now that they could raid. The only reason they wouldn't take advantage of an early thaw is if they were planning a big push and needed to gather the villages.'

'You're sure?'

'I'm sure. Liris used to tell me stories sometimes, when he was drunk. Stories of great raids, of full-scale battles fought in the old days. He called them glory-memories. They're so old even the old men weren't part of them. There was always talk of forging a new glory-memory, but Liris was against it. Too lazy, some said, but gossip from Crow Crag always said Corvus was ambitious. He'll want a glory-memory of his own. Plus, the Blessed One – I mean Lanta – she said they were recruiting a powerful man in Rilpor who would do more for the cause than Liris ever had. We know that much has come true. There's no way she'll pass up this chance now. Even if Corvus decided not to invade, she could probably get enough fanatics to follow her and come herself.'

Dom got that faraway look again. 'They're coming with everything they've got,' he said. 'Blood oaths and sacrifices and the Dark Lady's blessing. No quarter, and no prisoners. They're coming.'

The little group blinked and looked up the valley one more time in silence. They were high up in the foothills where the wind was still sharp and the trees grew twisted from its constant force.

'What about the Gil-beside Road?' asked Rillirin. It niggled that all their attention was focused on the Blood Pass. The obvious choice. *Corvus is clever enough not to be predictable. He knows all the ways down from the Sky Path.*

'They couldn't bring a full army down the Gil-beside,' Ash said. 'It's too narrow, too dangerous. It would mean they couldn't bring packhorses or mules, siege weapons, wagons. They'd be hauling everything by hand.'

'So it's unlikely,' Lim finished and Rillirin stared at the patchy snow and greening grass.

'But not impossible? Difficult, yes, but if you wanted to take a superior force by surprise, it would be an option.'

Lim grunted. 'No, not impossible. But we already have patrols out that way and Mace has a score of men camped at the Final Falls. We'd hear from someone if movement was spotted.'

His words were counterpointed by a faint horn call drifting on the breeze. Lim's eyes snapped to Rillirin. She nodded convulsively, her chest tight. 'That's them. That's a Mireces cow horn.'

'The straight advance after all. Can't say I'm not relieved,' Lim said.

'At least the waiting's over,' Dom said, but his shoulders were tense, worried.

'Ash, Dalli, eyes on the pass. I need to know numbers. Dalli, it'll take you two days to reach the West Rank, so try and get an estimate before you go. Ash, I'll send someone to relieve you at dusk. We want eyes on them constantly. We'll evacuate the village and stage at the charcoal pits at the edge of the valley, ready to move when the Rank gets there. You know the place?' Ash nodded. 'Good. Do not engage.' Lim's voice was fierce and the pair nodded, settling down in the lee of a fallen tree to watch.

'Everyone else, back to the village to help move supplies,' Lim said, clapped the sentries on their backs and loped off in the endless, mile-eating stride of the Wolves, Dom matching his pace, Rillirin crashing along behind.

Lim pulled ahead and so he didn't see Dom stumble, missing his footing on the slope. He grunted and limped a few strides before shaking off the pain and carrying on, but that wasn't what stopped Rillirin from going to his aid. It was the fact he was talking to himself, a heated, one-sided conversation with a voice only he could hear.

'No, I won't tell them that, I won't tell them anything,' he hissed. 'No, I don't. Stop calling me that.' Dom grunted and clutched his right arm to his chest as he ran. 'Fine, I promise. Just stop hurting me,' he said and then glanced back, saw Rillirin watching him and forced a smile.

Rillirin didn't smile back.

DOM

*Third moon, eighteenth year of the reign of King Rastoth
Charcoal pit camp, Blood Pass Valley, Mount Gil foothills,
Rilporian border*

It was dark when Dom woke. The cavern echoed with
bouncing, rushing laughter that slithered clammy fingers
beneath his clothes. He shuddered and pinched the inside of
his thigh to wake himself. Dream thigh. No luck.

As always, She was standing behind him, wearing a gown
that revealed more than it hid; it clung to Her curves and
stirred in the hot breeze to show flashes of leg and belly,
the dark curve of one erect nipple. Dom swallowed and
concentrated on Her right ear. It seemed the safest place to
look.

'We meet again, Calestar. Despite all your protestations,
waking and sleeping, you keep on coming back. Tell me
why.' He didn't – couldn't – answer and She smiled, reached
out Her left hand to touch the bracelet of scars around his
right wrist. He yelped and tried to pull away, but Her grip
was steel and the scars burnt a fierce red, an inner glow that

309

coursed fire through his veins. He ground his teeth together, fists balled.

'What, no screams this time?' She laughed and the flare of pain increased. 'You owe me screams, remember? You owe me everything.'

'Only until my oath is fulfilled,' Dom said through gritted teeth, tears in his eyes. 'Once I find Hazel's killers, I'm free.' The Dark Lady pouted like a spoilt but dangerous, oh-so dangerous, child. She released him and flounced away a step.

He bent over, arm between his knees. 'Dream,' he muttered between pants, 'just a dream.'

The goddess's laughter pealed off the rock as She bent down to see into his face. 'Do you really think pain like this is a dream?' She hissed, and for a moment he was sure Her tongue forked like a serpent's. Her golden eyes bored into his. 'Do you?' She asked again, almost puzzled, as the wreaths of fire flickered again up his arm.

'Wake up now,' Dom gasped, ignoring the smell of burning flesh, 'just wake up.' When he was a boy of thirteen he'd upturned a cooking pot on his bare foot. That sizzling, branding, burrowing pain was the worst burn he'd ever suffered. It was nothing like this. He bit his tongue and forced himself upright, swallowing screams. He wouldn't bow to Her.

'You are awake, Calestar,' the Dark Lady said, reaching out to his arm again. The flames danced over Her skin and She shivered with pleasure. 'You're as awake as you'll ever be worshipping that old hag. You're through the veil now, my love. You're in my world.' She gripped his biceps and dragged him towards Her so that their lips touched as She talked, breasts and belly moulding against him. Fire rippled around them and through the crackle and below Her voice he could hear screaming. It might have been his.

'I could give you such power, power you've never even imagined. I could take your foretelling and polish it into gold. You could see everything the world has to offer, see it and make yourself rich, powerful, ruler of the whole world. People would worship you, flock to hear your predictions. Women throw themselves at you,' She murmured, one hand cupping him. He gagged even as he stirred.

'Such power. And such pleasure. You could charge them any price, ask anything in return for your visions. I'd even take away the pain, so that you could simply reach out and pluck the future from the shadows like a man picking an apple. Don't you want that? Don't you want . . . this? Me?' She tightened Her fingers on him.

Dom leant back and looked into Her eyes. He could see all She promised, all that and more. His hips moved and She moaned, Her free hand sliding across his back. Images danced in his skull, of him in a crown, foreseeing flood and famine and being able to counter both, of knowing how to defeat an enemy before they even attacked, of who was responsible for Hazel and their child's death. It was all there, just out of reach. She could give him everything.

He leant in and kissed Her, felt the hot press of Her tongue into his mouth. He thought of Rillirin. And bit.

Dom thrashed upright with a scream, pushing with one hand, gagging and scrubbing the other over his mouth. The taste of blood was strong and he couldn't see: hair in his eyes. He scraped it clear and screamed again when he saw a figure looming over him; he stumbled to his feet, fingers scrabbling for his sword.

'Dom, it's us, Sarilla, Rillirin, all of us,' Sarilla said. 'You're safe, at the charcoal pits by the valley, remember?'

'What?'

'You're safe.'

'Sarilla?'

'Yes, Dom, Sarilla.' She held out a hand and Dom shied away. 'Sit down. Talk.'

Dom hesitated and then complied, eyes darting around the firelit camp, right hand cradled against his chest. He wiped a hand over his face, felt wet on his cheeks and sank back into his blankets. 'Didn't mean to wake you,' he mumbled. 'Can't get comfortable.'

'Start talking,' Sarilla said in that special way she had. 'You've told us the cause of the nightmares, now maybe you should describe what happens in them.' Dom blushed, glad it was dark. 'It'd help,' Sarilla added and the others gathered close, waiting.

'How do you know?' Dom grunted suddenly. 'How the fuck would you know what would help?'

'Listen, you little piss-stain,' Sarilla snarled, 'there's a war coming and no one can get any bloody sleep because of you screaming all the time. So start talking and maybe we can help you.'

Dom lurched to his feet, grabbed sword and blanket and marched past Sarilla. He got all of three strides before she gripped his shoulder. He could have pulled past but he stopped, frustrated and ashamed. He was behaving like a child and he knew it. So did everyone else.

'Talk to us, Dom,' Rillirin pleaded. Hands pulled him back, forced him to sit, and Sarilla kindled a candle and set it in the middle, driving back a little darkness.

'They're not nightmares,' Dom said, weary beyond words. He made a cutting gesture with one hand when they began to protest. 'They're not nightmares,' he repeated. 'What I told you at the temple, that the Dark Lady visits me at night, that's exactly what I mean. She visits me. I don't dream Her, I get . . . taken to Her.' Dead silence.

'Taken where?' Sarilla asked, looking as if she wished she'd never asked in the first place.

'No idea. A cave, cavern, huge place, cold, firelit. The gods are there.'

Rillirin pressed herself to his side and put her arm around his waist. 'The Waystation,' she whispered. 'The Blessed – Lanta talked of it. The place beyond the veil the Red Gods come to when They want to talk to mortals. To the priest-hood. Or you, I suppose.'

'All right, the Waystation,' Dom said, not giving a fuck what it was called. 'What They do to me there, I can still remember, still feel, when I wake up.'

'And what do They do to you?' Sarilla asked. Their faces were haunted in the feeble light, and Dom wondered what his must look like.

'Whatever They feel like. Normally it's the Dark Lady, but Gosfath shows up every so often. He's . . . more straight-forward. It's just pain with Him.' He coughed a laugh at the utter inadequacy of words. Just pain.

'And the Dark Lady?'

'That's where it gets interesting,' Dom said, trying for glibness and falling far short. He gave up and just said it. 'She's playing with me, trying to wear me down. Each night Her offers are a little bigger, a little grander. And each night Her punishments for my refusal are a little harsher. And that's when I start screaming.'

'What are the offers for?' Lim broke his silence. 'Why is She offering you anything at all?'

'I told you before, She wants my soul. It amuses Her to think I'll betray the gods,' he put his hand over the scars, 'and pledge myself to Her.'

Lim rubbed his chin. 'Surely She's going to a lot of effort just for one soul. Is torturing you really that much fun?'

Well, yes, probably, but mostly it's because if She gets me the veil tears and They can return. But I can't tell anyone that, can I? Because this is all my fault. Everyone who dies in this war is dead because of me. Because of that blood oath I swore.

Dom groaned and pressed the heels of his hands into his stinging eyes. *Hold on . . .* He lowered his hands. 'Maybe it's not that,' he said slowly, thinking it through as he spoke. 'Maybe She's doing it for another reason.'

Lim snapped his fingers. 'Distraction,' he said.

Dom nodded. 'Distraction. She doesn't want me finding out something else. She's trying to keep something hidden, hoping that if She occupies the godspace in my head, the Dancer won't be able to get in and tell me what I need to know.' Rillirin sat up straight, breaking contact with his ribs, and cold flowed in between them.

'Something about this whole thing stinks,' Dom said. 'We're missing something.'

'The situation in Rilporin?' Sarilla asked. 'You said poison could burn us all. It could be Rivil.'

'Could be, but I don't think so. I think it's closer; it's something here. Or coming here.' He hissed in sudden pain, clapping his hand over his right eye. 'Guess I'm right, then,' he muttered, looking away from the tiny candle flame and concentrating on the blackness.

'Why didn't you say anything before?' Sarilla asked.

'Because I don't want this to be all I am,' Dom muttered. 'And I'm sick of the fucking pity in everyone's faces.'

'Perhaps this is your war,' Sarilla said with uncharacteristic diplomacy. 'Perhaps you're not meant to fight physically, but to try and find out the Dark Lady's secrets.'

'No,' Rillirin said before Dom could protest. 'If She realised what he was doing, She'd tear his soul out and eat it. He can't; it's too dangerous.'

Lim locked eyes with Dom and Dom's heart sank. 'Is it something you could try?' he asked. It wasn't an order, and that just made it worse. Dom could refuse an order.

Rillirin was squeezed against him again and he put his arm around her shoulders, resting his chin on the top of her head. Lim's eyes were apologetic and firm – he wasn't retracting the question and Dom would have to answer it.

'Yes,' he said and Rillirin tightened both arms around his waist as though trying to squeeze sense into him. He kissed her hair. 'I can try.'

MACE

*Third moon, eighteenth year of the reign of King Rastoth
West Rank headquarters, Cattle Lands, Rilporian border*

The horse slithered to a halt outside the gates as the sun
rose behind the mountains, bowmen in the towers on either
side calling for identification. Mace watched from the tower,
wrapped against the cold and eyes burning from lack of
sleep.

'Dalli Shortspear of the Wolves. They're coming!' Her
voice was faint with distance, but still he heard the rust of
fatigue. She'd ridden hard, then.

The sentries waved her through and she urged the horse
through the wicket gate as Mace ran down the stairs from
the tower. A soldier took the lathered mount and held it still
so she could jump from the saddle, staggering as she landed.
Mace met her halfway across the killing ground.

'Lady Shortspear. Dalli. They're coming?' Her eyes were
moss green and veined and rimmed with red. She wiped mud
and sweat from her cheek and nodded.

Mace beckoned a loitering soldier. 'You, fetch Abbas and

316

Dorcas immediately. And some food and ale for our guest. My office, as quick as you can.' He hurried away and Mace ushered Dalli into the keep and up to his office. He paced while they waited for his officers, fingers drumming on the hilt of his dagger. When they arrived, he didn't bother waiting for them to sit. He strode to a table littered with maps. 'Colonels, thank you. Abbas, if you could take notes to inform the sub-forts afterwards, I'd be grateful. We can't wait for them.'

Dalli stood next to Mace, scanned the map and then pointed. 'We caught sight of them at the top of the pass two days ago. Ash and I had eyes on for most of the afternoon. Around four thousand by the last count, though I left before they were done appearing over the skyline, heavily armed and armoured, with enough horses to mount a cavalry charge and mules pulling siege weapons. I think we can confidently say five thousand or more.' She paused to cough, face reddening, and Mace handed her another cup from the tray.

'Five thousand?' Abbas squawked, looking up from his notes. 'They've never raided with more than five hundred. Are you sure, woman?'

Dalli exchanged a glance with Mace and he answered before she could retort. 'I've faith in the Wolves' ability to count, Colonel.'

'How soon can you set out?' Dalli asked Mace, ignoring Abbas with an obviousness that made Mace swallow a smirk.

He looked to Dorcas. 'Colonel?'

'Three days,' the colonel said promptly and beamed at his own efficiency.

Dalli puffed out her cheeks. 'Three days? We can't contain them for that long. You have to move faster than that.'

'Impossible.'

Dalli straightened up and glared at him. 'The Wolves will be dead in a day if we confront a force that size. There are little more than a thousand of us. You're only half a day from the mouth of the valley – how can it possibly take you so long to mobilise?'

Mace touched her sleeve. 'You must be exhausted,' he said as Dorcas bristled. 'Head down to the barracks for a hot meal and a rest. Believe me, I'll get them moving.' He pointed at Dorcas, then at Abbas. 'You, weapons and supplies. You, men and horses. I'll get the news to the other forts myself.' He looked at Dalli, then back at his staff. 'We march tomorrow.'

Four thousand at least. Say five and we're an even match. One on one. They'll have the high ground and Dalli saw siege weapons.

'We're taking three trebuchets; don't tell me we can't, I don't care how they get there. Dorcas, tell Colonel Bors he's in charge of logistics. If they need to leave now to arrive in time, get them broken down, loaded on to carts, and wave them off. Three trebs. In the valley. See it done.'

'Thank you, General,' Dalli said. 'I'll return to my people tomorrow. I hope I'll be leaving an hour ahead of you, no more.' She glared at Dorcas and then looked back at Mace and her face softened. 'Thank you for your hospitality. The bed and the bath will be most welcome, as will the food.'

'Anything you desire, my lady. You know your way around.'

When the knock came on his door, Mace was out of bed and armed. It seemed as though Dalli really did know her way around, for she poked her head into his bedchamber. 'General? Are you awake?'

'Lady Shortspear? Is something wrong?' he asked, conscious

he was nearly naked. The cold of the stone prickled through the soles of his feet and he suppressed a shiver.

She came in and closed the door; she stood staring at him in the red light from the banked fire. 'Aside from the fact I'll probably be dead in a couple of days?' she whispered. Mace sheathed the knife and put it back under his pillow. When he turned back to gesture her to a seat by the fire she'd already got her boots off.

Mace raised an eyebrow as she stripped out of everything bar her linens and breastband. She didn't speak and neither did he. There was nothing to say. He drew her to him, ran his fingertips up the firm muscle of her arms, over her shoulders and down her back. Goosebumps rose in their wake and Mace lifted the blankets to help her into bed.

Dropping his linens, he climbed in with her and her hand was warm and rough on his face, her mouth hot and insistent. She pulled him close, squirming out of her linens and breastband, and then pulled him in.

Mace lost himself in her, with her, and for a while at least they chased away the spectre of death.

GALTAS

Third moon, eighteenth year of the reign of King Rastoth
East Rank Headquarters, Grazing Lands, Listran border

'How many men follow the Dark Path?' Galtas asked as he dined in Skerris's quarters with his staff.

The general tapped the side of his nose. 'One hundred and three,' he said.

Galtas's eyebrows shot up his head and he whistled. 'That I did not expect.'

'It's a dangerous business, worshipping the true gods in this nest of vipers. Having men around me I trust has been essential. Over the years, others have come to see the benefits and rewards of the Path.'

Galtas tipped his wine glass in Skerris's direction in appreciation. 'The Mireces should have shown themselves by now, and all attention will be on the West. When we begin to move, none will suspect us. We march under Rilporian colours to aid the city, stand between it and the barbarians.' He refilled his glass, grinning around the table. 'Once they've defeated the West Rank, they'll advance on Rilporin.'

Skerris nodded. 'And we'll appear to oppose them.'

'Right up until we open up the siege engines on the walls,' Galtas confirmed. 'The only problem is your men. They'll never fight with the Mireces, and they'll never attack Rilporin. The Blessed One inferred you would have a solution.' Galtas spread his hands and sat back, waiting for Skerris to make or break Rivil's plan.

Skerris slapped his belly and belched. 'I told you, my lord, I'm an anointed priest of the Red Gods. We will simply force conversion on the Rank.'

Galtas cocked his head. 'They'll slaughter us if they're forced to renounce the Dancer. Slaughter us and go back on their oaths to the Red Gods in a heartbeat.'

Skerris looked at one of his men. 'Baron, would you renounce the Dark Path now your feet are upon it?'

The major blanched. 'No. Never.' His voice was thready, pupils wide and black in a face grey with anxiety.

'Even if you were ordered to?' Skerris pressed. Baron shook his head.

'What? I don't understand,' Galtas said.

'Baron here took his oath lightly, without true consideration for the gods. The Dark Lady . . . showed him the error of his ways.' Baron looked as if he might throw up. 'A soul once given to the gods can never be ungiven. Never. The Dark Lady has promised us victory. She's promised you an army. We force conversion on the Rank without them realising, afterwards welcome them on to the Dark Path and tell them their souls belong to the Red Gods. Some will rise against you and die. The Dark Lady will see to it. The rest will be yours.'

Galtas tapped a fingernail against his teeth, thinking. 'I like it, but how does it work? Surely they'll suspect.'

'You are Prince Rivil's emissary, are you not, asking us

for our loyalty in the trials and wars to come? Then we will swear that loyalty. An oath to the Lady, made in good faith, that we are yours to command.' Skerris winked. 'Who wouldn't swear that?'

'Men of the East, Prince Rivil's emissary has spent a week with us and you have shown him your valour as soldiers of our great country. We have spoken much these last days, myself and Lord Morellis and your colonels, and we have concluded that we can no longer keep this news from you. You are warriors and brave sons of Rilpor – you have the right to know.'

Skerris's parade-ground voice was so loud that Galtas took a step sideways and wiggled a finger in his ear. The Rank stood in orderly lines on the plain outside the main fort. Cloud shadows chased one another across the flat, feature-less expanse of green. He gestured for Galtas to take over the narrative.

'A week ago a Mireces army several thousands strong invaded Rilpor, crossing our border to engage the West Rank.' Galtas gave it to them straight – maximum impact.

Silence but for the lapwings curling and calling above and the murmurs as the news was passed to those who couldn't hear. Skerris's loyal Hundred were seeded among them.

'King Rastoth the Kind knows of the invasion and of the numbers the Mireces have brought into our land. We don't know whether the West Rank has engaged them yet. We don't know the outcome of any battle. The silence is worrying.' Galtas paused delicately to let the seeds grow.

'King Rastoth is reluctant to send reinforcements. He is unwell. He refuses to listen to the council or to Commander Koridam. He refuses to allow another Rank to march west.' Mutterings of discontent. Lovely. 'I know many of you have friends in the West Rank or have served there yourselves. I know you don't like to think of them abandoned by their king and country to fight and die against insurmountable odds.'

Skerris's face was a picture of sorrow and Galtas bit the inside of his cheek, letting the general take over the narrative with a slight nod. Skerris gestured at him. 'Lord Morellis came here at the prince's behest but without the king's consent, without permission or approval. Rivil sent the noble lord because he is afraid for his country. Because he is a soldier-prince seeking to aid his brothers, looking for a way other than this. But there is no other way.'

Galtas tried to look simultaneously contrite and worried. What he wanted to do was throw back his head and laugh. Skerris was a better actor even than Rivil.

'The west may fall. It may already have fallen and the plains and towns and villages, the herds and flocks that sustain us, the crops that feed us, may fall too, fall to the invaders. Our prince refuses to sit idly by and let our great nation be swallowed up, our people be slaughtered or enslaved, our brave West Rank annihilated. After much discussion, he resolves to march to war. He asks us, he begs us, to march with him.'

A rustle of noise, growing murmurs, shifting in the lines. Galtas stepped forward, past Skerris, and opened his arms to them. 'I can't promise the king won't seek to punish you for marching against his orders. All I can promise is that His Highness Prince Rivil will do all in his power to defend you.' He sliced his palm through the air, stilling them. 'But that's a problem for another day. This day I ask you to march with the prince into battle to save your brothers. To save Rilpor from the heathen. Will you?'

Skerris's loyal Hundred roared their approval and the

sound swelled as others were caught up in the moment, swelled and expanded until the East Rank was yelling its acclamation for Rivil and for war. Didn't hurt that Skerris's majors were roaring along with the rabble. A shaft of sunlight broke through the racing clouds and highlighted Rivil's standard with gold. The shouting thundered into silence.

'The gods bless him,' a voice called. 'The gods promise victory.'

The roar rose up again and Skerris let the fever run a few more moments before patting the air. The Rank quietened, but slowly. 'My lord, the Rank is with Prince Rivil, and it's plain to see so are the gods. We are yours to command in the prince's stead.'

All right, now for the tricky bit.

Galtas pulled a king from his pouch and held it aloft. Sunlight glinted off the gold. More cheers, the most enthusiastic so far. *He's paying us in gold? Where do I sign?*

'For your loyalty to the prince, for your faith in him and willingness to aid your brothers, I am authorised to name you the King's Rank, first among the army in all things.' He flipped the coin sparkling into the air. 'Pledge your loyalty to Prince Rivil and to the Lady, receive a king here and now, and tomorrow we march to war.'

Three small folding tables appeared on the platform behind him, three stools. On each table were two sacks, sacks that clinked hypnotically.

'King's Rank, line up to pledge allegiance and receive your gold,' Skerris bellowed and the Rank dissolved into three long queues, men shoving to be at the front in case the money ran out.

'Swear loyalty to Rivil and the Lady and prick the base of your right thumb with this nail.'

'I do so swear.'

'Receive your payment. Congratulations.'

'I do so swear.'

'I do so swear.'

'I do so swear.'

'I cannot swear.' Galtas's smile failed and his head snapped around to focus on the third table and the man in front of it. An older soldier, hair grizzled, painfully erect.

'Very well, soldier, you are loyal to King Rastoth and his orders, I understand that. Please stand over there. You understand you will have to be rotated to another Rank? Very well. Next.'

'I do so swear.'

'King's Rank,' Galtas shouted when all had pledged and those who refused were under informal guard – fewer than a hundred men, 'we thank you for your loyalty. The blood oath you have made to the Dark Lady and Gosfath, God of Blood, binds you to Them. Your souls are Theirs. We will have victory over the mad king and his armies, and over the Dancer Herself. Welcome, brothers, to the Dark Path.'

He stripped off his coat, revealing the blue shirt beneath. Skerris and his officers did the same, and the men standing in line below. It was a brave move from them; it was likely they'd be torn apart when the Rank realised what had happened. 'Our feet are on the Path,' they yelled.

The lapwings called, songs echoing over the held-breath stillness of five thousand disbelieving men. 'Traitor,' a voice called, 'fucking heathen traitor bastard.'

Shouts of fury and fear mingled on the air, their force a physical pressure against Galtas's chest. He held up his hands for silence, didn't get it. Men were shying away from the devotees in the Rank below, and four more shoved through the crowd, swords drawn, screaming curses. Galtas's eyes slid sideways to Skerris, who stood with his hands behind his back, gazing down at the sea of seething humanity. The men ran on to the platform, slowed, faltered, fell to their knees, gurgled and choked to death.

The Rank saw it, and they saw that no one had touched those men. Others, unable to believe it, jumped the corpses and bore down on Galtas. They died. One more made the charge, leaping up the steps and drawing his bow. Skerris turned to face him and spread his arms wide, inviting the arrow. The soldier fired and five thousand men followed its flight. The arrow hung in the air in front of the general's massive chest, twisting, humming.

'See the power of the Red Gods?' Galtas shouted. 'See Their ability to push away the hand of death from a man, to prevent his slaying even in battle? There is a war coming and you are soldiers . . .' He let that thought take root in their minds, thanking the gods for a quick tongue despite his own mesmerised disbelief.

'Think what you could become if your enemies could not kill you. We are warriors, and if we hold the Red Gods in our hearts, we are invincible.' Bullshit, of course. The Dark Lady was lending Her aid to bring these men to Her cause. Galtas doubted any of them would be unkillable when it came to it.

The men stirred and muttered as Skerris reached out and plucked the arrow from the air. He twirled it through his fingers and stuck it through his belt, a souvenir. Some laughed at his bravado; others were thinking hard about what they'd seen and what they'd been told.

'How many of you can say that you've seen the Dancer stop arrows in mid-air? How many of you can say She's intervened in your lives to the good in any way?' Galtas shouted. He held up a coin and gestured at the black-faced corpses scattered around them. 'Gold. Land. Women. Men, if that's your preference – I don't care. Servants, even slaves. All this and more when Rastoth is pulled from his throne and the Red Gods are ascendant.'

Galtas flicked the coin into the air and caught it. 'All this and more.'

TARA

Tara crashed through the brush as though the God of Blood
Himself was coursing her heels. She was lost, heading north
as near as she could tell beneath the trees. Rounding a mess
of rock and ivy she came face to face with a woman and a
half-grown girl. They were pointing spears at her sweating
face. Tara squawked and fell over, cracking her tailbone on
a stone.

'Ahh! Friend, friend,' she gasped, flailing her hands. 'My
name is Captain Tara Carter of the West Rank. I have information for the general.'

'The Rank marched to the Blood Pass. As you'd know if
you were of the West.' The woman poked her with her spear.

'They're coming down the Gil-beside Road, thousands of
'em,' Tara shouted desperately, flinching.

'No, they're not,' the woman said. 'They've been seen at
the Blood Pass.'

'Well, they've also been seen at the Final Falls. I know: I

328

was the one who saw them. I'm not fucking lying! I need to get to the West Rank.'

'The Gil-beside?' the woman repeated, fingers slackening on her spear. 'How? There isn't the room.'

'I don't know, but they are, thousands of them.'

'You'll never reach the pass in time. You don't know the way and you haven't the woodcraft. I'm Freya of the Wolves. I'll take your message.'

'No, Mother, let me go,' the girl said. 'You tell the other scouts. We've camped right in their path.'

'Cora, you're only thirteen,' Freya said.

'And fast. Look, if I lead her, I'm running away from these Mireces, aren't I? If I go back to the scouts, I'm in more danger.'

'Damn your logic, child.' Freya clicked her teeth together, looking back the way Tara had come and then deeper into the forest. 'Fine. Captain, Cora will lead you. Cora, remember everything you've been taught. Quiet, fast, leave no traces. No fires, no footprints in mud. Stay off the wider trails. You better learn fast, Ranker, my girl won't wait for you.'

Cora looked at Tara, pale but determined. 'You ready to run?'

Tara sucked in air and wiped the sweat off her face. *Not really, I'm fucking knackered.*

'When was this battle?' Freya asked, pressing a hand to her heart. Tara could sense the fear she was barely keeping under control. Cora was fidgeting beside her.

'Three days ago, a few hours after dawn. If you're right, then it's a pincer move, a sweep this way to catch the Rank between them and the pass.'

Freya puffed out her cheeks and then punched Tara's shoulder. 'You've come a hell of a way in three days, Captain. I'm impressed. Have you eaten?' Tara shook her head and swallowed the surge of saliva flooding her mouth. She'd been trying not to think about it. Freya pulled a small satchel from her back. 'Meat, cheese, some sour apples, a waterskin. Cora, you ate this morning, so the captain gets half of this tonight when you rest, then you split what's left between you tomorrow.'

'How much further?' Tara asked, fidgeting almost as much as Cora now.

'If you can keep up with my daughter, two more days. If you can't, well, she'll carry on ahead and take the message to our chief and your general. You just do the best you can. Getting through to my people and yours is the most important thing now. Stop for nothing.'

Cora stretched up and kissed her mother's cheek, and Freya crushed her in a tight embrace and then shoved her roughly away. 'Dancer's grace upon you, my love,' she whispered, tears glinting in her eyes. 'Run.'

Cora grabbed Tara's hand and started to move. Tara didn't even have time to thank the woman or wish her luck, though what she and the rest could do against the force Tara'd seen, she had no idea. Run and hide, she hoped. She disentangled her hand from Cora's and dropped a few paces behind, watching where the girl ran and copying her where she could. The pace wasn't as fierce as Tara's had been, but she knew the girl could keep it up for the rest of the day with barely a pause.

Tara fixed her eyes on the satchel on Cora's back. *Follow the food. If I drop back, I'll be even hungrier.* Tara had no intentions of dropping back.

GILDA

Third moon, eighteenth year of the reign of King Rastoth
Scout camp, Wolf Lands, Gilgoras foothills,
Rilporian border

Cam would be furious when he found out Gilda had trav-
elled with the scouts, but she'd felt the gods' guiding hand
in this and had listened, as she always did. She needed to
be here. If these Watchers could leave town to lend their
aid to their kin fighting in the forests and valleys, then so
could she.

The scouts knew the Mireces had been spotted in the
valley to the north and were debating whether they should
stay in position or go to fight when Freya sprinted from the
woods to the south.

'Run,' she screamed. 'All of you, run!'

The scouts leapt to their feet, grabbing weapons, shouting
questions drowned out by the blare of cow horns and screams
of triumph. A swarm of blue-clad men and a few women
zigzagged through the trees on Freya's heels and the scouts
lunged to engage. There were pockets of sporadic fighting

331

as the Mireces surrounded and clubbed the scouts. Didn't kill. Captured. *Please, Fox God, no.*

Gilda was lying beneath the low-slung branches of a fir tree and peered from her hiding place at the man and woman standing in the centre of the clearing. They were richly dressed and oozed power and arrogance. Corvus. The cast of his features matched Rillirin's. The respect the woman was dealt marked her as special, probably the priestess. The so-called Blessed One. They shared a waterskin and laughed, triumphant as though this was the sum total of the Wolves and they'd won a famous victory.

Men and women were dragged before them singly or in pairs to be hacked down while the woman chanted an obscene prayer of supplication.

Gilda's skin felt as though it was on fire as she crawled from beneath the fir. 'Parlay,' she shouted, stunning the clearing into silence. She knelt on one knee and bowed her head. 'Great King Corvus, do not slaughter these people, in the Dancer's name I beg you.'

Corvus looked her up and down and laughed. 'Let them live? They are my enemies and the enemy of my gods. None who are so will live.'

'Then take me instead,' Gilda said and stood, shoulders back, meeting Corvus's amused gaze with her own.

The woman drifted towards her, eyes glittering like a snake's. 'Do you know what we would do to you, old woman?' she asked.

'Your worst,' Gilda said and shrugged. 'What you did to Janis. What you've done to countless victims over the centuries. What's your point?'

The woman licked her lips. 'Bravado,' she said, dismissing Gilda's words. 'You'd scream louder than any of the others.'

Gilda shrugged again, because it seemed to annoy the bitch. 'No doubt I would. Again, what's your point?'

'Enough,' Corvus snapped, his voice a lash that goaded the Mireces into movement. They readied the next victims and the sword and axe swung, silver on the way down, red on the upswing.

A bright, deep peace filled Gilda's stomach and overflowed to tingle in every limb. She inhaled, raised her hands in benediction to everyone in the clearing, Mireces and Watcher alike. 'The Dancer spreads Her peace upon us all. We who die now have nothing to fear, for She will take us into Her Light. I pity you, king, and your toy priestess. You have to live in the filth of your petty religion. We do not. We are bound for the Light. Blessed Dancer, strong and true, to Your Light we consecrate ourselves. Honoured Fox God, swift and sure, shepherd our souls into Your Grace.' She tapped her fingertips to her heart.

One by one the Watchers relaxed, lowered weapons and fists and recited the prayer with her, fingers on chests, eyes on the sky and each other. It was all she could give them, unless she could convince Corvus to turn from the Blood into the Light.

The woman flicked back her hair and grabbed Gilda's sleeve; she turned to Corvus. 'Oh, Sire, let me keep this one,' she begged. 'She amuses me.' She looked back at Gilda. 'And perhaps she will take her place in sacrifice one day.'

Gilda's eyes focused on her, as though only just noticing her presence. 'Hmm? What did you say, dear?' she asked. 'I'm sorry, I wasn't listening.' The woman's eyes narrowed, her lips thinned, and Gilda looked away again, back to her people, her voice joining theirs as the prayer swelled again.

'Very well, Blessed One. I commend her into your care. As for the others, kill them. And make sure she watches. I want her to know how little her precious Dancer cares for them.'

'Our next move, Sire?' Valan asked. 'They'll know the pincer move's coming if that Ranker we've been tracking reaches them ahead of us. She's not here, that's for sure.' He wiped his sword clean on the coat of a dead woman.

Gilda's heart lurched when Corvus's gaze fixed on her. His smile was cold and cruel. 'I think we've marched far enough north to convince anyone in these woods we're heading for the valley. Time to change direction. Tell me, priestess, how far is it to Watchtown?'

MACE

Third moon, eighteenth year of the reign of King Rastoth
Blood Pass Valley, Gilgoras Mountains, Cattle Lands

Beautiful day to die.

The sun shone on the green of the valley and winked from the steel of the armies drawn up facing each other. The Rank's brass trumpets clarioned to the sky, incessant, demanding, and the archers began to move. The rain had eased with the dawn, but the ground was claggy. The green would vanish soon enough, trodden into a quagmire. Harder to fight in; easier to die in.

'The civilians are moving,' Colonel Dorcas observed and indicated the stream of men and women loping through the edge of the woods in their brown and green garb, splashes of chainmail and boiled leather. When they stopped, they were almost invisible.

'They weren't to move yet,' Mace said and swore. 'What have they seen? Abbas, send a courier down there. He's to leave his horse at the edge of the trees, though, I don't want him giving away their position.'

'Yes, General,' Abbas said and strutted off, polished stick held tight under one arm. Mace and Dorcas exchanged glances. Abbas really did need rotating to another Rank, preferably one off the edge of the known world.

'Come on then, you bastards,' Mace muttered. 'Let's see what you've got.' As if in response, clouds of arrows buzzed up from both armies, hung against the pale morning sun, and then flung down into the ranks of men. There was silence, before faint screams drifted on the lazy breeze.

'Give them ten volleys and then we'll try the cavalry,' Mace said. 'See if we can't break them early.'

The muscles in his legs twitched with the urge to run and fight, to help turn the tide, stop the war before it could really start. A flicker of white caught his eye: the enormous banner they'd made flapped and then hung still so he could read it. 'Your allies are in prison.' If Corvus had seen it, it hadn't had the desired effect. His Rank loosed another volley.

'It's down to us, then,' Mace whispered. 'Steel and will and discipline.' More screams and the lines becoming ragged, the edges nibbled away, a stream of walking wounded making their way back, others carried by their mates.

Another volley. And another.

The Rank's bowmen ran for the edges of the battle where the valley sloped and took up new positions behind wicker hides. Through the gap they'd left thundered the cavalry, five hundred huge and heavily armoured horses, a battering ram of steel and flesh.

The ground shook as the riders couched lances and bore down on the Mireces on their shaggy horses. Abbas was silent beside Mace, rapt. This was warfare for him, noble and picturesque. Well, picturesque up until impact, anyway. Then it was horses ripped open, men flung over the heads of their mounts, and the charge became a screaming, swirling mêlée that nobody could win.

To Mace's left, Dorcas picked relentlessly at a ragged fingernail with his small front teeth. The rest of his staff crowded on the little hillock. Majors and colonels – and generals, more's the pity – didn't fight in the lines unless there was no other choice.

'The cavalry is pulling back, sir,' Dorcas murmured. Abbas tutted. Horses and men disengaged and cantered heavily back down the field. The riders turned them, rested them for a moment, and went again.

'Horses won't stand much more of this,' Mace said as the impact shrieked through the valley. Mace stretched on to his toes and stared hard, trying to make sense of the chaos. Too many horses were down, but some of the Mireces' mounts had refused the charge. 'Go once more and then we'll have to pull them out. When we do, send the infantry in straight away. We'll take this hand-to-hand. They'll break. And, Abbas, have the cavalry dismount and form up with the infantry as a second wave.'

'They won't like that, sir,' Abbas said, aghast.

'I know they won't like it, Colonel, I also don't give a runny shit for their damned pride. They can prance about on their ponies when the war is won. Until then, do as I say.'

Abbas flushed and ripped off a salute. The final charge drummed across the valley, armour and horseflesh crunched into each other and he focused on it, ignoring Dorcas's smug smile around his chewing of his fingers.

'Come on, come on, break them. Break them, damn you.' Abbas's stick slapped against his boot top.

But neither side gained an advantage and as the forces broke trumpets blared the cavalry retreat. As expected, the

Mireces jeered the straggling line of horses, some riderless, and men, some horseless, as they began to disengage. The horses were exhausted, the mud sucking at their hooves as they straggled to the side to allow the infantry to prepare. A few dozen Mireces horses trotted into the open space and then lengthened stride. One last charge into Mace's unready infantry.

'Infantry to the fore and set spear, now,' Mace roared and his herald squeaked at his trumpet, spat desperately, and sounded the order. The trumpet call dragged the Rank's cavalry around to see the Mireces charging but they were tangled, spent, the horses blown.

Fuck it. Mace yelled for his horse and flung it into a gallop down the hillock, roaring for the cavalry to re-form. Men and horses milled and got in each other's way. Mace saw a knot of mounted men and steered around them, yelling for them to follow. They complied and herd instinct brought two dozen more warhorses charging after, some without riders. They galloped through the ragged gaps in the infantry line towards the oncoming force. Too late.

Mireces horses bounded into the front ranks of men, impaling themselves on planted spears, charging through those which hadn't been set and crushing the first three ranks of foot beneath their hooves and falling bodies. Riders leant from saddles to hack at arms and faces, forcing the maddened animals deeper into the First Thousand.

'It's a suicide charge,' Mace screamed, but his words were lost in the wind. Whose suicide, he wondered as his horse pounded through the mud. He didn't have a lance. He dragged his sword from its sheath and dug in his spurs. Screaming again, Mace led a score of cavalry around the mêlée and in from the flank, driving a wedge into the Mireces attack.

Break you fuckers, break. Mace gripped the pommel of his saddle as his stallion reared and kicked with lethal accuracy. A Mireces horse went to its knees, stunned, and Mace's mount trampled it and its hapless rider into claret smears.

His gaze was snagged by a laughing face in the chaos. Captain Crys Tailorson, who he'd left at the command post, threw himself out of the saddle of – Mace squinted – Abbas's horse and lunged into the infantry, yelling orders. The line stiffened, tightened up and surged back, closing with the exhausted Mireces cavalry.

'Hold them,' Mace screamed as he hacked into a man's back, stabbed a horse in the neck and forced his stallion deeper into the fray.

RILLIRIN

Third moon, eighteenth year of the reign of King Rastoth
Blood Pass Valley, Gilgoras Mountains, Cattle Lands

'All right, we're going. Keep low, they've archers up on the slopes and you're running right across their line of fire. You know what to do?' Rillirin nodded and Dalli clapped her on the shoulder. 'Don't drop your spear, you're going to need it.'

By the time Rillirin had worked up enough saliva to speak, Dalli was gone, sprinting down from the cover of the treeline into the valley. Rillirin sucked in air and followed. She ran with the others, hurdled a body, stumbled on landing and kept going, spikes of pain shooting from her ankle with each step. A hundred strides, eighty, fifty. A Wolf fell just ahead of her, blue-fletched arrow in her back. Dalli crouched lower, spear in one hand, small shield held up in the other. Rillirin copied her as best she could, the breath whistling in her throat.

Thirty strides, twenty, ten. Dalli threw her shield to one side and dragged a knife from her belt, came up behind a horse and slashed through its hamstrings. It screamed and its hindquarters collapsed; the rider rolled off and turned to engage her and Rillirin stabbed him in the belly with her spear, both hands locked around the haft, lunging with little training and an abundance of terror. His expression was one of pure astonishment as he grabbed at the spear lodged in his gut. Rillirin pulled it free and he fell.

She stared at him; then Dalli was dragging at her arm. 'Move,' she shouted and slithered forward towards the next horse, ripped open its belly, stabbed the rider in the side for good measure and was on to the next, bloody to the shoulders. Rillirin stumbled in her wake.

The Wolves wove among the Mireces' horses, killing and hamstringing where they could, laming where they couldn't. The animals panicked and pressed forward, tighter together, while the infantry stood firm on the other side, penning them in.

Don't look them in the eye, not their fault they're owned by Mireces. The horses were panicking, flicking out hooves, spinning on their hocks to find a way out. One stepped sideways on to Rillirin's foot and she shouted in pain, smashing the butt of her spear into its leg. It shrilled and reared, flinging its rider backwards on top of her. They thrashed in the mud, the man squirming until he flipped over and slammed a forearm across her throat.

Choking, hands slipping, spear gone somewhere beneath her, Rillirin flailed at him, found her knife and slid it in, scraped it off his hip and into his side. He stiffened, his eyes very wide as they stared into hers. She punched it in twice more and his mouth sagged open, revealing grey, empty gums. Too old for war.

She heaved him off her, stamped on the fingers he tried to snake around her leg, gagged on blood and dragged her spear from under his body. She could hear herself screaming, rage and triumph and fear and joy all mingling in a bright clarity, the grain of the wood, the sticky heat of the blood, the dragging of the mud each a distinct and blinding sensation.

Rillirin dodged a flying hoof and followed it back in, ramming her spear between the horse's hind legs into the bladder. The animal shuddered and screamed, its rider turned in surprise, and she thrust the spear into his lung, practically climbing the horse's collapsed rear legs to push him out of the saddle.

Hands grabbed him from in front and an infantryman dragged him into the mud. Sarilla's piercing whistle soared over the shouting and Rillirin slogged for the edge of the battle with the others. As they opened an escape route for them the surviving horses, panicked beyond all control, wheeled and galloped madly up the valley, scattering men and riders, trampling any who fell before them.

Rillirin slid to a halt on her knees next to Dalli and watched them go, red from crown to heels with hot, thick, sticky blood. 'We stopping?' she panted and Dalli's green eyes glittered in a red mask.

'Stopping?' she wheezed. 'Girl, we've barely started. If we're still alive in an hour, we can rest then. Up you get, take position between me and Tessa here. Spears work as a unit; we keep each other safe.'

The Mireces' siege engines opened up as they got into line, raining stones and rocks down on Wolf, Rank and Mireces alike. Rillirin looked for a shield and found a Raider instead. He had a shield, a huge thing he tried to smash into her face. Rillirin stumbled left and poked at him with the spear, pulled it back as he whipped the shield sideways to protect his flank and Dalli used the opening to stab him in the neck. He fell.

Rillirin gripped her spear in both hands and waited for the next, not stepping from the line and exposing herself. Dalli and Tessa were doing most of the work, but Rillirin did her best and didn't die. The Raiders flung themselves at the Wolves, and the Wolves gave, shifting back as a pack.

Rillirin caught a glimpse of Crys in the front line to her left, droplets of blood spattering one side of his face. His sword would have winked heroically in the sun as he held it aloft if it wasn't so bloodstained. But then he roared something and his Hundred wheeled, neatly splitting a few hundred Mireces off from the rest of their line. The Rankers moved like a shoal of fish under his command.

The Wolves stopped retreating and the Mireces came on, and then faltered when they realised they were surrounded. Rillirin felt her lips peel back from her teeth and she screamed a wordless challenge, advancing eagerly in step with the others.

Nine years of hatred, of fear and humiliation and shame, bubbled up and overflowed, and Rillirin shrieked at them again, daring them to face her.

Next to her Dalli parried a sword, the blade thunking into the spear's shaft near the tip. She reversed the arc and whipped the butt forward between the man's legs, practically lifting him off the ground. He whooped in a breath and fell like a sack of shit.

'Fuck you, Mireces,' Rillirin yelled at him. 'Fuck you and your mothers.' She slammed her spear into his ribcage and pinned him to the mud. *Fuck you.*

TARA

Bodies, dozens of them, most in Mireces blue, twisted in death beneath the twisting branches of the trees. No one else. No signs of life.

Cora kept on running so Tara put in a final spurt and grabbed the strap of her satchel, dragged her into the leaf litter and slapped a hand over her mouth. To her credit, Cora lay still, her only movement to shift her mouth away from Tara's hand so she could suck in air.

When she was sure it was safe, Tara rolled into a crouch and drew her sword. At her side, Cora pulled two knives, one in each hand. Tara was past being surprised by her. She held her fingers to her lips, eyes quartering the glade. Out in the brightness of the valley she heard a trumpet sound the rotation. First Thousand out, Second Thousand in. Gods, rotating already? How long had they been fighting? The Rank would be entrenched, committed now. Getting out just got a whole lot harder.

344

For the first time in – what? – two days, Tara felt in control. She slid through the trees, barely able to feel her feet any more they were so bloody, bruised and torn. She'd made the mistake of taking her boots off when they paused in the middle of the night. Couldn't see what they looked like – no fire, of course – but the cool breeze on them and a gentle exploration had revealed blisters of truly epic proportions, most burst at least once, and three loose toenails she'd just ripped off to spare the agony.

Cora was a comforting warmth at her back and Tara didn't worry about someone creeping up behind her. The girl's senses were keener than an owl's. The light grew as they approached the valley, the grassy sward painfully bright. Squinting, Tara examined the valley and the battle, found the command post and realised they had a clear run straight to it. She looked back. 'One more run?' she breathed.

Cora was watching behind them but she gave a brief nod, reached out without looking and found Tara's arm, tapping it twice. *Ready when you are.*

Tara tapped three times in response – *right now* – and set off, Cora her smaller, faster shadow. They burst from the trees and headed for the isolated hillock, Cora outdistancing her soon enough, but that was fine now. That was absolutely fine.

MACE

Dorcas had sounded the rotation to allow Mace to extricate himself from the battle and get back to the command post. He stood there now, arms heavy as lead, a vicious ache spiralling through his skull from the lump on the back of his head. His helmet was dented, too.

Fire arrows flickered through the sky towards the Mireces' siege engines. They weren't alight yet, but you never knew your luck.

'General. General!' a thin voice screeched.

He'd heard enough men screaming for him already today, and paid this one little attention. Wasn't coming from the battle.

'Mace! Mace! Fucking Mace!' That one penetrated. He glanced down the hill and did a double-take at the little girl labouring towards him. She was very red, elbows and knees pumping as she drove up the slope. Behind her, Tara slogged uphill, flapping a hand and urging her on.

346

'General Mace Koridam?' the child gasped, her hands on her knees, thin stomach heaving in and out. She spat out a mouthful of hair and wiped at the spittle on her chin.

'Yes, I'm Mace. Who are you?'

'General, Tara has news. Five days ago, just after dawn, an army of several thousand Mireces came down the Gil-beside Road. Tara was there; she saw it all. Only survivor.'

She heaved for breath and Mace found himself holding his. He felt his staff crowding his back, their dumbstruck silence.

'They overwhelmed the sentries and Major Costas's Hundred, but not before he sent Tara to warn you. They're coming north, hoping to catch you unawares. A crab-claw. No more than half a day behind, maybe a little more. But we ran pretty fast.'

Mace's mouth was hanging open. The girl hacked a harsh, dry cough.

'What are you talking about? How can there be another force? This is the largest army of Raiders we've ever seen. How can there possibly be more?'

'I don't know,' the girl grated. 'The Mireces were going to run into our scout camp on their way here. My mother sent me. She said I had to warn you, to make you believe somehow.' She swayed on her feet and Mace steadied her as Tara finally made her way to the hill's summit. 'You do believe me, don't you?' the girl asked, her eyes big and bright with sudden tears.

'Yes,' Mace said, 'I think I believe you. But I don't understand how this could be possible.' His fingers tightened on her shoulder. *My entire Rank is committed. All five thousand men. There's no reserve, no force left in the forts. There's no one to call on. We're fucked.*

'Everything she says is true, General,' Tara panted, then

dropped to one knee and vomited thin, watery bile into the grass. She wiped her mouth and stood back up. 'Five days, just after dawn. Major Costas would've held them off for as long as he could, but there were just too many.' She put her arm around Cora and the girl clung to her, exhausted.

'Lim Broadsword approaches,' Dorcas murmured and pointed down the hill.

'Mace,' Lim shouted as he jogged up, a bloody bundle clutched to his chest, 'we have a serious – Cora! What are you doing here? Where's your mother?'

'Uncle Lim,' the girl cried and burst into tears, running to him. 'There's Raiders coming down the Gil-beside; they're heading this way. And Gilda was with the scouts.'

Lim's face paled. 'Hush child, hush. Freya will have got them out. You know your mother. Hush now. Here, drink.' He handed her his waterskin and kissed the top of her head, then straightened and looked Mace in the eye.

I didn't offer her a drink. She's run gods know how far in the last few days and I didn't even give her some water. Mace could feel himself blushing, and it didn't help when Tara grabbed the skin from Lim's hands and emptied it down her throat.

'This confirms it,' Lim said. He dropped the cloth covering the bundle and revealed a human head. Mace jerked backwards. 'Look, he's an old man. His hair and beard have been dyed to make him look more youthful, but look at his wrinkles, the missing teeth. Must be sixty, maybe seventy. They all are.'

'The men coming down the Gil-beside weren't old,' Tara said. 'They looked like the best warriors the Mireces have.'

'Then this battle is a diversion,' Lim said, 'a ruse to weaken us so the reinforcements can finish us off. Rillirin says these men are likely blood sacrifices who've agreed to sell their lives as dearly as possible for their gods. That's why they're not retreating, why they're being pushed back but aren't breaking, aren't running. Their sole mission is to distract us until Corvus can get here.'

'But why?' Tara asked. 'Why not just send everything they've got against us at once? Why the subterfuge?'

'They've never fought a pitched battle before. They can't be sure they'll win, so they weaken us with expendable warriors and send in their elite afterwards to mop up any survivors.'

'What do you suggest?' Mace asked in a voice devoid of emotion. *Has any general ever fucked up as monumentally as this? I'll be vilified through the ages. If there are any ages to come. We're out of men and out of time. My Rank is going to die.*

'We can't contain a second force,' Colonel Bors muttered behind Mace. 'We must evacuate. Or – or parlay, negotiate a truce.'

'An immediate, full-scale retreat. It's our only option,' Abbas added. The wind brought the sounds of the battle clear to Mace's ears. Screams and the clang of metal, the thump and whine of the trebuchets firing.

'We can't fight a retreat all the way to the forts,' Dorcas said, blood on his lips, his fingernails chewed to the quick. 'There's nowhere to go. We have to defeat this army today and prepare to meet the other tomorrow.'

'We've no reinforcements,' Lim snapped, 'while the Mireces have a second army. We have to disengage.'

'A retreat would be a blow to the Rank's morale.'

'Fuck their morale, Dorcas,' Lim snapped, his arm around Cora. 'It's their lives I'm more concerned with.' He met Mace's eyes with a challenge and a plea. 'I've never let you down before. My people have never let you down. Don't let us down now.'

Arguments rose behind Mace, voices buzzing in his ears like bees and making as much sense. 'They won't let us retreat. As soon as they know we're making for the forts it'll become a rout. Without cavalry, we can't protect our rear,' he said as he looked down at the swirl and crimp of battle below. The horses wouldn't stand a slow walk burdened with an armoured man, let alone a cantering retreat. And they only had a few hundred anyway.

'We have to win,' Tara said. The voices faded. 'We have to win today. Now. We win and then we run for the forts before the other army arrives.'

'They'll besiege us,' Dorcas said.

'Or they'll leave a force just big enough to contain us. We've got supplies in the forts. We can rest and eat while they get hungry and then we can sally and slaughter them.'

'They might just pass us by,' Lim said. 'It's Rilporin they want, the alliance with Rivil. Either way we rest and then we follow them. Live to fight another day.'

'Half a day behind?' Mace clarified and Tara shrugged.

'Well, we didn't wait around to check, but they were fast-moving. I wouldn't think they'd be much more than that behind.'

He rolled his head on his shoulders, loosening muscles stiffening from the fight. 'Then we need to win in the next few hours if we're to have any chance of reaching the forts. Sound the all-out.'

'What?' Dorcas and Abbas said together.

'You heard me. Sound the all-out, put on your helmets and lead your Thousands into battle. They're not breaking and they're not retreating. We send in everyone and everything we have. We're going to annihilate them.'

Lim, Dorcas and his staff stared at him, dumbstruck. 'Do it,' he snarled and his officers sprinted for their horses.

CORVUS

*Third moon, year 995 since the Exile of the Red Gods
Northern Wolf Lands, Gilgoras foothills,
Rilporian border*

'Are you the high priestess of your goddess?' Gilda was
silent. 'I am high priestess, the Blessed One. I was chosen
when I had eighteen summers. My predecessor picked me
from all the acolytes before she went to the sacred fire. Is it
as much an honour for you as it is for me to dedicate your
life to your gods? How often does the Dancer speak to you,
command you? I commune with the Dark Lady often. The
power of Her voice reminds me constantly of my little, little
place in the world. Is it the same with you?'

Corvus bit his tongue to stifle laughter. Lanta's little place
in the scheme of things? Oh aye, modest as a week-old fawn,
that one, shy as a dormouse.

'I'm not playing "my gods are better than your gods" with
you, woman. Your hands are still red with the blood of
innocents. There's nothing to say to you that you don't
already hear in your nightmares.'

351

He saw Lanta's back stiffen. Was there something in that remark? Had the Rilporian touched a nerve? Interesting.

The land was nearly flat now as they threaded between the trees. They were out of the foothills and should only be a few miles from the plain. They'd found the River Gil the day before and were following it to the grasslands. From Watch Ford, it was a day's march to Watchtown and vengeance. Corvus's stomach fizzed with excitement.

'Why is it you think your gods didn't intervene?' Lanta pressed Gilda. 'If those people were as innocent as you say, why didn't the Dancer save them? Or fill them with holy fire so that they slaughtered us? Why did She command you into our power?'

'The Dancer never commands,' Gilda said. 'She teaches us independence and free will, patience and pleasure, and allows us to live our lives beneath Her guidance. We learn strength and resourcefulness from Her Son, the Fox God.'

'And how does She guide?' Lanta asked, tasting the unfamiliar word. They seemed so similar and yet different. Both walked tall, both sure of themselves, but Lanta wielded her power like a whip, whereas the old woman . . . it sat inside her, coiled and patient, to be used only in the direst need. Corvus was impressed. Apparently the old bitch didn't count this as direst need, even though she knew they were walking towards the destruction of everything she loved.

'Through encouraging us to work as a community, as family, through dreams sometimes, through silence and stillness. Her Son teaches us wit and ingenuity. When we sit beside the pools in the temples, or beside any running water or even beneath a canopy of leaves, that sense of timeless peace present in the trickle or the rustle is Her Voice. Have you ever seen the ocean?' Gilda interrupted her own spell, bringing Corvus out of his reveries. Lanta had the grace to shake her head.

'When I was a girl, to complete my training we made the trek through Listre to the ocean. A body of water without end, without limit, the sun sparkling on the waves, waves big enough to crash against the shore like the great ripples of grass the wind makes across the plain in late spring. That was when my soul opened and I knew the Dancer completely for the first time. That was my initiation. I sat on the shore for a day and a night and a dawn, watching the changing shapes and colours, the sounds it made, and I heard Her talk, and I listened.'

Was that wistfulness in the curve of Lanta's cheek? 'What was your initiation like?' Gilda said, breaking the spell again.

'After the old priestess chose me, I was honoured to perform her sacrifice, tying the sacred knots, bringing the sacred flame and setting it on her feet. She was transported with ecstasy.'

Gilda snorted. 'Sounds like she was transported with agony. So, that will be your end too, will it? Burnt to death by an ambitious young woman, someone who will climb over your still-hot corpse and into your king's bed to try and scrape herself some power?'

'It isn't like that,' Lanta snarled. 'It's sacred.'

And there isn't any climbing into my bed. More's the fucking pity.

'And that's how your gods talk to you, is it? Through pain?'

'But of course. What other way is there?' Lanta seemed genuinely surprised and Corvus had to remind himself it was all she'd ever known. Not that he'd ever heard the Dancer in his sixteen years in Rilpor.

Gilda put her hand on the Blessed One's arm and drew

her to a halt. She raised her face to the budding branches overhead. Corvus slowed and stopped, curious. 'Listen,' Gilda whispered. 'What can you hear?'

Lanta rolled her eyes. 'Birds, the river, the creak of branches.'

Gilda sighed with pleasure. 'That's the Dancer talking to you, if you can learn to listen.' She closed her eyes, smile beatific. Lanta screwed up her face but she was listening, straining to hear more than just the sounds of nature.

'There's nothing there, old woman,' she said eventually and there was irritation in her voice, but not enough to mask the disappointment.

Gilda inhaled a deep, slow breath and opened her eyes again, turning that smile on Lanta and on Corvus. 'You just have to listen,' she repeated.

'Sire? We've reached the treeline,' one of Corvus's scouts said, breaking the moment. 'Half a mile to the plain, maybe an hour's walk to Watch Ford.'

'And then a day to Watchtown,' Corvus said, his voice heavy with malice. Gilda's smile faded like the sun tumbling from the sky.

DOM

Dom danced right, blocking low to protect his left leg, spun on his left heel lunged back in and sheathed his sword in the man's armpit, dragged it clear and hacked off the foot of the Mireces to his left. The man sucked in a breath and squealed high through his nose, took a step forward, leaving his foot behind, and brought his weight down on the stump.

Dom winced at his shriek and kicked him in the face as he collapsed, sending him on to his back. He spun the sword in his fist, slammed it down into the belly, ripped it back out. No point going for the heart when he might miss, or get his blade stuck between two ribs. Belly'd kill him sure as anything. Just take a bit longer.

He'd a second of clear space, hauled in a deep breath and shook the ache out of his arm; then he scratched viciously at his right wrist. Fucking itching. An hour since the all-out had sounded and they'd finally got the Mireces on the back foot. Outnumbered and old, tired now, they'd started shuffling backwards.

The man who faced him next looked a hundred despite the dye in his beard. The axe he carried was no joke though, and although he spun it slowly and hacked with it even slower, he was big enough that it'd split Dom in half if he landed it. So Dom ducked, shield above his head to help it on its way, then drove up from the knees, shield boss slamming into the man's sternum. *Push him off balance, herd him back a step – hard to swing an axe when you're retreating.*

Defensive now, a little behind when blocking, eyes wobbling all over the place following the sword tip, the man had forgotten all about the shield. Dom lifted his elbow, exposing his flank for a second as he tilted the shield and drove it, rim-first, into the Mireces' face. Flash of silver from the corner of his eye and he rocked with the impact, but the man in front staggered back and that's what mattered. Teeth snapped, nose mashed flat, a snorting, bubbling grunt and Dom pulled the shield back into place and drove his sword into the side of the man's neck instead.

He went over backwards spurting and wheezing and Isbet and Lim stepped up to his flanks, Isbet's long spear punching through the Raider's throat and then moving to the next smooth as silk.

'Rotate,' Lim grunted, voice hoarse from shouting orders and screaming curses. Dom nodded and slid back between them, thankful for the rest. A dozen paces to the rear, sword ever at the ready, but his knee buckled and he went into the mud, shield flapping down. He watched Lim wade forward, blade flickering like the scales of a fish in deep water, in and out, around and down, leaving death in its wake. As though it wasn't his third rotation. As though he wasn't even feeling it.

The fingers of Dom's left hand released his sword and slid across the front of his chainmail, found the rip and dipped inside, came away glistening bright. 'Ah bollocks,' he muttered. Could feel the pain now, coming in waves like the wind through a tree canopy, hot and nauseating. Freed his hand from the strap of his shield and pressed it to the wound, felt something soft and vital pressing back. Corpse next to him, mouth wide and flies already busy inside it. Grunting, Dom tore the dead man's sleeve off, wadded it and stuffed it inside the torn chainmail, groaning. Took the man's belt and cinched it tight, holding the padding in place.

Sword as a crutch he forced himself upright, tight shallow breaths high in his chest, sweat in his eyes, mouth tasting metal and ash. The line in front of him buckled, began edging closer, and Dom hefted his sword.

'Not on my watch, you fuckers,' he shouted and pushed back into the throng, forcing his way through to the front and hacking madly at the blue-clad heathen bastards come to take his people and his land.

Blood slid down his side into his boot.

CRYS

Third moon, eighteenth year of the reign of King Rastoth
Blood Pass Valley, Gilgoras Mountains, Cattle Lands

Men were falling around him, and not from wounds. Exhaustion was slowing them all, friend and enemy alike. Men weren't fighting so much as holding each other up in a drunken dance of edged weapons.

Crys had long since lost all sense of fair play. When a Mireces slipped in the mud in front of him he slammed the edge of his shield down into his throat, staving in his windpipe and leaving him to suffocate. He faced the next, men either side moving with him, fighting in unison.

'Shoulders in,' he heard the call and swallowed bitter laughter, yelled it on down the line. The count followed, and when it reached ten the front line snapped their shields together, ducked their heads and put their shoulders into the back of the shields. Left legs stepped first, in time, and they battered into the Mireces, who pushed back. Left foot stamp and push. Right foot drives.

Inch by bloody inch, slipping and falling in the mud,

crushed by the second line stabbing over their heads, the First Thousand advanced. Shoulder screaming from the battering on the shield, legs shuddering as they stepped, straightened, stepped, Crys didn't hear the roar off to his right for a few seconds. By the time he did, it had spread through the First Thousand and the Second on their flank.

'Wolves have split them, sir,' a voice yelled in his ear. 'They've broken into two. They're surrounded on all sides.'

'Thank the Trickster,' Crys gasped. He raised his voice to the loudest rasp he could manage. 'They're going to be desperate now, lads, so watch for sudden surges, all right? Don't let them out; don't let them regroup. Let's finish this.'

His men raised a yell that spread along the line and even those who hadn't heard him were infected. The advance continued, shoulders in, left foot stamping, right foot driving, the second row stabbing over their heads into the mass of squirming, pushing Mireces screaming curses at them.

Nearly there. We're nearly there. Keep pushing. We can win this if we just. Keep. Pushing.

Crys tucked his head tighter in under the rim of his shield and concentrated on moving, every ounce of strength, every last fibre of his will condensed into one bright, sharp command: push. Soon enough, the quality of the sound changed. The noise coming from in front grew desperate, despairing. Crys chanced a look over the rim of his shield.

The Mireces were packed like herring in a barrel, those on the outside pushing back to escape Rank swords, those in the middle pushing out to save themselves from being crushed. On his right he saw Mace on a borrowed horse, yelling something at the Mireces. Looked like he was ordering them to surrender.

The Mireces were exchanging glances, edging towards the idea of laying down arms, of living, when one close to Crys began a shouted chant. 'Blood rises! Blood rises! Blood rises!'

He was killed, a blade in his mouth and punching out the back of his skull, but the chant spread and grew in strength until every man in blue was shouting it. They threw themselves at the shield wall, a last desperate attempt to break out of the ring of steel, and the Rank cut them down, stepping on and over the bodies, moving steadily towards the heart of the resistance.

Hundreds, and eventually scores, and finally dozens, and then none.

The field thundered into silence. Crys rested his shield edge-first and leant on it, heaving for breath, shaking, tears running down his face. Far as he could tell, every Mireces on the field was dead or dying. Thousands of them.

Nothing glorious about it, nothing beautiful or noble. There was no art of war, there was just this. Carnage.

The Rank fell still, and silent, and then, without being commanded, dozens began moving again, pawing through the bodies and giving the grace to Ranker and Raider alike. A swift and painless end in a world made of agony.

Crys wiped his face and, dropping his shield, pulled out a battered dagger. Choking on sobs, fighting just to stay upright, he picked his way across the battleground and began killing again. This time it was a mercy.

DOM

Third moon, eighteenth year of the reign of King Rastoth
West Rank headquarters, Cattle Lands, Rilporian border

'You're going to be fine.'

Dom blinked and focused. 'What?'

'You're going to be fine. It's wide but not deep. Nothing vital was torn. It's clean and stitched and bound. You'll live.'

Rillirin burst into tears and Dom was tempted to join her. The healer was already moving to the next cot along. 'Thank you,' Dom called. The healer raised his hand but didn't look back. The man's shoulders were slumped with fatigue and he was red to the elbows.

Every barracks in the four forts was given over to the injured. And nearly everyone was injured. There were men lying on the floor in between the cots. Rillirin protested when Dom sat up, hissing with pain.

'No. Look at him, he needs the bed. I don't.'

'The healer said—' Rillirin began and grabbed him as he swayed.

'The healer said I'll live. Come on, if you want to help,

361

then help me get him on the cot. Rillirin, the man's missing an arm,' he said, his voice low. 'I'm only missing some blood. Help me.'

Between them, they lifted the soldier into the cot. His face was slack with shock, blood loss and opium, not that there was much of that left. Dom slung his arm around Rillirin's shoulders and let her take a little of his weight, but not too much. She was a mass of bruises and cuts, her knuckles scabbed, shins and knees black from multiple falls, and there was a nasty cut along her forearm.

'This is the second time you've come out of a fight with fewer injuries than everyone else,' he grumbled as they limped together out of the barracks and into the fort's killing field, hundreds of campfires scattered across it, figures huddled under blankets everywhere they looked.

'And I didn't drop my spear either,' Rillirin said. 'Oh, wait, no, I did, but only once, and there was a man on top of me at the time.'

Dom stopped walking and pulled her tight to him. 'Don't,' he whispered, pressing kisses to her brow and cheek and nose and mouth. Her hands tightened on him and her mouth opened and Dom's heart stopped.

Rillirin glowed in the light from the nearest fire, the curve of her cheek highlighted in gold. She had a black eye and a cut lip, a rasping abrasion from her hairline to her ear that had ripped out a fistful of hair and she stank of blood and old sweat.

She was the most beautiful thing he'd ever seen. 'I love you,' he said.

Rillirin placed her palm on his cheek. 'I love you, too.'

His smile kissed her smile and they wended between the sleeping figures to a fire near the granary, arms around each other. 'Guess what?' he said, squatting next to Sarilla and scratching absently at his wrist. His heart was so full he didn't notice the silence or feel the blanket of numb horror that had settled over the group like a corpse's shroud.

Sarilla turned a haunted gaze on him before he could say anything else. 'Cam's dead.'

CRYS

Third moon, eighteenth year of the reign of King Rastoth
West Rank headquarters, Cattle Lands, Rilporian border

'So, Trickster eyes, eh? Bet that makes life difficult in the Ranks,' Ash said when Crys woke. 'Life in general, maybe.'

'What?'

'Your eyes. One blue, one brown, or didn't you know? Eyes of the Fox God.'

'Oh. Yeah. The unlucky boy, the untrustworthy man, the cursed soldier, they say. Heard them all. Though who "they" are who make all these predictions, I haven't a fucking clue.'

'Any of them true? Curses, I mean.'

Crys yawned and blinked up at the sky as the moon sailed from behind a cloud. The killing ground inside the fort had been packed with soldiers by the time they'd reached it, so they'd retreated to the watchtower looking east. It was unmanned and they'd coaxed the little brazier into life and collapsed in its warmth. Crys stretched and groaned as every muscle in his body protested.

'Probably. Janis is dead, isn't he?'

'Or maybe you're the reason we won today and got to safety before Corvus arrived to kill us all.' Crys grunted, unconvinced. 'All right, what d'the ladies think of them, then?'

That I'm unlucky, unmarriable, unfuckable. 'Why are you so interested in my eyes?' Crys hissed. 'I can't change them, can I?' He thought back to a long-ago card game. 'Unless I cut one of 'em out.'

'More interested in you, actually, though truth be told I quite like the eyes. Mysterious.' Ash snorted at himself and threw another lump of coal on the brazier. Sparks twisted into the night. 'You've done more than most men would: gone to Rilporin despite the danger, come back here despite the even greater danger. Why?'

'I told you. I have a lot to make up for.'

'Horseshit,' Ash said. 'Rivil's actions are not your fault. You weren't to know.'

'I was his friend: of course I should've known.'

'I said you had the eyes of a god, Crys, not that you are one. There's no way you could've known Rivil would betray us.'

'No gods here,' Crys said and yawned again. 'Just us soldiers.'

'I don't think you're just anything, Crys Tailorson,' Ash said and Crys snorted. 'There'll be lots of people having sex tonight,' he added. 'People celebrating they're still alive.'

'Your lot maybe. No women in the Rank, remember.' He settled himself more comfortably, suppressing another groan, oblivious to the change in the tone of the conversation.

There was a long pause and Ash took a deep breath. 'Not all men need women for loving,' he murmured and Crys's head swivelled to stare at him as Ash's meaning finally became clear. 'Want to celebrate not being dead yet?'

'What? What the fuck?' That's why he'd suggested coming up here instead of staying with the others? 'I told you I'd kill you if you touched me,' Crys snarled. His hand was on his belt, near his dagger. *Fucking pervert.*

'Which is why I'm not touching you, Crys. I'm asking you. I'm giving you the choice.' Ash's voice was measured, unashamed, and Crys was glad he couldn't see his face in the dark.

'It's illegal,' Crys said with as much dignity as he could muster. His mouth was dry.

Ash laughed into the crook of his elbow. 'Illegal? Says who?'

'King Rastoth,' Crys said in icy tones, unamused, 'the man we're fighting this war for.' He shifted away and glared into the night, folding his hands into his armpits. This was disgusting. He'd go back downstairs, that's what he'd do.

'I'm not fighting for the king. I couldn't give a fuck about him. We're fighting for our kin, for the man in the Rank next to us. The Dancer. And anyway, the king's laws don't often reach us out in the west. Why do you think they call us savages?' Ash ran a tanned hand through his brown curls and leant forward slightly, trying to see Crys's face. Crys twisted away. 'And besides, what harm in two people loving each other when they've survived one battle and know they've got another one on the way? We might be dead tomorrow. But if you don't like me—'

'It isn't that,' Crys interrupted and then snapped his mouth shut. *Fuck. Fuck fuck fuck.* Why'd he said that? He didn't like Ash. He didn't. He was a fucking man and he liked fucking women.

'Then what harm?' Ash repeated, interrupting Crys's internal insistence, his eyes soft and hungry in a way that made Crys's belly tighten. No one had ever looked at him like that. No one. Not the whores, not the girl in Three Beeches who'd been prepared to marry him before he joined up. No one. Crys could feel his pulse pounding through his chest. Incessant. Insistent. He couldn't look away.

'No one will know, Crys. Not that any Wolf would care, but I won't tell anyone.'

'I don't . . . I've never . . .' Crys tried, but found he couldn't form words. Ash's eyes were pools and he wanted to drown in them. He couldn't put voice to his feelings, couldn't articulate how Ash had woken something in him that he'd never known was there but uncoiled now, slid through every angle and joint of his body, flooding him with emotion. With need. A flowering of something that had started the very first time they'd met.

He shook his head, his eyes stinging. *Am I actually considering this? Get up and walk away, Crys. Court martial, execution. Walk away.*

He stayed.

One corner of Ash's mouth lifted in gentle mockery of a smile. 'Exactly, Crys. You've never. And seeing as we'll probably both die soon . . .' He let the words hang and then held out his hand. Not touching. Asking to be touched.

Crys stared at it, looked along the arm to Ash's chest, his neck, his face, his eyes. His heart was pounding in every part of his body when he laced his fingers through Ash's, their hands the same size, both calloused, both strong. Both with blood beneath the nails. Ash's breath shuddered out and jolted through Crys's chest. Fuck the king, fuck the law and fuck the Rank. This wasn't wrong. This was so right it hurt.

Chest tight, tears in his throat. 'What are we doing?'

'Only what you want to do, Crys. Only that.' They were still for a moment, and then Ash's free hand touched Crys's cheek. Heat flashed through Crys's body, his skin burning with contact. He turned his head and kissed Ash's palm, and Ash knelt up and forward and pressed his closed lips on to Crys's.

A sound that might have been a whimper came from one of them and Crys put his hand on Ash's chest, hot and damp. Ash's mouth was soft and any doubts Crys had fled into the night. He felt a hand slide around his ribs over the bandaging and stifled a groan at the jolt of pain. And then somehow, without him knowing how, Ash's tongue was in his mouth and Crys's world imploded. What was left in its place was a host of sensation and the knowledge, clear and bright as a silver bell, that nothing would ever be the same again and he didn't want it to be.

'I don't know what I'm doing,' Crys whispered when they came up for air, and there was embarrassment and amusement in equal measure in his tone.

'We'll work it out,' Ash said and slid his fingers under Crys's shirt, tracking the lines of muscle and the ridges of old scars, fresh bruising.

They kissed again, hungry this time, their teeth banging together, and when Crys touched Ash's skin it was like lightning through his fingertips. Slowly, inch by inch, they drifted down into the blankets and each other, discovering a whole new world in the darkness.

Above them, the stars wheeled in the sky, untroubled.

DURDIL

Third moon, eighteenth year of the reign of King Rastoth
Commander's quarters, the palace, Rilporin, Wheat Lands

The city was in uproar and the palace was sullen. The courts had been suspended and the nobles were gossiping, furthering the city's panic.

Durdil's lockdown had prevented Rivil leaving Rilporin and strenghtening the alliance with the Mireces, but it also tied Durdil's hands. Any correspondence he received the prince insisted on examining, using his status as heir as justification. Renik's latest report on the hunt for Galtas had reassured Rivil his friend was still at large and worried Durdil further.

'He's not on his estate, he's not in Three Beeches or Maresfield. He's not in the city.'

Hallos's bulk filled most of the window and he didn't reply. He stared across the deserted assembly place to the gates leading into Fourth Circle. They were shut and barred, Personals standing guard.

Durdil wandered to the map of Rilpor painted on the wall in vibrant colours. His eyes drifted west past the yellow

369

of the Wheat Lands, up the huge winding blue snake of the River Gil to the white-capped mountains, where his son would be fighting the Mireces. Or already had, perhaps. There'd be a message soon by carrier pigeon, a single sentence that would determine everybody's next move. A Rank victory would force Rivil's hand – he'd either have to declare himself or admit defeat. Durdil didn't think he'd admit defeat.

A Mireces victory would mean his son was likely dead and the Raiders could push on unopposed into Rilpor. He'd sent messages to the other Ranks to prepare to march to Rilporin's aid, and had received confirmation from North and South they were ready. Nothing from the East yet.

Durdil's eyes slid across the map. 'Allies in the east,' he murmured. 'No. It's not possible.'

Hallos turned from the window. 'What?'

'I haven't heard back from the East Rank.'

Hallos put his head on one side. 'I agree, it's not possible. It's a Rank, Durdil. It's five thousand men. If five thousand of your soldiers walked the Dark Path you'd know about it. They rotate every two years – how would you even get them all into the East at the same time?'

Durdil's eyes were fixed on the cross marking the East Rank's forts and Hallos's words came muffled through the buzzing in his ears. 'That's where Galtas is. It has to be. He's convincing the East Rank to declare for Rivil and rise against Rastoth.'

Hallos's hand came down on his shoulder. 'You're over-wrought, my old friend. You need to rest. Let me mix you a sedative.'

Durdil shook his hand off and indicated the map. 'The Mireces defeat the West Rank, march to the Gil and comman-deer the Rank's fleet, sail it to Rilporin to lay siege.

Meanwhile, the East Rank declares for Rivil and marches to the Tears, sails its own fleet to Rilporin to lay siege.' His hands came together in a cage around the bright gold dot of Rilporin. 'If they control both the rivers, the North and South Ranks will be forced to march overland to our aid, adding days to their journeys. At the same time, our lines of supply and escape are cut off.'

Hallos moved to stand by his side and squinted at the map. 'No,' he said, 'we can go out through the King's Gate and ride straight for the Listran border, the king's estate in Highcrop.'

Durdil's heart sank. 'All twelve thousand citizens of Rilporin, Hallos?' he asked. 'While the Palace Rank defends the city against its brother Rank and an army of heathens?'

He sensed Hallos's shame and took the bite from his words with a squeeze of the physician's arm. 'The king's safety first, I understand. He is your priority. But I am Commander of the Ranks. The safety of the whole country is my concern. I'll send another pigeon to Skerris in the east, and a courier to Renik at his last reported location. He'll have to go to the East Rank and sniff around, see what he can find out.'

'Prince Rivil won't like that,' Hallos said.

'Prince Rivil won't like what?' Rivil asked from the doorway, and the two men started like guilty children and spun to face him. Rivil gave them a tight smile and repeated his question.

'That we have no further news to share,' Durdil said, and wondered when lying to his prince had become the safest way forward. 'I'm sorry, Your Highness, but we are still unable to locate your friend, and we still await news from the west regarding the planned Mireces invasion.'

Rivil went to Durdil's desk and looked at its contents, picked up a couple of reports, juggled a couple of paperweights.

'About that,' he said, his tone curious. 'Tell me again where that intelligence came from.'

'The Wolves found a slave escaped from Eagle Height. She told them the Mireces were planning an invasion. My son questioned her; he believes her story is legitimate and took appropriate measures. The Raiders have a new king, Corvus. It seems he wants to make a name for himself.'

'An escaped slave,' Rivil said, putting one paperweight back on the desk and keeping the other, a lump of raw silver, in his hand. It was almost as big as his fist and Durdil had a sudden vision of how it would sparkle just before Rivil slammed it into his temple. He put his hand on his belt, next to his dagger.

'It seems she knew a lot. For a slave, I mean.'

Durdil sniffed. 'Well, from what I know, Mireces don't think of slaves as human. They don't even acknowledge their presence unless they're giving them an order. I can't imagine they'd feel it necessary to keep secrets from them.'

'Yes, secrets,' Rivil said, leaping on the word. 'Insidious, dangerous things. They always get found out in the end.'

Durdil matched him, threat for threat. 'Yes, Your Highness, that they do.' Neither of them blinked for a long second, and then Rivil grinned and tossed the silver from one hand to the other.

'Well, I'll leave you to your plotting. The king wants to thrash me at chess again.' He gave them a friendly nod and exited, and Durdil followed him to the door and closed it firmly. He puffed out his cheeks and swallowed hard. Too close.

At his desk he opened a drawer, took out a tiny slip of paper and wrote 'Renik, check East Rank' on it. He rolled it into a tube and tucked it into his jerkin. He'd visit the dovecote before he started his rounds of the Personals. The men were professional and dedicated, but even they were getting restless under the extended hours of guarding the palace without help from the Rank.

He straightened, and then frowned at his desk and moved a couple of papers aside. He glared at the closed door. 'On top of everything else, the bastard stole my paperweight.'

DOM

Third moon, eighteenth year of the reign of King Rastoth
West Rank headquarters, Cattle Lands, Rilporian border

Dom scratched his right wrist, the bracelet of scars itching, burning, maddening. When that didn't work, he brought it up to his mouth and nibbled. The itch didn't fade and he shook his arm hard, and then scraped it against the stone of the wall.

'Fuck's sake,' he said, frustrated. The Dark Lady's attempts at torture in the Waystation had been less effective than this. If it didn't stop soon, he'd lose his mind or hack his own arm off. Or both.

Dom gritted his teeth and pressed his back against the wall. There was a flicker of an image, a tantalising glimpse of something he recognised and couldn't place, like something seen from the corner of his eye, there and gone. The itch swelled into pain and burnt up his arm into his head, his right eye.

'No,' Dom muttered, 'no, not here, not now.' He stared around desperately, staggered into the stables and headed to

374

the end stall. The horse in there took one look at him and flattened its ears, prepared to kick him to death if he went in. There was a pile of hay opposite and Dom fell into it as the fire filled his eyes and the godspace in his head filled with images.

Dimly, he heard a horse whinny and a hoof hit a stall door, the sound of a bucket being kicked over. His back arched and he clenched his fists, his jaw. The pictures were clear this time, not confused or obscure. Dom knew exactly what he was seeing and what it meant. He fought the air into his lungs, felt the stitches on his wound pop as he thrashed, the pain of it tiny in the sea of agony washing through his skull.

Another image, so clear it was as if he stood before the horror of it, a helpless witness. Dom convulsed, a low wail juddering from his throat.

'You're the calestar. You.' Mace couldn't hide his disbelief. Half a dozen Rankers had witnessed the knowing, dragged him out of the hay when he stopped thrashing and taken him to the hospital. Lim and Mace sat either side of his cot.

Dom ignored Mace's incredulity. 'Corvus isn't coming,' he croaked. 'He was never intending to face us. He's going for Watchtown.'

Lim's face drained of blood while Mace's confusion deepened. 'They're all going to die,' Dom said. 'Watchtown is going to burn and everyone will burn with it. More deaths to tear the veil. It's nearly done now. They'll be back soon.' Tears slid into his hair. 'We've lost.'

'You don't really believe all this, do you?' Mace whispered when Dom laid his arm across his eyes. 'Visions and prophecies? Really? It's madness. He's . . . ill, some sort of brain imbalance. He's just raving, Lim, you must see that.' He coughed a laugh. 'You can't base a sound military strategy on the ravings of a madman, even if he is family.'

Lim's voice was very cold. 'Dom has foreseen all this and more. He saw Janis's sacrifice as it happened; he foresaw the invasion. If he says Corvus is going for our people, I believe him. And we're going to stop him.'

Dom sat up in the cot and world spun around him. 'We've lost,' he snarled, 'and they're all going to die. It's over.' He could hear the rustle of the Dark Lady's laughter and shuddered, digging his nails into his right wrist.

'Watchtown is made up of thousands of warriors, fighting for their homes and their children. They'll stop Corvus, but we need to help them.' Lim's voice was less sure in the face of Dom's conviction. If they lost Watchtown, they lost everything. They lost their future, their past, who they were.

'Look, I have no idea what's going on here,' Mace interrupted, 'but it's clear you're exhausted, Dom. I know you all believe in your calestar, in his prophecies, and I admit I'm stunned to learn you think you're him, but I have a Rank to command. Captain Carter's intelligence was that Corvus's army would be here sometime today. That is intelligence I understand and believe. Not this . . . whatever it is.'

Lim scraped his chair back. 'I understand, General. Good luck.'

Mace jumped up. 'What does that mean?'

'We'll be riding for Watchtown to aid our people,' Lim said. 'That's where Corvus is going, that's where we'll fight him. You'll be sitting here looking out at nothing if you stay, General, whereas you could help us if you marched with us. Please, Mace.'

Mace wavered.

'The veil is weak. So many dead, so many converts,' Dom said, his eyes blank. The words came through him, not from him, and he had no idea what he was going to say until he heard himself say it. 'All the east.' He pushed back the blankets and stood, brushed past Mace and wandered to the exit in bare feet. 'It'll tear soon, tear wide open. Rot in the east, madness in the capital, and a soul to claim.' He giggled and picked at the scabs on his wrist. 'You think I'm mad, you should see Rastoth. Blood rises.'

'Supposing I believe you,' Mace said thoughtfully, 'why didn't you see any of this before? Why let us run back here with our tails between our legs? If you'd known of the two forces earlier, we could have sent a Thousand up the Gil-beside Road and held them there.' He jerked his hand through the air. 'Gods, there are so many things we could've done. A Thousand could hold on the Gil-beside for weeks.'

'It comes when it comes when it comes,' Dom said. 'No stopping it, no controlling it most of the time.' He grasped at the air. 'The gods talk when They wish, not when I want Them to.'

'And normally it's never this clear,' Lim said, 'but now it is, and we should be thankful for that. We need to get ready to move. My father's dead, thousands of us are dead. I won't lose anyone else.' He collected Dom's boots from the under the cot and snatched the blanket as well. At the door he looked back. 'Make up your mind fast, General. Stay here and fight nothing, or march with us and fight Corvus.'

'You really believe him?' Mace asked.

'Dom's made his mistakes, General,' Lim said and Dom's face flushed, 'but I believe this. The Dancer has sent us a message that could save the lives of our people. I'll not ignore that.'

Lim gave Dom his boots and Dom concentrated on getting his feet into them. It was easier than looking into Lim's eyes and telling him the knowing hadn't come from the Gods of Light at all.

THE BLESSED ONE

Third moon, year 995 since the Exile of the
Red Gods
Watch Ford, River Gil, Cattle Lands

'It is confirmed,' Lanta said, opening her eyes and blinking at the glare of the sun. A whole night had passed while she'd communed. She allowed Corvus to help her to stand and gave no indication of the pins and needles consuming her legs as they took her weight.

Corvus handed her a waterskin and waited, edgy with impatience, for her to speak. Behind him were Valan and the war chiefs and Gilda, her lined face bright with curiosity. What had it looked like to her, Lanta's communion with the Dark Lady? The army was a carpet of blue on the green plain, most of them sitting or lying in the grass, enjoying the warmth, the softness of this land.

Lanta looked back at the mountains rearing behind them, then at the ford through the river, the water hissing and chuckling over the rocks.

'Your army was defeated, Sire.' Lanta pitched her voice

loud enough for the war chiefs to hear. 'Slaughtered to the last man.'

Corvus's nostrils flared. 'I see.'

'Their holy deaths served their purpose, Sire. The veil is washed in blood, weakening every day. The West Rank lost nearly half its men, and the Wolves were decimated. They have scurried back to the forts, hiding behind the walls in fear. But they will come for us soon.'

Corvus crossed his arms. 'Good. Will they interfere with our plans for Watchtown?'

'No. We have more than enough time for Watchtown's destruction. And when the West Rank does come, will we flee ahead of them?'

'We will not. I have a plan to end every last one of them with minimal losses to our number. The maps the Rilporian left with us have been most informative. As long as we destroy a few bridges to force them to stay on the south bank of the river, then when we strike they'll only have one place to go.' He brought his hands together. 'Into a trap.'

'Well?' Lanta snapped at Gilda, who'd for once lost her patronising smile. 'Does your goddess give you such detailed information?'

'Not to me,' Gilda said, 'but She talks to our calestar, tells him what we need to know.'

'Ah yes, the famous calestar. It isn't just the Flower-Whore who talks to him, though. Did you know that? Did you know the unspeakable torments he suffers at the hands of my gods?'

'I know,' Gilda said. 'And I am not surprised you would take pride in something like that. You speak as though your gods' penchant for torture is a good thing. You should be careful They don't decide to torture you.'

'I would welcome it,' Lanta said and Gilda's expression showed polite disbelief.

'We are days away now, Blessed One, just days from Rilporin. Did the gods say anything of our allies? Does the prince keep true to his word?' Corvus pressed.

Lanta glared at Gilda a moment longer before turning her attention on the king. 'He does. His allies in the east are confirmed. They will join us in sacking their city and claiming their king. The Red Gods will be ascendant, Sire.'

'Then let us bathe this land in the blood of heathens to welcome Them. Valan, sound the advance and get the army over the ford. I want us just out of sight of Watchtown by nightfall and ready to tear the place to pieces by dawn tomorrow.'

'Your will, Sire,' Valan said.

Corvus offered Lanta his arm. 'You have knelt in trance for many hours, Blessed One. Are you able to walk or shall I have the men assemble a litter?'

Lanta put her hand on his arm and stood. 'I will walk,' she said, ignoring the fizzes of pain behind her knees. 'My feet are on the Path, and every step I take is consecrated to the gods. My pain is my gift to Them.'

Corvus inclined his head. 'You are a teacher to us all, Blessed One.'

'You should try being joyful,' Gilda said as she walked behind them. 'The gods like Their people to be happy. Maybe the Dark Lady would appreciate that instead.'

'I have been in the presence of my goddess. Do not profane the moment with your ramblings, or I will have your fingers cut off.'

Gilda said no more and they walked in the midst of their army over the ford on to the Western Plain. Towards Watchtown and glory. 'Soon, Sire,' Lanta murmured, 'soon the Wolves and the Watchers will be annihilated, Rilpor subjugated, and the gods will take Their rightful place in the world again. Soon, all Gilgoras will bow to Them and to you.'

And soon enough to me.

Blessed One.

Queen.

GALTAS

Third moon, eighteenth year of the reign of King Rastoth East Rank headquarters, Grazing Lands, Listran border

'Messages from Rilporin, my lord,' Skerris wheezed, panting in the doorway from the climb up the stairs.

Galtas beckoned him in. 'About fucking time. I was getting worried. Well?'

Skerris poured himself into a chair and mopped his face with a square of linen. 'Sent by pigeon, so they're brief. Durdil requests again my confirmation of orders received, that we will march to Rilporin's defence if needed.'

Galtas smirked. 'I think we can safely say yes to his request. And the other?'

'From Corvus via the prince. Must've used one of those pigeons you left with him. The West Rank has fallen.'

Galtas stiffened. 'The Mireces won? Shit.' He wandered back to the window and looked down on the men nailed to the posts in the parade ground. Most of them were dead now, but a few were still twitching. They were a constant reminder to the Rankers that their souls no longer belonged to them. 'But how can Corvus know that? He wasn't there.'

'That many deaths, whether Mireces or not, will have caused a ripple in the veil. The Blessed One may have detected it.'

Galtas scrubbed his hand through his hair. 'The last thing we need is a fucking Mireces army at our heels,' he muttered.

Skerris shifted his arse in the chair. 'Then the promise of the Western Plain—'

'Was empty. We expected the West Rank to defeat the Mireces, of course. But an invasion gave us the perfect excuse to mobilise troops – you – who could then secure Rivil's throne when he killed Rastoth and announced his faith.'

'I see,' Skerris said. 'There was more, my lord. "Wheeler dead. Palace lockdown."'

'Shit,' Galtas repeated. He paced the room, mind spinning; Skerris was content to watch without interruption. Lockdown would fuck up everything. Rivil wouldn't – couldn't – risk killing Rastoth during lockdown. Durdil suspected too much as it was. And who'd killed Wheeler? Wheeler was one of theirs.

Galtas froze, icy fingers down his back. What had Wheeler told his killer before he died? How much did Durdil know? Was the message even really from Rivil, or was he in a dungeon awaiting trial and this was Durdil's way to draw Galtas out?

'Our feet are on the Path,' Skerris said. 'Take a deep breath and think it through. We've got options and time. At the moment, the Mireces are the least of your problems. We need to get Rivil out of the city. Forget assassinating Rastoth – the man can die anytime we choose. Without Rivil, we have no coup.'

Galtas made himself sit. 'Durdil's too canny to lift the lockdown,' he said. 'It hamstrings us and he knows it. He'll have used Wheeler's death as the perfect excuse. Rivil's a prisoner in a very gilded cage.'

There was a rapid knock at the door and it burst open before either of them could speak. 'Men from Rilporin. Palace Rank,' a soldier said. 'Mile down the road and coming fast.'

Skerris swore. 'Knife the sacrifices, cut them down and sink them in the shit pit, now,' he snapped. 'Then get the men practising ladder drills. I want them loud and sweaty and too busy to talk by the time they get here. My lord, I suggest we find you a hiding place.'

'Fuck,' Galtas said as he put it together. Durdil had blamed Wheeler's death on him. The perfect excuse to haul him back to Rilporin and ruin any alliances or plans he'd made, while also keeping Rivil right where he could see him.

'The infirmary, Major Renik. Just a few men in at the moment,' Skerris boomed cheerfully. 'Over-enthusiastic drilling – you know how it is. We were so shocked to learn of the death of Prince Janis,' he added. 'Please, Major, you would do me a great favour if you assured Prince Rivil of the East Rank's absolute loyalty.'

'Of course, General,' Renik said. 'In times such as these, loyalty is more important than ever. We must all be ready to make the ultimate sacrifice for Rilpor.'

Galtas lay under a blanket with bandages around his head and over both eyes. His hands and forearms were swathed in linen as well. He heard boots approaching, and Skerris's stentorian breathing.

'What happened here?' he heard Renik ask and willed himself to lie still, relaxed.

'Ah, a particularly nasty accident,' Skerris said. 'The private was working in the forge when a kiln exploded. The poor man's hair caught fire. Terrible burns to his head and scalp.' Skerris's voice dropped. 'Tried to put out the flames with his hands. Still, he remains as cheerful as can be expected, eh, private? Our physicians are optimistic.'

Galtas waved his bandaged hands vaguely.

'I hope you will be soon recovered, private,' the major said. Galtas waved again. The footsteps moved away. 'And you've received no visitors, no correspondence from the capital in recent weeks?' he heard Renik say.

'Nothing, Major, except that from Commander Koridam, of course. Who is it you're looking for?' Galtas lay still as the voices were cut off by the closing of a door. Durdil had suspected them ever since they'd brought Janis back without his legs. Seems the old bastard had decided to do something about those suspicions. He couldn't move on Rivil, but he could isolate him from his allies and cut off his means of communication.

Galtas relaxed in the cot and waited for someone to come and tell him Renik and his Hundred had gone. The major's assurance on Skerris's behalf of their loyalty would be all the confirmation Rivil needed that they were coming. He'd know to get out of Rilporin. He'd find a way to lift the lockdown. And if he didn't, well, the Lady's will.

GILDA

Dawn was the pink inside of a lip across the ocean of grass as they marched the final miles to Watchtown.

'Blessed One, we would all fight harder with words from the gods.' Corvus was vibrating with energy and excitement, infecting the men around him and spreading ripples of bloodlust through the army.

'The Dark Lady has words for them all,' Lanta said. 'Bring the Dancer's whore to witness our power at first hand. Besides, I want her close when her people and her temple are trampled into the mud.'

'I'm a little too old to be a whore,' Gilda said from her place behind Corvus. Her face was impassive despite what the day would bring. 'And even in my youth, I only ever had eyes for one man. But please, if it makes you feel better, call me anything you like.'

Lanta glared her into silence and stalked through the fringe of the army, her heavy blue skirts hissing through the grass.

387

She favoured some with smiles, others with the touch of her hand. Behind her, men stood taller in the gods' favour.

'Why do you antagonise her?' Corvus asked Gilda as she was led past him.

The old woman put her head on one side, her eyes alight with mischief. 'I'm old, I'll be dead soon. Why shouldn't I? Besides, it annoys the holy fuck out of her.'

Corvus blinked and the corner of his mouth twitched. 'She may well torture you,' he found himself saying. 'If not for her, you'd have died with the others.'

Gilda's face darkened. 'With the innocent, you mean? I'd have been pleased to die then; I couldn't think of finer people with whom to fly to the Dancer. But She has other plans for me, plans which don't include me dying at your hands. So I'm free, am I not, to do as I please?'

'Your goddess has told you that you're to live?' Corvus asked, almost shocked at her casual confidence.

Gilda's smile was enigmatic. 'It won't be you who kills me, Madoc of Dancer's Lake, and it won't be poor, misguided Lanta. The Lady of Light has told me this.' She inclined her head briefly and followed in Lanta's footsteps, leaving Corvus reeling at her mention of his birth name.

Gilda raised her hand to her amulet as she walked. *Sweet Dancer, let me be right. I don't want to die like Janis did, nailed upside down to a post. Not without seeing Cam and my boys again. Not unless I must.*

But it wasn't just her death that was coming, was it? By the time this was done, she might well be the last Watcher in the world. She caught up to Lanta and stood beside her on a small hump in the grass, looking out over the army scattered before them, the army that had come to destroy her people. She wondered again how she could turn this tide, or whether the Dancer had put her here simply to bear witness. If the latter, she prayed she had the strength to do so.

Lanta inhaled and faced the army, arms raised to embrace them all. 'You who are the army of the Red Gods, you whose feet walk the Dark Path swinging the hammers of Their just vengeance, hear me. The Dark Lady and the God of Blood have spoken. Our great people are destined to destroy the heathens and kill their false gods, to take these wide plains and thick forests for our rightful home. The feet of the Red Gods will leave Their bloody prints in Rilpor's green plain. Their red hands will stretch forth to crush the unbeliever, to topple the towers of Rilporin itself.'

The men strained towards her in the lightening air and even Gilda felt the pull on her emotions. Oh, this one was good.

'But before They descend to live in glory among us, we must prove our faith. We must prove our dedication to Their cause.' Lanta gestured with theatrical passion. 'Out there lies the walled and protected Watchtown, the nest of our enemies. Out there lies hate and bigotry. Out there lies death and glory. Theirs is the death, and yours is the glory!'

The roar was so loud that Gilda had to put her hands over her ears. *Please, Watchtown, hear this and prepare your walls. Where are your scouts? Where are your patrols?*

Lanta turned her triumphant gaze on Gilda. 'Well, old woman? Now do you see my power?'

Got you. Gilda raised her eyebrows. 'Your power? I thought this was the power of your gods,' she said and saw shock pass over Lanta's flushed features.

'Of course it's Their power,' she stammered. 'But I channel it so that our people can understand. The gods are complex. They don't reveal Their intentions easily.'

'Indeed. You've a gift for speaking, Blessed One, a gift for manipulation. Is that your gods' power?'

'Don't test me, old woman,' Lanta warned, stepping close so that her face was in Gilda's. 'You're my prisoner, not the king's. *Mine*. And I'll do with you whatever I see fit.' Gilda saw the thought blossom in the other woman's eyes. She had time to move, even to duck but she stood still, hands folded before her as Lanta pressed a flat palm at the army to hush them and then slapped Gilda hard in the mouth, the flat crack echoing out across the multitude.

Gilda stumbled back a step as blood sprang from her lips. But only a step. *Don't give her more than that.*

Lanta looked up at the pink dawn. 'Well, Dancer? What have you to say to that?' she shrieked and the army held its breath. Lanta grinned and looked back at Gilda just as the old woman bunched her fist and swung.

Her knuckles slammed into Lanta's right eye and buckled her legs. She screamed with pain and shock and Gilda had the satisfaction of seeing tears stain her perfect, satin cheeks and red blood pump from her nostril.

Gilda looked out at the stunned army and shook the pain from her hand. 'That's what the Dancer says,' she shouted into the silence and cackled. Guards pinned her arms and dragged her from the prostrate woman curled on the grass with her hands pressed to her face.

Corvus's second, Valan, ran forward and hauled her to her feet. Lanta shook off his supporting hand and wobbled in a circle, taking in the slack horror of the warriors, the blank eyes of the king, the triumphant grin on Gilda's lined face.

'Blessed One,' Valan hissed, 'respond to the challenge.'

But Lanta did nothing. Gilda knew she wouldn't kill her now. Oh no. She had to exact her vengeance first, had to balm her skinned pride, make Gilda pay for the shame and humiliation. Gilda doubted this one would kill her even if the Dark Lady Herself came out of hell to command it. Not now.

Slowly, Valan's words penetrated Lanta's shock. She forced a smile for the army, raised one hand in a dismissive wave, gave a slight shrug. *Captives, eh? Rilporians.* It wasn't enough. They were waiting for more and Lanta didn't have more. Gilda tried not to snigger and failed.

'Take her away. She'll face the Dark Lady's inquisition,' Lanta said and they all heard the ripple of disappointment, of confusion, from the assembled Raiders. 'You men, do your duty to the king and the gods.' And Lanta walked unsteadily away.

Gilda stood sucking her knuckles in a ring of steel, waiting until her guards began to feel like idiots for menacing an unarmed old woman. 'Well,' she said brightly to the man in charge, 'either your goddess is as powerless as you say mine is, or She doesn't get involved in petty struggles. What do you think?'

'Shut up,' the guard snarled, shoving her hard. 'The Dark Lady sees everything. She'll have a punishment waiting when the time is right. Now move.'

'I'd've thought that was the right time,' Gilda said and their silence confirmed it. 'So, the Blessed One got that wrong then, did she? Interesting. Wonder how many times that's happened.'

In the distance, Watchtown's horns sounded a triple blast. The guards exchanged uneasy glances. 'That means you've been spotted,' Gilda said. 'Time to die.'

'Their time, not ours.'

Gilda smiled again, though there was no humour left in the day. 'Perhaps.' She walked between them in Corvus's wake, the army streaming around them, flowing like a flood to lap at Watchtown and wash it away.

Gilda examined the reddened flesh of her knuckles with intense satisfaction. It wouldn't change the outcome of today's battle – nothing she could do would ever change that – but the Dancer had long ago taught Rilporians free will and resourcefulness, and that sometimes a fist was better than words.

RILLIRIN

Third moon, eighteenth year of the reign of King Rastoth
Road to the River Gil, Cattle Lands

Rillirin jogged through the trees. She was at the back of the group now and starting to lose touch with the stragglers as they flitted like shadows through the forest. It was the second day of the march and the pace was still relentless, even the injured Wolves pulling ahead of her now. She dashed angry, tired tears from her eyes and focused on the terrain, skipping over tree roots and stumbling into rabbit holes. She wouldn't fall behind. She couldn't.

Dom had had the knowing and told Lim what he'd seen, and then, before they could even gather the survivors to break the news, he'd stolen a horse from the stables and ridden south. He was going alone to Watchtown and nobody knew why, least of all Rillirin.

He hadn't even told her he was leaving.

A stone turned under her boot, her spear got tangled between her legs and she went down hard, grunting as pain exploded along her ribs, her knife hilt burrowing into flesh.

Rolling on to her back, she stared up at the sunlight through the canopy of green leaves, one hand pressed to her side, sucking in air.

Godsdamn bloody forests. Stupid trees. Rillirin wished she was back in Watchtown – a Watchown at peace – bustling with life that comforted her with its similarities to her childhood at Dancer's Lake, and even, if she was honest, its reminders of Eagle Height. She'd hated that place, hated everything about it, everyone in it, but these endless trees with their treacherous roots, the sudden outcroppings of rock that broke the trail, the creaking, rustling silence was driving her mad. Too different to anything she knew.

Then again, she'd known nothing about a battle and she'd survived one, hadn't she? Maybe she could learn to love living in the woods, a semi-nomad Wolf woman, never settling anywhere for long. Or maybe they'd rebuild Watchtown, begin the slow process of repopulating it, a new generation of Watchers.

It was no good. No matter how hard she tried to think of other things, her mind kept rushing back to Dom, racing alone into the jaws of the Mireces. 'Why would you do that, Dom Templeson?' she asked the trees, an angry creak in her voice. 'What else do you know? Why do you need to be the one who faces Corvus?'

There wasn't time to be tired, she knew, but she couldn't get up right now. Just couldn't. She wondered if the West Rank had decided to follow them. Mace had been discussing it with his staff when the Wolves had set out. She hoped they'd come.

'Rillirin, are you all right?' It was Seth Lightfoot, Dalli's cousin. He reached down and lifted her to her feet without effort. Hours of running had done little to dent his energy.

He put his hand to her cheek. 'Are you hurt?' he asked, and his hand was hot on her face, invasive.

Rillirin's skin crawled and she pulled away. Seth's mouth turned down. 'I'm fine. Just turned my ankle on a stone.'

'I dropped back a few miles, checked our trail. The West Rank's coming.'

'Thank the gods,' Rillirin said. 'How long to Watchtown, do you think?'

'At this pace, two days. If we wait for the Rank, closer to three.' He didn't need to tell her that was too long. Watchtown would've fallen by then. Might already have fallen.

Dom, alone in the ruins of Watchtown, surrounded by the dead.

Dom, for some reason known only to himself, confronting Corvus as Watchtown burnt.

Dom, cut down by Raiders before he got within a mile of the main army.

Dom.

'Can we go faster?' Rillirin asked, circling her foot to test the ankle. Sore, not damaged. Could she go faster? Yes.

'Some of us, but not enough that we could risk engaging Corvus if he's still there. We have no idea how many men he has, but they'll be his best warriors. But Watchtown is strong; our people are strong. They won't fall.'

The conviction sounded hollow in Rillirin's ears, but it was all they had. She rubbed her ribs a last time and started moving again, twinges of pain in her calves and thighs. *Got to get to Dom. Must go faster.*

DURDIL

Third moon, eighteenth year of the reign of King Rastoth
The palace, Rilporin, Wheat Lands

'May I see?' Rivil held out his hand and Durdil passed him Mace's report.

Durdil summarised it for Rastoth as Rivil read. 'The West Rank was victorious, Your Majesty. They slaughtered the first Mireces army to the last man in the Blood Pass Valley, ordering the all-out to force the victory. The Rank suffered heavy losses but retreated in good order to the forts to recuperate.'

'Excellent, excellent,' Rastoth boomed, slapping weakly at the arm of his throne. 'Excellent, isn't it, Marisa?' he asked the empty chair at his side. Rivil twitched.

'First Mireces army?' the prince questioned, pausing in his reading to assess Durdil.

'Yes, Your Highness. A reconnaissance patrol spotted a second army venturing down the Gil-beside Road and heading directly in-country. When General Koridam found out, he and the surviving Wolves set out in pursuit. I have heard nothing since.'

'So there's a second invading army in Rilpor and a shattered, exhausted Rank is the only one in pursuit?' Rivil rolled up the report and slapped it against his palm. 'Not good enough. We need to mobilise reinforcements.'

This was where all Durdil's suspicions would be proven correct. Galtas was still missing and Renik had confirmed he wasn't with the East Rank. To effect Rivil's rebellion, Galtas's only other option was to travel into Listre to hire mercenaries. Rivil would announce he'd secured aid from Listre and that would be the final part of the proof Durdil needed.

Durdil's hands tightened on his belt and he moved into parade rest to keep from fidgeting. Any second now.

'Father, we should call a Thousand from the North, South and East Ranks to bolster the Palace Rank's numbers and ensure the Mireces are defeated.'

Durdil blinked. *What?*

'As you think best, my boy.' Rastoth waved him on. 'I leave the matter entirely in your hands.'

What?

'Your Majesty—' Durdil began.

'Thank you for the report, Commander,' Rivil said smoothly. 'We will keep you informed.' Durdil didn't move and Rivil's gracious smile turned quizzical. 'Was there something else, Commander?' he asked.

Durdil's movements were jerky as he bowed and backed towards the door. He paused there as Rivil turned his back on Rastoth and began penning a series of messages. On the throne, Rastoth looked on in blissful ignorance and mumbled platitudes to his dead wife.

'Forget Rastoth, I think I'm the one going bloody mad,' Durdil said, his fingers scraping through the stubble on his head. 'How can he do that? How can he just give the security of the country to Rivil while I'm shitting well standing there? I'm the bloody Commander of the bloody Ranks!'

'Durdil, calm down. You'll rupture a blood vessel.' Hallos forced him to sit and put a glass in his hand.

'We're going to have to tell him,' Durdil said eventually. 'We're going to have to tell Rastoth about Rivil's conversion, his alliance with the Mireces, everything. Six pigeons left the roof an hour after that audience,' he added. 'I counted. And you know what? They all circled and headed east. All six. You can write quite a long message if you send it on six pigeons.'

He broke off and put his free hand on his chest, taking deep breaths against the slowly tightening band of steel around his ribs. *Bloody heart twinges. Now is really not the time.*

Hallos was at the window of his study. 'Durdil? You'd better come and see this.'

'Why? Is it the Mireces army come to murder us in our beds?' Durdil asked sourly. He drained the glass, grunted and refilled it.

'They're opening the gates.'

Durdil dropped his glass and crunched heedless through the shards shattered on the flagstones as he ran to the window. He shoved Hallos aside. There was a cheer and people poured through the gate from Fourth Circle into the assembly place. Nobles, court officials, lawmakers, plaintiffs. Hundreds of people flooding Fifth Circle and entering the palace and courts. A Hundred from the Palace Rank marched in last and filtered into the palace. The Personals would be relieved at least.

'Lockdown's over,' Hallos said quite unnecessarily.

'Then we're out of time. Rivil's making his play. We need to make ours, convince Rastoth his son's a traitor.'

Hallos nodded. 'I'm with you. We'll make him listen.'

The door swung open. 'Commander Koridam?' Lieutenant Weaverson wobbled into the room brandishing his pike with an air of miserable bewilderment. 'The heir commands you are to be confined to quarters for the duration of this emergency. There are concerns over your ability to effectively counteract the Mireces threat. If you would accompany me please, sir.'

Durdil looked from the boy to Hallos and fought the urge to laugh. 'Speak to him,' he hissed. 'Make him listen. Today. Now.' Weaverson herded him to the door. 'And send some fucking pigeons to the Ranks.'

'The pigeons are to be used only by the royal family,' Weaverson said apologetically. 'There are concerns that unauthorised pigeons and messages have been sent.'

Yes, and we all know by who, Durdil thought as Weaverson pushed him gently out of the room. *Unauthorised pigeons.* The need to laugh rose in him again. *Mace is coming. Mace is coming with the Wolves and Hallos knows the truth.*

It wasn't enough and he knew it; in his bones he knew it. Rivil had outsmarted him.

'Lieutenant, I commend your loyalty to the king and the heir. Tell me, would you defend them with your life?'

'Of course, sir,' Weaverson said without hesitation.

'Good. Remember that. I've a feeling you may have to do that very thing very soon.'

'The Mireces, Commander?'

'No, lad,' Durdil said. 'I think it's going to be a lot closer to home than that.' He hesitated in the entrance to his quarters and grabbed Weaverson's pike. Startled, Weaverson snatched it back and dropped into a fighting stance. Durdil held up both his hands. 'Good. Stay sharp. I think someone's going to try and kill the king.' He closed the door in Weaverson's face and leant his back against it. After a moment he heard the lock turn from outside. He slid down the wood on to the floor and put his head in his hands.

'All down to you now, Hallos.'

CORVUS

The battering ram they'd hauled all the way from the forest was useless, the gates too well built and propped with timbers on the inside. Scaling ladders were little better against walls built with an overhanging lip. Instead, Corvus had them pile the ladders against the gates along with some clay jugs of pitch, dropped handfuls of dry grass and some old rags on top; then they threw a torch into the mess.

The wood exploded into flame and his archers poured fire arrows into the gate and over the walls. Others aimed for the jugs of pitch, and each time one exploded the fire jumped higher up the gates. There were whumps as thatched roofs caught and Watchers disappeared from the walls to fight fires inside the town. More archers picked off any who tried to throw down water.

Fire everywhere, at the walls, in the town. They wouldn't take much more of this. It'd be over soon, one way or the other. The smoke coiled so thick in the early-morning sky that a second night had fallen. Fitting for the Watchers to die without the light of their goddess on their faces.

Corvus stood with his army just out of bowshot and watched the gates burn, split and curl in on themselves like dying spiders. He sent the ram team forward again, his archers forcing the Watchers to keep their heads below the wall. The gates were so weakened it only took four swings before they splintered and broke. A stream of Watchers poured through the breach and killed the men on the ram. To be expected.

But now there was Corvus, King of the fucking Mireces, with an army of thousands of Raiders, all of who had sworn blood oaths to exterminate the Watchers. Roaring, Corvus lunged through the smoke and fire of the gates, his men howling behind him, howling into Watchtown.

The Watcher was older than him by two decades, but fast and deadly, the tip of her spear countering his every thrust and hack. She wore a brooch that showed her to be the town's elder, and it winked in the light from a nearby fire as she deflected a slash down into the packed earth of the road and recovered faster than he did, following the arc of her parry so that the butt of her spear slammed into the side of his neck. Pain, and weakness up into his head so that his tongue went numb, and down into his arm.

Air, and its lack, as his neck muscles squeezed, constricting his windpipe. Corvus stumbled a step sideways, his sword drooping in his hand. Hazel eyes burnt into his and Corvus knew himself for a hog ready for slaughter.

Her hands pulled back on the spear, her shoulders setting for the killing blow and still there was no air in the world. He wobbled, pulled away and the Watcher stepped forward, driving with the tip of her spear and all the strength of her shoulders and hips, unstoppable.

An arrow appeared in her shoulder and the strike missed, the tip digging a furrow through Corvus's cheek as it passed. Air rushed into his lungs and he straightened as she over-balanced. 'My feet are on the Path,' he croaked and drove his sword into her belly.

He coughed and wiped his eyes, sucked in air thick with smoke that made him cough again, and stepped over the woman. She was keening, a high-pitched wail that grated along his nerves, her hands pressing at the wound. He ignored her, waited for Valan and some others to catch up, and pressed forward.

Flames everywhere, leaping high from buildings left and right, shouts and screams adding to the chaos. An empty alley to his left and he was five strides past when men and women erupted out of it and drove into his squad, hacking into them with swords and spears. Four of his men went down in the first flurry.

A man like a bear drove a club at Corvus's head, an axe in his other hand swinging at his knees at the same time, and Corvus had no time to decide. His hand did it for him, sword swinging to parry the axe, head ducking, hoping. Not enough.

The axe opened the front of his right shin and the club damn near took off the top of his head and Corvus was horizontal in the air, sword flying from his fist. The Watcher reversed his swings. The club would punch him into the ground and the axe would follow, burying itself in him. He could see it happen, no way to stop it. He made a wild grab, somehow got one hand around the club arm and jerked it down with him. The breath slammed from his body as he landed, and a second later the Watcher overbalanced. He landed on his knees next to Corvus and Corvus snatched at the club, got his hands around it and used it to block the axe arcing for his face.

Wood chips sprayed his eyes and yelling mouth and the Watcher leant his weight on the axe, forcing it down. Corvus thrashed his legs but no help came. His exhilaration at finally being in Watchtown died as rapidly as he was going to. The axe head grated sideways along the club and Corvus twisted with it, letting the man's weight take it across. The axe thunked off the end of the club into the dirt, the Watcher bending over him. He straightened, freeing the axe, and Corvus poked him in the face with the handle of the club, just hard enough that he flopped back off his knees on to his arse.

In the sliver of space Corvus got a knee under him and both hands on the club's handle. He swung, awkward, not much power, and clocked the Watcher along the side of his head. The man rocked and Corvus got to a foot, heaved himself up, kicked the man's axe away and beat in his skull with the club, blow after blow until his head was red pulp and smashed white bone. Then he spat on the corpse. Then he clubbed it again.

'Sire, are you all right?'

Corvus brushed Valan's hand off his shoulder and heaved in air. 'Keep going,' he ordered, glaring at his surviving two men. 'And keep a fucking eye on the alleys.'

GILDA

Gilda stood beside the Blessed One and wept as Watchtown
burnt. 'Fly to the Dancer,' she whispered, 'and know Her
grace.'

'They'll know the Red Gods' might first,' Lanta said.
'They'll know pain and suffering and the deaths of their
children.'

Gilda faced her: 'Shall I break your nose this time, or
would prefer another black eye?' and was gratified to see
Lanta stumble backwards. A guard appeared at her side with
a dagger. The corner of Gilda's mouth twitched and she
opened her arms. 'Be my guest.'

Lanta pushed his hand down. 'No. She wishes to avoid
the pain of seeing any more of her people die. She's a coward,
but she will watch.'

'Aren't you worried your king will be killed in there?'
Gilda asked. 'Watchtown is made of many warriors, the
streets littered with traps, blind alleys and murder holes.'

'We walk the Dark Path,' Lanta said, serene and confident. 'We will do and die when commanded. If Corvus's destiny is to die in there, then die he shall.'

The sky was a riot of sparks and black smoke lit from beneath with a hellish orange glow. She couldn't imagine anyone getting out of there alive, Watcher or Raider. Her throat was raw and her eyes stung with smoke and tears and something in Lanta's words made her repeat them in her head.

'Oh,' she said quietly. 'I didn't realise.' Lanta stared down her nose at her. 'You'll take command of the army if Corvus dies, won't you? I mean, you'll leave the tactics and the fighting to the warriors, but you'll have overall control. This will be your army. In fact, it would probably suit you better if he did die, wouldn't it? No pesky king wresting away your power.' She paused to cough. 'What's the plan? Corvus dies in Watchtown and you marry Rivil, make yourself queen?'

There was a glint of fear in Lanta's face, there and then gone. Gilda had touched a nerve. 'Mireces do not marry, and priestesses do not become queens,' Lanta said, haughty.

Gilda folded her arms. 'Yes, but this is a new world, isn't it? If you manage to bring back your psychotic gods and rule this land, why, anything could happen. So what if Corvus lives? Will you stab him in the night? Or do you just not care which of them makes it on to the throne? You're not fussy, perhaps, about who gets between your thighs?'

Lanta backhanded her and this one Gilda didn't see coming. It spun her in a half-circle and dropped her to one knee. Her cheek and eye were throbbing. *Definitely touched a nerve.*

Gilda clambered to her feet, feeling her age. Smoke tickled the back of her throat. 'Would the gods approve your ambition?' she croaked and coughed.

Lanta seized the plait of her hair and jerked her head back. A slim knife was in her hand and she pressed it under Gilda's chin. 'If you speak to me like that again, I'll have you blinded and your tongue chewed out of your head. There are men in our army who enjoy that sort of thing. Do you understand me?' Gilda looked into Lanta's eyes and saw nothing but absolute honesty in them. 'Do you?'

'I do, Blessed One.'

'Then watch your town and your people die, and don't speak to me again.'

Gilda did as she was told.

DOM

Dom sat on his horse and listened to it crop the grass. Behind that sound was the crackle of fires still burning in the ruins of Watchtown. Behind that, the echoes of screams. And behind even that, the endless whispers of the Dark Lady, dripping poison into his ear, rotting the edges of his mind, clouding his ability to think.

Corvus's route was easy to follow. Thousands of men marching left a trail fifty strides wide in the grass. Over the ford, through Watchtown, and on towards the bridge at the West Rank harbour. Into the boats and down the Gil to Rilporin.

The day was bright but he was blind to it, blind to the flags of flame still rising from Watchtown's homes. All urgency had left him. There was something he had to do, somewhere he needed to be, but it was hazy, unimportant.

A ripple of smoky air blew hair into his eyes, tickled a strand over his stubbled cheek. The burning in his wrist couldn't be ignored, and as he stared without seeing he picked savagely at the scabs. When his fingers became too slick to find purchase, he brought his arm up to his mouth and chewed.

Sometimes his vision flickered and he saw the cavern, the Waystation to the Red Gods' Afterworld. Other times She showed him what had happened here, the smoke and battle, the slaughter, the temple where Gilda had raised him desecrated and burning, corpses in the godpool, blood on the walls. Individual deaths, of warriors and children alike, danced across the backs of his eyeballs, and the memory of their screams echoed in his head. An endless parade of corpses matched only by the real ones littering Watchtown.

The horse shifted beneath him; Dom dismounted and wandered through the shattered gates. The heat beat at him like a drum from shops and houses burning on both sides. It smelt of stale smoke, old blood and roasting pork. Pools of blood blackened and cooked into plates with the consistency of frogspawn. And bodies. Burnt, hacked, stabbed. Men, women, children, goats.

He wandered to the assembly place at the centre of town, where judgements were given and marriages celebrated. They'd made a stand here and they'd died in heaps and drifts like snow messily shovelled away.

'Is this not beautiful? Is this not the Afterworld on earth?' The Dark Lady stood in the centre between the dead in the blue and the dead in green and brown, smoke curling like a living thing around Her, flames dancing on the edges of Her shadow. 'Now you see clear, little calestar. Now you see me, here in the world.'

'I see death,' Dom mumbled around his wrist. The source of the itching was there somewhere; he just had to get to it.

'And yet you rode so hard to come here and see it.' She

glided towards him and Dom backed away. She stepped closer anyway. 'Was this what you wanted to see? What were you going to do here? Tell me.'

'Whatever I had to to stop it.'

The Dark Lady tutted. 'No, you weren't. You were racing here for another reason. My reason. Say it.' She took hold of his hand and drew his arm away from his teeth. Her fingers brushed the scabs, the raw flesh oozing clear liquid, and the itching faded, fell away. Dom's eyes closed in an ecstasy of relief.

'Is that better, my love?' She whispered, Her lips brushing his. 'Is that what you wanted?'

'Yes.'

'Then tell me why you came here. What were you to do?'

Dom's hands were on her waist, thumbs stroking the muscles of her flanks. Her golden eyes bore into his, demanding, promising. He bent his head and kissed Her, their tongues twining around each other, Her breasts soft against his chest.

'Beautiful,' She murmured, Her finger over his lips to break the kiss, 'but you are avoiding my question. Why did you come here? You will answer me.'

'To do your will,' he whispered and She licked her lips. 'Whatever that will may be.'

'Well done. Now tell me why.'

Because She was there, and here, and inside him, and She was never going to go away, he knew that now, he understood it in a sudden rush. It was over. He was Hers. She was endless and eternal and beautiful and terrible and he had no more strength to resist. With the knowledge came a certain peace, blanketing the fear, the guilt, the shame.

'I give up,' he whispered through bloody lips. 'I give up,' he said again, louder. 'I'm yours.' He inhaled Her scent of blood and smoke and closed his eyes, focused on the place in his head where the gods spoke and broke it open to give it to Her, to spill every last secret he had, even that one. The one that would end everything.

He packaged up his soul and he held it out for Her to take.

There was an explosion in front of him, light and heat and the tang of lightning and Dom fell backwards, hit his head on the stone and curled on to his side, waiting for the Dark Lady to claim him. That She would he had no doubt.

Instead a tender hand caressed his back and the scent of flowers filled his nostrils, chasing out the stench of burning. 'Hello, Calestar,' the Dancer said.

Dom looked up and recognised Her, and rage coursed through his veins, pounded in his head. 'You come to me now?' he screamed as She cocooned him in peace and light, Her face sad and beautiful and just as blinding as the Dark Lady's, just as loved and hated when all was said and done.

'You come to me here, in the graveyard of your people, among the corpse fires of my family?' He swung at Her and She avoided the blow; then She swept him up into Her arms.

'I come when you need me. I always have.'

'No, you come when your plan's in danger of failing,' Dom shouted as She soothed away the pain and left balm in its place. He was empty without it, without something to strive against. So he strove against Her and Her endless demands, Her unending love.

'That's what you care about, not me. You don't give a fuck about me.' He paused, coughing. 'Why are you doing this to me?' and now his voice was cracked, failing. Like the rest of him.

'I love you, Calestar, as I love all people. I love those who walk my Sister's bloody path, and I welcome any who come

411

to my Light.' She rocked him as he would a babe. 'I come now because your faith is weak and you need to be strong. And because you must understand the rest now. What has been dark I will illuminate. And I do it because I must. Because you are my beloved. And I'm sorry.' She smiled, flickers of light dancing through and over Her face and form, and then She cupped his chin and kissed him.

The knowledge of what he was to do was an axe chopping into his mind, a lash scourging his soul into tatters and Dom screamed, screamed and wept and flailed against Her embrace. No, he wouldn't. He fucking couldn't. Not that. Not any of it.

'You must be strong, Calestar,' the Dancer whispered, releasing him. 'This is only the beginning.' And She brushed Her fingers on the raw wound of Dom's wrist and the itching returned, worse than ever.

GALTAS

Third moon, eighteenth year of the reign of King Rastoth
East Rank headquarters, Grazing Lands, Listran border

'My lord, we've had a veritable flock of pigeons from the prince,' Skerris said. He passed over the slips of paper, each numbered so the code could be deciphered.

'This is it, Skerris, I can feel it,' Galtas said. 'Rastoth the Mad's time is up.'

'Long live King Rivil the First in the gods' bloody embrace.'

Galtas unrolled each paper in turn and compared the letters and numbers to the cipher he had inked on to the inside of his money pouch. '"Lockdown lifted. Durdil imprisoned. Command is mine."' Skerris slammed his palm on the table in excitement. '"West Rank still coming" – that's unfortunate. "Will try for Rastoth."'

'He's got balls, that one,' Skerris rumbled approvingly. 'Utterly without allies and still going for the king. And the last one?'

Galtas held it up. '"Bring everything you've got."' He rubbed his hands together. 'Well, that would be five thousand

413

highly trained soldiers, a priest of Gosfath, several chests of gold and the blessing of the Red Gods, wouldn't it?' He tipped his head back and laughed. 'Think it'll be enough?'

They raised a glass to Rivil and the gods and Skerris summoned his staff and told them the news.

'I gave a job to my tailor in Three Beeches for just this occasion, my lord,' Skerris said when the jubilation had muted. 'From afar it would be best to appear a loyal Rank, but I wanted some indication of our true allegiance, so I've had these made up.' He pulled a cloth badge from inside his uniform. 'Couldn't get anything in blue, of course, but I've built up a fair store of woad and I've got some lads dyeing the others already. Delivered this morning.'

Galtas studied the white patch. An embossed R hovering over a wide black line that curved and narrowed. 'A Dark Path?' Galtas queried. 'That is a bold move, General. Are these tailors of yours to be trusted?'

Skerris waved away his concern. 'John and Mara Tailorson have worked for the East Rank for years. I've made sure to request some odder things during my time here, so they suspect little.'

Galtas crumpled the badge in his fist. 'John and Mara Tailorson of Three Beeches? They're here now?'

'Yes, my lord. Why, do you know them?'

'You could say that. I swore to kill their son; he nearly destroyed all my years of work, but he slipped through my hands. I wonder if I could beg them from you?'

Skerris frowned at the ceiling but then a broad grin split his face. 'Take them. At least that way I don't have to pay them, and it spares any awkward questions over my design, I suppose.' He slapped Galtas on the back. 'I wish you joy of them.'

*

414

'John and Mara Tailorson, is it?'

The woman took several pins from her mouth and stuck them in a cushion. 'That's us. What can we do for you, sir?'

'I've some news of your son, Captain Crys Tailorson.'

Mara pressed a hand to her heart and called for her husband. The room they'd been given to make repairs to the officers' uniforms was small and well lit and Galtas could see Crys's resemblance to his father immediately.

'John, love, the lord has news of our Crys.'

'Is that true, milord? Why, we'd be so grateful for any news, troubling times like this. Last we heard he'd joined the Palace Rank.'

'That's true,' Galtas said, closing the door behind him and examining the piles of jackets and shirts. 'This is very fine work, madam.'

'Thank you, milord. So Crys is safe then?'

'Hmm?' Galtas looked up. 'Safe? Oh no, Mara, Crys isn't safe. Crys is dead. But don't worry, I'll send you to meet him.'

John didn't even move as Galtas drew his sword and punched it through his chest. He fell hard, skull bouncing from the floorboards and his features never losing their expression of disbelief. Mara's scream echoed to the rafters.

Galtas crouched by the dying man and studied his face. He stroked John's hair out of his eyes with gentle fingers. 'My name's Galtas Morellis. I didn't quite get around to cutting Crys to bloody ribbons like I swore to do, so in the absence of his hide to carve my name into, yours is just going to have to do.'

Mara unfroze and ran at him with a pair of cloth shears and Galtas flicked his blade out and hacked it into her ankle as she came. Her shriek climbed the scale and she pitched on to her face, howling. Galtas punched her into silence. 'Lie there nice and quiet now, there's a good girl. I promise I won't forget about you.'

'Dancer . . . Dance—' John Tailorson tried. 'Cryssssss . . .'

Galtas pushed his face right into John's so the man was cross-eyed looking at him. 'That's right, John Tailorson. This is all the fault of your son. All Crys's fault. All of it. What I'm going to do to poor old Mara over there' – he pointed, then swung his finger to indicate out of the window – 'and then what's going to happen to young Richard and young, very young, and very beautiful apparently, Wenna Tailorson, back at your shop in Three Beeches, well, you can lay that blame on your son as well.' Galtas sat up and patted John's cheek.

'Untouched, little Wenna, I'm guessing. Makes sense if she really is only thirteen. But rest easy knowing she won't die pure. Might not die at all, if she pleases me.' Galtas hawked and spat into John's gaping mouth. 'But then, I have such particular tastes. How likely is it that a child can satisfy them all?'

Mara started screaming then and Galtas punched her again. 'Do be quiet. This is going to be tricky and I need to concentrate. I told you it'll be your turn soon enough. And anyway, if I'm going to try the daughter, it's only fair to see what the mother has to offer first.'

He looked back at John. 'Well,' he said brightly, resting on his heels and ripping at the bloody shirt with his knife. 'Let's get started, eh?'

John couldn't really manage anything other than a bloody gurgle, but Galtas took it for acceptance anyway. 'I'm afraid I'm going to have to make this quick. It doesn't do to keep a lady waiting, and we've got a king to kill.' John gargled again, and Galtas bit his bottom lip in concentration and got to work.

CRYS

A forced march like this, with wounded, would've gone down in the history books if it wasn't for the fact they were too late.

'A day, maybe two ahead of us. They'll have hit the Rank's harbour by now, commandeered what they need and scuttled the rest. They're sailing; we're walking. We'll never catch them.'

Crys's voice was scratchy with thirst and fatigue and he looked for Ash in the throng of Wolves sitting, kneeling and sobbing in the grass in front of the blackened shell of their town.

Tara drifted gently to her knees and then leant on her hands, head hanging down. 'These poor people,' she muttered. 'Came to fight with us and lost everything they have in the process. How many of them are there now?'

'A few hundred survivors,' Crys answered, his voice dull. 'Gods, even the children,' he said as a woman staggered out

417

of the ruins with a bundle clutched to her chest. 'Sweet Dancer, they killed everyone.'

'Dom? Dom, are you here?' The voice was thin and faint with distance and had been repeating the same question for the best part of an hour. If Dom was there, he was dead or deaf or both. He wondered whether Dom'd made it in time to be killed by Mireces, whether that was what he'd wanted. Or had the madness of the Dark Lady's torments broken his mind and he didn't know what he was doing any more? Ash had told him of the nightly visitations and Dom had taken to sleeping alone a mile from camp before the battle just so everyone else got some rest.

Crys shuddered. Alone in the woods, in the dark, with the Red Gods haunting you. He looked again at Ash and wanted nothing more than to go and wrap his arms around him. The one thing he couldn't do. 'I'm going to look inside,' he said abruptly.

Tara's lip curled. 'Why?' He didn't answer and Tara didn't push.

Crys threaded through the grieving Wolves to Ash and pulled him into a quick hug. 'All right?' he whispered.

'No,' Ash said. 'Not in the least.' They stepped apart and Crys felt a flush of guilt that he couldn't comfort his lover.

'I wish—'

'Don't,' Ash said. 'Thank you, but I have my people. What's left of them anyway,' he added bitterly. Crys hovered at his shoulder for a few seconds and then retreated from the rawness of their pain, berating himself for a coward.

Feeling a sudden urge to hide from everything, he made his way into the town, gaping at the scale of the destruction. Barely a building left standing. They hadn't just killed the people, they'd gutted the town, torn it apart in a whirlwind of savagery. He could hear Rillirin calling for Dom to the north so he made his way into the eastern quarter, the furthest from the main gates, where the fire might not have spread so much.

The town had begun to smell, a miasma that coated his tongue and the back of his throat, but Crys found himself walking with his hands outstretched to either side, palms down. 'Lady Dancer, sweet and true, take these people into your Light. Lord of cunning, holy Fox God, end their trials and bring them now to rest.'

He blessed the dead as best he could, not being a priest, blessed them from the heart and the smell and the horror began to melt away until Crys saw only the Light and he knew their souls were safe in its peace.

The houses were less burnt here, some looming strangely untouched as the road opened out and Crys recognised the town's assembly place. They'd fought hard here, making use of firing platforms on the roofs and alley traps, using the width of the assembly place to fight in step, and they'd taken their share of heathens with them.

Crys was turning back when movement caught his eye. The flapping of cloth, that's all. It flapped again, too regular a motion in this erratic wind, and Crys pulled out his knife and crept closer on soft feet. He rounded a mess of corpses and his eyes made sense of what he was seeing. Crys sheathed his knife and crouched down.

'Hello, Dom, it's me, Crys. Remember me?'

Dom stopped scraping at his forearm with a piece of splintered wood and his gaze wandered up to Crys's face. He recoiled. 'Hello, Fox God,' he said and fainted.

DOM

Third moon, eighteenth year of the reign of King Rastoth
Watchtown, Western Plain

'Easy, man, easy. There's nothing to fear. Here, drink some water.' A dribble of wet on his lips. He swallowed. 'Good, good. A little more.' He swallowed, mouth and water tasting of flame and blood. 'Do you remember your name?' the voice continued and a small frown creased Dom's forehead. This voice . . . it wasn't *the* voice. A man's voice?

'Who?' he managed to croak, his eyelids refusing to lift.

'It's Crys, Crys Tailorson, do you remember? I brought word of the death of Prince Janis some weeks ago?'

'Watchtown?' Dom forced one eye open, squinting in the glare of daylight at a blurry outline. A warm breeze shook his hair, brought the tang of smoke to his nostrils. So thirsty, skin tight, sore with heat. Dom managed to unglue his other eyelid and focus for the first time.

'Watchtown's gone, my friend. There's nothing left. No survivors. Just you.'

Dom hacked out a cough and drank again. Corpses every-

420

where, some in Mireces blue, most not. 'How did I get here?' he asked, not remembering. Crys was outlined in bright light, making it hard to focus on him.

'You had a knowing in the West Forts, remember? You told Lim and the general that Watchtown was going to be destroyed. Then you stole Mace's prize hunter and rode here alone.' Crys gave him some more water. 'What were you going to do? Did you see it happen?'

Dom pushed up on to his elbows and stared at the carnage. It was bewildering, absurd in its excess. 'No, I was too late. They're gone. I missed them.'

'They're waiting in the Light for you, Dom.'

'Not them,' Dom said.

'Then who?'

'Doesn't matter now.' Dom cleared his throat, looking away from the massacre with guilty relief. 'You were here earlier, weren't you? You saw the knowing? Did I speak?'

Crys shook his head and Dom gusted a sigh. 'Fine, you need to tell Lim. Don't think Mace'll believe me, but you can try. It's all falling apart in Rilporin. Rastoth's madness is increasing and he's given Rivil command of the defences. Water.' Dom drank and tried to collect his scattered thoughts. So tired, the light so bright around Crys. 'There's no one left to oppose him. Durdil's under arrest. The East is moving. Chaos.'

'Calestar? What else? What else?' Crys's voice was rising, whining in Dom's ears like mosquitoes. A leap of smoke and flame across the square, a roof falling in. He felt the rumble through the earth, up into the bones of his spine, shivering through his lungs. It was still burning. Everything was burning.

Dom grabbed Crys in a tight embrace. 'You shine. Do you know why?' Crys didn't answer. 'Shine with godlight, Crys Tailorson. Shine like *Him*. You have to believe.'

Crys pushed him away hard but it didn't matter. Dom's eyes were full of the fire now, fire roaring, eating houses, eating bodies. It filled his face and head, filled his brain, went searing down his right arm to his wrist, up into his right eye.

The knowing came, and so did She. She wasn't quite here in the world, but She was close enough, a flickering presence on the other side of the shadowy veil that was so thin now, so thin, and he could no more hide the knowing from Her than he could hide from himself.

CRYS

'Dom? Calestar?'

Crys shook him but whatever had happened, he was out. Dom had smiled, reached out as though he was taking someone's hand, someone only he could see, and passed out again. Crys, feeling like a traitor, picked up one of the few lumps of unburnt wood lying nearby. He didn't want to hurt Dom, but Dom wasn't right in the head. Or at least, something in Dom's head wasn't right.

This business with the shining again. He'd thought it just a one-off, part of Dom's condition. He'd forgotten all about it. Godlight? What did that even mean?

'Dom?' he whispered again. Dom's eyes opened and Crys scrambled back, yelping, tripping over his feet and sprawling on the stone.

'Run, little god,' Dom grated through a throat full of jagged metal. 'Run away now, little fox.'

'No,' Crys said. His heart was pounding through his chest,

423

but this was someone he could help. 'Concentrate on the Light, Calestar. Feel the Dancer's sun on your face. Focus on that.'

Dom giggled and brought his arm up to his mouth, biting into the skin as though it were an apple fresh from the tree. His other hand wandered in front of his eyes and then made a grab for the wood. Crys snatched it back.

'Find Lim, tell him everything I've told you,' Dom said suddenly in his own voice. Crys knelt in front of him. 'Leave now. Go before I stop you.'

'The army's out there, the rest of the Wolves. Let me get you some help, get your family. Rillirin's here.'

'No! Not Rillirin, not any of them. Leave me. Don't let them find me. I can't go with you and they can't stay. They have too much to do. They can't help me.'

Dom squeezed his palms against the sides of his skull, making a noise like a sick cat. 'Don't let me follow you. I'll stop you. I'll do anything I have to to stop you telling Mace and Lim to stay out of—' His words were squeezed off into a grunt that rocked his whole body.

'Stay out of what?' Crys tried and Dom snarled and lunged at him, coming up off the ground faster than Crys had ever seen a man move. He yelped and thumped Dom on the shoulder with the wood. Dom fell back and then rose, lips pulled away from bloody teeth, his eyes red. Inhuman.

'Harder,' he hissed but then he lunged again, his fingers reaching for Crys's throat. Saliva ran down his chin. 'Stay out stay out stay—'

Crys leant back, took a double-handed grip on the stick, and clubbed Dom in the temple so hard the wood cracked in half, the loose end spinning away into the dusk. Dom thumped on to the stone and Crys lay him on his side beneath a pilfered blanket stained and stinking with soot. He checked Dom's pulse and wiped away the trickle of blood from his temple, left him his waterskin and the last of his rations. Then he ran.

MACE

'What will you do?' Mace sat with Dalli on a small rise and they stared across the grass towards Watchtown. 'I can't believe it's still burning,' he added as smoke twisted into the sky from points in the town.

Wolves were wandering the plain, some going to the temple. It hadn't been burnt, but by the looks on their faces when they came back out, it hadn't been spared either. They hauled the gates to the temple compound shut and dropped the bar across.

Others had gone to the copse a couple of miles away to sit beneath the trees and come to terms with their loss. Not that you could ever come to terms with something like this.

Dalli was warm against his side and she'd cried without shame for a long time until her eyes were red and her face was blotchy and puffy. He kissed it anyway, because she was as beautiful in her grief as she was any other time.

'What can we do?' Dalli said in a thick voice.

'I mean, do you want vengeance more than you want to preserve the lives of those you have left? You can march with us and we can find Corvus and his army and rip them to pieces, or you can stay here and grieve and try to find a way forward.'

Dorcas was below, frowning up at him, but Mace didn't give a good godsdamned fuck about how he looked, the General of the West Rank with his arms around a crying Wolf. The decision had been unanimous in the end, to follow the Wolves to Watchtown and try and save it.

With the initial flood of grief over, Rankers were moving among the Wolves, offering comfort to those they knew and had fought beside in the valley. They were all war-kin now, he supposed, and he held Dalli tighter because of it.

'It'll be Lim's decision in the end,' she said, bringing him back to the present. 'We'll take a vote. Maybe those who want to fight will go, and those who don't will stay. I think the chief's past giving us orders. We need to make up our own minds.'

'And you?'

Dalli twisted to look up at him, her smile fragile and her eyes fierce. 'Oh, I'm fighting, don't you worry about that. I had parents, a cousin and two young nephews in there. I don't want to know what happened to them, but I damn well want to kill someone for them.'

'I'm so sorry,' Mace whispered. 'You sign up as a soldier or take the Wolf oath, you know the risks. That's the chance you take. But the others, the innocents . . .'

'They're always the ones that get hurt,' Dalli agreed. She gestured. 'What's happened here, that's what Corvus and Rivil want to do to Rilporin. How many people there?'

'Thousands.'

'Thousands,' she echoed and it sounded like a death knell.

South of Watchtown, between the temple and the copse, a giant swathe of daffodils nodded in the sun. Many had been trampled and some were past their best, but the cheerful colour, so at odds with everything else on the blasted plain, did lift his spirits a little. New life budding beside the ashes of the old.

'We'll march in the morning,' he said. 'Will your people have made their decision by then?'

'I think so. I'll speak to Lim and Sarilla.'

'Later,' he said as she made to get up. 'Stay with me a while.' He wrapped both his arms around her as she settled back against him and kissed the top of her head. 'Just rest a little.'

DURDIL

'They searched me – they actually searched me before they let me in here,' Renik said, red with outrage. 'What do they think I'm doing, smuggling weapons in here? And yes, the men on your door and the king's are the honour guard who went west with Janis.'

'Then they're traitors. Provoke them into any insubordination you can, arrest them and confine them. When Rivil asks where they are, tell him you don't know. Two can play at secrets.' Durdil drummed his fingers on the table. 'What else?'

'With respect, sir, that won't work. I've already tried replacing the men who guard the king; Rivil himself told me to keep my nose out of palace business, said the king's safety was now his concern and no one else's. I can't get a man in edgeways and believe me, sir, I've tried.'

Gathering the reins of power into his own hands, isolating the king from his most loyal soldiers, removing his closest advisers and any who'll tell him the truth. Cutting off

429

communication with the Ranks who could aid him. Durdil could almost admire how Rivil had gone about it. *It's what I'd do if I was a traitorous, heathen fuck-puppet with an army at my back and absolutely no comprehension of the hell I'm about to unleash on my country.*

But I'm not. I'm the man who has to stop him. While confined to quarters. Marvellous.

'What else?' Durdil asked again, pushing away bitterness and fatigue.

'Sir, Prince Rivil has made a public proclamation that the Mireces were defeated by the West Rank and the war is over.' Renik's voice was a monotone. 'No one is to worry and life in Rilporin is to continue as normal.'

'He's done what?' The horror in Durdil's voice made Renik wince. The room tilted crazily and bile rose in Durdil's throat. He shoved his chair back from the table and put his head between his knees.

'Sir? Sir, are you all right?'

'Major,' Durdil said to the floor, 'start stockpiling weapons. Buy up every sword, dagger, spear and bow available in Rilporin and any that come into the docks. I will give you a letter making my personal income available to you.' He sat up carefully. 'Check the outer wall and engage masons to make any necessary repairs. Stockpile food in the barracks. Make sure the Rank is very visible doing all of this.'

'You want to panic the city?' Renik asked.

Durdil stood up and wobbled, putting one hand on the table to support himself. 'Yes, I want to panic the bloody city. I want them terrified and demanding the palace tells them what's happening, demanding that reinforcements be sent for. I want rumour to be rife in the docks and the quarters. I want nobles fleeing the city to their estates – they're fucking useless anyway. I want Rastoth to hear about all of this and retake control from his son, then order my release so I can organise the defence.'

Durdil's hands were shaking and he clasped them together behind his back as he stalked to the window. 'What's the latest from our agents?'

'The East Rank is moving,' Renik said, his reluctance obvious. 'The whole Rank, sir, not the Thousand Rivil said he'd requested. We've a man keeping watch on the Tears and he sent one of the North Tower One birds, came in this morning.'

Durdil grunted. His whim to have another flock of homing pigeons that didn't return to the palace but somewhere else in the city had finally proven its worth. There weren't many of them, and of course they had to be sent out in the first place, but some information was flowing into his hands again, albeit at a trickle.

'So, the eastern Listran border is unguarded and Rivil has an entire Rank moving to his command. And yet he tells the people the war is won. All right, I want this news spreading as well. Leak it at the docks and within an hour no one will know who started it. Why's the Rank moving if the war's won? Is there another threat we don't know about? You know the type – they're usually the rumours we're trying to suppress.'

'We also have an agent in Shingle and three travelling west, one on the river, two by horse. They've all got tower birds and they're instructed to put their location and the date on the message and send it back as soon as the Mireces are spotted. It'll give a little warning.'

'And there's no way you can get to the dovecote? A message to the North and South Ranks?'

Renik was already shaking his head. 'Dovecote's guarded day and night.'

Durdil slammed his fist on the wall by the window and pressed his forehead to the cold glass. 'Not enough. It's not enough. I don't know what's going on in the palace. Is Mace coming? How many men does he have? How many Mireces? Three thousand Palace Rankers against five thousand from the East, plus the Raiders. Maybe a thousand merchants and tavern-brawlers and fishermen will stand on the walls with us and the City Watch when they see what's coming, but I can't see them making much difference . . .

'All right, it'll take longer, but I want you to send men on horseback to the South Rank and demand two Thousands from them. Also send men by horse as far as Three Beeches so they avoid the East Rank, then get them on the Tears up to the North Rank as well. Another two Thousands from them. All forces are to set out within one hour of receiving the correspondence. Understand? One hour. Forced march to the harbours, then they sail without stopping, day and night. Leave the siege weapons, leave the horses. All haste or Rilporin falls.'

'Yes, sir,' Renik said and Durdil brightened. They just needed to hold them off for a week, ten days at the most, and four thousand Rankers would be ramming swords up their arses.

'All right, good. The market is being dismantled?' The market that covered Rilporin's killing field was vast and cumbersome and would take days to pull apart, but if the enemy broke through the gatehouse they'd be fish in a barrel, trapped between First and Second Circle's walls and vulnerable to arrow volleys and even small catapults.

Their losses would be horrendous and . . . and Renik wasn't saying anything. Durdil came back to the table and sat. 'There's no need for it to be pulled down, sir, because the Mireces aren't coming. Apparently.'

'Gods fucking damnit,' Durdil said with quiet vehemence. 'Right, burn it down. Make sure it's late at night and make sure you set multiple fires. The whole thing needs to go up at once. If enough of it's damaged, they'll have to pull it all down. Keep it away from the houses, but when you turn out to help fight it, recommend those stalls are knocked down immediately to prevent the spread of fire into a residential area.'

'You want me to set fire to Rilporin?' Renik whispered.

Durdil rocked his hand from side to side. 'Only a bit of it,' he said. 'Look, Rivil's going to know this was me. As soon as it's done I expect I'll be arrested and charged with treason, so pay attention. Colonels Edris and Yarrow can probably be trusted, and possibly Major Vaunt as well. Hallos can absolutely be trusted, so I'd make him your first confidant and sound out the others as you go. If they come to you willingly with ideas of defence or concerns about the prince, you can probably confide in them. But remember Wheeler, and be careful. The defence is going to be down to you, so watch for Rivil stabbing you in the back when you least expect it.'

'We can get you out, sir,' Renik said, leaping to his feet. 'The men are loyal to you, not Rivil. We can storm the palace and—'

'Concentrate on defending our city for now,' Durdil interrupted. He clenched his fists. 'It really doesn't matter what happens to me as long as Rilporin stands, and stands in the Light.'

MACE

Third moon, eighteenth year of the reign of King Rastoth
Yew Cove, River Gil, Western Plain

The bridge at the West Rank's harbour had been destroyed, all the boats taken or set alight, and the bridge at Pine Lock had been felled as well. The river was beginning to curve south, adding miles and hours to the march. They needed to cross.

Almost a hundred Wolves had refused to go any further. Those who'd lost too many in Watchtown and the battle; those who'd lost their stomach for the fight. Two dozen others had announced their intention to follow the Gil all the way back to the Sky Path in the mountains, massacre the Mireces women and children left in the villages, and free the slaves. If the Wolves had no one to go home to, neither would the Raiders.

Mace felt a flicker of disquiet at the memory, and at the memory of the ice in Lim's voice when he wished them good hunting. Even Dalli had approved. Mace wondered if he'd want to do the same if Rilporin fell, or if every man in his Rank was dead. Maybe.

Dusk was chasing them down when they finally came in sight of Yew Cove.

'Bridge looks good, sir,' Tara said. 'The Wolves are checking it now.'

'About bloody time,' Mace said. 'Alright, form up tight. I want us over this bridge at speed – we don't want half our force on one side getting ambushed and half stuck on the other.'

'Yes, sir,' Tara said and jogged away, her voice rising as she gave orders.

There were no candles being lit in Yew Cove, no smoke rising from chimneys. Dead or fled, Mace supposed. He prayed the latter. Pine Lock had been a butcher's yard.

Mace strained his eyes in the gloom and saw the Wolves flitting through the first few houses lining the road to the bridge. The muscles in his legs tensed to run and he found he'd donned his helmet without noticing. They were clear all the way to the bridge, clear on to it, and the Rank was packing in tight to follow when shouts and the clash of steel eruped from the far side of the bridge. Rags of flame wove from between the houses on the far bank as Mireces with torches poured out of concealment. Arrows whickered in both directions and the Wolves didn't have the numbers to hold the bridge. The Mireces locked shields and pushed them back.

'Get your arses off the bridge and we'll hold them here,' Mace roared, bulling his way through the Rank to the front. 'Fucking move,' he added as arrows crossed the water and found homes in his soldiers.

'Behind! Behind!' Dorcas's voice shrieked, so high-pitched he sounded like a woman. Mace lurched around and peered over the heads of the Rank.

'Boost,' he demanded and three men around him hoisted

him up. 'Shit on this,' he breathed. 'How many armies do these cunts have?'

A force of Mireces that looked in the gloom to be thousands strong was sprinting from the town towards them. There was nowhere to go – they couldn't cross the bridge and the road back on to the plain was blocked with advancing Raiders.

'Here,' a voice called, 'over here, now!' Soldiers began streaming towards the source of the voice and Mace caught a glimpse of a young man beckoning desperately from a house. 'Now,' he shouted, 'there's a way out.'

'Careful,' Mace yelled but no one was listening. It was dark, arrows were thudding into them and they were trapped between two forces. The boy's way out was all they had. Despite his protests, Mace got caught up in the sudden stampede, unable to slow the tide or extricate himself.

He found himself in the boy's house. 'Straight down. Trapdoor. Tunnels,' the boy was repeating, over and over. 'Straight down, trapdoor, tunnels.'

Yew Cove, also known as Smuggler's Cove, was honeycombed with tunnels beneath the town and Mace found himself running along one, the sounds of stamping feet and shouts to hurry bouncing from the rough earth and wooden walls.

They passed storerooms stacked with barrels and bundles, sailcloth, salted fish, brandy, all lit by torches in wall sconces. More storerooms, empty now and without light, and then more, those empty too. The pace slackened; no one knew where they were going or even if there was another exit, and Mace slowed, stopped.

He turned in a circle, dragging in air. Crys was close by and he grabbed the captain. 'Where are the townsfolk?' he demanded in a hoarse whisper. 'If everyone's hiding, where are they? These rooms are all empty.'

Crys swivelled very slowly on his heels to look behind him. As he did, his eyes reflected yellow like an animal's in the torchlight. 'It's a trap,' he said and pointed.

A growing orange glow lit the walls further down the tunnel and they could hear the tramp of feet and the jingle of war gear.

TARA

Third moon, eighteenth year of the reign of King Rastoth
Yew Cove tunnels, River Gil, Western Plain

They'd run until the tunnel widened and split, then split again and they were cut off from each other. Tara sprinted around a corner and into a mob of yelling men; they were in a storeroom, no way out except the way they'd just come in.

'Form up, prepare to defend,' she shouted, dragging three or four of them into a line with her. Dalli was there, Rillirin too, a weird mix of Wolf and Ranker that didn't move together the way she wanted.

The Mireces didn't allow them much time to organise. They took the corner at a run and barrelled straight into the front line and Tara's ranks buckled, threatening to dissolve. 'Hold,' she screamed, 'hold, you fuckers.'

A Raider lunged at her with a sword, and Tara parried, riposted, and they fenced for a few seconds in the flickering, confusing torchlight. She thought she saw an opening, a split second when the man's arm came away from his side and exposed his flank. Tara pressed hard, attacking the same

438

spot, waiting for the same mistake, and when it came she slid forward, sword tip ripping through his sleeve it was so close and finding a home in the man's liver.

He screamed and dropped his sword to clutch at hers and Tara obliged him by twisting and withdrawing the blade, slicing into his fingers as she did. He dropped to one knee and she kicked him in the chest, sending him over on to his back, skull bouncing from stone and interrupting his second, bubbling scream. Another Raider swung his sword down and cleaved the man's skull, shutting him up, and Tara gaped and then hacked him in the neck as he tried to free his blade from imprisoning bone. No point letting an opening like that go to waste.

She heard Dalli scream her name but was pressed, harried from two sides until another of her men slid into a gap and took one of them for his own. Tara chanced a glance and saw Crys charging out of the tunnel the Mireces had come out of, hacking into them from behind, fighting his way to Dalli's side. He killed like a crazy man, his eyes glowing in the firelight.

Their line pressed forward, found a little more space and more men slid into the front rank, engaging the Mireces, separating them from the others and cutting them down. They swept past Dalli and Crys, leaving them to end the wounded they left behind, and drove the Mireces back into the tunnel until they broke and fled back the way they'd come.

Her men set off after them and Tara ordered them back. 'Don't. Could be an ambush. Keep going forward: we need to find the others.' She beckoned to Crys. 'Where did you come from?'

He gestured vaguely. 'Heard the shouting, came looking,' he said, showing his teeth in a grin. 'Come on, we don't want to get left behind.'

RILLIRIN

*Third moon, eighteenth year of the reign of King Rastoth
Yew Cove tunnels, River Gil, Western Plain*

'They're coming again!'

Rillirin lunged in the near darkness. The Raider brought his sword up to meet her spear and there was the thunk of metal kissing wood. Before he had a chance to force her spear up, she swung around and thrust at the second man, trying to catch him off guard.

He forced her back easily – too easily. Already she was against the tunnel wall. She threw herself towards him with a howl, aiming for his throat, snarling as she spun and hacked, feet skittering over the hard-packed earth, breath whistling in her throat, arms burning.

But Rillirin was no warrior and they all knew it, most of all her. Spots of fizzing colour danced before her eyes and her aching lungs couldn't drag in enough air. She staggered sideways out of range, tripping over someone else and catching an elbow in the ribs.

'Fucking move,' Crys snarled and shoved her away to gut

440

a howling Mireces. He glanced at her, then reached out and yanked her arm so hard her shoulder popped. An axe slammed into the ground where she'd stood and Crys swung her into the wall and leapt past, stabbing the man in the shoulder. He squealed and dropped his axe and Rillirin choked on the stink of guts as Crys opened him from cock to throat.

'You fighting or falling asleep?' Crys growled and Rillirin sucked in a breath and darted up to his side, spear flailing. This tunnel was deeper than the others, leading steeply downwards, and it was dank, slime coating the walls, puddles forming on the ground, filling with blood and piss.

Mireces, Wolf and Ranker strained and hacked at each other, screams and curses echoing and bouncing until everything was noise, flickering orange and black shadows and confusion.

Crys was gone, chasing three Mireces down a side tunnel and howling like the damned, and Rillirin leant on her spear, panting and spitting out a mouthful of hair. A grunt as a Raider hefted his sword and she whooped in a breath and brought the spear up in both hands, caught his blade high above her head and started to parry when she felt a hand grab her shoulder from behind and a tearing pain through her lower back. A soft jingling as the Raider behind her pulled the knife out of her chainmail and her flesh, and a rush of heat down her back and leg.

Rillirin's knees slammed into the ground. The dots were joining up in her eyes, her back hot and wet and sloughing life. She was staring along the tunnel where Crys had vanished but he wasn't coming back. No one was coming to save her.

She looked up without much interest at the Raider before her. Her left hand was pressed to her back but the blood kept coming, hot and thick between her fingers. And something else, something hard sticking up from her belt. Her fingers closed around it and as the Raider readied the death stroke, she drew her knife and shoved it up under his chin, through his tongue and palate, wrenched it back out as he stumbled, and into the side of his neck, knife awkward in her left hand and the grip slippery with blood.

He dropped to all fours in front of her and Rillirin stabbed him in the back so he slammed face down into a puddle. She heard the wet crunch of his nose hitting the ground and then someone fell over her in the dark. The Raider who'd stabbed her. He thrashed on top of her, trying to get the knife. She had nothing left now. She felt him peel back her fingers and rip the handle from her grip, then he stiffened, rocked, and slumped against her back, bathing her in blood.

Dalli, her spear red along a third of its length. She lunged over Rillirin and drove the spear's blade into a Mireces' chest. It skittered over a rib before biting deep and lodging. Dalli tugged, the man stumbled forward, tugged again and then ran him back into the wall, waggled the spear and finally freed it.

She left him gurgling in a heap and dragged Rillirin to her feet, over a second body and back along the tunnel into a storeroom to huddle against the back wall. Rillirin had lost her knife, somehow still had her spear.

'Where are you hurt? Rillirin, where are you hurt?' Dalli hissed.

'Where've you been? Where'd Crys go? I was alone.'

'Shit. Rillirin? Focus on my voice. Where are you hurt?'

'Everywhere. I'm dying.' Light exploded in her head and she focused on Dalli in shocked outrage. 'You hit me.' She started to cry. 'You bitch, you slapped me.'

'Stop whining, it's just a scratch. I'm going to rip off the bottom of your shirt and use it to wad the wound, all right? Hold up your mail, come on.'

'Scratch?' Rillirin whispered and Dalli grunted and nodded, tearing at the bottom of her shirt.

'Deep breath now.' A hiss, a hiccup and a strangled groan. 'Good girl,' Dalli said and wrapped the bandage tightly around Rillirin's waist, dragged her mail shirt back down and tightened her belt across the wound.

'Ah!'

'Hush, it's done. You can sit still for a minute.' Dalli's head came up and she cocked it, listening, bloody fingers over Rillirin's lips. She dragged herself to her feet. 'I'll take rearguard. You just get moving.' She put a hand in Rillirin's armpit and hauled her up.

She couldn't leave Dalli to face them on her own, but she was so dizzy she couldn't see straight. *Just a scratch. It's just a scratch.* 'Don't lose touch with us,' she mumbled. She pointed a shaking finger. 'This tunnel. Sure they went this way.'

Dalli nodded and turned away into the dark.

MACE

Mace couldn't wait to get out of the tunnels and find that little piss-weasel boy who'd sent them down here. Never mind that he'd probably been coerced into doing it, didn't matter that the Mireces had undoubtedly threatened his family, Mace was going to take great pleasure in finding him and popping his head off his shoulders.

The Mireces hacked at him with a double-headed axe bigger than Mace's head and he took it on his shield, grunted and twisted his arm so the axe fell away. Took a man's hand off at the wrist, blocked a sword, came back for the axeman and opened his scalp, severed an ear and thunked into a shoulder. Shield up to block number four's sword, backplate grating against the wood as his shoulder blades tried to dig their way through the wall.

Breath rasping in his chest and number four came back at him again but he was limping and Mace hammered into him so he had to step back on his damaged leg. The step was short and wobbly and Mace punched his shield boss into the man's face, slammed the bottom rim down on to his knee and shoved him away. He went down choking on his teeth and Mace screamed his defiance, but he was away from the wall now and there were still two more, and the shouts of others coming from the bend in the tunnel.

'Come on, cock bastards,' he yelled, hacking at the fifth man as the sixth circled, trying to get behind him. Blow to the back of his knee, buckling his leg, and he blinked in pain as his knee slammed into the stone. He swung behind him with his shield, wanting only to find some space, pushed back up to standing as the fucker in front of him ran his sword into his belly.

Screech of metal as his breastplate held and the sword careered off, slicing into the underside of his upper arm as it passed. Mace hissed – no armour there and he could feel the hot rush of blood already. Twat was off balance now though, not prepared for his strike to miss and Mace punched him in the face with his sword hand, headbutted him for good measure and got air between them, pushed him back with his shield and hacked into his waist with his sword. This one didn't have plate, not even chainmail, and the boiled leather parted like silk under his blade.

Not sure how many were dead, how many might get back up, and still one more circling, circling. The torch was guttering and shadows were leaping, making the corpses at his feet seem to move. His arms were shaking, hot nausea in his throat, knee throbbing.

'Motherfucker,' the last Raider snarled, spit flickering across Mace's cheek. 'Motherfucking fuck.' Mace set his feet, sucked in a whistling breath, and then blinked when the man's head vanished.

Tara's face appeared through the fountain of blood, grinning. 'Close call?' she asked, the sibilants hissing like snakes around the wall. 'Nice job,' she added when she counted the bodies. 'I'm glad you're not dead. But time to go.'

'Take their torch,' Mace said, hands on his knees as he panted, 'and next time I call, hurry the fuck up, would you?'

'I'll do my best, sir.' She slipped her free hand under Mace's uninjured arm and hurried him along as the shouts of Mireces grew louder behind them. They slithered into the group of Rankers and the men set their shields and blocked the tunnel, buying them time.

Mace unbuckled his pauldron with stiff fingers and wrapped a bandage awkwardly around his arm, tying it with his teeth. Tara rebuckled the shoulder plate as violence erupted in the tunnel behind them.

'Pass word forward and back. Keep the column tight, look for any exit to the surface and take it. We need to get in the open and fight the way we know best. We don't get out, we all die down here.'

DOM

'Rillirin!' Dom was on his feet by the time his eyes opened, his lungs tight from the shout. The moon peeked from behind wisps of cloud, the landscape bone-white and eerie, the shadows soft charcoal. Disoriented he knelt, one hand pressed just above his jutting left hip against the shadow of pain.

'Stay out of the darkness,' he mumbled. 'It's coming.' He rocked on his knees. Was it a dream or a knowing? Everything hurt so much he couldn't tell any more.

Movement, a woman threading between the fallen timbers across the square. He lurched back to his feet, hope making him dizzy. 'Watcher?' Then, thready on an exhalation: 'Rillirin?'

'Not quite, my love,' She said and Dom groaned. He rubbed his eyes hard, but She was still there. 'What are you doing, little calestar?' She asked.

What I have to. 'Don't know. Doesn't matter.'

The Dark Lady tutted. 'Sounds like you've given up, sweet one. Why?'

447

'Nothing I can do.' Dom sighed. 'No way to help.'

'So sad, to be so useless. Come to me and you can help. Just step forward, embrace me and I can take all this away from you.' She came closer, feet whispering through ash, naked and glowing in the light of the shrouded moon.

Somewhere east of him, Rillirin was bleeding in the dark, his family were fighting and maybe dying and he was here, in the ruins of Watchtown, dealing with this.

'Haven't you had your fun yet?' he muttered as he fought not to back away. He had a dagger in his boot, a sword on the ground beside his feet. They were both useless against Her, but he felt a distant pleasure that he'd even thought about them.

'I wasn't sure you'd be able after the Dancer threw you out of the world,' he added. 'I bet that was unpleasant.'

'I must admit it's taken me a while to come back, my love,' the Dark Lady said with a dismissive wave of Her hand. She stopped so close to him Her breasts brushed his chest. Dom rocked back on to his heels and She shifted forward on Her toes, maintaining the contact. Her pupils dilated and Dom's lip curled with disgust.

'Your prancing girl is quite the weaver of shields. Do you want to know how I did it?'

'Through the last knowing, the one when the Fox God was here, I could feel you scritching around in my head like a flea-ridden rat.'

'Yes, through the knowing,' She said, amused. 'Your mind and your soul are directly connected to the worlds of the gods. That's how your Dancer controls you.'

'That's how you control me, you mean.'

The Dark Lady laughed and cupped his chin, kissing him. 'I'm not controlling you, my love,' She whispered against his lips, 'She is. She's the one putting you through all this, giving you the ability to see me. If She cared, She could take it all away, take away your gift so that I am hidden to you – me and all the others. Gosfath, the Fox God, the Dancer Herself. But She doesn't. And so I but do what it is in my nature to do.'

She kissed him again, Her tongue whispering against his, and Dom felt the heat stir in his belly. His hands were pressed to Her shoulder blades, pulling Her closer. Her skin was as smooth as butter, as silk, hot and yielding, the muscles in Her back tensing as he stroked them. Her kiss sent pulses of warmth through his body, washed away his weariness and replaced it with hunger.

He didn't think about what She'd said. He concentrated on the kiss, losing himself. She was a good kisser. Nearly as good as Rillirin.

He twisted away. 'What do you want?' he asked, his voice a growl; She pouted and nibbled his jaw. He jerked his head back but didn't step away, didn't let go. Her skin touched his despite the barrier of his clothes, and he felt himself harden against her thigh. It would be so easy just to give in. She traced a finger along his cheek, into the hollow beneath the bone. If he let go She'd catch him, hold him, take away his pain and replace it with pleasure such as he'd never known.

He kissed her again and She responded, arms around his neck, left leg hooking behind his calf. She bucked Her hips and Dom moaned, inhaling the scents of moonlight and musk and blood, one hand on the curved muscle of Her arse. A sharp sting in his lip and he winced, pushed Her away, spitting in the grass. Blood.

The Dark Lady's lips peeled back to reveal curved fangs. A forked tongue licked out and was gone. 'Still you deny me?' She hissed. 'Still you haven't understood the price? You belong to me. She's *given* you to me. And I will have you, body and mind and soul.' She grabbed his arm and spun him so that She stood pressed against his back, tall suddenly, taller than him and cocooning him in Her arms. She pointed. 'Look out there. Look at the world, at the beauty of it. We can rule it, me, my brother, and you. You would be our voice in this land and all would kneel to you.'

'I don't want people kneeling to me,' Dom forced himself to say. It was like leaning back into the embrace of a great, muscled mountain cat. Soft, with coiled power lurking beneath its skin. And so very wild.

'Don't lie,' She murmured into his ear. 'Not to me.'

'I don't want people kneeling to me when the price is so high,' he amended, watching the silver moonlight bathe the plain. Something was moving out there. Stalking.

She kissed the side of his neck. 'And now, at last, after all of this time, we come to it,' She said. 'It always comes down to the bargain, to what you're willing to pretend you didn't do in return for power.' She kissed the other side of his neck, below the ear, and Dom shivered. 'Name your price.' Her hand trailed down his chest. 'Tell me what you want.' Her voice was husky, needful.

Dom collected his thoughts and marshalled his courage. 'You and your Brother dead in a ditch for crows to feast on?'

She tutted and turned him about to face Her again, and now She was small and delicate, Her eyes vulnerable. 'You wound me.'

'If only that were possible, Lady, you would learn exactly what I want.' Her hands were busy at his belt and he took them, held them still, and then stepped back, every muscle in his body screaming at him to step forward instead.

'There's nothing else you can do to me, my love,' he said. 'You can't hurt me any more, not without killing me, and I know you won't do that. If I'm dead, you can't get into the world, can you? Your Blessed One doesn't have the power.' He giggled and chewed on his arm while the Dark Lady pouted.

She gave him a seductive smile and swayed towards him. Dom held up his hand. 'No, not that either. I've no interest in fucking you despite your very obvious charms. So to answer your question, Lady, there will be no bargain. Not tonight, not ever. You can break me, and you can hurt me, but you cannot have my soul. So why don't you just leave me alone?'

'Because you're too much fun,' the Dark Lady whispered and backhanded him hard enough to hurl him through the air, over the water trough and into the rubble beyond. There was a moment of freedom in the flight, when his flailing limbs let go of everything. The air whistled over his skin and cleansed him of Her touch.

But then he landed hard, smashing through the fallen frame of a window, the oiled screen flapping around him and broken wood slicing into his lower back and shoulder, and She was standing over him again, moonlight limning Her skin. He reached for the pain instead of Her, willing his cock to wilt.

'Gosfath,' She called. 'Gosfath, you can have him now.' The movement on the plain stuttered and reappeared a stride from Dom's feet and he yelped, squirming backwards through the rubble. Gosfath reached down and curled a taloned hand around his ankle, dragging him back to the clear space by the water trough. Dom clutched at rubble and burnt beams, hooked his fingers around the trough for a few seconds, but there was no denying that pull.

And then Gosfath stood him up. 'Fight,' He rumbled, grinning. 'Fight, little man.'

Dom stared up at him, light-headed with hilarity at the proposal. The Dark Lady had a faint smile playing across

Her lips. 'Well done, my brother,' She murmured. 'Go on then, Calestar. You want to play games with gods? Then play.'

Might be time for that knife, then. Dom slid it from his boot and crouched. Gosfath laughed and the Dark Lady tapped two fingers into Her palm in mocking applause. There was wet on Dom's face and his guts bubbled, close to shitting himself, but he had a lifetime of training on his side. What did the God of Blood have? Dom giggled and then lunged, feinting with his right hand to draw Gosfath's gaze and then stabbing with his left, aiming for the groin. No point fighting fair when you were fighting a god.

Gosfath wrapped His hand around Dom's face, squashing his nose with His palm until Dom couldn't breathe, and picked him up from the grass, feet dangling. Dom swiped for the god's forearm, felt resistance as though he'd run his knife across a whetstone, and then the world slammed him in the back and drove the air from him.

Gosfath let go of Dom's face and pinched the knife between His thumb and forefinger, and He showed it to Dom as he wheezed on the ground, and then He drove it through Dom's left palm and into the ground.

Dom's back arched and he'd have screamed if he had any air in his lungs. Then Gosfath pulled the blade back out, licked it, and tossed it aside, launching in with His talons instead.

'This is our world now,' the Dark Lady said, calm as if She was watching spring lambs playing king of the hill. 'You understand me, Calestar? Our world. And you're right, we can't kill you yet. But we can make you wish you were dead.'

As always these days, Dom woke tasting blood. His blood, the blood of his people, blood of innocents. The pain was constant, racking his body, an old enemy close to being a friend.

He rolled on to his side and then reached his hands and knees, pausing to retch as the world flipped and danced around him. He gasped, the pain in his left hand stinging and intense. He sat back on his haunches and looked at it, looked at the wide red mouth in his palm and the smaller one on the back of his hand, the dried blood crusted down his fingers and up his forearm. He licked it thoughtfully. The gods' wounds never lasted past waking. If they did he'd have died a thousand times already. His eye was drawn to the grass where he knelt. It was black and dead, blighted. As though something had poisoned the soil.

Or Someone. And that's when Dom realised. They'd been here last night, not in the waypoint between the real world and Red Gods' Afterworld. Not in the flame-lit cavern. They'd come to him in the living, waking world.

She'd even told him to his face. This is our world, She'd said. After a thousand years of exile, the Red Gods had pierced the Dancer's veil. Enough blood had been spilt, enough men had pledged their souls, and the veil had torn asunder.

Whatever Dom had or hadn't done to his soul, whoever it belonged to now, there was no denying the return of the Gods of Blood. He rocked back and forth on his knees, chewing his arm, and he laughed madly as he wept.

CRYS

Third moon, eighteenth year of the reign of King Rastoth
Yew Cove tunnels, River Gil, Western Plain

Crys bit, hard as he could, and thrashed his head from side to side. The man on top of him was screaming, pushing and slapping at his face, but Crys wasn't letting go. On his back in filthy, bloody water, the only light that from a dying torch forty strides away, they fought, grunting, punching, squealing, until Crys managed to bring up his legs and cross them around the Raider's torso.

Still had two fingers in his mouth so he clenched his jaw even tighter and jack-knifed straight, slamming his legs and the Raider down into the water, keeping hold of the arm. A crunch of gristle as the shoulder ripped and hot blood spurting against his tongue when the fingers came off: the Raider's scream went up in pitch as he was folded backwards in Crys's legs and then Crys sat up, spat the fingers at the bastard, fumbled for his knife in the dark and stabbed him in the belly over and over, seven, eight, nine times, until the screams were whimpers and the thrashing just twitching.

Bodies everywhere and this whole section of tunnels dank with water inches deep. Crys kicked free of the dying man and sloshed to his feet, spitting heathen blood into the water.

Voices with Mireces accents and the tinge of orange light from a second tunnel. Crys grabbed his sword and backed off, down the tunnel where Ash had gone with the others, leaving him behind, but there was movement from that direction as well and it didn't sound friendly. He threw himself into a corner, pulled a corpse on top of him and lay still, heart hammering.

'Gos, the gods must hate you,' a voice said, loud and uncaring if anyone heard, 'else you'd be dead and with Them by now.'

'Must admit I'd prefer the Afterworld to this shithole, but what can a man do, eh?' The two men shook hands. 'Surprised you're still alive.'

'Will of the gods,' the first voice said. 'How are we doing?'

'All going to plan, as near as we can tell. The sappers up top should be in position by now, ready to—'

'Wait. Ssh – shut the fuck up. I heard something.'

Crys's breath stopped and he forced himself not to tense. The corpse's arm was over his face, hiding the glint of his eyes as he watched the Mireces fall silent and scan the corpses in the chamber.

'Spread out. Check they're dead,' the first speaker said and stepped over a tangle of limbs to pull the bodies apart. He carried a spear which he plunged down into each corpse as other Mireces sloshed through the water, stabbing weapons into men.

The one called Gos was getting closer and Crys breathed slowly through his nose, panic flaring in his gut, biting back a scream, a plea for mercy. He had the element of surprise. He only needed to leap up, take out this one and break for a tunnel, didn't matter which one. Fastest runner in the North Rank, Crys Tailorson, right now probably the fastest in Rilpor given the motivation.

The man whose fingers Crys had bitten off made a mewling sound and the Mireces' heads snapped towards him. 'Fucking hell, it's Benn,' Gos said. 'You silly twat, you had us going then,' he said and peered down at him. 'Won't make it,' he said and drove his sword into Benn's chest and then his throat. Crys whimpered, the sound muffled by the corpse's arm, and shut his eyes.

'All right, may as well take a break here,' the first speaker said.

'Bit wet, Maris,' Gos said, splashing water with his foot.

Maris grinned and shoved at a corpse with his toe. 'Pull up someone to sit on, then, Gos, you need to keep your haemorrhoids out of the chill.'

Crys opened one eye and saw the Mireces, nearly a score of them, stack corpses on top of each other to make benches and settle in for a rest. He suppressed a shiver and gritted his teeth against the cramp beginning in his calf. *Get me out of this alive, Trickster, I'll do anything you want.*

'Water's rising,' Gos muttered, rousing Crys from his frozen stupor. 'Must be a storm in the mountains.'

'Or the lads are doing their work,' Maris said and slapped his knee. 'Let's be about killing some more heathens then, eh? Rested long enough, I'd say.'

Their voices were muffled and clanging because Crys's right ear was submerged in the creeping, icy water. His shivers were uncontrollable now and only the gloom and the Mireces' chatter kept them from noticing the vibrating pile of corpses in the corner. They'd thrown another one on top of him some time during the last hour, a body that didn't live up to its expectations as a seat, shoving Crys further down into the water and sending a bolt of pain through his cracked ribs.

And now finally, finally they were leaving. But they stood up without hurry, stretching, grunting, adjusting their weapons, pissing on the corpses like dogs marking territory. A thin tendril of yellow bloomed into a paler rose in the water and warmed the side of Crys's face. Water was nearly at his nose. If they didn't go soon he'd have to move or drown, and the fuckers seemed to have forgotten why they'd got up.

The water was in Crys's nose and he opened his mouth, felt it flood in, tasted blood and piss and cold, gagged, but had just enough of an airway. *Fuck off. Fuck. Off.*

Finally they trooped past him, shadows and light bouncing from their torches and disappeared down the tunnel. Crys counted to ten, then heaved at the bodies, wrenched his head out of the water and staggered to his feet, leg numb, ribs creaking as he gasped for breath.

A man stood opposite, staring at him in surprise, cock in hand as he pissed. 'What?' he managed and Crys grabbed up his sword, sloshed across the cave and rammed it under his ribs. Still kept pissing though, even as he fell on to his knees. Crys kicked him face first into the water and stood on the back of his head until the bubbles stopped.

Crys shuddered with cold and with a strange, twitchy energy. He took the man's dagger and stuck it in the back of his belt, put a second into his boot, and then he crept after the others. He'd tasted their piss and nearly pissed himself with fear. Now he wanted their blood and he meant to get it.

RILLIRIN

Third moon, eighteenth year of the reign of King Rastoth
Yew Cove tunnels, River Gil, Western Plain

Lim slammed the man into the wall, forearm across his throat, and pulled back his elbow to run him through.

'Friend! Friend friend friend,' the man gasped and Lim jerked him forward into the meagre light of a guttering torch. 'Crys, I'm Crys.'

Lim blew out a breath and let him go, but didn't bother apologising. 'The fuck you been?' he growled.

'Lying under a pile of corpses trying not to drown while the Mireces had a nice chat. You? I've been looking for you for hours.'

'Running, fighting, running. Hiding.'

And then Ash shoved Lim out of the way and scooped Crys into his arms. Rillirin lay propped against the wall and watched while they kissed as if no one else was there, murmuring into each other's mouths and ears. She blinked owlishly. *Good for you.*

Rillirin was beginning to suspect Dalli had lied to her. She was cold, and not just because she'd got wet falling in puddles. Spots drifted lazily in front of her eyes and her hearing faded in and out. She had no energy, no will to move, and hadn't even twitched when Crys burst into their hiding place.

In fact, Rillirin was pretty sure she was dying. It felt as though they'd been underground forever. They were lost, split off from the other groups, and every hour it seemed another attack came, another couple of warriors picked off. It'd be terrifying if she wasn't so shitting tired.

And then there was the noise, the noise that Rillirin knew she'd heard before but couldn't place. A never-ending thumping echoing through the tunnels. It was like the earth's own heartbeat but for its stuttering irregularity and it had been going on now for hours, winding everyone's nerves so tight that someone was going to break. Muffled crying carried through the damp air and far away, the sound bouncing from the walls, she could hear fighting.

The men and women crouched at the entrance to their storeroom tightened their fingers on their weapons and pushed themselves up the walls to standing. She watched as Dalli checked her spear yet again and then thumped its butt on to the ground again and again, in time with the thumping echoing along the tunnels.

Rillirin sat up straight. 'I know what it is,' she said. No one turned to face her. 'Ash? Dalli, I know what that noise is.'

'Is it important, because we've got incoming,' Dalli said and set her spear. Ash leapt to her side, Crys behind him, and everyone in the room who could prepared to fight.

Rillirin forced herself up the wall to standing, leaning on her spear. 'Yes,' she whispered as the Mireces howled into the room, 'it is important. You need to listen.'

The Mireces attacked.

MACE

'I was raised at Dancer's Lake,' Rillirin said. There's a cave system there we used to store sailcloth and rope in, but it kept flooding with meltwater from the lake. So a dam was constructed. This is before I was born, but we had to maintain it to keep the waters out of the caves.'

'Why do I need to know this?' Mace interrupted. 'We should be looking for an exit.'

'My brother Madoc – Corvus – worked on the dam before we were taken by the Mireces. He understands the mechanics of it. That thumping sound? They're breaking the dam that keeps these tunnels from being flooded by the river. They're going to drown us.'

Mace looked at her, so pale with blood loss that the punch to the face she'd taken wouldn't even bruise. Then he looked at the people around her, holding her up. Grim-faced and silent, it was plain they all believed her.

460

'That's ridiculous,' Mace protested. 'They wouldn't drown their own people. They—'

'We've never seen groups of more than fifty down here,' Tara said. 'It's quite likely they haven't got more than a few hundred warriors. Shit, they might even have dressed the townsfolk up as Mireces to make it appear they had superior numbers. Either way, looked like more than it was in the dark, and that boy yelling about an escape route was enough to get us moving. Then all they had to do was follow us down here and keep harrying us, keep us moving away from them and deeper underground. Corvus probably offered the folk here a deal – lead us into a trap and they wouldn't get slaughtered.'

'Corvus was sixteen when he was taken,' Rillirin said before Mace could respond. 'He knows Rilpor, knows its stories and Smuggler's Cove is one of the most famous. They sailed through here on your boats: you think he wouldn't have checked out the truth of it?'

'But the Mireces down here with us . . .?' Mace tried as the awful truth grabbed him by the throat.

'They're pledged to die for the Dark Lady,' Rillirin croaked. 'If they think they can take us with them, they'll drown and gladly.'

'We need to get out, now,' Lim said, not bothering to whisper any more. 'We have no idea how long it'll take them to smash that dam. And we need to tell the Rank without them panicking.'

'But which way do we go?' Ash asked. 'None of us have found a tunnel that leads upwards.'

'Then we go back the way we came, if we can remember it,' Rillirin grunted. 'Straight through the fuckers. We've been moving downhill ever since we were forced in here. All they had to do was push us downwards.'

'So now we push back,' Tara said, cracking her knuckles.

'Does anyone remember the way out?' Mace asked. They were silent. 'Then we head uphill, Mireces be damned. It's our only hope. Get ready to move.'

Rillirin stuttered a laugh. 'I can't even walk. I'm not going anywhere.'

'Dom needs you. You're coming with us.'

Ash's eyebrows disappeared into his fringe as he looked at Crys. The soldier stared at them all in turn, a weird light in his eyes. 'She comes,' he insisted. 'And we go back the way we came.'

'He's right,' Lim said. 'We take the fight to the Raiders. Tell the Rank it's a final, all-out push to break through.'

'The Rank is scattered through who knows how many miles of tunnels. We can't get them all together,' Tara said.

'Then start passing the message, get it sent along as fast as you can and get them piling back here at the double,' Mace said. 'Rillirin, count to a thousand. When you're there, tell me and that's the signal to go. Regardless of how many have made it to us. Lim, Tara, Crys, we'll form the advance and once we start moving, we don't stop for anything.'

Mace rolled his shoulders. 'We need to keep this secret. If the Mireces suspect we're planning a push, they'll do all they can to disrupt it. Tara, get some lookouts at the bend down there. The rest of you, keep them quiet when they get here.'

'Don't stop for anything once you start,' Rillirin said. 'A straight run for the surface, as fast as you can. There's only a few hundred of them, Tara said, so you'll be fine.'

'Stop saying you,' Crys said, 'it's us, all right? You're coming with us.'

'We might not break them,' Mace said. 'We might just drive them before us. That means as soon as they're out they

462

turn and hold us underground if they can. They'll block the trapdoor.'

'Then we don't let them,' Tara said. 'We do this like a ladder drill, stick so fucking close to them we can smell their shit as they climb the tunnel in front of us. We can climb ladders faster than they can run on the flat. Classic bridge-head tactics – we come up swinging and we make a space, let the next man up and the next. Don't give them time to organise, don't give them time to breathe. When they come up into that house we come up one stride behind them. If we don't we're dead.'

'That's our plan,' Mace said. 'Send word now. Go.'

'Oh goody,' Rillirin mumbled, 'another battle.'

'Rillirin, make that count two thousand. I've a feeling we're going to need every man we can find.' Mace groaned and flexed his leg until his knee clicked. Run a few miles fighting a battle, uphill, then sprint up a ladder and defend a bridgehead. All the while trying not to drown, dragging a half-dead girl and wearing fifty pounds of armour.

'Join the Ranks, see the world, die in the dark,' he heard Crys mutter.

'All right,' Mace said with a warning look at Crys, 'let's get ready.'

TARA

Third moon, eighteenth year of the reign of
King Corvus
Yew Cove tunnels, River Gil, Western Plain

Tara's sword was gone, lost in a corpse somewhere in another tunnel, another life. She'd taken a hatchet from a body and strapped a lightweight spearman's buckler on to her left arm. Crouching in the dancing light of torches, dried blood a mask down her face, hatchet swinging idly by her side, she was terrifying.

And terrified.

Men were flooding into the tunnels behind her, loud and panicked as the news spread. Lim and Mace were doing their best to quiet them.

The Mireces around the next bend must number fifty or more. Tara's assault force was thirty. She rubbed at the cut on her forehead, wincing, and shook out her shoulders. 'We can't let them know about the others, or that we've guessed the ruse. If we do we'll have an all-out assault on our hands,' she hissed. Men and women nodded, grim.

'Time to get massacred then,' Crys said, sounding almost cheerful.

Tara blinked at him. 'If you like. Personally I'm going to kill eleven of them and then run like a rabbit.'

'Eleven?' Crys thumped his chest. 'I'm killing twelve.'

'Pussies,' Sarilla grunted. 'Fifteen.'

Tara found she was grinning, and then that she was running and howling down the tunnel and around the bend.

The Mireces'd heard them coming, of course, and there were far too many of them, but Tara kicked water into the face of the first and chopped her hatchet into his jaw as he blinked. Bottom of his face came off and she was on to the next, taking his swing on her buckler and hacking low, into the side of his knee. Sarilla's sword flashed past Tara's hip and took him in the chest as he fell and they were pressing forward again, tight in a wedge and slowly being surrounded.

Tara jerked up her left foot as an axe swung for it, kicked the man in the elbow, landed close on his off side and the hatchet went in at the waist three times, then sought out the spot below the ear and ended him.

Chest heaving, she ducked under her buckler and nearly got her shoulder smashed, the impact huge and numbing her arm. But Crys was on the man's other side and he couldn't defend against them both and she hamstrung him while Crys aimed for his head. Between them they cut him on to his knees in the water and Tara chopped the hatchet into the back of his neck.

More yells, shouts of Mireces alarm, and Wolves and Rankers poured into the tunnel, Mace and Lim and Ash in the lead, fighting like a six-armed beast as they waded towards the cut-off group.

Tara ducked a swing, but took the next two on her buckler as the man battered at her, driving her into the ground like a nail. Her arm would break soon, the blows were so heavy, and she was stuck in the press of bodies, couldn't slip sideways and he knew it, grin splitting his beard. He cackled as he readied for the next strike and all Tara could do was poke at him with the head of the hatchet: no room to swing.

The sword came up like the sun and Tara charged him, one step only but she dropped her hips, angled her shoulders behind the buckler and slammed up against his chest. His strike wobbled and missed and now he was too close for the blade anyway, shoving at her with his free hand and she screamed in his face and kept pushing: no other ideas except to be too close for him to stab her.

And then two swords sprouted from his chest and a long arm wrapped around her waist and dragged her away. Mace.

'The fuck, Major?' Mace growled.

Tara blinked. 'Major? You're promoting me?' she asked as Rankers poured around them and killed the last of the Mireces in this section.

'Figured it'd be the only way to force you to listen to my orders. Now move. This is it. We've got the momentum; we're making the break. Run.'

'What's the count?' she panted.

'Not enough, but they're on the back foot and the sounds from the dam just got a lot scarier. So move.'

Tara turned into the line the others were making, the tunnel for now free of living Mireces, and together they began, again, to run, the press of Wolves and Rankers behind them forcing them on, faster and faster. No stopping now, even if she wanted to.

DURDIL

Third moon, eighteenth year of the reign of King Rastoth
Commander's quarters, the palace, Rilporin,
Wheat Lands

Durdil was writing another letter he'd never be able to send anywhere when a commotion erupted outside his door.

'No, no, what are you doing? You—' Hallos's voice raised in a shriek and suddenly cut off, a brief scream and then a triple thud against the door.

Durdil leapt from his chair, wooden plate in one hand, eating knife in the other. He flattened himself behind the door and waited for it to open. It swung in and he held his breath. No one entered.

'Major Renik and Hallos the physician,' Renik said. 'Time to go, sir.'

'Step inside,' Durdil ordered even though he knew speaking would give away his location. He had to make sure it was really them, that they weren't being coerced.

Renik's hands appeared around the door first, outstretched and empty, spattered with blood, and he came in sideways,

467

facing Durdil and presenting himself as the largest possible target in a show of good faith. Hallos copied him.

Durdil threw himself against the door, expecting it to ricochet off someone else, but it slammed shut.

'The Mireces have been sited at Shingle. They're marching overland and will be here by tonight. The East Rank left its harbour two hours ago – it will also be here by tonight. Galtas Morellis leads them. We suspect Rivil's been co-ordinating them from here, sir, getting the intel in from the West Rank and forwarding it to the East, ensuring both his forces arrive at the same time. Didn't get a chance to destroy the market, it was supposed to be tonight but I suspect we're going to fighting by then.' Renik ran out of breath and stopped talking.

'We're rescuing you,' Hallos added in case Durdil hadn't grasped the situation.

'Your sword and armour are outside, sir,' Renik said. 'I think we're going to have company soon.'

Durdil gestured to Hallos to open the door and studied his body language as he exited, just in case there was an ambush waiting. He decided not, threw the plate and knife to one side and followed Renik out. His armour was stacked next to the bodies of four guards. Durdil raised an eyebrow. 'Nicely done.'

'Hallos got one. The man's a bloody menace with a scalpel.'

Hallos beamed. 'Knowing where to knife someone is somewhat a speciality of mine,' he chuckled and Durdil grabbed him by the coat.

'You're nervous, I can see that,' he said, 'but I need you to shut up and do as you're told, all right? Chatter at the wrong moment is extremely likely to get us all killed.'

Hallos sucked one end of his moustache into his mouth and chewed it. 'I understand,' he said, the edge of hysteria fading from his expression. 'Sorry.'

Renik helped Durdil on with his armour and gave him the highlights. 'Rivil is in control of everything. I haven't seen the king for three days, Rivil says he's ill but Hallos isn't allowed to tend him.'

'Is he dead?'

'Wouldn't think so. Rivil would announce that as soon as he could, wouldn't he? No, Rivil's got him locked up somewhere.'

'If we kill Rivil, the Mireces will come anyway. They're fighting for the gods. But if Rivil kills Rastoth, then Rivil becomes king and we become traitors for opposing him. He'll be within his rights to trample Rilporin into submission. So our priority is the king,' Durdil said. 'Protect the king, and then capture Rivil if we can.'

'Yes, sir,' Renik said as Hallos came hurrying back down the corridor.

'Someone's coming,' he hissed.

'Let's move. King's quarters, queen's quarters, Janis's quarters, in that order,' Durdil said and hurried in the opposite direction. 'After that we'll be searching room by room.'

They sprinted down the corridor and around a corner, ducked into a servants' passageway and Renik drew his sword; servants shrieked and dived for cover and, with luck, none of them would waste time looking over Renik's shoulder and recognising Durdil.

Hallos was spry for such a burly figure, and the trio ran down corridors and across audience chambers, through the kitchens and along the plush corridors of the king's wing until they reached his chambers. There were no guards outside.

Renik went in first, sliding left and Durdil ducking right. Empty.

'Marisa's chamber,' Durdil panted, 'he might be there.'

And there he was, with four guards stationed at her door, and Renik and Durdil put on a last burst of speed down the length of the corridor. One of the foursome turned to open the door and something silver blurred past Durdil's ear and sank into the guard's thigh. He howled and fell, clutching at the scalpel in his leg.

Durdil reached them and drove his sword whining through the air to a man's neck. The guard slammed his sword up two-handed to block it and Durdil's other fist came up and punched his dagger into the guard's armpit. The man shrieked and the sword dropped from nerveless fingers and Durdil chopped him on to his knees, left him there bleeding and spun to the next, slicing through the vertebrae at the top of his neck where his helmet didn't come down low enough.

Renik finished the third and grabbed the fourth by his uniform and dragged him up. 'Where's Rivil?' he demanded as Durdil slid past them into the queen's suite.

'My feet are on the Path,' the man screeched and Durdil heard the sound of his throat being slit over Hallos's exclamation of disgust.

Rastoth was huddled on Marisa's bed with the coverlet pulled up to his chin. Durdil dropped to one knee in front of him. 'Your Majesty, you are in mortal danger. Will you allow me to escort you to safety?'

The door slammed shut behind him and Rivil stepped forward. 'My father has me to protect him,' he said softly, 'and besides, it is you who brings violence here, not me. You have killed my men.'

Durdil's fingers tingled with adrenaline and everything became very still and silent. 'You are a traitor to your father, to your king and to your gods, Prince Rivil,' he said. 'You have nailed your feet to the Dark Path and exchanged Light for Blood. You seek to kill your father, overthrow his government, subjugate his people and outlaw worship of the Gods of Light. I'm afraid I can't allow any of that to happen.'

'Well, don't you know a lot all of a sudden.' Rivil smiled and stepped forward, his sword gleaming, his armour polished. 'Who told you? Was it Wheeler, before you killed him?'

'Wheeler really didn't tell you who we had here? No, it was Captain Crys Tailorson, Your Highness. The good captain told me everything when he was here in the palace beneath your very nose. He's the one who killed Wheeler before he escaped.'

Rivil stilled, genuine surprise flitting across his face, and Durdil leapt. Rastoth shrieked as their swords clashed together once, twice, and then they separated, circling like dogs as Renik hammered at the door.

'Sire, stay out of the way,' Durdil called as Rivil lunged at him again, trying to force him sideways, clear a path to the bed. Durdil refused to be moved, taking a blow on his pauldron instead that numbed his arm. Rivil pushed, hammering again and again at Durdil's shoulder, Durdil's blade intercepting most of the blows but not all. He gave ground, Rivil taller than him, stronger than him. Younger than him.

'What are you doing to my boy?' Rastoth suddenly squalled and Durdil felt something hit the back of his helmet. A pillow. Rastoth was throwing pillows at him.

'Your Majesty, the prince is trying to kill me in order that he can kill you,' he shouted as another pillow bounced off his elbow. *As long as he doesn't throw the—*

The coverlet drifted down over his head, blinding him. Rivil laughed; Durdil lunged, his sword tip scraping across armour. The door burst open, Rastoth shrieked, Rivil cursed and he heard footsteps sprinting through into the next chamber.

471

He fought his way out from under the silk. Rastoth was lying twisted on the bed, hands glistening red and pressing at a bubbling wound in his chest.

'Hallos,' Durdil screamed, and followed Renik through into the next chamber, down the stairwell and into another servants' corridor.

Carnage. A cook was sitting splay-legged on the floor, wailing and trying to stuff his guts back into his belly, a butler was face down with his spine showing through his coat, and further on Renik was staggering along the corridor, leaving a succession of bloody handprints on the wall.

'Where?' Durdil gasped and Renik pointed with his sword.

'Straight on,' he gasped and slid on to one knee. 'Sorry.'

Durdil ran, his lungs screaming, the image of Rastoth bleeding beating in his head, and slammed through the door without slowing, sword and arm crossed over his face in a vain attempt at protection.

There was no one there. Three corridors branched off, no indication in any of them which way Rivil had gone. But one of them led outside. Durdil took that one, his gait heavy, legs slowing now, and burst out of the main doors of the palace into the assembly place. It was crowded and people were staring in shock and horror at the woman and child lying bloody on the cobbles.

'What happened?' Durdil shouted and there was screaming when people saw him, sweaty, bloody and armoured, sword in hand. 'What?' he yelled and someone pointed at the gate into Fourth Circle.

Durdil ducked to his right and looked down the King's Way. Prince Rivil was galloping down it, a straight run for the distant gatehouse and the twin armies that were even now advancing towards the city.

Durdil threw his sword on to the ground. 'Shit,' he roared.

'You, signal the guards, see if you can get the message to the gatehouse to drop the portcullis now. Nobody leaves the city and I mean nobody. Including royalty.' He gestured. 'Including him.'

The guard gaped and then nodded, sprinting for the gate tower leading into Fourth Circle. They'd be too late, Durdil knew it, but they had to try. He picked up his sword, sheathed it, and headed back into the palace.

Renik was injured, and Durdil had seen enough chest wounds to suspect the king was dying. He'd have to trust his men to stop the prince.

CRYS

Third moon, eighteenth year of the reign of King Rastoth
Yew Cove tunnels, River Gil, Western Plain

Crys watched his dagger sink into the man's throat. He'd regret the throw soon enough, missing the extra steel in his free hand, but for now he had to push forward, make space for the hundreds of men crowding in behind him. Mace to his left, fast and deadly with the short sword despite his exhaustion. Ash on his other side, Lim and Dalli, Sarilla and Tara. They were all there, making up the front row, doing what each of them was bred for.

Crys stabbed into a chest, felt a heartbeat shiver up his sword into his hand as though he held it, and pulled out, letting the man fall, leaping the body to find another to kill, all the fear, the guilt bubbling up and up and overspilling. He heard himself shriek fury, the men and women around him responding, pushing on, killing and dying and breaking the line.

Crys's sword tip raked open a face and he caught a glimpse of brown teeth before black blood gushed. The man screamed and Mace punched the wound, dropping him, stamping him into the stone. He'd be but smears of flesh on rock when they'd all passed over him.

Crys ducked a swing wild and big, dragging Mace down as well or the axe would have lodged in his face. They responded together, Mace cutting into the man's groin, Crys into his axe-arm so the weapon clattered down and he followed it, screeching. Crys stepped, stamped, tripped and fell forward into the arms of a Raider with just one eye, the other a bloody black hole in his head. Moment of surprise when the Mireces caught him and shoved him back upright, then they were hacking away at each other. 'Lady,' the Mireces grunted as Crys's sword found his belly.

'Not down here, fucker,' he snarled and took off his head. 'This is the Fox God's lair.'

The tunnel split into two, both sloping upwards, and men poured along each. Crys saw Sarilla stumble against the outcrop between the two tunnels and go down on one knee and heard Lim shout his wife's name but neither of them could reach her and then Crys was down the right-hand tunnel and there was no fighting the current. The Rank had the bit between its teeth now – they stopped for nothing and no one.

Crys snatched a knife from a Raider's hand, grinned and stabbed it into his face, through the cheek into the mouth, through the eye, the mouth again. Screaming around steel, muffled, gagging, and down he went; the tunnel was so narrow there were only three of them abreast and the Mireces finally, finally, broke into a run, turning their backs.

Crys thrust his sword into the air. '*Run,*' he shrieked. He brought his blade slashing down across a Mireces' back, hurdled the body and chased down the next.

RILLIRIN

*Third moon, eighteenth year of the reign of King Rastoth
Yew Cove tunnels, River Gil, Western Plain*

Rillirin was at just over eighteen hundred in the count, huddled against the wall to avoid the hundreds of men crowding into the tunnels and storerooms, when the roar sounded from the tunnel ahead and more and more men started pressing forward. The count stuttered and faltered and she winced up to one elbow to watch.

There'd been a flood of humanity as the message was passed forward, but not enough. Nowhere near enough. There must still be thousands in the tunnels ahead, running towards the dam instead of away from it.

'Shit.' Dalli had wrapped fresh bandages around her wound, but the pain was monstrous and unrelenting, the blood still seeping, and she was so cold. She pulled herself up the wall to sitting and watched for a few more seconds. 'Shit,' she said again, dragging herself to her feet, left hand pressing her side. She grabbed the splintered spear from the water, water that was nearly up to her knees now, and pushed her way into the mass of men jamming the tunnels ahead of her.

'Dom. Got to get back to Dom,' she muttered, swaying and dizzy and so, so cold. Rillirin paused and looked back behind her. She raised her voice. 'This way, down here, back towards the exit,' she yelled as loudly as she could. 'We're breaking out. Come back.'

Ahead were screams and clanging echoes and the last of the torches. Only the dimmest sliver of light illuminated the hell ahead of her. She could barely make out the slower, injured figures hobbling determinedly after the army. The hairs on her arms and nape stood up and she sensed the water rushing on them. Knew it was coming. Somehow just knew.

A whimper choked its way out and she limped faster, grinding her teeth against the pain, fizzing spots in front of her eyes. Running footsteps and a few men dashed past her from behind and joined the crowd. She struggled forward, passed a couple of the slowest wounded and saw two black mouths open ahead of her.

Panting, she looked from one to the other, then a stab of movement between the two caught her attention and she inhaled, choked on her own spit, coughed, broken spear wobbling about in paltry protection.

'Rillirin?'

'Sarilla? Fucking thank the gods.' Rillirin limped forward. 'Hurt?'

'A bit. Need to move though.'

No way Rillirin could help her, state she was in, but she held out her hand anyway, groaned when Sarilla used it to drag herself to her feet. 'Let's go then, eh?' she managed, wondering if this made them friends now after all this time.

They staggered down the right-hand tunnel, hands on each

other's shoulders to keep themselves upright. Rillirin couldn't take a full breath and her ears buzzed, muffling the sounds ahead.

The tunnel wound on, black on black, Sarilla's breathing beside her harsh and stumbling, a high whine in her chest. Twists and turns and they reached the back of the army, still shoving forward, waving steel they couldn't use, hollering to hurry, keep pressing, gonna drown back here cunt-faces.

Rillirin led Sarilla into the mob, worming her way into gaps whenever they appeared, bloody fist tight on Sarilla's shirt. She could just see the glow of torchlight ahead when a cold wind blew against her back and the faintest rumble tickled the soles of her feet, her eardrums.

'Run, run,' men shouted and the shoving increased, voices high-pitched, desperate.

She was crushed against the man in front of her, her cheek slamming into his backplate with shocking force, and her fingers slipped from Sarilla's shirt. She caught a wooden finger, tore the whole thing from Sarilla's hand as they were swept apart, and she had a last glimpse of Sarilla's white, terrified face through the tangle of bodies, swallowed and gone beneath them.

She reached for her, mouth wide in a scream, and a sword hilt clubbed her crown, an elbow crunched into her chest and robbed her breath and she stumbled two paces, looking back and straining, Sarilla's crippled hand there and then gone.

A knee or elbow into the wound in her back and all her breath stolen, all her reason, as the agony flared up and down and into every limb and there was no air in the world to wail. Mouth sagging open she reached back, straining still for Sarilla's hand, until a short Ranker shoulder-barged her and she lost her footing, fell to her knees.

Men were tripping over her, boots slamming into her ribs, one shockingly into her nose to set off explosions of colour and pain. She raised a hand to her face, grunted as the fingers of her other hand were crushed beneath a heel, and roaring filled her head and body.

Someone fell over her. The water was a screaming animal filling the tunnel behind but he hooked a long arm under her belly and hoisted her up on to his shoulder, arms and legs dangling, and staggered on. Seth. Out of nowhere, Seth.

'*Sarilla!*' she screamed. 'Stop, go back, it's Sarilla,' but Seth ran, the water close now and then he was dodging right, into a sliver in the tunnel wall that he had to jam her through, skinning her arms, hips and shoulders, and force himself through after. He grabbed her wrist and dragged her across to the far wall. Trapped.

Rillirin was sobbing, crying for Sarilla, for Dom, babbling to the Dancer through waves of pain. Seth hauled her up on to a shoulder-high ledge and scrambled up after her, kicking jars and bottles out of his way. He pulled her head against his chest so she wouldn't see the water coming and she closed her eyes, put her head beneath his chin, Sarilla's wooden fingers clutched to her chest.

Wouldn't die alone. At least there was that.

CORVUS

Third moon, year 995 since the Exile of the Red Gods
Rilporin, Wheat Lands

Four thousand Mireces warriors drawn up in a square outside Rilporin, and a quarter of a mile north across the field, five thousand soldiers of the East Rank.

Corvus, Valan, Lanta and the other war chiefs rode the horses they'd stolen in Shingle forward to meet their allies. They stopped at the centre of the road leading all the way to the gatehouse and Rivil and Corvus leant out of their saddles and gripped forearms.

'King Corvus, welcome to Rilpor.'

'Prince Rivil, or is it King Rivil now?' Corvus said, noting the battered armour and the man's sweaty hair. 'You've had some trouble?'

Rivil waved away the comment. 'Nothing I can't handle,' he said, 'and it's Prince Rivil for now, but I expect the scarlet of mourning to be flying from those towers by tomorrow. The king is grievously wounded.' He patted the hilt of his sword with smug glee.

480

Corvus inclined his head. 'This is excellent news. The gods will be well pleased. For my part, you have my finest warriors and the West Rank and the Wolves have been taken care of.'

They stared at the city in silence for a while. The great gatehouse's portcullis was down, the iron-banded gates firmly shut behind it. The two towers either side of the gatehouse bristled with men, and more stood silent and watchful along the wall.

'Formidable defences,' Corvus said, leaving unspoken the fact that Rivil was supposed to have ensured the gates were open on their arrival. The Lady's will.

'We have the numbers, Sire,' Rivil countered. 'And once Rastoth is dead, they will be resisting the rightful King of Rilpor. They'll open the gates.'

Rivil twisted in his saddle and stared at Corvus's army. 'How many?' he asked.

'Nearly four thousand.'

'I had hoped for more,' Rivil murmured.

Corvus beckoned Lanta. 'The prince worries we do not have enough men,' he said and Lanta laughed, the sound high and girlish. Her cheeks were flushed and her eyes sparkled with genuine delight.

'Prince Rivil, we have something far greater than warriors,' she said. 'We have the gods.'

'Of course—' Rivil began but Lanta cut him off.

'No, Sire, you don't understand. The gods have returned to Gilgoras. The veil is torn. The Dark Lady and Gosfath, God of Blood, walk the world again.'

Rivil's mouth was hanging open and his retinue urged their horses closer, stammering questions. Lanta raised her voice to include them all.

'Our presence in Rilpor, as true worshippers of the Red

Gods, and your conversion, Prince Rivil, yours and the lord's and the East Rank's, has combined to weaken the Dancer's grip, the power of Her shields. Rilporians' lack of faith and our true belief are powerful tools. The destruction of our army of the Blessed, every one a living sacrifice, in the Blood Pass Valley began to tear the veil, and the annihilation of the West Rank and the Wolves upriver thinned it even further. But in the end it was the breaking of the calestar that finally allowed our gods to return.'

'The calestar? The Wolf prophet?' Rivil asked as Galtas and Skerris muttered prayers of thanks in stunned voices. 'What has he got to do with anything? Isn't he a myth?'

'The calestar is the Dark Lady's tool, Your Highness, and he is very much a living man. Well, for now, anyway. The calestar is broken, lost, my lords. His mind drowns beneath a torrent of images and the torments of the gods. Whether the Dancer or the Dark Lady, all he'll ever see now is what They show him.'

'He is godblind,' Corvus said, a delicate shiver running up his spine and Lanta nodded affirmation. 'His torture must be exquisite, his mortal mind lost in the mysteries of the gods.'

'It will break him,' Lanta confirmed. 'His mind will shatter into a thousand pieces. And when we find him, when the Dark Lady delivers him up to us, we'll see Their power tease his very soul into threads, watch Their hands snap those threads one by one. Watch him unravel.' Her voice dropped to an exalted whisper. 'And none who see it will be able to deny Their power. And he will tell us such things, such secrets and dreams, visions of the Afterworld seen in waking life. He will be a living reminder of the power of the gods.'

The Rilporians were mute with shock and awe and Corvus relished that it was they who'd known it first, that the Dark

Lady had chosen to reveal Their return to the Blessed One before anyone else.

'What must we do?' Rivil stammered. 'To properly welcome them, I mean.'

Corvus raised his arms to Rilporin. 'Break the city, slaughter its inhabitants, and destroy the Dancer,' he said.

'With fucking pleasure,' Rivil said fervently. He gestured and Skerris wheeled his horse and kicked it into a heavy canter towards the waiting army, the blue patch on his sleeve catching Corvus's eye.

'East Rank! Trebuchets! Loose!' he roared.

King, prince, lord and Blessed One sat their horses under a clear sky and a bright sun and watched the three trebuchets send the first artillery shots of the siege into Rilporin's walls.

The war was only just beginning.

EPILOGUE

DOM

Third moon, eighteenth year of the reign of King Rastoth
Watchtown, Western Plain

Dom sat with his back against the water trough in Watchtown's assembly place, legs splayed before him, right wrist crammed into his mouth, teeth seeking the source of the burrowing, itching, burning. It was in there somewhere. He'd find it. Just a little deeper.

The bodies around him were bloating in the sun, millions of flies feasting, buzzing, rising and falling in clouds from corpse to corpse.

Dom watched as men and women flipped and tumbled deep underground in dark water, bouncing off walls and each other as they flailed with heavy steel at floors and other people, until eventually they spoke streams of bubbles and then spun, limp and agape, boneless in the rush of water.

More pictures, of a man in a crown covered in blood, a soldier gaunt by his bedside, a beautiful woman carving open a man's belly in honour of the gods.

The gods. The Dark Lady and Gosfath, God of Blood,

Their hands forever upon him, Their wills forever bent to crush his.

So beautiful. So black and red and beautiful.

Blood streaked Dom's chin as he ate himself. And he laughed and laughed at the pretty pictures.

ACKNOWLEDGMENTS

I'm not entirely sure where to start with this, as writing thank yous means I've actually written a book, and I still can't quite believe this isn't a dream. If it is, please don't wake me up.

I owe a huge debt of gratitude to my family – Mum, Dad, Sam, thank you for letting me grow up in libraries and books and the inside of my own skull, and for never stifling my somewhat odd imagination. Without you, this may never have come to be. My favourite phrase as a child (and to some extent still today) was 'I could be a . . .' followed by whatever took my fancy at that moment. Well, 'I could be an author' has finally become 'I am an author' and much of that is down to you.

To all my extended family, from Scotland to Belgium to five minutes down the road, cousins, nephews, nieces, aunts and in-laws, you've all cheered me on and supported me through the craziest fourteen months of my life from agent to editor to published book – you've been amazing and I'm so grateful for all your help and excitement for me and for *Godblind*.

And to Mark, the best husband I could ever hope for, you're my best friend and greatest teacher. Not only that, you've been my biggest fan and most steadfast supporter and you never complained about the hours I worked or the number of times you had to do the housework on your own so I could write. Your belief in me has got me through some really difficult times and I promise to always do the same for you. *Godblind* is as much a product of your love and patience as it is of my brain. You mean everything to me, love. Thank you.

And to the people who took the slightly chaotic mess that was the original book and helped me polish and improve it – Harry Illingworth, literary agent extraordinaire, who worked tirelessly on my behalf to get *Godblind* into the right hands – you're a legend and I couldn't have done it without you. Thanks for your belief. And Natasha Bardon, editor, publishing director and all-round babe, you waited out my whining and pleading with the patience of a saint and then made me do it your way anyway – turns out it was the right way and *Godblind* is the richer for it, so you have my undying gratitude. This doesn't mean I won't whine and plead next time, though. Just so you know.

Thanks also to Cameron McClure at Donald Maass for your efforts in getting *Godblind* to North America, and to Louisa Pritchard and The Marsh Agency for your foreign rights work in France, Germany and the Netherlands.

The support I've received from other authors I've met in the last year has been incredible – publishing really is one big crazy family, so thanks to you all for the advice, the nudges, the laughs and the introductions. Mark de Jager, for taking me under your wing, Stu Turton, for the laughs and the beers, and Ed Cox and Jen Williams for your wisdom and hellos at conventions. And to all at Birmingham Writers'

Group for the collective creative knowledge and all the Doctor Who chats.

And finally, to the people we've lost in the last few years who would have been so proud – you're in my thoughts and my heart always. Thank you for making me me.

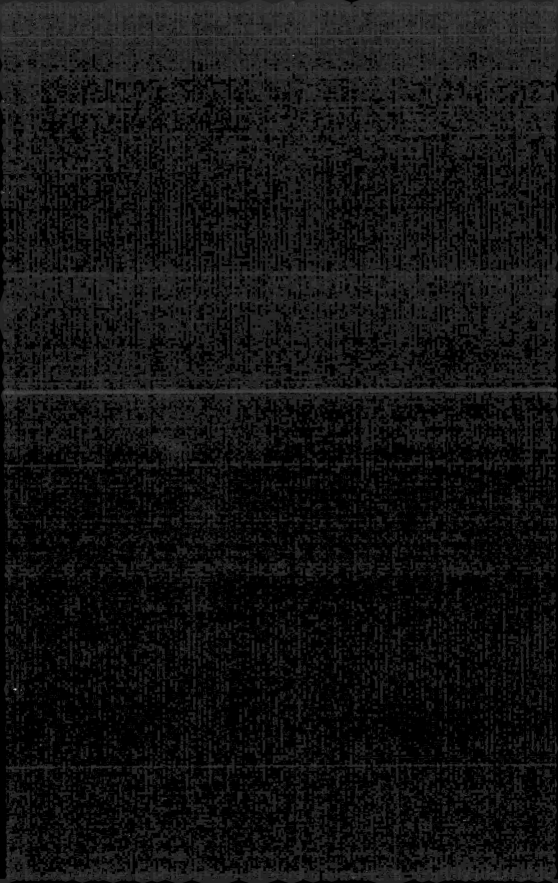